The Hat on the Bed

BOOKS BY JOHN O'HARA

JOHN O'HARA

THE HAT
ON THE BED

RANDOM HOUSE · NEW YORK

Of the twenty-four stories in this book, nine first appeared in *The New Yorker,* five first appeared in *The Saturday Evening Post,* and one appeared in *Show.* The remaining stories are herein published for the first time.

To William Maxwell

CONTENTS

The Hat on the Bed

AGATHA

Both dogs had been out. She could tell by the languid way they greeted her and by the fact that Jimmy, the elevator operator, had taken his twenty-five-cent piece off the hall table. Or was it Jimmy? Yes, Jimmy was on mornings this week; Ray was on afternoons and evenings. Jimmy liked dogs, Ray did not. The day was off to a better start when Jimmy took the dogs for their morning walk; it was nicer to start the day with the thought that Jimmy, who liked dogs, had exercised them, and not Ray, who made no attempt to conceal his distaste for the chore. Ray was paid a quarter, just the same as Jimmy, for taking the dogs down to the corner, but Mrs. Child had very good reason to believe that that was *all* he did—take them to the corner, and hurry right back without letting them stop at the curb.

"Good morning, boys," she said, addressing the dogs. They shook their tails without getting up. "Oh, you're such spoiled boys, you two. You won't even rise when a lady enters the room. Muggsy, don't you *know* that a gentleman *always* stands up when a lady comes in? You *do* know it, too, and you're not a very good example to your adopted brother, are you? How can I expect Percy to have good manners if you don't show him how? Percy, don't you pay a bit of attention to Muggsy and his bad manners." The dogs raised their heads at the sound of their names, but when she finished speaking they slowly put their heads back on their paws. "Oh, you're hopeless, the two of you. Really hopeless. I don't see why I put up with two such uncouth rascals."

She proceeded to the kitchen door and pushed it open. "Good morning, Mary," she said.

"Good morning, Mrs. Child," said the maid. "I heard you running your tub. Will you have toast this morning?"

"Just one slice, please. Maybe two slices, but bring me my coffee first, will you?"

"Yes ma'am."

"I didn't see any mail. Was there any?"

"Got it here on the tray. Which'll you have? Marmalade, or the blackberry jam?"

"Mary, you're not cooperating at all. You know perfectly well if you mention marmalade or jam, I'll *have* marmalade or jam, and I'm trying not to."

"Oh, if I don't mention it you'll ask for it."

"I'm such a weak, spineless creature. All right, you mean old Mary Moran, you. You know me much too well. I'll have the blackberry jam. Were there any packages?"

"None so far, but United Parcel don't usually get here before noontime. That's the way it works out. Some neighborhoods they only deliver in the afternoon, some in the morning. I guess they have a system."

"And speaking of other neighborhoods, when am I going to be able to lure you away from Mrs. Brown?"

"Oh—I don't know about that, Mrs. Child," said Mary Moran. "Will you have your first cup standing up?"

"No, I'll wait. I'll be in the livingroom," said Mrs. Child.

Mary Moran would have been expensive, and there really wasn't enough work to keep her busy, but Mrs. Child knew that Mary's other employer, Mrs. Brown, had been trying to persuade her to give up Mrs. Child and work full-time for her. It did no harm, every once in a while, to remind Mary that she had a full-time job waiting for her with Mrs. Child—and subtly to remind Mary that she had been with Mrs. Child a good two years longer than she had been with Mrs. Brown. There were a lot of things Mary could not do, but in what she could do, or would do, she was flawless. Mrs. Child did not need Mary Moran at all, when you came right down to it. The building provided maid service of a-lick-and-a-promise sort, and you could have all your meals sent up and served by the room-service waiters. But Mary Moran was acquainted with every article of clothing that Mrs. Child possessed; she was a superb laundress of things like lingerie; a quick and careful presser; very handy with needle and thread. She could put together a light meal of soup and salad, and she could do tiny sandwiches and a cheese dip for a small cocktail group. But she would not serve luncheon or pass a tray among cocktail guests; not that she was ever there at cocktail time, but as a matter of principle she had made it one of her rules that serving was not to be expected of her. She was not very good about taking telephone messages, either; it had taken Mrs. Child two years to discover that Mary was ashamed of her handwriting and spelling. Nevertheless she would have been an excellent personal maid, and Agatha Child never gave up hoping that she could lure—lure was the word —Mary away from the Browns, whoever *they* were beyond the fact that they had a small apartment on Seventy-ninth Street and were away a good deal of the time. It would have been worth the money to have Mary Moran on a full-time basis, not only for the work she did, but because her coming to work full-time would have been an expression of the approval that Agatha Child suspected that Mary withheld.

"We haven't talked about that for quite some time," said Agatha Child.

Mary Moran had just brought in the breakfast tray. "What's that, Mrs. Child?"

"About your coming to work for me full-time."

Mary Moran smiled. "Well, it suits me, the way it is," she said.

"You'd make just as much money. And don't you find it a nuisance, to finish up here and then have to take the bus to Seventy-ninth Street?"

"I usually walk. I enjoy the walk. I get a breath of fresh air."

"Do you know what I think? I think you have a gentleman friend that you have lunch with. You almost never have lunch here."

"Well, there may be some truth to that. We have a bite to eat. It's on the way."

"Oh, my guess was right? How fascinating. Tell me about him."

"No, I don't think I'll do that."

"Of course not. It's none of my business, and I don't want to appear inquisitive. But of course I'm dying of curiosity. You've been with me eight years and this is really the first time we ever got on that subject."

"Well, you made a good guess for your first try."

"Is he Catholic?"

"No ma'am."

"You'd rather not say any more."

"Rather not. It's him and I."

"Yes. Well, I won't badger you any more. I just want to say that I hope he appreciates you, and if you ever feel the need to talk to someone about it—about him."

"Thank you, ma'am."

"Remember, I've been married three times."

"I know that, yes."

"And I'm a lot older than you. Probably fifteen years."

"Not quite. I'll be forty-one."

"Well, almost fifteen years. How did you know my age? Did you see it on my passport?"

"No ma'am. Your scrapbook, where you have that newspaper cutting of when you eloped and all. The big green scrapbook."

"Oh, yes. That's a dead giveaway, isn't it? Well, what difference does it make? Anybody can find out my age if they want to take the trouble. All they have to do is go to the Public Library, and there it is in big headlines, seventeen-year-old heiress and all that tommyrot. Never lived it down. But that's where I can be of help to you, Mary, in case you ever *need* any help."

"They'd never put *me* in the headlines, whatever I did."

"You can be thankful for that," said Agatha Child.

"Will you want me to—changing the subject—will I send the black suit to the dry cleaner's, or do you want to give it another wear?"

"I guess it could stand a cleaning. Whatever you think," said Agatha Child.

"I had a look at it this morning. It's about ready to go."

The day's mail was fattened up by the usual bills and appeals. She put a rubber band around the unopened bills, for forwarding to Mr. Jentzen, who would scrutinize them, make out the appropriate cheques, and send her the cheques for signature. She saw Mr. Jentzen just once a year, at income tax time, when he would deliver his little lecture on her finances, show her where to sign the returns, and have one glass of sherry with her. On these occasions Mr. Jentzen could almost make her feel that he was paying for the sherry and for everything else. Bald, conscientious Mr. Jentzen, who looked like a dark-haired version of the farmer in Grant Wood's "American Gothic," and who in some respects knew her better than any husband or lover she had ever had, but who politely declined her suggestion that he call her Agatha. "Not even if I call you Eric? It's such a nice name, Eric." And so unlike Mr. Jentzen, she did not add. She could have gone right ahead and called him Eric; she was, after all, at least five years older than he, but she knew that he was afraid of even so slight an intimacy because he was the kind of man who would be afraid to get entangled with a woman who had had three husbands and an undetermined number of gentlemen friends.

It occurred to her now, as she doubled the rubber band about the bills, that her life was full of small defeats at the hands of people who rightfully should have obeyed her automatically. Mary Moran, Eric Jentzen, and Ray the bellboy were three she could name offhand who refused to yield to her wishes. With Ray the bellboy it was a case of attitude rather than outright disobedience; he did what she asked, but so churlishly that his obedience became an act of defiance. Mary Moran, crafty little Irishwoman that she was, was practically an illiterate but she was adroit enough to avoid a showdown on the question of giving up the Browns. And Eric Jentzen used his sexual timidity to keep from losing the arrogated privilege of lecturing her on her extravagances. (It was quite possible that Mr. Jentzen got some sort of mild kick out of that safe intimacy.)

The dogs were now sitting up. "One little piece of toast is all you're going to get," she said. "No, Percy, you must wait till your older stepbrother has his. See there, Muggsy? If you'd taught him better manners he wouldn't be so grabby. One piece is all you're going to get, so don't bother to look at me that way. Down, boys. I said down. *Down,* God damn it! Percy, you scratched me, you son of a bitch. You could cause me all sorts of trouble, explaining a scratch like that. *If* there was anybody I had to explain to." She lit a cigarette and blew smoke in the dogs' muzzles. "Now stay down, and don't interrupt me while I see whose sucker list I'm on today."

Two of the appeals were for theatrical previews at twenty-five dollars a crack. By an amusing coincidence both contained similarly worded personal touches. "Do try to come" was written across the top of the announcements; one was signed with initials, identifiable by going down the list of patronesses; the other was signed "Mary," and didn't mean a damned thing. Mary. What a crust a woman had, to sign just Mary and expect people to know who Mary was. Agatha Child went through the list and discovered three Marys behind the married names and one Mary who was a Miss. "I'll tell you what you can do, Mary dear. You can invite me to dinner and the benefit and shell out fifty dollars for me and some likely gentleman, and I *will* do-try-to-come." She dropped the announcements in the wastebasket. She immediately retrieved them and went over one of the lists again. Yes, there it was: Mrs. W. B. Harris, the wife of her second husband. What a comedown that would be for Wally, if he should ever learn that she had seen that name, which once she bore, and it had failed to register. True, she had always given the name the full treatment: Wallace Boyd Harris. True, too, there were so many Harrises. One too many, or two too many, if it came to that, which was how she happened to become Agatha Child. For the second time she dropped the announcements in the wastebasket, but at least they had given her some amusement. Wally Harris, afraid of his own shadow—more accurately, afraid of the shadow of her first husband. Well, it hadn't been a mere shadow; more like a London peasouper that lasted four years. Four dark, miserable years that she could recall in every detail and had succeeded in suspending from her active memory, by sandwiching the whole period in between her first marriage and her third, so that it was worthless even as a wasted segment of her time on earth to cry over. He was an intimate man, Wally, wanting to know everything about everything she

did, until there was nothing left to learn except all the things
she felt and could not tell him, that no one can tell anyone unless she is asked the right questions, at the right moment, in the
right tone of voice, and for the right reason which is love.
Finally he had learned just about every fact of her marriage
to her first husband and had accidentally discovered a few
facts about the man who was to be her third. All that time
that he had consumed in pumping her about Johnny Johns, in
contemning Johnny Johns, in emulating Johnny Johns—a little
of that time, only a little, Wally could more profitably have devoted to the maneuverings of his friend Stanley Child. When
the blow fell and there was that tiresome scene that Wally had
insisted upon ("I want you to hear everything I say to Stanley"), the thought kept running through her mind that Wally
hated Johnny much more than he did Stanley. Despite the fact
that she had been having her affair with Stanley right under
his nose, Wally managed to bring up Johnny Johns, whom she
had not seen or heard from in five years. "I thought you were
all through with that kind of thing when you got rid of that
Johns fellow," said Wally.

"I was—to marry you," she said. "Johnny could have
been very unpleasant about *you,* don't forget."

"That lightweight," said Wally, unmistakably implying
that Johnny was incapable of sustained indignation. Two years
later Wally married the present Mrs. Harris, the lady of the
patroness list, and immediately started having lunch with Stanley again. By Wally's lights it was all right to resume the friendship with Stanley Child as soon as he remarried, but not before. The friendship in its second phase was stronger than it
had ever been, and it did not include the wives. "Wally and
I are going over to play Pine Valley . . . Wally got me an invitation to Thomasville. Will you be all right?" At first she was
not all right, at all; it was not her idea of fun to sit in a New York
apartment while the two big boys, her husband and her ex,
went off to play. She was not worried about what they would
say about her; Stanley Child was simply not the kind of man
who would discuss his wife with another man on any terms,
and insensitive though he may have been about many things,
Wally Harris would know better than to mention Agatha except

when it was unavoidable. No, it was not the fear of their talking about her that annoyed her; it was her growing conviction
that she could be the wife of two men and yet remain completely outside their lives, one after the other and the two
together. In olden days they might well have fought a duel
over her; in the fifth decade of the twentieth century they
played golf together and tacitly denied her existence.

It was a dismal record for a girl who had only wanted to
be liked, who had only tried to be pleasant to people. She
loved Johnny Johns now, today, so many years later, but she
had not even believed at the time that she was marrying Johnny
for love. He was a screwy boy who would come charging into
Canoe Place late Saturday nights, arriving alone and always
leaving with some other boy's girl. Nothing vicious about him;
he made no phony promises, and he nursed no hard feelings
against the girls who refused to ditch the boys they had come
with. To such steadfast types he would say, "Okay, but you
don't know what you're missing," and it was as close as he
ever came to the surliness of some of the other wolf types. At
this point in her reminiscing she smiled.

Canoe Place, a Saturday night after a dance at the Mea-
dow Club. He came and sat down beside her—actually in back
of her—pulling up a chair from the next table. "Aggie Todd,
I've a bone to pick with you. I hear you said I wasn't a wolf."

"You heard I said you *weren't* a wolf? Were not? Why is
that a bone to pick with me?"

"You trying to ruin my reputation?"

"You're getting me all confused," she said.

"Did you or did you not say I was not a wolf?"

"I said you were not," she said.

"That's what I heard. What right have you got to go
around saying nice things about me?"

"Huh?"

"The first thing you know, all the mothers and fathers will
start approving of me. Then where will I be?"

She was young, and not very quick. "Oh, now I get it," she
said. "You glory in a bad reputation, is that it?"

"I sure as hell don't want to turn into a Henny Ramsdell."

"You won't, never fear." This was fun because Henny
Ramsdell at that very moment was seated on her left.

"Or a Bucky Clayton." Bucky Clayton was sitting across the table, looking at them and straining an ear to hear what they were saying. "Take a gander at Bucky, trying to read our lips."

"I know," she said.

"Why did you rush to my defense, Aggie?"

"Because I think—well I *don't* think you're a *wolf.*"

"Well, one of these days maybe I'll say something nice about you." He was a little more serious, and started to rise.

"Why not now?"

"All right," he said. Then, "No, I guess not. I don't want to turn your head."

"Ah, come on, turn my head, Johnny."

"You really want me to?"

"Yes."

"All right, but you asked for it, Aggie. I think you're the only girl in this whole damn bunch that I give a hoot in hell about."

"Is that truc?" she said.

"It's true."

"Scout's honor?"

"Now don't push it. Yes, scout's honor. Come on, let's dance. Mr. Ramsdell, boy, I'm taking your girl away."

"The hell you are," said Henny Ramsdell.

"The hell I'm not," said Johnny. "Come on, Aggie, while you have the chance."

A week later they eloped, and during the next four years all the predictable mishaps of their kind of marriage came to pass. There was, in addition, a handicap that the pessimists had not counted on and the optimists had not foreseen: she was too young for companionship with most of the young wives in her set, and as a wife she was no longer compatible with the unmarried girls who were her contemporaries. It came down to a problem of often not knowing whom to have lunch with, and Johnny, working downtown, was impatiently lacking in an understanding of the problem. "You would never think," she said to Wallace Harris, "that a thing like that would make so much difference, but it does."

Wallace Harris was a bachelor, a few years older than Johnny. "Do you mean to say you're lonely?"

"That's *just* what I'm saying."

"Why don't you have a child?"

"We did. I never saw it."

"Sorry."

She had not been very bright about Wallace Harris. She had had no curiosity about him, and when she drifted into an affair with him she was all but shocked to discover that he had always been promiscuous, that women by the dozen had succumbed, if that was the word, to his availability. It was difficult to believe him as he told her the number and kinds of women who had slept with him, but she could not wholly doubt him since she was now one of that list herself. What made it difficult to believe him was her unthinking acceptance of the notion that roués had fun, and inevitably were gay; but for Wally there seemed to have been no fun, only a succession of women who used him as much as he used them. As for gaiety, one of his outstanding characteristics was a total lack of it. In this respect, however, she came to understand his success with women: he was so lacking in gaiety that a woman would automatically credit him with discretion and reliability. But poor Wally was essentially nothing more than a well-scrubbed male, who never needed a haircut or a manicure, and would have been far happier without women if the men he liked had been able to do without them too. He would never have been clinically curious about her life with Stanley Child as he had been about Johnny Johns; without asking, he would guess that Stanley's demands on a woman were much like his own—and he would have been right. He understood Stanley, but Johnny Johns was a lightweight . . .

Agatha Child heard herself say, "What? What?"

Mary Moran was standing in the doorway, with the jacket of the black suit over her arm and holding up the skirt. "I didn't mean to startle you, ma'am."

"Oh—I was off somewhere," said Agatha Child. "What is it, Mary?"

"Well, I was wondering if maybe there's a little hole in the skirt we should have rewoven."

"A hole in it? Let me see."

"Right here, ma'am, just back of the knee. You musta caught it on something."

"Yes. I wonder if it'd be worth it. Reweaving is awfully expensive."

"Now if it was a country suit, you wouldn't care so much. But you don't want to go around with a hole in your skirt in the city."

"I forget how much they charged the last time I had something rewoven. I paid four hundred dollars for that suit, when was it, three years ago?"

"You had this three years, that's right. It's a beautiful suit, no doubt about that. I think it's worth getting it rewoven."

, "It's too bad you can't wear my clothes. I'd give it to you, then I'd have an excuse to buy myself a new one."

"No, I could never get into this. I was always too big an eater."

"You *could* have a nice figure, if you'd take off about fif- teen pounds. You really ought to be ashamed of yourself, Mary. That's all since you've come to work for me."

"Aach, and if they don't like me this way it's too late for me to change."

"Too late? Nonsense. Forty-one. If I gave you a course at Elizabeth Arden, would you go through with it?"

"Me at Elizabeth Arden's? Huh."

"Well, any place."

"Thanks just the same. I got the determination, if I want to starve off the fifteen pounds, but I'd only put it back on again."

"Do as you please," said Agatha Child.

"And what about the suit, ma'am?"

"Have it rewoven, of course. And tell them not to take so long. The last time I think they took over a month."

"That was a big cigarette burn, in your gray."

"You don't have to make excuses for them, Mary. Just tell them what I said."

Mary Moran left, saying no more. If she had stayed longer, said any more, Agatha Child would have fired her. The woman had snubbed her twice within the hour, less than an hour, actually. Agatha, at the thought of time, glanced at the little gold and enamel clock at her side. It was twelve-twenty-two, according to the clock—which obviously had stopped during the night. She reached for the clock to wind it, but it had *not* stopped; the winder took only one full turn. She held the clock to her ear, and it was steadily ticking away. Was it possible that she had been sitting here for an hour and ten minutes? Had she fallen asleep after her coffee and cigarette? She looked for her cigarette. It was not in the ash tray, and yet she remembered having a cigarette, blowing the smoke at the dogs.

Casually, so that Mary Moran would not come in and catch her in the act of looking for the cigarette butt, she bent over to the right and then to the left of her chair. The cigarette was on neither side. She leaned forward, and there it was, having burnt itself out and formed a small crater in the carpet. She *had* been asleep, and once again she had gone to sleep with a cigarette burning, just as she had done while wearing the gray suit, which Mary Moran knew about, and one other time that the maid did not know about, all within a space of six or eight weeks.

She picked up the cigarette butt and put it in the ash tray. Then she dipped a napkin in the glass of icewater and tried to rub the blackened crater in the carpet so that the burn would not show. This was only partially successful. The crater remained, and some of the piling was permanently blackened.

It was no time to panic; it was a time to face facts, to look at things calmly. She would begin by admitting that this was the fourth, not only the third, time that a cigarette had given her some kind of trouble recently. The third time, fortunately, was in a taxicab. The fourth time—a week ago—was here in the apartment, when she went to the bathroom and found a merry little fire in the tin wastebasket. She extinguished that fire easily by putting the basket under the bathtub tap and letting the water run. The contents of the basket she flushed down the toilet; the scorched basket itself presented a bit of a problem, which she solved by wrapping it in newspapers and taking it down to Madison Avenue and dropping it in the city basket. Mary Moran noticed that the bathroom basket was missing. *She* noticed everything. "I got tired of it," Agatha Child told her. "I threw it out with the trash last night."

"It was kind of pretty," said Mary Moran.

"Cheap," said Agatha Child. "I saw a nicer one at Hammacher's."

"Oh, one of them with the mirrors all around it?" said Mary. "Mrs. Brown has two of them."

"Yes. The other basket was here when I took this apartment, and I don't know why I kept it so long. But yesterday I decided I couldn't look at it one more day."

It was the kind of explanation that would satisfy Mary Moran, with her unspoken but unmistakable opinion of Agatha Child as a frivolous woman. The same opinion had made credible the explanation for the burn in the gray suit. "I'm almost sure that it was some awful woman at the cocktail party I went to yesterday. She carried a long cigarette holder, and I noticed her waving it around."

Explanations were imperative. Agatha Child had heard of some woman who had been asked to leave some apartment-hotel because she was a fire hazard, falling asleep and setting fire to her bedclothes. It would not do, it would not do at all, to let Mary Moran know that Agatha Child had had any such experiences.

Agatha Child rose and sauntered to the livingroom door, listened, heard Mary Moran humming a tune, which she did when she was busy. Now quickly Agatha Child got a bottle of ink and a fountain pen and went back to her chair. She carefully poured ink on the crater in the carpet, watched it soak in, then sharp and loud she exclaimed, "God damn it! Oh, God damn it."

Mary Moran appeared in the doorway. "Something the matter?"

"Look at the mess I've made. Trying to fill my pen."

"They can get that out."

"I wonder. I know they can get the stain out, but look how deep this is. One of those places where the dogs have chewed the carpet. Boys, you really do try my patience sometimes. Oh, well this was my fault, no use trying to blame the dogs."

Brilliant. Inspired. At the moment of pouring the ink she had not even thought of the dogs and their, or Muggsy's, habit of digging holes in the carpet. It was the kind of inspiration she would not have had if she had not refused to panic. Face facts, look at things calmly.

"Will I phone the rug man?" said Mary Moran.

"Yes, will you, before you leave? And I won't be here this afternoon, Mary. I've just decided to blow myself to a new suit."

"Another black, ma'am?"

"Anything but. This is something for spring," said Agatha Child. "Do you think I'm mad, Mary? I *am* a little mad, aren't I?"

AUNT ANNA

He was a big man, a good six foot two-and-a-half or three, and probably two hundred and thirty pounds. Just standing there on the dock he was impressive in spite of his attire, which was so careless that especially in a man of his size there was defiance, belligerence, to the way he made himself look. He wore a cotton work shirt of faded blue, khaki pants that were ripped in a couple of places and rolled up at the cuffs, old surplus Marine Corps combat shoes of reverse calf, and a yellow safety helmet. They were honest clothes, but he wore his belt low, so that his belly flopped over the brass buckle; in the back his shirt was not tucked in and on one side the shirt-tail was almost out. His safety helmet was on the back of his head because he had neglected to adjust the harness inside that would make the helmet fit.

He was watching the progress across the bay of a dory with an outboard motor. A young man was steering the boat, and a middle-aged woman sat erect in a spot halfway the length and halfway the width of the dory. She had a paper shopping bag in her lap which she held on to with one hand while keeping the other hand on top of her blue denim hat.

The man on the dock made no sign of greeting. He remained standing in the same position as the crossing ended; the woman gave the boatman a dollar bill, got out of the boat at the float beneath the dock, and walked slowly up the ramp. She halted when she was a few steps from the man.

"Well, aren't you going to say hello?" she said.

The man reached in a shirt pocket and took out a crumpled

cigarette pack. It was so crumpled that at first he could not find the last remaining cigarette. He threw the pack in the water and held the cigarette up to see if the paper had been broken. The cigarette was bent in a couple of places, but it was smokeable. He lit it, took a deep inhale, and now for the first time spoke to the woman. "I thought you's gonna be here an hour ago," he said.

"He couldn't get the thing started," she said.

"Charged you a dollar," said the man. "I remember when they used to row you across for a dime. Yeah, and they took about the same length of time."

"I don't think that kid could row that far."

"Row that far? He didn't look to me like he could spin the flywheel."

"Well, he finally did."

"Do you want to stop in Paul's for a beer?"

"There's some in the icebox, unless you drank it all," she said.

"I put in a couple six-packs," he said.

She followed him in the direction of the parking lot. "You get enough to eat while I was away?"

"Lay off," he said.

"I was only asking you a question," she said. "Did you eat home, or go out someplace?"

"I done both. I ate home, and a couple times I went over and had something at Paul's." They reached the car, a twelve-year-old Cadillac that had a cracked window criss-crossed with friction tape in one of the rear doors. The edges of the fenders were crumbly with rust, and a hub cap was missing, but still it was a Cadillac, a big car.

"You didn't get rid of this," she said, sitting in the car. "What happened with getting the Falcon?"

"He wouldn't allow me but only three-fifty on this," said the man. "I read an article where they pay five, six thousand dollars for a car this size. In South America. One of those South American countries. So why should I part with this for three-fifty?"

"Well, if they pay that much maybe we could put this on a ship and get a free trip to South America," she said.

"Listen, if I could get the time off that's what I was think-ing of doing. I went through the Canal in '43, when I was in the Seabees. That's quite a place, South America."

"I don't have any objections," she said.

"Well, you been away almost three weeks," he said. "Stay home a while."

"I'd be ready to leave again tomorrow, if we could go to South America. Free. Maybe make a little profit, if they paid you five or six thousand for this. How much would it cost to ship this?"

"Oh, maybe three-four hundred dollars, I don't know for certain."

"But it'll never happen, so what's the use of talking about it? You'll end up taking two hundred for this, and I won't get my little Falcon till I'm too old to drive it. If you had any idea what this was to park."

"I don't have any trouble."

"You don't weigh a hundred and twenty," she said. "You just want a big car, that's all."

"Well, I tell you this much," he said. "You won't get me driving around in like one of them Fiats."

"Let's change the subject. Was Margaret all right? Did she keep the place clean?"

"I only saw her Sundays. Yeah, the place looks all right."

"Did she make your bed every day?"

"Uh-huh."

"She put the dishes away and all?"

"Uh-huh."

"You didn't pay her, did you?"

"I didn't know I was suppose to. I understood you were."

"I was, but I thought maybe you might have. Forty-two dollars, we owe her."

"Will we get it back?" he said.

"How?"

"Well, didn't that brother-in-law of yours offer to pay you anything?"

"For God's sake, Harry. My own sister."

"Your own sister, but he's your brother-in-law. He could offer to pay something."

"He did offer, but the expenses mounted up. He'll be a year paying off his debts, and he needs every cent for those children. A widower with three young children, not one of them old enough to work. But he sure is wonderful with them, I must give him credit. They do everything he says, and they're so neat and clean. You never saw any three children so neat and clean, well behaved."

"Was that him, or your sister?"

"It was both. But they didn't go to pieces when their mother took sick. Little Ann, she did the dishes before she went to school every morning, and she's only twelve. Maxine made the beds, she's only ten. And Roddy, you oughta seen that little seven-year-old boy trying to help out with the garbage can and one thing another."

"I guess he better get himself another wife pretty soon, with three kids that age," said Harry.

"That's what I told him," she said. "He asked me if I thought it was right. 'Henry,' I said, 'the best proof of how well you thought of Betty is if you get married again.' "

"I don't get *that*," said Harry.

"If a man stays single, that doesn't prove he thought highly of his wife. Half the time it just proves he always wanted to be single."

"Well, he isn't much for looks," said Harry. "A long, skinny drink of water. He won't get another as pretty as Betty."

"He got Betty, didn't he? Henry Dumaine has a lot of personality, never mind the looks."

"How do you mean, personality? Would you go for him?"

"Me? He was married to my younger sister."

"Yeah, well I heard of *that* happening," said Harry.

"Oh, sure. You heard of everything happening," she said. "I phoned you the night of the burial."

"I was home, unless—Tuesday I was bowling."

"Anyway, you weren't home, because I phoned you. I tried you again Wednesday, too."

"What for?"

"I wanted to stay there a while longer. There was a lot of things I wanted to take care of. But I said I'd be back here today, so I came back. I'm going over there again next week for a few days."

"No, you're not," said Harry. "You done your share, now let Henry start looking for somebody else."

"No, I said I'd go over again next week. I'm the only one that knows where everything is, and I have to show this woman he's getting to help out."

"What the hell do you think you are?"

"I'm those children's aunt, my younger sister's children, and that's all there is to it. You could of got the day off to come to the burial if you tried hard enough. You could of reported sick."

"You can't hold that against me. I'm the foreman, and if I don't show up the work don't get done. Done right, anyway. And somebody has to make up that forty-two dollars."

"If you weren't such a helpless we wouldn't had to spend the forty-two dollars. I'll pay you the forty-two dollars out of my savings account, if that's the way you're going to talk."

"I'm no chiseler. I'll pay it. But you're staying home."

"It's only across the bay and five miles by car."

"It might as well be Saskatchewan. You're staying home." They had reached home, a gray shingled, story-and-a-half house on the slant of a hill, with a propane gas tank near the kitchen door, and ruts in the grass made by the Cadillac. "Where's your suitcase?" he said.

"I left it over at Henry's. I knew I was going back."

"You had it all planned."

"I could of told you over the phone," she said. She slightly raised the shopping bag. "This is an angel cake I brought you. One of Henry's neighbors gave it to him, but he said to take it with me. He doesn't like to have the children eating too much sweet stuff, for their teeth."

"So that's what I get for my forty-two dollars. A cake I could buy at the supermarket."

"You don't have to eat it if you don't want to." She carried the cake into the kitchen and put it away.

"Are you coming up to the room?" he said.

"All right," she said.

He had been deprived of her for three weeks and his

need was so urgent that she was surprised by the response it created in her. She had known what to expect and was reconciled to it, but she found that she wanted him as much as he wanted her. He was almost someone new. But he was not someone new. The someone new was over on the other side of the bay.

"Well, I guess you won't go back now," said Harry.

"I have to, Harry. It's those children."

He was in a better humor. "You're a stubborn bitch," he said.

"You don't have to curse at me," she said. "Just because I want to do something for those children."

"Toss me one of those cigarettes," he said. "Maybe I don't have the personality, but I know *you*, all right."

"You only think you do," she said.

"Huh," he chuckled. He took a couple of drags on his cigarette, one on top of the other, and crushed it out. He stretched out and lay on his right side. "Wake me up around ha' past seven, will you?"

"What do you want for supper?"

"I don't care. Maybe a pot roast," he said.

In the morning she caught the bus that took the long way round to the other side of the bay, an hour's journey. She walked from the bus stop to Henry Dumaine's house and let herself in by the kitchen door. At about ten o'clock she heard someone downstairs. "Is that you, Mrs. McNamara?" she called.

"It's me. Mrs. Phelps?"

"I'm just finishing up the upstairs."

"Can I help?"

"Why don't you put the coffee on and I'll be down in a minute," said Anna Phelps.

Mrs. McNamara was a sturdy woman, who looked as though she could do everything about the house; but sitting at the kitchen table, smoking a cigarette, she seemed to be waiting to be told what to do. "You certainly do resemble your sister," said Mrs. McNamara.

"Well, we used to when we were younger. She was four years my junior, you know," said Anna Phelps.

"I wouldn't of said that. In fact, toward the end there Betty aged. Of the two you look the younger."

"I guess that's because my husband and I don't have children. It's wonderful to have them if you're healthy, but Betty was sick much longer than she let on."

"I have five myself, but thank the Lord I was blessed with a strong constitution. I have nine grandchildren."

"All your children married?"

"All but the one that's a priest, naturally. I have my boy Paul, a Vincentian, teaches at St. John's University, Brooklyn, New York. I'm probably older than you think. How old would you say? Give a guess."

"Well—fifty-two?"

"I'll be sixty-three years of age on the twenty-fourth day of October. I didn't have glasses till I was fifty-five. I don't need them now, except to read. These are bifocals."

"I was judging by your hair, and your complexion," said Anna Phelps.

"They say worry puts the lines in your face, and it's true. I know I was never one to worry, even when Mr. Mc-Namara had to stay home from work all that time. He was home over a year before he finally passed on. Just suffering, and no money coming in, but I didn't let it worry me."

"I guess you have your religion," said Anna Phelps.

"Oho, indeed I do, thank the good Lord," said Mrs. McNamara. She dipped the lighted end of her cigarette in the bottom of her coffee cup, got up and put the cigarette butt in the garbage pail and rinsed out the cup and saucer. "Henry said you'd be over some time next week," she said.

"Yes, but I talked it over with my husband and he said I might as well help you get started today. I can stay a couple days and by that time you'll know all the ropes. Harry said what was the use of waiting till next week? If I was gonna be any help, this was the time." Anna Phelps watched Mrs. McNamara taking in the lie.

"He sounds very considerate, your husband," said Mrs. McNamara.

"Oh, yes. Good-natured, like most big men."

"Mr. McNamara was a big man, over six foot."

"Uh-huh. Harry Phelps is, too. Six two-and-a-half in his stocking feet, and weighs well over two hundred. He can pick *me* up with one hand. He's a foreman with the telephone company."

"So I understand, from Henry. I guess he must be one of that Phelps family from over on the Point."

"Yes, Harry was born there. So were we, of course. Betty and I. We're Point people."

"I know," said Mrs. McNamara. "But Henry comes from Pawtucket."

"Originally from Worcester, Mass, but raised in Pawtucket. They moved around, the Dumaine family. That's how Henry happened to first meet Betty. Betty was just starting out as a telephone operator when Henry came along. That was when he was still working for the telephone company, a traveling auditor, went from place to place."

"That wouldn't have been much of a life for a couple of newlyweds."

"No, that's why Henry took this job here."

"Well, they think the world and all of Henry at the bank. I know that. He's in line for cashier, that's according to my eldest son, Desmond. Desmond has the management of the Inn, that's where Rotary and Kiwanis meet, and Desmond hears everything that goes on around town."

"Oh."

"The men at the bank, the directors, they finally got wise to the fact that one third of the population are Catholics, French extraction mostly, but they never had a Catholic working there before Henry. You know those French, they're thrifty, but it was Henry Dumaine got them to start putting their money in the bank."

"Yes, I never thought of that," said Anna Phelps.

"And your sister, Betty. Was she an asset! She was as much of an asset as Henry, to some extent. You know they say that about converts, that they're more devout than some were born in the Church. Not always the case, but true in her case. You saw that church the day of the Mass. Over half filled, and on a weekday when everybody has to go to work. That's what they thought of your sister."

"It was a wonderful turnout, that's for sure," said Anna

Phelps. She was beginning to see that this woman, so pleased with herself, who had seemed to be waiting to be told what to do, had in fact been waiting to get across a few points of her own. And she was getting them across. "Betty never talked much about it, religion, at least not to me. She just did what Henry said."

"Oh, that's not the way it is, Mrs. Phelps," said Mrs. McNamara. "You have to convince the priest that it's *you* that wants to turn Catholic, otherwise he won't baptize you. Henry had something to do with it, but Betty had to be sincere."

"Uh-huh. Well, as long as she was happy," said Anna Phelps. She got up and rinsed out her cup and saucer. "You'll want to do things your own way, but I thought I'd show you where Betty kept everything. You notice the knives and forks, the sharp things, they're all kept up here, that's so the younger ones don't cut themselves. My little nephew tries to help out, and he does, but Betty kept the sharp things out of reach."

"Uh-huh. I took notice to that. I'll make my changes gradual-like, to give them a chance to get used to me. I guess Henry told you, I'll be coming in late in the morning and stay to cook their supper. But I don't want them to get *too* used to me, Mrs. Phelps. I told Henry, I said it's his duty to start looking around for somebody to take Betty's place. Someone more her age."

"You mean, to get married again?"

"Yes, sure. He said he had some conversation with you about it and you had the same idea, so I just wanted to let you know. He oughtn't to have any trouble finding a nice Catholic woman, most likely a widow. There's two or three would jump at the chance, but Henry don't have to take the first one that comes along. You know, *we* have to be sure it's *permanent*."

Even before the children came home from school the two women had gone through the house and covered all the details of running the household. "I could almost go home on the late bus," said Anna Phelps. "But I think I'll stay and cook supper for them. I'll get them off to school tomorrow, and if I don't see you in the morning, thank you very much and good luck."

"You'll be here tonight, then?"

"Yes, I'll be here, if you want me for anything. Then I'll

get the ten-fifteen bus in the morning or else maybe get that boy to take me across the bay in the outboard, if I can find him. I'll leave you my number in case you want to call me."

"Uh-huh. Well, I'm glad we had a chance to talk," said Mrs. McNamara.

"Yes, I'll feel better knowing you're in charge," said Anna Phelps.

There was no further excuse for lingering, and Mrs. McNamara left.

The children were delighted to see their Aunt Anna again so soon. Her return was an extension of the holiday that her visits always seemed like but particularly in the recent three weeks of their mother's illness and death. She had not brought them presents this time, but she gave each child some money. At supper they groaned when she said she was leaving in the morning, and the boy, Roddy, had to be told to stop bawling. "Why'nt she stay if she came back?" he said.

"Now you be a good boy, and I'll come over a lot," said Anna Phelps. "And next summer if you're good you can come stay with Uncle Harry and I. We can go for rides in his great big car."

"Where to?" said the boy.

"Oh—Pawtucket, to see your Grandpa and Grandma. And a lot of places."

"If you're good," said Henry Dumaine. "Now it's time to say goodnight, son. And girls, your homework."

"Does Uncle Harry have a TV at his house?" said the boy.

"Of course," said Anna Phelps. "And by next summer we'll have a brand-new one."

"I wish we had a TV," said the boy.

"Maybe this Christmas," said the father. "Now enough stalling."

The children went to their rooms. "I guess I'll get them a TV," said Henry Dumaine.

"They're nice to have if you don't let them have it on all the time."

"School doesn't want them looking at it week nights, and I'm in favor," said Henry Dumaine.

"So am I."

"If I'm not strict with them now they're liable to take

advantage," said Henry Dumaine. "And they have to get used to Mrs. McNamara."

"They will," said Anna Phelps.

"Well, I hope so," he said. "That's why I was thinking—don't make them any promises about coming over. You know what I mean? Let them get used to—"

"Oh, I know, Henry. You want them to get used to Mrs. McNamara. I won't interfere."

"You wouldn't interfere, Anna. But I don't want them—you know—counting on you. That way they'd never get used to Mrs. McNamara, and they're going to have to. At least for a year or so."

"Well, I could stay away entirely, if that's what—"

"No, I don't want that. Not a bit. But you were never here much before, and then these past few weeks, they're too young to realize."

"Realize what, Henry?"

"Well, that with me a widower, it's a different proposition than if Betty was still in the house."

"We didn't realize it, either, the night of the burial," she said.

"I don't know what came over me," he said.

"Well, I was willing," she said.

"I've been ashamed of myself ever since."

"What for? It was always there between us."

"Yes, I guess it was. For you? Was it there for you?"

"Yes, and you knew it and Betty knew it."

"No she didn't," he said. "She never had the slightest inkling. And you're wrong, Anna. Maybe we liked one another, but that's all it ever was. If there was anything much before, we had several chances. I've been analyzing it, and it was just two people overcome by emotion and the one emotion led to another. But you went straight back to Harry Phelps. Don't tell me you and Harry didn't have relations when you went home yesterday."

"I won't tell you anything, since you know so much. Got it all analyzed and figured out. But did you ever stop to consider why I only came here once or twice a year? An hour away by bus?"

"Harry."

"Betty, not Harry. She didn't want anything to get started. And I don't know what you're talking about, those chances you mentioned."

"Well, I could have gone over to the Point."

"That. But here Betty never left us alone for five minutes. She made sure of that."

"Betty trusted me," said Henry Dumaine.

"Like a hole in the head. Henry, Betty used to think you could have any woman you wanted, from her own sister right on out. Young or old, big or little, rich or poor. She knew about your reputation before she ever met you. The other operators. But that didn't keep her from going for you."

"That was when I was single," he said.

"Oh, hell, I don't care when it was," she said. "Now all I care about is if those children have a good home. That's really all I care about. And I'm not going to stand in the way. You could even marry the McNamara woman if she was ten or fifteen years younger."

"Her? I wouldn't give her a tumble if she was thirty. How did you ever get that idea?"

"I spent the whole day talking to her. She'd like it, even if you wouldn't."

"She's over sixty, and I'm forty-seven," he said. "You're getting yourself all wrought up because you have some kind of a guilty conscience. Not only Tuesday night, Anna. But what you came here for. Why you came back so soon and didn't let me know."

"All right," she said. "But at least I'll admit it. You pretend you want me out of the way, but you don't. Will you admit that much?"

"You admit it for me," he said. "You got it all analyzed."

"Then you the same as admit it, why don't you come out and say so?"

"That I go for you? I proved that, didn't I?"

"Yes," she said.

There was a long fraction-of-a-minute of silence.

"That's all I wanted to know," she said.

"Do you mind if I ask you a kind of a personal question?"

"That all depends," she said. "Ask it."

"Was Harry Phelps always so crummy-dirty and sloppy?"

"He didn't used to be when he was young. He was quite a dresser. Why?"

"Oh, I don't know. I just used to think you were more refined."

"Well, when we were first married Harry used to go to New York City for all his suits. But then he began to let himself go. Now he don't care how he looks. And it doesn't do any good to talk to him about it. I don't have the slightest influence, not the slightest. And Christ knows I tried."

"Well, you don't have to go to New York to have good taste in clothes," said Henry Dumaine.

"I couldn't agree more," said Anna Phelps. "Either you have good taste or you don't, and all you can feel is sorry for those that don't." She crossed her leg and smoothed her skirt down over her knees. "Little Ann *and* Maxine, they both have it, to the *nth* degree."

"And why not?"

"Well, if that's a compliment . . ." She smiled, and he smiled so that she could be sure.

EMINENT DOMAIN

The Langendorfs and the MacMahons exercised a private version of the right of eminent domain over the Whitney property. The Langendorfs lived on Second Street, the MacMahons on Main, which paralleled Second. Between Second and Main there was an unnamed alley. Instead of going to one of the nearby corners, a MacMahon would go out his back gate, cross the alley, cut through the Whitney property lengthwise, and cross Second to the Langendorfs' front yard. It helped, of course, that the three families were friends and it helped even more that Mrs. Langendorf was Albert Whitney's sister. Actually she was a half sister, but that was close enough.

As a boy Gerald Higgins spent all or part of every summer with the MacMahons, who were his grandparents. He had no contemporaries in the Langendorf family, but he was often sent on errands to the Langendorfs', and in fact the Langendorfs would telephone the MacMahons to ask if Gerald would run an errand for them. Consequently he used the trespass privilege over the Whitney property many times in his boyhood, and he was well along in years, fourteen or so, before realizing that he had never been inside the Whitney house—except the kitchen. Mrs. Whitney and Beulah Bader, the Whitneys' hired woman, had occasionally interrupted him on one of his errands to invite him to have a glass of lemonade or a piece of huckleberry pie; but even on such occasions he had usually stayed on the Whitneys' back porch, where they kept the icebox. At fourteen he had begun to notice more and more of the subtleties of social relations, and to the discovery that he had never been in the front part of the Whitney house he added the observation that he could not recall that his mother, his father, or his grandparents had ever gone calling on the Whitneys.

It was not of itself much of a discovery; in Lyons, Pennsylvania, you could be friends with a family and still not have them to your house or go to theirs. There was that kind of relationship: friendly, but not close. And in some houses they never used the front room, the parlor, except at the time of a death, a wedding, or the annual visit by the pastor. The Whitneys, however, did use their parlor every day, every evening. They most certainly did. Gerald Higgins, passing their house in the early evening, would often see Albert Whitney reading the Fort Penn paper that came in the mail, and smoking a cigar. The cigar was forbidden in those front parlors that were opened only for special occasions. The Whitneys, when they had friends in for a game of cards, would use their front parlor instead of the diningroom. Sometimes on a summer evening Gerald Higgins would be passing the Whitneys' house and he would hear their Vic playing Harry Lauder's record of "She's My Daisy," the same recording that his grandfather enjoyed so. It was hard to understand some of Harry Lauder, who did nothing to smooth out his Scottish burr. Was he singing, "I'd rather lose m' *straps* than lose m' Daisy" or "I'd rather lose m' *stripes* than lose m' Daisy"? Stripes, most likely, meaning chevrons. To Gerald Higgins, growing up with ragtime and jazz, Harry Lauder was a bore, and he replied to a Lauder record with a popular, very risqué parody that began, "I love a lassie/ a bony, bony lassie/ she's as thin as the paper on the wall." He could never finish it in front of his grandparents. It was very risqué, and very popular, and he had a feeling that it would not have shocked Albert Whitney, who smoked cigars in his front parlor and played cards without lowering the parlor shades . . .

Bert Whitney, as the older people called him, had a job as manager of the Valley Lumber Company, which was owned by the Langendorf family. Any business enterprise that went by the name Valley was likely to be owned by the Langendorfs. The Langendorf general store was called Langendorfs' but the lumber company, the brick yard, the water company, and a real-estate firm, all named Valley, were nominally separate from the store, which was almost a hundred years old. If anything happened to one of the Valley enterprises, the Langendorf name would still go on as it always had, symbolized by the store. Old Mr. Fred Langendorf was not sentimental about many things, but he was sentimental about that. He had sold his shares in the Valley Power & Light Company at a profit, and suspended the Valley Wagon Works at a loss, but the general store was not for sale at any price, and everyone knew it.

Everyone knew, too, that Bert Whitney owed his job to two people: to his grandfather, who had come to Lyons and stayed there in the early part of the previous century; and to his half sister, who had married Mr. Langendorf when the old man was a middle-aged widower. Bert Whitney was third-generation Lyons, representative of a family that had escaped mean poverty and never quite got rich. They had always had enough to eat; on the other hand Albert Whitney's father, Lawrence Whitney, had mortgaged his house to get his son through Franklin & Marshall; in eighteen years Lawrence Whitney had failed to stash away enough money to pay for Bert's college expenses. The mortgage was still outstanding four years later when Bert's half sister married the widower Langendorf. As a wedding present to his wife Fred Langendorf retired the mortgage, and Lawrence Whitney, free of debt, soon gave up the struggle that had ceased to be a struggle.

The next in an unending series of presents that Fred Langendorf gave his wife was to place her younger half brother in charge of the lumber yard. It had been Lawrence Whitney's hope that Albert would study law, but Bert had no taste for the law—or for study. Nor was he particularly good at selling; but all the lumber yard needed to survive was an order-taker. The carpenters and builders, the railways and the mines would buy what they needed, and they did so in sufficient quantity to make the lumber yard a profitable business. All that Bert Whitney had to know was what stock he had on hand and keep it from getting too low; his customers usually came to the yard and helped themselves to what they wanted.

Bert ate a good breakfast every morning and was at the office at eight, went home for dinner at half past eleven,

returned to the yard an hour later to do business with the
independent carpenters who used the noon hour for their small
purchases, and at five o'clock he was through for the day. The
tennis court, for which as a subscriber he had a key, was on the
property adjoining the lumber sheds, and Bert could get in a
set or two nearly every spring and summer day. He was one
of two men in the town who could chop a ball so that it
would go over the net and come back over the net on the re-
bound. He was also a keen trout fisherman and a better than
fair shot. He had a very pleasant life, and his one regret, for
which he could not blame himself, was that he had not had a
son to whom he could teach the chop stroke, the tying of a
trout fly, the timing of the second shot when going after quail.
He had one daughter, Amy, to whom he taught the rules of
lawn tennis, but she was so lacking in the competitive spirit
that she was no fun to play with. When she finished high
school she went off to Fort Penn to become a trained nurse,
and her father was thereby relieved of the responsibility of her
education and of the problem of what to say to her when they
were alone together.

Amy Whitney was more like her mother, the former Jobyna
Ortlieb, whose father was a blacksmith at the old Valley Wagon
Works until his death. Jobyna's education ended with the
eighth grade, not because the Ortliebs were poor, but because
Jacob Ortlieb would not have a female in his house who knew
too much. Jobyna went to work with the thirty-five other girls
in the shirt factory and at the end of a year she knew too much
about certain things that she had no business knowing about at
all. Her father was not aware of the kind of conversation that
went on among the factory girls, or of the privileges that the
girls' foreman exercised. Jobyna Ortlieb was an apple dumpling
of a girl, and after a year of her share of the foreman's attentions she quit her job. Her mother backed her up in her refusal
to go back to the factory. "If she comes home some day
knocked up it'll be your fault," the mother told the father.
This argument carried weight, and Jobyna then got a job as
cash girl in Langendorfs' store. By the time Bert Whitney
finished college Jobyna was a full-fledged clerk, bringing home
forty dollars a month and entitled to the employees' twenty-five

percent discount on nearly everything sold at Langendorfs'. She sang in the Lutheran church choir—a mezzo-soprano— and was president of the Busy Bees, her sewing club. She was happy in her job, with its daily contacts with the customers and the promise of a secure lifetime if she did not find a husband.

She could almost forget the ugliness of her year at the shirt factory, but it came back to her when Bert Whitney asked her for a date. She had not had many dates, and although she had known Bert all her life, he was now a college graduate and requests for dates with her did not come from boys who had been to F. & M. or Lebanon Valley, Dickinson, Bucknell or State. A Lyons boy asking her for a date was more likely to be one who had had no more education than she, and if he came to her house with a fifty-cent box of chocolates he seemed to think he had made a down payment on her for life. She wanted something better than that. On the other hand, there was the question: what exactly did Bert Whitney want? She knew from the factory experience what men could want, and she did not want that, either. But if she was ever going to get anyone better than the box-of-chocolate swains, she had to start somewhere with the Bert Whitneys. She therefore agreed to let Bert walk home with her after choir practice, then to come to her house on a Wednesday evening, then to escort her to the band concert in the Grove, and then to kiss her as they sat on the front porch. Something told her that in the world they then entered, she was more knowledgeable than Bert. That, or Bert was behaving with such gentlemanly restraint that this would not be like the ugly ordeals with the factory foreman. In the succeeding months she watched Bert fall in love with her, and somewhere along the way she fell in love with him. The Busy Bees gave her a shower, her mother gave her a cameo brooch, her father gave her—or, just as good, returned to her—five hundred dollars. After the wedding trip the bride and groom took up residence in the Whitney house on Second Street, just across the street from Jobyna's former boss, Mr. Langendorf.

It was a full year before Jobyna realized that she might as well have moved to Pike's Peak. No one came to see her, and she did not feel right about taking up again with the girls of the Busy Bees. She had a feeling that Bert would not like them to return her calls. Not that he ever said anything derogatory about them. But the husbands of the married Busy Bees were not among Bert's friends. They pitched horseshoes; he played tennis. He was a Mason; they belonged to the P. O. S. of A. They slept in their underwear; he wore pajamas. They said ain't; he never said ain't. They spoke Pennsylvania Dutch; he knew only a few words in it. They saw each other; he never saw any of them. Jobyna would have liked the company of the married Busy Bees during her pregnancy, but to seek them out then would have seemed like asking for help, and when her daughter was born she was grateful for the help of Dr. Samuel G. Merritt. She needed all the help the doctor could give her, and he later admitted that he had needed a lot of help from God.

She was never again able to hold on to a baby long enough to have it brought forth whole and alive, and the older Amy got, the more precious she became to her mother. Bert never complained, but from the pleasure he took in showing his friends' sons what to do with their wrists in casting, where to hold their thumbs on a shotgun, how to grip a tennis racquet, it was obvious that he missed having a boy of his own. It was less obvious but apparent to Jobyna that he *tried* to love Amy, and she pitied him for having to make an effort to feel what he did not feel. For Jobyna it was so easy to love Amy, therefore sadder that the girl's father was missing that joy.

Jobyna Whitney could not teach Amy to play tennis, but from her Amy learned to cook, to sew, to market. It went without notice by the girl's father, but at fifteen Amy Whitney six or seven times a year would take over the cooking and other such household duties when Jobyna had to take to her bed with periodic pains. Amy would have to be excused early from the morning session at school to give her time to prepare her father's dinner. She was a good student, she made up whatever she missed, and the only thing she minded was when her duties at home took her out of biology class. She got 100 in every biology exam and her teacher apologized for giving her a mark of 99 for the year. "If I gave you a hundred that would mean you were perfect," he said. "Nobody's perfect. I tell you

what I'll do, Amy. I'll give you 99-plus, then the only person
that ever gets a higher mark will have to be perfect, so?" In
junior and senior years Amy did moderately well in chemistry
and not so well in physics, but since the same man taught
biology, chemistry, and physics, she always had one subject that
she enjoyed more than others. In senior year Prof Hunsberger
told her she must study medicine. "You wish me to, I will
speak to the father," he said.

"Well, I'd like to be a doctor, but I'm a girl."

"I speak," said Hunsberger. He called on Bert Whitney
at the lumber yard. Hunsberger was a fellow alumnus of Franklin & Marshall, of the same time but not a classmate.

"What can I do for you, Hunsie?" said Bert Whitney.

"Whereabouts do you send Amy to college, Bert?"

"I didn't know she wanted to go. College. You mean four
years, or Normal?"

"Not Normal, Bert. Don't send her to Normal. She wants
to be a doctor, an M.D."

"A doctor, no less. No, Hunsie. If she wants to go to
Normal, I can manage that. But pre-med, and then medical
school. I'm not a rich man."

"Neither was your father, Bert. And Amy could maybe get
a scholarship. Maybe you send her up to State."

"My father had to mortgage his house to—"

"*You* mortgage *your* house," said Hunsberger.

"And you mind your own business, Hunsie. I remember
now, she got good marks in biology, but cutting up frogs is a
long way from studying medicine. Is this your idea?"

"Cutting up frogs is a long way from studying medicine.
But you make it longer than it is. This young girl has ability
and wants to learn. Wants to learn, Bert."

"Do tell? It'd cost at least five thousand dollars before
she got through, ready to start earning some money."

"I go to Mr. Langendorf, or *Mrs.* Langendorf then."

"You keep your nose out of my family affairs, Hunsie. If
you say one damn word to my sister or my brother-in-law, I
won't even let her go to Normal."

"This is a sin, Bert. A sin."

"Then the Lord will punish me. I'm very pleased with

Amy. She's done well all through High, she's not a bit flighty. But she doesn't want to be a doctor. I know her too well for that. She just said that to please you. She's a very polite girl. We always saw to that."

Hunsberger shook his head. "And yet they call us the thick-headed Pennsylvania Dutch."

"Didn't you ever hear of the stubborn Yankee? That's what we are, a few generations back. I don't mind being called stubborn when I know I'm right. You just don't understand women, Hunsie. They try to please everybody, and you can't do that in this world."

"I'm in this world, too, Bert."

"No, you're always looking through a microscope, too busy to see what's going on around you. You better concentrate on your amoebas. By the way, are you going down to Lancaster next week? You fellows are having your twenty-fifth reunion."

"I was never to a commencement since I graduated."

"But your twenty-fifth reunion. You don't want to miss that."

"My fiftieth, I miss that too, if I am living yet. I was not one of you Chi Phi boys, Bert. Four years I only saw one football game. Saturdays I was clerking in a store. One dollar and fifty cents."

"I didn't have it so easy myself. That's the trouble, Hunsie. You have some idea that I'm a rich man."

"No, not now any more. I think you're a poor man, Bert."

"I'm not sure just how you mean that, Hunsie, but I don't want to get sore at you. So if you're not going to buy any lumber, I'm going to close up for the day."

It was a particularly inopportune moment for Hunsberger's appeal. Apart from an automatic resistance to such a radical notion as sending his daughter to medical school, Bert Whitney had certain notions of his own which would require financial assistance, inevitably by Fred Langendorf. Hunsberger encountered opposition that was confused with alarm, and Bert Whitney was proud of his self-control in his conversation with his old college acquaintance. For a year or more Bert Whitney had been turning over a scheme that if successful could make him independent of Fred Langendorf, although the first money would have to come from Langendorf himself; the bank would not be likely to make a loan for such a scheme. And the sum needed was five thousand dollars—minimum. The project was one for which Bert Whitney felt he was uniquely qualified, with his interest in athletics and games. He even had a name for it: the Olympia (if the movie theater could call itself the Bijou, pronounced By-Joe, an ancient Greek name would catch on in time).

The scheme, which Bert preferred to call a plan, was to get hold of some land back of the lumber yard, clear it, grade it, and construct four or six tennis courts, a trapshooting range, a swimming pool, a refreshment stand, men's and women's toilets, and eventually a pavilion that could be used for meetings and —not to be mentioned at first—mixed dancing. The land was only three blocks from the very center of town, whereas the Grove, where picnics and band concerts were held, was at the far edge of town and offered nothing but a stand of trees and a bandstand. In wintertime Bert would flood his tennis courts to provide skating rinks that would be safer than any of the nearby dams, and, again, closer to the center of town. People would pay small sums to use the various facilities, but the profit would come from the refreshment stand and the sale of sporting equipment, tennis balls, blue rocks, guns, skates. It would be a wholesome, family place where absolutely no alcoholic beverages would be served—certainly not in the beginning—and rowdyism would be strictly forbidden. Bert Whitney could envision a respectable, well-policed amusement park that on some future day would rival Willow Grove of Philadelphia, and Lyons might become famous as the site of Olympia. He would be the George C. Tilyou of Nesquehela County, without having gipsy fortune tellers or questionable side shows. Both railroads would have to do their share when he began to expand, but he would never let the common stock pass from his hands. It was, after all, his original idea. Hunsberger was up against a man's dream.

Fred Langendorf was usually described as being all business, a description that he earned in business dealings but that was not completely fair to his private generosity or his personal amiability. He was physically a rather frail man, ill equipped by Nature for the wrestling and the running and jumping, the camping out in the woods, the swimming in the coal-stained creeks that his boyhood companions enjoyed. Nor was he by temperament a player of games, a hobbyist. He was able to keep a lot of figures in his head, and his whole face would brighten up when he was called upon to perform his trick of adding three columns simultaneously. As an arithmetical gymnast he had no rival in the town; quail shooting and euchre he left to men like his wife's half brother.

"It's easy to see you gave this a lot of thought, Bert," he said.

"Been thinking about it and thinking about it," said Bert Whitney. "As I said a minute ago, it's too bad the bank can't go into it."

"Oh, they could, you know. Up to the value of the land."

"The assessed value," said Bert Whitney.

"Well, maybe a little more than that."

"But nowhere near five thousand dollars."

"No, nowhere near that," said Fred Langendorf. He put a finger in his ear and wormed some wax out of it. "How would you want this money, Bert? Would you want it all at once, or say half this year and half next, after you see how you're progressing? You'd be better off taking half now, you know. Then you'd only owe me twenty-five hundred and say two percent. Twenty-five fifty if it was a total loss."

"I'd have to have the whole amount now, Fred. I couldn't do it on less."

"And your job at the yard."

"Won't suffer, I promise you that," said Bert Whitney.

Fred Langendorf tried the other ear. He produced a wad of wax that stuck to the tip of his little finger. He studied it carefully for a long moment and then flicked it into the wastebasket. He was frowning, but he said, "All right. You have to give a man a fair chance, otherwise where would any business be? I'll make out a cheque and a promissory note. From then on it's up to you, Bert. But don't come to me for any more. Five thousand dollars cash is a very large sum of money. And keep me out of it. They'll guess you got the money from me, and you can't keep them from guessing. But if anybody asks me am I behind you in this scheme, I'm going to tell them no. I'm lending you five thousand dollars at two percent, and what you do with the money is your own business. That's what I'm going to tell them."

"Is it all right if I mention your name at the railroad companies?"

"No, Bert. You can't use my credit in this scheme. In fact, Bert, you be at the bank at ten o'clock tomorrow morning and I'll give you the cheque and you can deposit it right away."

"That sounds as if you didn't trust me."

"If a half a dozen people saw that cheque they might get the wrong impression. You have your money, Bert. Be satisfied with that, now, and don't ask for any extra. By the way, I understand Amy took second in general average. That's fine."

"Yes. What made you think of Amy all of a sudden?"

"Oh, I happened to. Maybe a little more than just happened to, but I don't believe in interfering in family matters. So I guess that's all today, Bert."

Amy Whitney, with the twenty dollars she got from her Uncle Fred and Aunt Lorena Langendorf and letters from Prof Hunsberger and Dr. Samuel G. Merritt, went to Fort Penn and enrolled as a student nurse at the big hospital.

One day in the summer of 1918 Gerald Higgins was taking a basket of grapes to the Langendorfs'. He had picked the grapes from his grandparents' arbor and now he was delivering them to Mr. Langendorf, who was convalescing from some illness. Gerald Higgins was fifteen, getting, he thought, a little old to run errands of that sort, but Mr. Langendorf was a nice man and Gerald's resentment vanished when he saw the old boy. Mr. Langendorf was sitting in a rockingchair, fully dressed in a white linen suit, his starched collar too loose around his scrawny neck, his spotted hands fluttering as though beating time to an inaudible tune.

"You ought to be out in the Glen on a day like this," said Mr. Langendorf.

"I guess I will go, later," said Gerald Higgins.

"I never learned to swim," said the old man. "That water was so cold, I couldn't stay in long enough."

"It's pretty cold, all right," said the boy.

"Watch out for snakes, too."

"We do. Billy Reifsnyder killed a copperhead the day before yesterday. That was the second one he killed this summer."

"It's been so dry. We need rain. Did you see Amy?"

"Amy Whitney? No. I didn't know she was home."

"Yes, she's home. On your way back, if you see her tell her I'm expecting her."

"Yes sir, I will," said the boy.

The old man reached in his pocket. "A little something for you, Gerald. Just between you and I." He held a silver dollar between thumb and forefinger; his other fingers were curled up on the palm of his hand and the hand shook so that as Gerald Higgins reached for the coin it fell to the floor. "Excuse me. You'll think I don't want to part with my money."

"Thank you very much, Mr. Langendorf," said the boy. "I'll tell Amy you want her to come over."

"Come again, Gerald. I always like to see you."

On the way home the boy knocked on the screen door of the Whitneys' kitchen. A voice from inside said, "Just put it on the porch . . . Oh, it's Gerald. I thought it was the groceries." Beulah Bader, her arms covered with flour, came to the door.

"Is Amy in?" said the boy.

"Amy! You got a visitor!" Beulah had a loud voice.

The boy could hear someone running down the back stairs, then Amy appeared. "Oh, hello," she said. "You wanted to see me about something?"

"Mr. Langendorf said to tell you he was expecting you."

"It's Gerald! Little Gerald. Why I never would have recognized you in your long pants. When did you get them?"

"I had them for over a year, pretty nearly. Mr. Langendorf said—"

"I know, I'm getting ready. Come in and sit down, have a glass of lemonade. Or would you rather have some grape juice?"

"I have to go, but thanks."

"Haven't you got time for one glass of lemonade?"

"Well, all right I guess so."

"Come on in out of the heat. Beulah, will you bring us a pitcher of lemonade in the front room?"

"I got my hands all sticky with dough," said Beulah Bader.

"Beulah's baking, but you go on in the front room, Gerald, and I'll be in in two shakes of a ram's tail," said Amy Whitney.

The Whitneys' front room was unlike any the boy had seen in Lyons. The chairs and sofa were covered for the summer, but the room gave the immediate impression of being in active use. There was mail on the secretary and spots of ink on the blotter. There were photographs of baseball and football teams on the walls; group photographs, and action photographs; not the sort of pictures that hung in Lyons front parlors, although there were the customary severe-looking men and women in oval frames as well. There was a large lithograph of the Franklin & Marshall campus. The boy counted four silver loving-cups of various sizes, and an elaborately designed beer stein stood alone on the top shelf of the secretary. A massive walnut cigar humidor rested on a mother-of-pearl inlaid taboret. The rugs had been taken up and the room was comfortably cool. The room was more like the boy's father's den than like any front parlor in Lyons.

"I brought a little sugar in case this is too tart," said Amy Whitney, setting down the tray. "Sit wherever you'll be comfortable."

"Thank you."

"I'm glad I saw you before I leave. Don't you wish you were going along? I'll bet you do."

"Where to? I didn't know you were going anywhere."

"You didn't? I was sure the whole town knew. I'm going overseas. I joined the army. I'm a nurse. A lieutenant. Don't you read the paper? It was in last week."

"I just got here Saturday," said the boy.

"Yes, my father just got out of the army and now I'm going in. So we can still hang the service flag in the window. I'm the only woman from Lyons in the army."

"I didn't know Mr. Whitney was in the army."

"Don't you ever hear *anything* in Gibbsville? My father was a first lieutenant. You should have seen him in his uniform. He had boots and spurs, and a swagger stick. He went in last September and he just got out in June. He was so disappointed, poor Father. Just about to go overseas, and they discovered he had kidney trouble. Didn't you know any of this?"

"I wasn't here in September. I had to go back to school," said the boy.

"Well, I don't think it'll last long enough for you to get in, but it might. I'll send you a German helmet when I get over there. That's because when you were a little boy, maybe you don't remember this, Gerald, but when you were a little fellow you and I used to play catch. Do you remember that? In the alley?"

"Sure, I remember."

"You must be what, now? Fifteen?"

"Yes."

"I thought so. You were about seven, then, and I was seventeen. That's just about when it was, the year before I went in training."

"For what?"

"To be a nurse. Didn't you know I was a trained nurse? I haven't seen much of you these last six or seven years. I guess I wasn't home much when you were here. Do you like the girls, Gerald?"

"Oh—well, some I do, and some I don't."

"Have you got a sweetheart in Lyons?"

"No!"

"Lyons girls too countrified for you?"

"They sure are. Dumb hicks."

"Well, don't be too sure about that."

"Oh, some of them are all right, I guess. One or two."

"Who, for instance?"

"Oh, I don't know."

"Ask me no questions, I'll tell you no lies, huh?"

"Uh-huh," said the boy. He had become conscious of her femininity during the latter part of the conversation, an awareness of resources of experience that he had not expected her to have. In the great division between girls who did and girls who did not, he now placed Amy Whitney among the girls who did.

"What are you thinking?" she said.

"Nothing. I wasn't thinking about anything."

"Oh, yes you were, but I'm not going to pursue the subject," she said. "You have eyes that give you away, Gerald. Did any girl ever tell you that?"

"No."

"Well, you have."

"So have you."

"Why Gerald Higgins. I have? Can you read my thoughts?"

"You were trying to read mine."

"And I did," she said. "Well, Mr. Mind-Reader, unless you want some more lemonade I guess I ought to go over and see my uncle."

"I had enough, thanks."

"If I send you a German helmet will you write to me?"

"Sure, if you want me to."

At this moment Bert Whitney appeared in the doorway. "Ah, I see you have a caller. Hello, Gerald."

"Hello, Mr. Whitney."

"How's everybody up at the MacMahons'? Is your mother here?"

"No sir, she's coming later. August."

"It is August," said Bert Whitney.

"Oh, that's right. Well, later in August," said the boy.

"How is your father? Keeping well?"

"Yes sir, as far as I know."

"Didn't I hear he was in the army?"

"The Navy. He's a senior lieutenant, the same as a captain in the army."

"And where is he now?"

"In Chicago. Great Lakes Training Station."

"Have a glass of lemonade, Father?"

"No thanks. If it lasts much longer they may get you into it. I suppose you wouldn't mind that."

"No, I wouldn't mind. I wish I was."

"Don't be in any hurry. It isn't all bands playing and pretty girls throwing kisses at you. Your mother asleep, Amy?"

"Yes, I gave her a pill a little while ago."

"Think I'll take a little tonic myself," said Bert Whitney. He opened a door in the taboret and got out a bottle of whiskey and a tumbler. He filled half of the tumbler and drank the whiskey in two gulps while his daughter and the boy sat silent. "Tonic," said Bert Whitney, to no one. "Amy, you have a lot of things to do this afternoon, so I guess you better start doing them."

"Yes. I was just getting ready to go over to Uncle Fred's."

"Oh, you're going over there? What do you want to go over there for?"

"I'll tell you later," said Amy Whitney.

"You mean not in front of Gerald? Good Lord, he's a MacMahon, and they all know I have no use for Fred Langendorf. They know why, too. Don't you, Gerald?"

"No sir. I guess I better be going."

"All right, Gerald. And I'll send you the helmet the first one I see. Goodbye."

"Goodbye, Amy. Goodbye, Mr. Whitney."

"The last time I saw you," said Amy Whitney. "Do you remember when that was?"

"Yes I do," said Gerald Higgins. "It was at your house in Lyons, the day before you were going away to be a nurse in the army."

"August 1918. And what are you doing now?"

"Right now I'm at Princeton, getting my M.A. And what are you doing, Amy? Are you still a nurse?"

"No. I'm in New Jersey, too. East Orange. Married to a doctor I met in the army. I have two children. Are you married?"

"No."

"I didn't think you would be. Either that, or you'd be married at nineteen. You were a rooty kind of a kid. I can remember thinking that even then. I wouldn't have been one bit surprised if you'd made a pass at me. I fully expected you to. Maybe I was a little bit disappointed that you didn't."

"Well, I'll make up for it now."

"No, you don't have to be gallant with me, Gerald. I'm fat and unattractive, but at least I know it."

They had a moment of silent, candid looking-into-each-other's-faces, the boldness relieved by a smile for nostalgia. Their chance encounter took place in a Childs restaurant on Fifth Avenue. "A long way from little old Lyons, P A," she said. "Wonder how many people here ever heard of Lyons."

"Not many, I guess," he said. "But we wouldn't know the places they came from either."

"I guess not. Do you ever get back there?"

"Oh, once in a while, to visit my grandmother. And I've been having correspondence with Robert Millhouser. Remember him?"

"Sure. The big scandal when he killed his wife. That's what he gets for marrying a girl not even half his age. But I guess he's paying for it, the poor old thing."

"That you can be sure of," said Gerald Higgins.

"I never go back. There's nothing to bring me back any more. I'm the last of the Whitneys, and I never had much to do with my Ortlieb cousins. They looked down on us."

"Looked *down* on you?"

"*You* know. The reverse of what it should have been. The Ortliebs worked with their hands, the Whitneys were all desk workers."

"Where is your father now? I know your mother died, but I lost touch with your father. Did he stay around Lyons?"

"Long enough to die, that's all," said Amy Whitney Robbins. "He would have lasted a few years longer if he hadn't hit the booze, but he never gave much consideration to anyone else and he ended up not caring what happened to himself. A man that never gave a thought to anyone else. The one thing I wanted to be in life, a doctor, he kept me from being. And why? Because it interfered with his plans. Do you remember Olympia Park?"

Gerald Higgins laughed. "Olympia Park, sure. Two tennis courts and an ice cream stand. Olympia Park. The courts are all overgrown with weeds, but the uprights are still there, to hold the nets."

"A memento of my M.D. My biology teacher in high school tried to persuade my Uncle Fred Langendorf to pay for my education. Pre-med and medical school. But my father wanted the money to build Olympia Park. So I became a trained nurse instead of a doctor. But at least I met my husband through that, so I guess I shouldn't complain. But I do complain, whenever I stop to think of it. That father of mine with his grandiose ideas, he never did anything he could be put in jail for, but he took five thousand dollars from Uncle Fred and bought that land and built those tennis courts, but there weren't enough people in Lyons that cared about tennis, so he

took what was left and put up that dance pavilion. Four miles
away was Midway."

"I remember Midway very well."

"My father thought Lyons people would rather walk to his
place than ride to Midway. He never stopped to think that the
young people wanted to get away from Lyons, even if it was
only four miles away. Midway got the Lyons people and the
Johnsville people, and Olympia got nobody."

"That was the summer I didn't go to Lyons. My family
went to Ventnor that summer, near Atlantic City."

"He had two dances at his park. The first one, people
came out of curiosity. The second, nobody came. He lost money
on both dances, and finally gave up. Flat broke. Five thousand
dollars down the drain, and I was emptying bedpans at the
hospital. I could have filled those bedpans with my own tears,
whenever I thought of that money. I never would have gone
home again if it hadn't been for my mother. You knew Uncle
Fred Langendorf."

"Sure. I liked him."

"People misjudged Uncle Fred," said Amy. "They used
to go on about how he was money-mad, but I could tell you a
few things. He tried to help my father get on his own feet,
lent him that five thousand dollars knowing he didn't have
much chance of getting it back. Believe me, no one else in
Lyons would have lent Bert Whitney that kind of money,
but Uncle Fred did. And a lot of men would have been good
and sore at my father for losing it all, but Uncle Fred let him
keep his job at the lumber yard." She paused, marshalling
thoughts that she probably had never tried to organize before. "I wrote Uncle Fred a letter from the hospital and told
him I had this chance to be an army nurse but I needed his
advice in the matter. He supported my mother while my father
was in the army, and he gave Father his job back when he got
out, although my father was saying awful things about him. So
he wrote back and said he thought I ought to do whatever
my conscience told me to do, and I knew by that that he was
telling me to go ahead and join the army. He never believed in
interfering in other people's lives, but he as good as told me
that I owed it to myself, it was a wonderful opportunity to see

something of the world and at the same time do something for my country. He didn't come out and say these things, but it was what he meant. Well, he was right. I met my husband overseas, and we got married after the war was over."

"And now you live in East Orange," said Gerald Higgins.

"Not very far from Princeton. You ought to come and visit us sometime. Remember how you used to walk through our yard?"

"It was a good short cut, till your father stopped us."

"My father stopped you? Stopped who?"

"Everybody, I guess. Me. My grandmother. My aunts. He wrote my grandfather a letter. I never saw the letter, but Grandpa said we all had to stop going through the Whitneys' yard."

"I never knew that, Gerald. This is the first I ever heard of that."

"I think he put a padlock on the back gate, the alley gate. Yes, I'm positive of that."

"I wonder why he'd do a thing like that," said Amy. "My mother could have got away by the front gate."

The young man was silent.

"You knew my mother was a little out of her head, didn't you? Didn't the MacMahons ever tell you that?"

"No."

"Oh, that's why you looked surprised. Yes, my mother began acting strangely, oh, back when I was in High. She'd stay in bed for days at a time and later on she'd hardly ever come downstairs. I had to get out of that house or I would have gone a little coocoo myself. My father wouldn't send me to medical school or any place else, so I went into nurse's training. I guess if the truth be told, I was a little afraid of my mother. It wasn't natural for a person to sit in her room, rocking away. She was always good to me, mind you. She never slapped me the way mothers did their children. But she began acting rather peculiar when I was around sixteen or seventeen. I remember one day she said I ought to quit my job. But I didn't have a job. I was going to school. I asked her what she meant by that, and she didn't even remember saying it. But she said it again one time, and she said certain things that I don't want to repeat, poor thing, but if anybody would have heard them—well, she had some idea there was something going on between Prof Hunsberger and I. Poor old Hunsberger, my goodness. Did you ever remember Professor Hunsberger at Lyons High? He was science teacher, and taught me more than any other teacher I ever had."

"Did he keep you after school, Amy?"

"Oh, come on. What kind of a thing is that to kid about? He was the last person you'd ever think that of. You're almost as bad as my mother."

"I was only kidding," said Gerald Higgins.

"Well it could have had serious consequences, if it ever got out what my mother was thinking."

"Yes, especially then."

"She told me I ought to go to work for Uncle Fred, only she called him Mr. Langendorf, and I took her seriously. I asked my father if we were that hard up, and he said to pay no attention to my mother. She was living in the past, he said. Well that was putting it mildly. As far as I was concerned, she was living in the past and he was living in the future, with his big scheme to build an amusement park. With money that I should have had for my education. You never had to worry about that, going to Princeton, and the MacMahons were very well-to-do. I guess your own family, too. I'm going to see to it that my children never have to worry about that. By the time my daughter is eighteen we'll have enough saved up for her to go to Vassar or some place like that, and the boy, it depends on whether he wants to be a doctor or what. My husband got his M.D. at Northwestern, but we thought of sending the boy to P. and S. So far he hasn't shown much interest, but he's only nine. He looks so much like my father you'd almost take him for a son instead of a grandson, and he has that same athletic ability. Albert Whitney Robbins. He's never been to Lyons. Vacations we go to Toms River, so it may be years before Whitney ever sees my old home town, if he ever does."

"You call him Whitney?"

"Yes, because I never liked the nickname Bert or Al," said Amy. "Look at that poor woman over there, near the window. She's had what they call Szymanowski's Operation. Didn't do her much good, though, did it?"

"I don't know. I didn't see her before they operated," said Gerald Higgins.

"You're such a smart aleck," she said. "But I'll bet you never heard of Szymanowski's Operations. I should have been a doctor. I'll always regret it that I wasn't. But that father of mine, believe me. One thing they can never accuse me of and that's selfishness. There I'm more like my mother. That is, up to a certain point. I'd never let conditions affect me till the only thing left to do was go up in the attic and hang myself. Were you in Lyons when they found her?"

"Yes," said Gerald Higgins.

"Somebody could have stopped her. If not my father, Beulah Bader should have. But there was another selfish one, that Beulah Bader. She never went out of her way to be helpful. When one of us'd call her she'd pretend not to hear us. Just go right on doing whatever she was doing."

"Yes, I know what you mean," said the young man.

"Uncle Fred was paying her twenty—dollars—a week. Can you imagine?"

EXTERIOR:
WITH FIGURE

As the years, the decades, go by, it is not so remarkable that the most interesting member of the Armour family should turn out to be Harry Armour, Mr. Henry W. Armour, himself. His wife and his children all had a shot at being interesting, and they all did behave or misbehave in ways that had one or another member of the family always being talked about. If it wasn't Kevin, it was Mary Margaret; if it wasn't Mary Margaret, it was Rose Ann; and if it wasn't either of the children, it was Mrs. Armour, one of the first women in town to have her own car, and the first woman in the county to be involved in a fatal motor accident. It is strange, then, for me to say now that in my younger days my principal recollection of Harry Armour was of a man who was always going for walks, but whom I seldom saw walking. He would stand in front of someone's house, apparently admiring the rose bushes, or I would see him watching the telephone linemen at work, his hands clasped behind his back while he stood at a nonconversational distance from the workmen. As it happens, I often rode horseback with Harry Armour, but I do not think of him as a riding companion. I think of him as a man who could stand and look at nothing by the hour, and that, of course, is a visual record that I wish to correct.

I say it is not so remarkable that this man should turn out to be interesting. And why do I say that about a man who seemed almost lifeless? Well, in view of what has happened to his family, he becomes interesting either because of his influence on their lives—or because he had no influence whatever. One's first guess, and the once prevalent one, would be that Harry Armour had no influence.

He looked like a butler, or at least like a non-comic butler in a serious play. He was, of course, smooth-shaven, *clean-shaven* at all times. His skin had a polish rather than a shine, and though he was not a thin man, the skin was tight over the cheekbones and the bridge of his nose and the jaw-line. His lower lip protruded slightly because the upper lip was pulled in and down. He was fairly tall, perhaps five foot ten, and broad-shouldered, but he had the appearance of solidity rather than of muscular strength. His clothes were exquisitely tailored, of sombre materials, and you could be sure that he was not a man who put on his jacket and waistcoat in a single operation, and that he made sure his pocket flaps and lapels were lying flat before he put on his overcoat. He would have his gloves on before he left the house, and his hat on in the vestibule. He wore a starched linen collar that was called, I think, a Dorset; it was a turn-over, perhaps two inches high, showing none of the knot of the necktie. He went on wearing Dorsets long after even the oldest men gave them up.

Dressed for the street, he would go for one of those walks of his, but I cannot remember how he walked—short steps or long, fast or slow. The logical conclusion is that he walked very slowly, since I never saw him on foot more than five or six blocks from his house, and whenever I saw him he was standing still and *maybe* admiring a rose bush, *maybe* fascinated by the digging of a sewer, but more likely, I thought, totally unaware of the beauties of the petals or the efficiency of the laborers.

It is a curious thing about the old-fashioned small town, where everyone was supposed to know all about everyone else, that there were so many people whose privacy was impenetrable. It was known about Harry Armour, for instance, that he and a brother had owned some mineral rights which they sold to the big coal company for a great deal of money. Mrs. Armour, with money of her own, also got her money from coal mining. But having established themselves in their large new house on Lantenengo Street, the Armours made no further effort to get into society, and in my generation there were those who believed that the Armours got their money from meat-packing. Such was not the case, as I knew because my father was an usher at Harry Armour's wedding, had known Harry Armour all their lives, and hardly ever spoke to him. If I had had a little active curiosity I might have found out a lot of things about Harry Armour, but my father died when I was nineteen, and I never knew what went on between the two extremely reticent men. We were Catholics, and so were the Armours, and I guess that when Harry Armour was choosing his ushers, he picked my father because he was a doctor, handsome, a bit of a dude, a member of the Gibbsville Club and of the Gibbsville Assembly, and a North-of-the-Mountain boy like Armour himself. I do not believe that there was ever any feeling of friendship between the two; on the other hand, Mrs. Armour had a younger brother, who died before I was born, for whom my father expressed what amounted to affection. "Ray Reilly was the best of *that* lot," he said.

One day, when I was about twelve or thirteen, I was told that I was wanted on the telephone. I naturally expected that the call was from one of my contemporaries, but when I said "Hello," the voice at the other end of the wire said, "James, this is Mr. Armour. Would you like to go riding with me?"

The Armour son, Kevin, had a high-pitched, through-the-nose voice. His father had bought him a good saddle horse, but Kevin was afraid of horses and I knew it was not he calling. Nor was it the kind of practical joke that my friends would think up. "What did you say, Mr. Armour?" I said.

"Riding. Would you care to go riding with me tomorrow?" said Harry Armour. "You could stop for me at our house, four o'clock, after school."

"Yes, thank you," I said.

"Fine, fine. Goodbye," he said.

To my surprise, my father was not at all surprised. "You be polite to Mr. Armour," my father said. "He's not a very good rider. Don't show off."

"Why does he want *me* to ride with him?"

"Because his horse needs the exercise," was my father's oblique answer.

"And Kevin is afraid of horses," said my mother. "He dreads it."

The next day I arrived at the Armours' house around four

o'clock. They had a combination stable and garage; one box stall, an open stall, and room for three cars. It was a handsome brick building, a simpler version of the main house, with a cupola and a golden horse for a weathervane. Mr. Armour, smoking a cigar, was looking up at the weathervane when I rode up the driveway. "Hello, James," he said. He turned and spoke to the chauffeur-groom. "Jerry, bring my horse out."

Jerry led the chestnut, already saddled, and stood at the horse's head while Mr. Armour mounted. He did two or three wrong things that revealed his lack of experience with horses, but once he was in the saddle he smiled, and I had never seen him smile. "All right, where shall we go?" he said.

"Anywhere," I said. "I don't care."

"Out to The Run?" he said.

"All right," I said.

"Where do you usually ride to?"

"Oh—all over," I said. "Sometimes out to The Run. But you haven't been riding much, have you, Mr. Armour?"

"Not lately, not since I used to ride with your father."

"Then maybe we'd better not go all the way to The Run," I said. "There and back is pretty far for the first day. You'll get sore."

"Sore? Oh, you mean in the seat," he said.

I was slightly embarrassed to be making any kind of reference to the rear end of a man who was the father of one of my contemporaries. "Maybe halfway would be better," I said.

"Yes, I think you're right," he said. "Thanks for reminding me."

He was not a good rider and never would be one. He asked me, on our rides during that winter and spring, to correct him when he did things wrong, and I made a lot of suggestions that he adopted. But you cannot be taught to ride well any more than you can be taught to dance well. It has to be there. Someone must have told him that a rider should fix his sight between the horse's ears, and it is true that when you are learning to jump horses, that is one of the things they tell you. But we were not jumping our horses—thank God!—and yet Mr. Armour always rode with his eyes staring at that point between his horse's ears. As soon as he was in the saddle he al-

ways tightened up and stayed that way throughout the ride. I
never suspected that he was afraid of the horse; it was not the
tension of fear. It was determination to stay on the horse's
back for five or ten miles while he and the animal got their exercise. I taught him, for instance, to post to the trot, and
watching him do it I was reminded of the pistons in an automobile engine. In the six or seven months that we rode together we never galloped and we seldom cantered, although
the chestnut had a nice, free canter. I will say this for Mr.
Armour: although he held a tight rein, he was not cruel with
the curb or with his spurs. In the beginning he carried a bone-
handle crop with a silver ferrule. It was brand-new, like his
tweed jacket and checked breeches and boots and derby, all
from Wanamaker's London Shop in Philadelphia, expensive
and faultless. I knew to the dollar what he had paid for everything, because I had priced them all, hopefully. He wore a stock
—so did I—which on him was a continuance of his Dorset collars. I tried to think of some way to get him to stop carrying the
crop; four reins were enough in the hands of a man who rode
so tight. Then one afternoon he dropped it and I rode back and
picked it off the ground without dismounting. "It sure is a nice-
looking crop," I said, overacting a little.

"Would you like to have it, James? I'll give it to you. It's
yours."

"Honestly? You mean it?" I said.

"Make you a present of it," he said. "I don't see why I
carry it anyway, I'd never use it."

"Well, thanks. Thank you very much," I said.

Our conversations, such as they were, always took place
on the way home. My mare had a good fast walk, faster than
the Armour chestnut, and sometimes Armour would have to go
into a slow trot to keep up with me, a fact which did not help
conversation. In the winter months we usually were riding in
the dark on the homeward half and were safer riding single
file, and that, too, was a conversation deterrent. But in the
spring months we did a little talking. As a matter of loyalty we
refrained from any mention of his son, the obvious person to
talk about. The next logical person was my father, but what
can a boy say about his father to a man whom the father

sometimes cut dead, sometimes merely nodded to? But in the only conversation that I remember clearly we touched upon both his son and my father. "Are you going to study medicine?" said Mr. Armour.

"I don't know," I said. "I don't think so."

"But you ought to. Think how proud your father would be," he said. "He wants you to, doesn't he?"

"Oh, sure. But I'd rather be something else."

"What?"

"A writer," I said.

"A writer? Of what? Of stories? Books?"

"Yes."

"Well, I suppose there's good money in that, if you make the grade. But nobody in your family was ever a writer."

"Not that I know of."

"Then why do you think you could be one? How would you go about it?"

"Don't ask *me*," I said.

"Well, you'll probably change your mind."

"What does Kevin want to be?"

"Kevin? He never told me. He may turn out to be a gentleman of leisure, but I hope not. It's better to be doing something."

That was one of our last rides together. The Armours went away for the summer, to their cottage in Ventnor, and when the fall came I went away to school. So many new things entered my life, things and people, that I scarcely ever thought of Mr. Armour. It certainly never occurred to me to ask about him. I may have seen him at the late Mass when I was home on vacation, but we had no conversation. In fact it was two or maybe three years later, when the Armours had a birthday party for Kevin, that I next visited their house and learned that they had sold the chestnut. After I finished prep school, and my father died and I went to work on a newspaper, I would sometimes see Mr. Armour on one of his walks, and by that time he had become, to our crowd, somewhat of a character.

We had various characters. The drinking judge. The drinking mother of one of the girls in our crowd. The lecherous

father of a boy and girl. A retired army colonel who wrote un-
printable—though not obscene—insulting letters to the newspapers. A retired Navy commander, another drinker, who suddenly appeared at my house one day to give me all his old
tennis balls, which were stamped with a fouled anchor. A man
who was related to quite a few of our crowd, who had locomo-
tor ataxia and was half blind, but attended most of the club
dances. An awesomely respectable lawyer, married, and his
schoolteacher lady friend. Among our group the first names or
titles or our nicknames for the characters became synonymous
with special weaknesses, such as alcoholism and lechery or
physical handicaps. The commander, for instance, never knew
this, but when we began to have drinking parties we always, at
some point during the evening, recited: "Here's to the commander, he's true blue/he's a drunkard, through and through/
so fill him up a bumper and celebrate the day/if he doesn't go
to heaven, he'll go the other way/so it's drink, chucka-chuck
chucka-chuck, so it's drink, chucka-chuck, chucka-chuck." He
had taught us the toast, and if we saw him on the street one of
us was sure to say, "Chucka-chuck." I don't think there was
any meanness in these criticisms of our elders, although there
was plenty of scorn in our laughter at the lecherous father of
the boy and girl, and a Goddard—the name of the pious lawyer—was in our code language a hypocrite. Sometime during
this period Mr. Armour became a character, but his name did
not become symbolic of anything. In an extremely dull way he
was unique.

Things were happening to members of his family. Mrs.
Armour had her automobile accident, skidding into a man on a
motorcycle. No charge was preferred against her, but it was
generally believed that some money changed hands. Then
Kevin, practically in secret, developed into an expert shot and
from the age of sixteen he was high gun at county and state
matches. He had never displayed any other signs of coordina-
tion, and this accomplishment astonished us. He was sought
after by older men, and he spent so much time in their company that he grew bored with us, his contemporaries. He was
winning a lot of money on bets, and at eighteen he was a heavy
drinker. He managed to get admitted to the University of Vir-

ginia, and there, with his guns and his Wills-Ste. Claire, he remained for two full—very full, as we used to say—years. His
family had no control over him, although they did not try very
hard or very long. They threatened, but only threatened, to stop
his allowance, and his reply was to win fifteen hundred dollars
in a live bird match. If he had not been so stupid, so totally lacking in a sense of humor, he would have been insufferable; but
when Bob Reynolds, the kidder in our group, asked Kevin who
was buried in Grant's Tomb, Kevin thought a moment and
caught on. "You trying to razz me?" he said. He was not easily
distracted, and he therefore played a competent game of bridge
and a safe game of poker. One of the girls in our crowd was
madly in love with him and made no bones about it, but when
Kevin was away on a shooting trip she would call the rest of us
until she found someone to take her out. She was much higher
than he in the social scheme, but he would not marry her because she was not a Catholic. I doubt that Kevin could have
explained what was meant by the Immaculate Conception,
but he was a staunch Catholic. At Mass he would take out
his beads and I know he was saying his Hail Mary's because I
could see his lips moving, but I do not think he prayed. He
thought he was praying.

The praying one in the Armour family was Rose Ann,
three years younger than Kevin and a colleen specimen; creamy
white skin, blue eyes, black hair, a voluptuous little figure. She
was ebullient, a laugher, at parties, but in church she read her
Missal and was acutely attentive to the ritual on the altar, ob-
livious of the people in her pew and of the other worshipers.
There could be no doubt that she was devout. Still it came as
almost as big a surprise to me as to our Protestant friends when
Rose Ann became a novice in a convent in upstate New York.
Mrs. Armour wept on my mother's shoulder and I gathered
that they were not tears of joy. Apparently Mrs. Armour
would have been willing to donate her other daughter, Mary
Margaret, who had the misfortune to look exactly like Mr.
Armour, to the service of the Lord. Mary Margaret already
had the appearance of a young mother superior, but Rose Ann
was *pretty*. It was a scandal in reverse, so to speak, and the
only really amusing thing about it for me was to listen to several

of the Protestant girls who said they wished they could become
nuns. "They cut off all your hair," I told them, thereby dis-
couraging some vocations.

Then one day Mr. and Mrs. Armour quietly left town and
nothing was heard from them for three or four weeks. Neither Mary Margaret nor Kevin volunteered any information,
but it was reported that Mr. and Mrs. Armour had gone abroad
and that they were accompanied by Rose Ann. My mother
was in on the secret and I suppose my father was too, but not
until the whole town had the story did my mother reveal any
of it to me. Something—I was not told what—had occurred at
the convent, a couple of weeks before Rose Ann was to take
the veil. Mr. and Mrs. Armour were sent for, and they made
their sudden arrangements to have Rose Ann go abroad with
them.

Mr. Armour stayed in Europe a couple of months, then returned home alone. Mrs. Armour remained with Rose Ann for
about a year, then she too returned alone. Meanwhile no one
had had a word from Rose Ann, not even a post card to indicate her whereabouts. Meanwhile, too, Mr. Armour had resumed his walks, his starings at nothing, which for him were so
normal that in this unusual situation he seemed to be hasten-
ing the restoration of usual, normal conditions. He had returned, and because of his unapproachability and the neighbors'
tact during a delicate period, he had considerably reduced the
inquisitiveness of the neighbors when Mrs. Armour came home.
They had gotten used to seeing Mr. Armour around, and some
of their curiosity was dispelled or simply evaporated.

Betty Allen, a friend of Rose Ann's, telephoned Mrs. Armour to say she was going abroad and would like to have Rose
Ann's European address. It was a bold move, but Mrs. Armour
gave her the address. "I'm sure she'd love to see you," said
Mrs. Armour. "She had a nervous breakdown a year ago, you
know, but she's fine now. Living with this French family about
forty kilometres outside of Paris. Her appearance has changed.
She's put on much too much weight, but there'll be time to do
something about that after she gets her health back. I'll tell her
to expect to hear from you."

Betty went to see Rose Ann, and her report was con-

tained in a long letter which I read. Betty was genuinely fond
of Rose Ann, and the accuracy and incompleteness of her account of her visit had to be judged on a basis of friendship.
Nevertheless it was, I recall, a sad letter. Rose Ann had indeed changed in more ways than in her appearance. She was
stout, said Betty, and during the three days of Betty's visit
Rose Ann ate enormous meals and drank a great deal of wine
—without, Betty added, getting tight. Rose Ann wanted to know
all about the boys and girls in the old crowd, and she surprised
Betty by recalling things that had happened to us when we
were small children. But she was hazy or completely wrong on
things that had happened more recently, even where they concerned members of her own family. She had Kevin, for instance, in love with a Philadelphia girl whom Kevin had never
had a date with. Then when Rose Ann calmly spoke of Mary
Margaret as her dead sister, Betty had to fight back the tears.
On the last day of Betty's visit they went for a walk together,
and at one point Rose Ann led Betty to a barn. "I didn't want to
frighten you," said Rose Ann. "But we were being followed. It's
all right now. He's gone."

Betty spoke good French and was able to form a judgment
of the middle-aged couple at whose house Rose Ann was a
paying guest. They were childless. The husband owned a garage,
the wife had been a trained nurse, and Rose Ann was not the
first paying guest that had been sent to them by Rose Ann's
doctor. The doctor came out from Paris once a fortnight and
had a meal with Rose Ann and the couple, then he would
chat with Rose Ann while the couple were doing the dishes.
They were a decent, hard-working couple, frankly pleased to
have the extra money from their p.g., equally frank about their
personal attitude toward Rose Ann as a commercial proposition.
It was not for them, they told Betty, to provide anything but
peace and quiet, a clean room, and good plain food. They referred to Rose Ann as a *malade à domicile*.

When Betty returned home she went to see Mrs. Armour,
and I learned about their conversation from Betty herself. "You
may have thought I should have told you about Rose Ann,"
said Mrs. Armour. "I didn't, for a reason. I wanted her to see
you just as you are, and I didn't want you to go there all self-

conscious, making forced conversation. I wanted you to be your natural self, or she'd have noticed the difference right away."

"It was a shock, though, Mrs. Armour."

"Yes, I'm sorry," said Mrs. Armour. "But I wouldn't have given her address to anyone but you."

"I hope my visit did some good."

Mrs. Armour shook her head. "Who knows? She never even mentioned your visit the next time the doctor went to see her."

"I met Dr. Claverie, you know," said Betty. "He was awfully nice."

"I know you did, and he said the same thing about you."

"It was amazing how much he knew. I mean, the questions he asked me, you might have thought he was there all the time I was with Rose Ann."

"Like her thinking she was being followed?"

"And the kind of things she remembered and didn't remember."

"He is an amazing man," said Mrs. Armour. "I just hope he's the right man. She never goes to church, and I should have thought he'd encourage her to go. Such a deeply religious girl. I know I always turn to the church when I have something troubling me."

Betty changed the subject. "When are you going to see Rose Ann again?"

"When Dr. Claverie lets me. Whenever he sends for me. I have no idea when that will be."

It was about a year later that the French psychiatrist sent for Mr. and Mrs. Armour. Rose Ann was dead, drowned in a canoeing accident in one of those narrow, swift, deep little streams that the French call rivers. They brought her body home for burial, and my mother and I were kept busy explaining to our Protestant friends that the Church was satisfied that Rose Ann had not committed suicide, otherwise there would have been no requiem Mass. I was not exactly telling a lie, but I did not believe what I was saying. The church, which was large, was nearly half filled with the young and the no-longer young. What is sadder than the death of an unhappy young girl? I did not go along with those of my friends who said that Rose Ann was better off. Why, there is some hope even for a girl whose lungs are filled with water. I was an honorary pallbearer, and I cried all through the Mass and the blessing of the body. At our house, after the burial, my mother said to me, "Were you in love with Rose Ann?"

"No! God damn it, *no!*" I shouted.

There was something in my profane outburst that my mother took personally, and she slapped my face. Well, she was right. I was protesting against her lack of understanding. My mother was old enough to forget that Rose Ann was us, the young. "Don't you *dare* speak to me that way," said my mother.

"I'm sorry for swearing," I said.

I have no recollection of even *seeing* Mr. Armour at the church, at the cemetery, or at lunch at his house after the funeral. He was there, of course; it is just that I have no recollection of him, although I must have shaken hands with him at least once and probably muttered some words of condolence. This failure of my memory was not caused by my grief, but rather by his failure to say or do or look anything that would make me remember him. On the other hand, I do remember that on the very next afternoon I saw him standing at a street corner three blocks past his house. He appeared to be reading the collection sign on a mailbox—a box that he must have passed a thousand times. He was wearing overcoat and scarf, and he had no letter in his gloved hand.

Mary Margaret Armour, whom we sometimes referred to as Horse Face, kept her sister's death alive much too long. I, we, wanted to have Rose Ann as a secret sorrow. We would not forget her, but we did not want to be reminded of her whenever three or more of us got together. Mary Margaret refused to cooperate. At a bridge party, two months after Rose Ann's funeral, Mary Margaret announced that she had had the nicest letter from some teacher of Rose Ann's and wanted to read it to us all. "Very nice," a few of us said, when she finished reading it.

"Well, *I* thought so," said Mary Margaret, implying that we had failed to appreciate the letter. A few weeks later, at another party, she announced that she had had another letter, from someone else.

"Oh, for God's sake, Mary Margaret," said Betty Allen.

"What?" said Mary Margaret.

"Do you *have* to?"

"No, I don't have to. And I don't have to stay here, either. *You,* Betty Allen, I know all the horrible things you said about Rose Ann."

No one said a word. Sixteen young people at four bridge tables sat in indignant silence. It was a lot of silence. Mary Margaret looked around, saw no relief or assistance, and again turned on Betty Allen. "I could kill you."

The hostess, Nan Brown, stood up. "Mary Margaret, I'm terribly sorry, but I'm going to have to ask you to leave. You're being very unfair to Betty, and—"

"Ask me to leave? That's a laugh. I wouldn't stay in this house another minute. Kevin Armour, are you coming with me?"

"Nan, do you want me to go, too?" said Kevin.

"No, of course not," said Nan Brown.

"That's the kind of brother I have. Lily-livered son of a bitch. *Stay!"*

Betty Allen stood up. "I started this, Nan, and I'm very sorry. I'll apologize to Mary Margaret if she'll apologize to me. Then we can forget the whole damn—"

"I don't want your apology and I'm not going to forget one single word," said Mary Margaret. She left.

"I'm sorry, everybody," said Nan Brown. "Maybe I could get Mother to take her hand."

"Whoever is dummy at the other tables can sit in for Mary Margaret," someone suggested. "It'll slow things up, but . . ."

Play was resumed, and for the rest of the evening the score was kept for Mary Margaret, in her name, and on the final count it turned out that she had won second prize, a small silver ash tray with the figure of a Scottie in the center. I don't know if anyone else thought of it, but I wanted to inquire if the dog was supposed to be a bitch. However, I kept quiet.

"Will you give this to Mary Margaret?" said Nan Brown to Kevin.

"I will not. Give it to the third. Who was third?"

"Third? Why, third was none other than Mr. James Malloy," said Nan.

"I'll take it," I said. "I always wanted a Scottie."

"You knew it all along," someone said. "When you were my partner you got set four tricks, doubled and redoubled, and that's part of Mary Margaret's score."

"Well, I wanted that Scottie," I said. "Not to mention the fact that you, you dumb bastard, you left me in that bid and never even mentioned your hearts."

Some rough kidding always took place in our bridge games, but on this occasion it was urgent and nervous; we all knew that Mary Margaret Armour could be extremely unpleasant, in the best of circumstances.

She stayed away from the country club and declined all invitations—which I must say were extended half-heartedly after her behavior at Nan Brown's. Through political pull she got a very minor job in the Court House, and I would occasionally see her in the speakeasies and roadhouses, drinking with politicians and county detectives, and semi-pro athletes, all men who considered two fifty-dollar bills a fortune. More than once, when she spoke to me, I caught her making a face at me and whispering something to her companions. She would have started trouble for me, but her companions happened to be men who liked to see their names in print, favorably, and my job had me covering some politics, some sports, and general assignments. Often, very late at night, I would see her driving her Chrysler convertible home alone, going like hell and unmistakably stewed. She was sore at the world, and nobody liked her much either.

The Armours, mother and children, took turns in getting talked about, but I moved to New York and the doings of Mrs. Armour and Kevin and Mary Margaret were of no interest to me at that distance. Mrs. Armour had an operation for cataracts. Mary Margaret eloped with a county detective, then had the marriage annulled. Kevin was sued for breach of promise by a switchboard operator in a Reading hotel. The case was settled out of court for five hundred, a thousand, maybe two thousand dollars. Such items were conveyed to me from time to time, and between times I heard nothing. It became a custom, very nearly a tradition, that the only information concerning the Armours that was passed on to the Gibbsville colony in New York was bad news. To break the monotony I once asked how Kevin was getting along with his shooting; had he won the State championship? Oh? I hadn't heard about that? Hadn't anyone told me that Kevin had had to give up shooting because of an abscess in his ear? And that the real reason was not an abscess in his ear, but that he had been barred from competition because he had grown careless with guns? At a match near Allentown he had accidentally blown a hole in the ground with a 16-gauge pump gun that had one live shell left in the magazine; at another match he accidentally killed a valuable pointer.

If there was any good news of Mary Margaret it was not made known to me.

There are, most definitely, such things as hard-luck-people, hard-luck families; at least it is a working thesis that misfortune is repeatedly attracted to certain families like the Armours. At first the incidence of misfortune is looked upon as a phenomenon; then it becomes a wry joke; and then, self-protectively, we hesitate to bring up the family name for fear of hearing one more bit of evidence that bad luck begets bad luck, that we too, once started on a run of bad luck, may have to endure not only a single disaster but a lifetime of it. As something of a mystic and very much of an overprotesting enemy of superstition, I deliberately deprived myself of information about the Armours, and years went by, twenty years, thirty years, during which I created a practical non-curiosity about them. I did not know which of them were alive, which dead.

Then one day last winter I read a small item in a newspaper that I bought on the train from New York to Washington. It stated that Kevin Armour had been sentenced to prison for defrauding some woman who had entrusted him with fifteen thousand dollars' worth of securities. In Washington I was meeting a boyhood friend, and by this time I was so insulated against the Armour bad luck that I mentioned the newspaper article. "Yes, they finally caught up with Kevin," said my friend. "This time they really nailed him."

"Have they any money left?" I said.

"Who?"

"The Armours," I said.

"The Armours? There aren't any more Armours. Kevin's

the last. Mrs. Armour died ten or fifteen years ago. Mary Margaret not long after. The sauce did it to her, although I will say it took a lot of it."

"And old Henry W.?" I said.

"Lived to be eighty-four. He died last year in a veterans' home."

"Veteran of what?"

"The Spanish-American War, I think. Yes, it must have been. Anyway, that's where he died."

My friend in those few sentences had wiped out the Armour family, and if I had once been afraid of them and their bad luck, I was afraid no longer. My friend and I talked a little about them, their individual personalities, their money, their scale of living, and we exchanged the usual commonplaces about the evanescence of wealth. I did not want to spend much time talking about the Armours; I wanted to think about them, and I have done so.

I had not seen any of them in more than thirty years, consequently had only an out-of-date recollection of the physical appearance of Mr. and Mrs. Armour and Kevin and Mary Margaret. They had traveled many miles—no matter where— and lived through three decades, more or less, and I had to invent the grossness that would have come into the faces of Kevin and Mary Margaret when youth was gone, the ravages to the faces of Harry Armour and his wife when old age set in. It was not much of a pastime; they refused to hold still for my fanciful portraits of them, kept returning to the mental photographs I retained from the days when I had known them well.

I discovered that I had learned, by 1930, all that I wanted to know about the Armours, perhaps all of value that there was to know. Mrs. Armour, a flighty, silly woman who had killed a man with her motor car, was no less flighty for having had bad eyesight. Mary Margaret, trying to trade on the tragic death of her pretty sister, was not much different from the self-indulgent lush that she made herself into. Kevin, submissive to a faith that his lazy mind would not accord the respect of curiosity, would at twenty-five have stolen from a woman if he had needed the money. And even poor Rose Ann, for whom I had once wept ("Weep not for me, but for yourselves and for your children"?), had got only as far as laughter would take her.

And Harry Armour. Henry W. Armour himself. Harry Armour. Henry W. Armour. Mr. Armour. He was—what? A man who stood and looked at nothing? I do not know. I wish I knew. I want to know, and I never can know. I wish, I wish I knew.

THE FLATTED
SAXOPHONE

Something happens to the tone of a tenor saxophone when it is played out-of-doors; they always sound flat, especially at wedding receptions, when the guests are queued up for the exchange of mutterings with the bridal party. The dancing has not begun, and the orchestra seems neglected and lonely and the tenor saxophone is expressing the musicians' self-pity. Later, when the bride and groom have done their turn (to a two-tune medley of "I Love You Truly" and "Get Me to the Church on Time"), and general dancing is under way, the flatness of the tenor sax is not so noticeable. It gets lost in the babble of human voices, especially the women's voices, and the musicians have stopped feeling sorry for themselves, the tenor sax therefore has nothing to express, the orchestra plays "From This Moment On" at the cadence of the Society Bounce, and if the tenor sax is flat, so too may be the champagne, but it does not matter much.

"The way I look at it," said George Cushman, "if I want good champagne, I've got some at home. And if I want to hear good saxophone, I'll find out where Bud Freeman's working."

"I didn't hear a word you said," said Marjorie Cushman.

"That's perfectly all right," said her husband. "I'll repeat it, word for word, but if I do you're going to say it wasn't worth repeating—and you'll be right."

"Oh, we're in *that* mood," said Marjorie Cushman. A man came to their table and asked her to dance. "Now don't let anyone grab my chair."

"I'll put my feet up on it," said George Cushman.

"You don't have to do *that*," she said. "Just keep an eye on it."

"I'll keep an eye on you, too," he said, but she did not hear him.

He was now alone at a table for six, and a man and a woman separately asked if all the chairs were taken. "Sorry, all spoken for," he said. A third person, a young man in a cutaway, simply put his hands on the backs of two chairs and started to walk away with them.

"Hold on, sonny boy," said George Cushman. "Bring them back. Just put them right back where you found them."

"Sorry," said the young man, and replaced the chairs.

"And try asking, next time," said George Cushman.

"Why should I?" said the young man, and went away.

"Yeah, why should you, you little jerk," said George Cushman. "With your soft collar and your A. T. Harris cutaway."

A woman seated herself in the chair next to him. "You look lonesome all by yourself, Georgie," she said.

"Oh, hello, Becky," he said. "Yeah, I'm just sitting here eating my heart out, thinking of my lost youth."

"Our lost youth," said Becky Addison.

"No, I wasn't thinking about your lost youth. Just mine. If you want to think about yours, okay. Do you miss it?"

"Not terribly," she said.

"You know, neither do I. Mine, I mean. Not yours. How many weddings have you and I been at? The same weddings, I mean."

"You and I? Oh, dear," she said. "Well, we started going to the same weddings over forty years ago."

"Right."

"And those first years, there were a lot of weddings," she said.

"A powerful lot. Everybody got married, everybody."

"Just about," she said.

"Excuse me, Becky," he said. "Waiter, you wouldn't want to do us a special favor and bring us four Scotches and water, would you?"

"Hello, Mr. Cushman. Yes, sure. I'll bring you a whole tray full. You don't remember me, but I worked at your daughter's wedding."

"Good for you, glad to see you again," said George Cushman. The waiter interrupted his passing of champagne to go to the bar.

"You must have done very well by the waiters at Sue's wedding," said Becky Addison. "Most of them, if you ask them to get you a Scotch, they'll say yes and that's the last you ever see of them."

"It's funny, I don't remember this fellow at all. They were paid by the caterer, but then I gave each of them a five-dollar tip. So now we can have Scotch. That's called bread cast on the waters, Becky. I know you never read the Bible, so I'm explaining it to you. Where is the great man?"

"Charles? My lord and master?"

"Well, who else?"

"He's in Mexico City," she said. "I see Marjorie. Looks lovely."

"She *is* lovely, and she's my wife, and I am devoted to her, and I am not good enough for her, and nobody knows what she sees in me."

"You don't have to lay it on that thick, not with me," said Becky Addison.

"No, I guess not," said George Cushman. "Have a cigarette?"

"I've quit," she said.

"No special reason, I hope," he said.

"No, not really. That is, I haven't been forbidden to smoke. Combination of hysteria from reading all those things in the magazines, *and* I *was* smoking too *much*. Sixty cigarettes a day. So I quit, and I've gained ten unnecessary pounds."

"In how long?"

"Nine weeks tomorrow," she said.

"Nine weeks. Speaking of which, we never did finish guessing how many weddings we'd been to."

"No. Well, the weddings we went to and were in, including our own. Those years there were a lot of big weddings. And lately, the last few years, our children's weddings and our friends' children. An average of five a year, do you think?"

"Times forty. Two hundred. It somehow seems more than that," he said.

"But I don't think you and I have been to two hundred of the same weddings, have we? Maybe we have," she said.

"Pretty close to it," he said. "And the funny thing is, we nearly always sit together, at least for a little while. Did you come alone?"

"Yes," she said. "I didn't go to the church. Did you? I suppose you did."

"Try and keep Marjorie from missing any part of it. Yes, we were there. Marjorie burning up because we didn't have any special pew to go to. To *think* that Ann Bartholomew, her own second cousin, didn't have us sitting with family. Well, maybe Marjorie has a point. There were plenty of people there I never saw before."

"Weren't there? I mean, *aren't* there? Looking around here I don't know half the people our age," she said.

"Why don't you and I get married, Becky? Would you like to toy with that idea?"

"I did, once," she said.

"Oh, that was when we were in love. Christ, that was that greasy kid stuff."

"Mm-hmm."

"It doesn't take any real imagination to think about getting married when you're twenty years old."

"Eighteen and twenty-one, I think we were," she said.

"At that age, and especially you and I, we didn't know what you did next except get married. God, how long would we have lasted? Two years, do you think?"

"Two or three," she said. "Or as soon as we found out we didn't love each other. Thank God we found it out without getting married."

"I know, and that makes it so much better now," he said. "Would you leave Charley now?"

"No, I don't think so," she said.

"Well, you don't have to ask me if I'd leave Marjorie. Like a shot, would be the answer."

"Then why haven't you?" she said.

"I don't know. I could give you plenty of reasons. *She* gave me plenty of reasons."

"But they were never good enough reasons, were they? You wanted to stay married to her, so you did."

"Yes, that's true," he said. "But I'd leave her now, like a shot. To marry you, that is."

"Georgie, I know what's behind this," she said.

"You do? What?"

"It's a very romantic notion," she said. "It's not young-romantic. It isn't that. But it's as desperate as young love."

"It's more so," he said.

"Yes," she said. "The feeling that we'd be happy together with what time we have left."

"You guessed it," he said. "And we would be, Becky."

"We might be. We probably could be," she said. "If we could get up right now and walk out together, if that's all there was to it. But two old crows like us, Georgie. All that time we'd have to spend with lawyers. Your lawyers, my lawyers. Marjorie's. Charles's. Who gets what? Charles would want the Andrew Wyeth, but I'd want it too. By the time we got through all that we'd both be exhausted, you and I. And we'd start asking ourselves, what the hell *for?*"

"Jesus, you're practical," he said.

"I am now. You would be later," she said. "Neither one of us is strong enough to go through all that. Or what we feel isn't strong enough, this loving each other dearly. And that's what it is, Georgie. Loving each other dearly. The dear, wonderful love of two old friends."

He nodded. "You're right," he said.

She put her hand on his. "Come on, dance with me," she said.

"Good," he said, and got to his feet. Then, "Let's wait. I promised Marjorie I'd guard these chairs."

"All right," she said. "Oh, look. Our friend, with there-must-be-sixteen Scotches. I've never *seen* so many Scotches."

"I told you, bread cast on the waters," said George Cushman.

"One, two, three, four, five, six, seven, eight, nine, ten, eleven, twelve, thirteen, fourteen, fifteen, *sixteen,* seventeen, eighteen, nineteen. Nineteen Scotches," she said. "You didn't really want to dance, did you, Georgie?"

THE FRIENDS
OF MISS JULIA

The old lady stood waiting at the receptionist's desk. It was a circular room, with niches in the wall and in each niche, under a pin-spot, was displayed one or another of Madame Olga's beauty preparations. Two or three women were seated, not together, on the curved banquette against the wall. High above and behind the receptionist's desk were the hands of a hidden clock, imbedded in the wall, with the Roman numerals signifying 12, 3, 6, and 9, with brass studs substituting for 1, 2, 4, 5, 7, 8, 10, and 11. According to the hands of the clock the time was five minutes to ten.

The old lady looked at the vacant desk, and turned to the other women, but they volunteered nothing. Then a curved door opened and a chic young woman appeared. "Oh, it's Mrs. Davis," said the young woman. "And you have Miss Julia, don't you?"

"Yes, at ten o'clock," said Mrs. Davis.

The young woman looked down at a large white leather appointment book, which lay open on the desk. "Just a set, wasn't it?"

"Yes, that's all," said Mrs. Davis.

"Well—I don't know what to say," said the young woman.

"Did you give my appointment to someone else?"

"No, it isn't that," said the young woman. "We're having quite a mixup here." She lowered her voice. "The trouble is— Miss Julia was taken suddenly ill."

"Oh, I'm sorry. I hope it's nothing serious."

"Well—I'm afraid it is. I'm going to have to cancel all her

appointments. But I could take care of your set if you don't mind waiting. I mean I could squeeze you in, since you're already here. It just happened about fifteen or twenty minutes ago. We got a doctor from next door, he's in there now."

"Oh, it does sound serious. Is it the heart?"

"It must be," said the young woman. "They sent for the ambulance. Taking her out the back way. Miss Judith is in a real flap, worrying about Miss Julia and the customers and all."

"Well, never mind about me," said Mrs. Davis.

"Oh, I'll fit you in, but you may have to wait a little while. Have a seat, Mrs. Davis, and I don't think you'll have to wait *very* long. But don't say anything to the other ladies, please. They don't know what's going on back there, and Miss Judith gave us orders. But I know Miss Julia was always a friend of yours."

"Was?"

"They're not very hopeful," said the young woman. A light flashed on the young woman's desk and she picked up the telephone. "Yes?" she said. She listened, replaced the telephone, and now addressed the other customers. "Ladies, I'm terribly sorry, but that was Miss Judith, our manager. We're going to have to cancel all appointments for today."

"Oh, come *on*," said one of the customers. "I drove all the way in from Malibu this morning. You can't do this to me."

"What's the big idea?" said a second customer. "I've had this appointment for over a week, and I have seventy *people* coming for dinner tonight. What are you going to say about that? Damn whimsical, if you ask me."

"I'm sorry, Mrs. Polk, but *all* appointments are cancelled," said the young woman.

"Well, give us a reason, for heaven's sake," said the first woman.

"The reason is—all right, I'll give you a reason. Our Miss Julia dropped dead, if that's enough reason for you. Do you want to go in and take a look yourself?"

"You don't have to be rude," said the first woman. "Are you closing for the day?"

"Yes, we're closing for the day," said the young woman.

"Well, when you open up again I hope there'll be some changes around here," said the first woman.

"Oh, go to hell," said the young woman. By mutual instinct she went to and was embraced by Mrs. Davis, and the other women left. The young woman was weeping, and Mrs. Davis guided her to the banquette. "She was so nice, such fun, Miss Julia."

"Always very jolly," said Mrs. Davis. "Always some little jokes to tell."

"It was so *quick,*" said the young woman. "I was talking to her only five minutes before."

"That's a mercy, when it's quick," said Mrs. Davis.

"I was going to have lunch with her today," said the young woman. "We always had lunch together every Wednesday. Every Wednesday since I worked here, we always went over to the Waikiki. That's a Hawaiian place over on South Beverly?"

"Yes," said Mrs. Davis. She rested a hand on the younger woman's shoulder.

"Every Wednesday, without fail. We always sat at the same booth, and she and Harry Kanoa, the bartender, they used to carry on a conversation in Hawaiian. She could speak it a little. Did you ever know she was a hairdresser on the *Lurline?*"

"The boat?" said Mrs. Davis.

"I forget how many trips she told me she made," said the young woman. "But a lot. She always wanted to go back to the Islands. She was going next October. She had me almost talked into going with her. I've never been to the Islands."

"No, neither have I."

"I'm all right now, Mrs. Davis. I just suddenly couldn't hold it in any longer."

"That's all right, dear. Do you good."

The young woman smiled. "You called me dear. You don't even know my name, do you, Mrs. Davis?"

"I guess I don't, no."

"It's Page. Page Wetterling. I always have a hard time convincing people, but it's my real name. My mother always liked the name Page. Some of the customers thought Miss Judith gave me the name because I had to page people, but that wasn't it. I have it on my birth certificate."

"It's a pretty name," said Mrs. Davis.

"Listen, I'll ask one of the other operators if they'll give you a set."

"Oh, don't do that, Page, I only have it done to occupy the time. It's something to do."

"But you have pretty hair. Let me speak to Miss Frances. Did you ever have her?"

"No, I never had anyone but Miss Julia."

"Miss Frances is really the best. She's the one all the other operators go to to do their hair, but she doesn't have the personality."

"Yes, I know which one she is," said Mrs. Davis. "But I'd just as soon go without it today."

"Well, do you want me to put you down for your usual time next Wednesday?"

"Yes, you might as well," said Mrs. Davis.

"Does it make any difference who?" said Page Wetterling.

"None. They gave me Miss Julia the first time, two years ago, and I stayed with her ever since. It's only something to do."

"I'll let you try Miss Frances."

"You better ask her first. Maybe she won't want to be bothered with an old lady."

"Oh, listen. Don't you think they all know what you gave Miss Julia for Christmas? I could tell you some big movie stars that are nowhere near as generous. She'll take you."

"All right," said Mrs. Davis.

"None of them are going to be working today, but they'd gladly give you a set before they go home. We're closing up. I'm going to type out a little notice to put on the front door."

"Then do you get the day off?"

"No. I have to be here to answer the phone, change appointments. I get my lunch hour is all. I'd rather anyway, something to do, like you say."

"I guess I didn't mean it the same way."

"Oh, I know what you meant, Mrs. Davis. A lot of the ladies only come here for something to do. Do you want me to try and get you an appointment somewhere else? I know the girl at the Lady Daphne's. Or if you wanted to try George Palermo's, but he's down there near Bullock's Wilshire."

"My hair can go without," said Mrs. Davis. "But thank you, Page. Here."

"What's this? Five dollars? You don't have to give me any-

thing, Mrs. Davis. I wouldn't take it. Absolutely. Listen, if it
wasn't for you I'd of really blown my lid. Not that I worry
about my job. I have other offers any time I want to leave
Madame Olga's."

"Then let me take you to lunch. Would you like to have
lunch at Romanoff's?"

"I'd love to, but you don't have to do anything for me,
Mrs. Davis."

"It'd be my pleasure. I guess we ought to reserve a table.
Can you make an outside call on that phone? Tell them it's
Mrs. Davis, Walter Becker's mother-in-law. Or Mrs. Walter
Becker's mother."

"Is that so? I didn't know you were related to Walter
Becker. That's the television producer Walter Becker?"

"Yes, he married my daughter. He's always trying to get
me to go to Romanoff's, but I never do unless I'm with him or
my daughter. I guess they know me there, but mention his
name to make sure."

Page Wetterling made the telephone call and hung up. "A
very nice table for two, they said," she said. "I'll meet you
there at ha' past twelve. Okay?"

The old lady was tired when at last she could present herself at the restaurant. She was taken to her table—a good location, but not one of the very best—and she ordered a glass of
port wine. She knew she should have ordered sherry, but she
was past caring about such things. The proprietor came to her
table. *"Nice* to see you, Mrs. Davis. Hope you enjoy your
lunch," he said, bowed, and passed on. If he noticed her
preference for port over sherry he gave no sign. He was less
impassive, as were the other men at the very best tables, when
Page Wetterling entered the room. She was a handsome girl
in the marketplace of pretty women, but she was unknown to
the men in the restaurant; a new face, no handsomer or prettier than the others, but new and unidentified.

"You want to know something? I've never been here before," said Page Wetterling. "I'll have a—oh—a Dubonnet."
The waiter left to get her drink, and she did a quick survey of
the room. "Some of these women are trying to place me. They
can't remember where they know me from."

"I thought a girl like you would be here every day," said Mrs. Davis.

"Never was here in my life before," said Page Wetterling. "My husband could never afford it, when I was married, and since then whenever I dated a man that had the money, we always went some place else. My first visit to the famous Romanoff's and I was *born* in Southern California. Whittier. Do you know where Whittier is?"

"I've heard of it, but I've only been here a little over two years. All I know is Beverly Hills and Holmby Hills and Westwood. And Hollywood. I was there a few times to watch them televise."

"What did you do after you left the salon? Did you find something to kill the time?"

"It wasn't easy. I went to the jewelry store, but I didn't have any intention of buying. Then to the toy store and I spent some money there, on my grandchildren. Then I stopped in at the drug store and had a Coke. Mostly to sit down, though. Then I went and sat on a bench at one of the bus stops, till it was time to come here. What did you do? Were you kept busy?"

"Oh, was I? The elevens and the eleven-thirties and the twelves started coming in, piling up one on top of the other. I could have made easily a hundred dollars on tips if I could have sneaked in a few customers. But Miss Judith sent all the operators home. Nobody paid the least attention to the sign on the door. Some of them didn't stop to read it, but others came in and tried to bribe me to sneak them in. One woman offered me fifty dollars. I wonder what *she's* doing tonight. You don't spend that kind of money for a little family party at home. They all went away mad except a few of them. Miss Julia's regulars. But even one of them acted like a perfect bitch. Pardon me for saying that, but that's what she was. You'd of thought Miss Julia was some kind of a machine, that broke down just to louse up this woman's schedule. If I didn't get away from women once in a while I'd begin to hate them all. And you know, they more or less *have* to be nice to me. I make all the appointments, and for instance if two women want to have a permanent for the same time, I can tell one of them that she can't have that time. Or I can call up and tell a woman she has to change her time, and there's nothing she can do about it. Miss Judith can't be bothered with those small details. Oh, that one that threatened to have me fired this morning. Wait till she wants a favor. Do you like women, Mrs. Davis?"

"The majority. Not all."

"Well, if you had my job you'd learn to appreciate the nice ones. But believe me, they're not in the majority. You saw two of the worst examples today. And *I* saw one of the nicest ones. *You.*"

"Thank you," said Mrs. Davis. "I guess most of them wish they looked like you, Page."

"But those that can't, why don't they try to develop a nice disposition?"

"Why aren't you a model, with your looks and all?"

"I was, but that's for the birds. I like to eat, not starve myself to death. I eat as much as most men. I eat a steak three or four nights a week, and wait till you see what I put away for lunch. That's why most of the models I know have such lousy dispositions. They don't get enough to eat. And my doctor told me when I was still married, he said standing around like that all day, and undernourished, if you *got* pregnant, if you *could,* you were undernourishing yourself and undernourishing the baby. Well, I didn't get pregnant, thank goodness, but I quit modeling."

"Wish to order luncheon, ladies?" said the captain.

"I know what I want, Mrs. Davis," said Page Wetterling. "I want the chicken pot pie, with noodles. I was never here before, but I heard it was good here."

"I'll have that, too," said Mrs. Davis.

The girl was stimulated, and all through the meal she was entertaining. She made no pretense of a blasé indifference to the movie and television stars, and she consumed even the crust of the chicken pot pie.

"A fruit compote?" said the captain.

"I'll have that," said Page Wetterling. "You have some, too, Mrs. Davis. You didn't eat half your chicken."

"All right," said Mrs. Davis. "You'd think *I* was trying to be a model, but I never eat much."

The girl smiled at the old lady's little joke. "You know,

you have a wonderful sense of humor. If more women had a sense of humor, but the women that come into the salon, and places like this, if they had a sense of humor they wouldn't be so cranky all the time. Oh-oh, we're getting a visitor. I think it's your son-in-law, from his picture."

"Hello, Mom." The speaker was a heavy-set man in a blue suit with only a hint of lapels, a very narrow blue four-in-hand, a white-on-white shirt with a tab collar. He leaned down with the heels of his hands on their table.

"Oh, hello, Walter. This is my friend Miss Wetterling, and this is my son-in-law, Mr. Becker."

"I see you finally got here under your own steam," said Walter Becker. "Or did the young lady bring you?"

"No, it was her idea," said Page Wetterling.

"Where did you two know one another, if that's a valid question?"

"I work at the beauty salon where Mrs. Davis goes."

"I see. Then you're *not* in pictures or like that? I thought I didn't recognize you. I was just saying to Rod Proskauer. Well, Mom, I just came over to say hello and pick up the tab. Nice to see you, Miss?"

"Wetterling. Page Wetterling."

"Uh-huh. Mom, I see you this evening, right?" Walter Becker returned to his table—one of the very good ones.

"He calls you Mom," said Page.

"Yes."

"What's your daughter like? She never comes in our salon."

"No. She used to, but her hairdresser opened up her own place. I went there when I moved to California, but it was twenty dollars for practically nothing. Madame Olga's isn't cheap, but I don't want to spend twenty dollars every time. Ten is bad enough, for a person my age. It's sheer waste of money. Most of my life I didn't have money to spend in a beauty parlor. I gave myself a shampoo maybe once a week, maybe not that often. With soap, too. No Madame Olga special preparations. But out here I got into the habit, and Miss Julia was nice."

"Yes. We'll all miss her. She used to come in some mornings and just hearing her describe her hangover—maybe it was hell for her, but she kept us all laughing."

"I know," said the old lady. "Well, I guess you have to get back and answer the phone. I'll take you there in a taxi, it isn't much out of my way."

"I certainly do appreciate this, Mrs. Davis. How about you being my guest next Wednesday? I'll put you down for an eleven-thirty, how would that be? Then you won't have all that time in between."

"Well, I'd like it, but are you sure you would?"

"Of course I would. I'll take you to the Waikiki. They have American food, if you don't go for the Polynesian."

"Oh, I don't much care what I eat," said Mrs. Davis.

As the next Wednesday got nearer, Mrs. Davis was tempted to cancel her hair appointment, and thus to relieve the girl of the obligation of taking her to lunch. What pleasure would one so young and pretty get out of taking an old woman to lunch? But Page Wetterling was a warm and friendly girl, and if *she* wanted to get out of the engagement, there were ways of doing so, right up to the very last minute.

"When you're through with Miss Frances, I have my car. We can ride over to the Waikiki together," said Page, after greeting the old lady. "That is, if we still have our date?"

"Oh, that'll be nice," said Mrs. Davis.

The Waikiki consisted of many small rooms rather than a single large one. Bamboo was used everywhere in the furniture and the decorative scheme, and the lighting was dim. From a loudspeaker came the tune "South Sea Island Magic," insistently but quietly, and the patrons and staff all seemed to know each other—or to be about to. "Hi, Page," said the bartender.

"Aloha, Harry," said the girl. "Oooma-ooma nooka-nooka ah-poo ah ah."

The bartender laughed. "That's right. You're getting there. A little at a time. Hey, Charlie. Table Four for Page and her guest."

"Table Four? You mean Table Two," said the waiter Charlie.

"No, I mean Table Four," said Harry.

"Page sits at Table Two," said Charlie. "You're losing your grip, Mr. Harry Kanoa. Where were you last night?"

"Table Four, Table Four," said the bartender.

"I do want Table Four, Charlie," said Page.

"All right, sweetheart, Table Four you want, you can have it. Anything your heart's desire. You bring your mama today?"

"No, this is a friend of mine. Mrs. Davis. This is Charlie Baldwin."

"Of the Baldwin Locomotive Baldwins, no relation to any other Baldwins," said Charlie.

"I don't know what he means by that, but he always says it," said Page.

"Go to the Islands, sweetheart. You'll soon find out," said Charlie. "Care for native dishes or American today? Mainland, I should say. We have statehood. Goodie, goodie. Drinks, ladies? We don't make money on our food, only on drinks. Ha ha ha ha. Page? A double frozen Daiquiri? Or have a Statehood Special. It's almost the same as a Zombie. No more than two to a customer."

"I'm a working girl."

"No profit today, huh? Mama, you want to try a Statehood Special?"

"No thank you," said Mrs. Davis.

"No sale. Well, then, what do you want to eat? Have the Charlie Baldwin Special. I recommend it. I made it up. It's roast pork with baked pineapple and an avocado with Russian dressing. You like it, Page, so why don't the both of you have it?"

"All right, Mrs. Davis?"

"Not the pork, thank you. Maybe an avocado salad?" said Mrs. Davis. "And some iced tea, please."

The old lady liked the Waikiki. The atmosphere of gay informality was just fine—so long as she could sit back and enjoy it without having to take part in it. Nearly everyone who came in knew Page Wetterling; a few stopped to express their regret at the passing of Julia. Mrs. Davis wanted to come back again, but in order to do so she would have to invite her new young friend to Romanoff's.

"Would you like to go to Romanoff's next Wednesday?" said the old lady.

"Listen, I'd like to go there any time."

It was understood that they would have lunch together every Wednesday, alternating the restaurants, and the arrangement was satisfactory to both women. In a few weeks the old lady had heard a great deal of Page's past and current history; it took a little longer for Mrs. Davis to tell much about herself. "I gabble, gabble, prattle," said Page. "I tell you more than I ever told my own mother, and that's for sure."

"I like to listen," said Mrs. Davis.

"Where does your daughter go for lunch?" said Page. "I keep thinking we'll run into her at Romanoff's."

"I guess she goes to Perino's. There, and a French place on Sunset Boulevard. She doesn't care for Romanoff's. She says the men get all the attention there. She likes to get all dressed up when she goes out."

"But a lot of women go to Romanoff's."

"I don't know. She has some reason," said Mrs. Davis.

"You give me the impression that you don't like it very much in California."

"I guess I'm still new here," said the old lady.

"Did your daughter make you move here?"

"My son-in-law. Walter Becker. He was the one. He was for years making a nice living with the radio, the TV. But then like it happened overnight he suddenly owned or part-owned three TV shows, and he sold them for a big profit and now he's in business for himself. Walter is a rich man. A Rolls-Royce car. A home in Beverly Hills on the other side of Sunset back of the hotel. Contributes to charities. It's impossible for him to go broke again. He gets a certain amount for life as a consultant with the CBS. I give him credit, he worked hard for it. But I don't know. He didn't have to make me move out here."

"Why did he, then?"

"He didn't want to have Walter Becker's mother-in-law living in a little apartment in New York City. I loved that apartment. I had a sittingroom for if I wanted to have some ladies in to play cards. A nice bedroom to sleep in. I never had to complain about the heat. They kept it warm no matter what the temperature was outside. It wasn't big, but to me it was big enough. I had two radios. One in my bedroom that I could listen to taking a bath, and one in the kitchen. And a 21-inch TV in the sittingroom. If I didn't feel like going out I could send around to the delicatessen. They delivered. Sometimes I didn't go out for two or three days. Old people are supposed to get lonely, but I wasn't. My whole life I grew up in an apartment that wasn't big enough for our family. I and my two sisters slept in the same room, my three brothers in their room. I got married and I slept in the same bed with my husband over thirty years and my two daughters they had the same bed in their room. That was supposed to be the diningroom. Then my husband passed on and my both daughters got married and I moved to a smaller apartment. Such a pleasure, a genuine luxury I had. Within easy walking distance of 149th Street, if I wanted to shop or go to a show. I was the envy of the other ladies."

"It sounds perfect," said Page.

"Uh-huh. But Walter wanted me out here. My daughter, too, but more Walter. He wanted a grandmother for his children. His mother died young, so it was me."

"You were still their grandmother, whether you lived here or back East."

The old lady shook her head. "With Walter it has to be seen. He has to show people every room in the house and everything in all the closets. 'My wife has sixty-four pairs of shoes,' he says to them, and he opens the closet door to prove it. The same way with a grandmother. A grandmother in New York isn't the same thing as a grandmother in the house!"

"But it must be nice living with your grandchildren," said Page.

"They're getting used to me," said the old lady. "They never saw me till two years ago I came here. My own daughter had to get used to me." She nodded in agreement with herself. "And *I* had to get used to *them*."

"Did you make any new friends here?"

"Here is not so easy to make new friends," said Mrs. Davis. "At my age it's too late to learn to drive a car. I have to take a taxi everywhere. The other ladies are in the same situation. My daughter would take me in her car if I asked her, but I don't like to ask her."

"You were really happier in your little apartment," said Page.

"I admit it, but I don't want to say anything to them. They think they're doing the right thing. My son-in-law took me to the TV studios, introduced me to Red Skelton and Lucille Ball and many more. Walter said I would have something to write about when I wrote to my friends. But then he asked me to show him the letter and I couldn't hurt his feelings. I wrote a letter to my friend Mrs. Kornblum, a neighbor of mine in the same building, but I couldn't show it to Walter. It was a homesick letter. I said Lucille Ball was nice, but I'll bet not as good a stuss-player as another friend of ours, Mrs. Kamm. Stuss is a game of cards we used to play. Walter asked me did I tell my friends about him owning a Rolls-Royce. I would never do that, brag about my son-in-law. One of our friends made herself obnoxious bragging so much about her son getting elected state senator. The Senator, she called him. You would of thought he was Jacob Javits instead of just a senator in Albany."

"Wouldn't it be easier if you got yourself a little apartment here?"

"I don't want a little apartment here. I just want to go home to my own apartment, East A Hundred and Fifty-third Street, The Bronx, New York. Or one just like it."

"Then go," said Page Wetterling.

"What?"

"Just go, Mrs. Davis. Just tell your daughter and your son-in-law that you're leaving next Tuesday."

"How many times I thought of that, Page. How many times."

"But did you ever say anything to them?"

"No. I wouldn't know how. They think they're doing everything for me. It would be like a slap in the face to them."

"Well, didn't you ever slap your daughter when she was little?"

"Many times. A good slap was what she needed, and I gave it to her. And her sister. And their father, too."

"You never slapped Walter Becker, though."

"No. Sometimes I felt like it, but I never did."

"But you're not afraid of him?" said Page.

"Of *him?*"

"Then slap him. I don't mean with your hand across his·

face. But tell him you're going back to New York. And don't let him give you a con. Don't let him argue with you. Buy your ticket on the plane and write to Mrs. Kornblum that you're coming."

"Not Mrs. Kornblum, but Mrs. Kamm would have room for me. Page, you're putting ideas in my head."

"Not me. It's all your idea. I'm just giving you a little push. Do you have the cash?"

"Plenty. They give me a hundred dollars a week spending money. Why, were you going to offer me the loan?"

"Yes."

"You're a true friend, and for such a young girl to know so much," said Mrs. Davis.

"I can't take all the credit, Mrs. Davis. Miss Julia knew you were miserable."

"That's why she was always trying to cheer me up."

"She had a big heart," said Page Wetterling.

The old lady smiled. "Don't you give *her* all the credit, either, Miss Page Wetterling."

"Why, I don't have any idea what you're talking about, Mrs. Davis."

"I'll put it in a letter," said Mrs. Davis.

THE GLENDALE
PEOPLE

No place in Florida is very highly situated, but from Dale Connell's cottage it is possible to see the Gulf of Mexico while seated on the screened porch. It is a somewhat obstructed view; between the cottage and the water there is a busy highway, and across the highway a row of cottages not unlike Dale Connell's, and in back of them is the narrow beachfront. But the Gulf of Mexico is there, flashes of it between the cottages, and above the cottages a thin blue arc that is the horizon. When the traffic is momentarily halted by the red light, you can even hear the surf sometimes during the day, and late at night and early in the morning the small attacks of the waves upon the sand are continually audible and very helpful in producing sleep.

The cottage is the best he could do for the money, and Dale Connell is reasonably content. He has a livingroom, bedroom, bath and kitchen. Some of his neighbors use their livingroom as a bedroom, but Dale Connell is alone and does not need a second bedroom. Some of his neighbors envy him the luxury of the livingroom that is a real livingroom and not a part-time bedroom with a convertible couch. Dale Connell has room for what he calls his stuff—his souvenirs and framed photographs of movie actors and actresses—and when the weather is not at its best he can entertain indoors. Having a nice place to receive guests, being a bachelor, and always wearing a jacket when he goes for a walk—these items set Dale Connell apart from his neighbors. It is also known that he is writing a book, and his neighbors are a little envious of that, too. It would be wonderful to have the knack of writing a book, or doing *something*.

The neighbors look upon Dale Connell as a very lucky man, and because they do, so does he, and he has made friends with dozens of people whom in the past he would have ignored, the kind of people he spent most of his life avoiding. They are what he used to call Glendale people, married couples from the Middle West who had come to California to save money on overcoats and tire chains, bought small bungalows in Glendale and Burbank and less well known places like Watts and Anaheim. They could truthfully write home and say they picked their own oranges in their own backyards, that there were hummingbirds outside their bedroom windows. They went, with a hundred thousand like them, to the annual Iowa get-togethers in Griffith Park; they queued up at the radio stations to attend the Breakfast at Sardi's and Queen for a Day programs. Some of them became Townsendites, some of them went in for food fads, some were devoted to Aimee Semple McPherson. They all had false teeth and took high colonics. And about once a week they would provide the Los Angeles newspapers with a murder; about once a quarter they would commit a murder that showed imagination, like the man who killed his wife by forcing her leg into a box of rattlesnakes. Dale Connell had given them the name Glendale people, although they could have been described as Culver City people, Santa Monica people, Santa Ana people. He just happened to have spent more time at the Warner Brothers studio and had passed through Glendale on his way to work, month after week after day. The appellation had nothing to do with his own name, which in any event was a name he had adopted along the way.

His present-day friends, those he would once have called Glendale people, are his own age. That is, they are anywhere from the middle fifties to the middle seventies. He is not unmindful of the fact that he is more tolerant of Glendale people since he became their contemporary. He does not mind living in the midst of Glendale people so long as he does not have to live with them in Glendale.

Most of the men he used to know are dead, and those who survive have lost touch with Dale Connell, do not even know that he is alive. When he dies, and the highlights of his career appear in his obituary, there will be people who will say that they thought he was dead; others who will wonder why they never heard of him; others who have heard of him and will say they wish they never had; and a few who will laugh and say unkind things not unkindly. Dale Connell is aware of all that. In the morning, when he has finished with the breakfast dishes and put on his double-breasted blazer and wrinkled Panama, and walks the eight blocks to the out-of-town newspaper stand, he opens his New York papers to the obituary pages before turning to the entertainment and book sections. He is precisely fair in his personal epitaphs of old acquaintances; he knows what they would say about him, and his thoughts of them are measure-for-measure gentle and severe, plus the embarrassing triumph of having for a while outlived men who lived better lives than his own. But there is never any severity in his judgments of women whose death notices he reads. He has forgiven every woman who ever gave him a bad time, and all the numerous women he has known are now creatures of equal rank in a company formed by his memory. No matter how unique and individualistic each of them may have been at the time, they all are banded together now, rather like a bundle of love letters tied in red ribbon, resting in the bottom drawer of his bureau under his New York shirts.

On his way home from the newsstand he carries his Panama, gripped by the brim, in one swinging hand, and tucked under the other arm are the newspapers and his stick. Many of his friends carry canes, not tucked under their arms but used for support, and they are cheap, despised pieces of wood. Dale Connell is fond of his Malacca, with its initialed brass ferrule, bought for him at Swaine, Adeney's by an Englishwoman from whom he had expected at least an Asprey cigarette case. Another Englishwoman, who could not really afford a walking stick, had given him a Dunhill gold lighter with a watch in it. The Malacca makes him think of the second woman's generosity, even though the lighter has long since been pawned; but the giver of the Malacca had been generous in her way, too, and Dale Connell will have something to say about the unpredictability of Englishwomen when he comes to that part of his book.

He works on his book in the mornings, after he has read the newspapers, made his bed, and prepared the instant coffee.

The actual writing is not as easy as he thought it was going to be. He has been at it for five years, and he has taken twenty-five hundred dollars from a New York publisher who will not advance any more money until Dale Connell shows him some manuscript. Any publisher would be glad to bring out the memoirs of Dale Connell, and Carson Burroughs was extremely enthusiastic when Connell wrote and told him that he had started a book. "You realize, of course," Burroughs had replied, "that even today we may have to tone it down. However, I promise you that we will do our utmost to retain the validity of your memoirs. Meanwhile, when do you think you will be able to show us the first five hundred pages?" Six months passed, and Dale Connell had got nothing down on paper. "I have torn up everything I have written so far and am off to a new start with an entirely fresh approach," he wrote Burroughs. "Could you see your way clear to advancing me another thousand?" He got no immediate answer to this letter; instead he got a surprise visit from Burroughs.

It was more than a surprise; it was something of a shock. He came home one morning and an enormous Cadillac convertible was parked in front of his cottage. It had Florida license plates, but Dale Connell knew no one who owned a Cadillac. Most of his Florida Glendale people owned no car at all. The shock came when he opened the screendoor of his front porch and was greeted by Burroughs.

"Hello, Dale," said Burroughs. "I thought I'd drop in and see how you were coming along."

"Drop in? Are you in town?"

"Palm Beach. I flew over this morning."

"Is that your car?"

"Hired. Your letter was forwarded to me. I guess my secretary didn't know you were on the West Coast and Palm Beach is on the East Coast. Anyway, she thought she was using her head. And she was."

"Of course. Will you have a drink, or would you like some coffee?"

"I'll have a cup of coffee with you, but don't go to any trouble. I'm chiefly interested in your memoirs. How're they coming?"

"Well, as I told you in my letter, I've got a whole new fresh approach. I wasted a couple of years trying to lick it, but it wasn't altogether waste. I learned how it *shouldn't* be done. You see, I was never a writer before. I used to dictate everything to a secretary, or into a Dictaphone."

"When you were in Hollywood? You have quite a few screen credits. Didn't you write those scripts?"

"Original-story credits, they were. I used to dictate them, and I could always get a secretary to put them in shape. All they cared about was the story line. Very different from sitting down and writing a book, I found out."

"Well, why don't you get yourself a tape recorder and get going that way? I can always find somebody to whip it into shape, once we have the stuff. I'm perfectly willing to advance you another thousand dollars if I have something to show for it, but I have to convince my partners. That's why I came over to see you personally. Hell, if you just sit down and tell the story of your checkered career, Dale, you'd have a real blockbuster. I admit that. Married what? Four times?"

"Five. The first one nobody knows about. That was back in Ohio, when I was twenty years old. I married my piano teacher, she was twenty-eight."

"You didn't stay married to her very long."

"It was annulled. I blew town and joined the Canadian army. Then right after the war I married—"

"Gaby Perrier? Right?"

"Right. She divorced me to marry the Bolivian, and I married Valerie Vale."

"Beautiful. I always thought the most beautiful girl Ziegfeld ever had. Tragic, of course."

"Yes, at least it turned out that way. You knew what her trouble was?"

"Booze, I always heard," said Burroughs.

"No. That's what everybody thought. No, it wasn't booze."

"What was it? Dope?"

"Not dope, either."

"Well, come on, give. What was it?"

"Wait till my book comes out," said Dale Connell.

"You son of a bitch, what kind of a come-on is that? All

right. Then you married Sylvia Rumson and you divorced her because she put you in a novel while you were still married to her."

"Is that the way it was, Carson?"

"Well, wasn't it? She did put you in a novel."

"Was that me, or was it somebody else? Everybody said it was me, but was it?"

"Wasn't it?"

"If I told you who the guy really was in that book, you'd call me a liar. I divorced Sylvia, but I didn't have to pay her any alimony. I didn't even have to pay for the lawyers. If you think back a minute, the next two years I lived like a prince, a maharajah. Not bad for a young guy from Ohio that didn't have a job or anything. No, the guy in that book wasn't me. I won't tell you who it was, but I'll tell you this much. He was a banker. Wall Street. Sylvia disguised the character in the book to make him look like me, but all those details were the banker, not me. In other words, Sylvia pulled a fast one on both of us. Oh, she was quite an operator, Sylvia. You ought to know."

"Not me."

"Oh, yes. You. She told me about you, Carson. Some kind of a convention in Chicago, and you drove back together in your car. I think you had a Marmon."

"Well, that was before she was married to you, so you can't hold that against me. Then you married Kitty Romaine."

"Married Kitty Romaine, was divorced by Kitty Romaine, married her again two weeks after the divorce, and was with her when she died."

"And she was the real love of your life."

"No. Not that I didn't love Kitty, because I did. But she wasn't the real one, my big number, as we used to say then. No, you wouldn't know who that was even if I told you."

"Is that going to be in the book?"

"Yes, without mentioning her name."

"Oh, happily married?"

"No. She's a nun."

"A nun? You were in love with a girl that became a nun? What was she before that?"

"Nothing. A schoolgirl. I used to walk home from school

with her. Carry her books. We used to talk. Her father was a doctor, the greatest man I ever knew, although he had no use for me. Coached the high school football team, and he'd scrimmage with us in his street clothes. He could do anything. Box. Shoot. Play the piano. Sing. Serve Mass. And keep up his practice. Had the first automobile in town. But he only had one child, a daughter. Dark brown hair and blue eyes. Everybody said Doctor Callaghan should have had a son, but he had only this one daughter and I guess no young guy ever measured up to her father. Oh, she was pretty. She could have been the belle of the ball, but she never went out on dates. I'd walk home with her during the winter and spring, when there was no football practice, and we'd stand and talk at their front gate. How I was going to be a big song-writer, and have my own orchestra, and travel all over. Or else maybe I'd go to Western Reserve and study medicine. She never believed that, but she'd pretend to. I always wanted to *talk* to *her,* and I did. By the hour. She really didn't have very much to say, but she had intelligent eyes and I always knew she was listening. They sent her East to school, and that was the year I ran off with the music teacher. I never saw Agnes again after she went away to school. Never heard from her. Never heard from her to this day, not that I expected to after the big scandal. And yet I guess I did expect to hear from her. I wanted her to forgive me. I haven't been inside of a confessional since I was nineteen years old. I never went to confession when I was in the army, when the chaplain would come around the night before we were moving up. Agnes was the one I wanted to forgive me, not some Canuck priest." He was silent.

"This is a new side of you, Dale," said Burroughs.

"No it isn't."

"No, I guess maybe it isn't," said Burroughs. "If you get this down the way you tell it, it sure would surprise a lot of people."

"It sure would," said Dale Connell. "It would spoil my reputation. Maybe America isn't ready for that."

"Maybe not. But if I advance you another thousand dollars will you spend some of it on a tape recorder?"

"Make it fifteen hundred and I'll promise to buy one."

"That's more like the Dale Connell I know. All right. Fifteen hundred, but that'll be all until I get five hundred pages of manuscript."

"How much is that in tape?"

"I have no idea. You send me the tape and I'll have it transcribed, and when you have five hundred pages I'll advance you another thousand. Making thirty-five hundred advance royalties."

A few days later a tape recorder arrived from Miami, with it a Carson Burroughs calling card on which was written, "Start talking—good luck—C.B."

During the next few days Dale Connell studied the instructions and learned to operate the apparatus. As a toy it was amusing. He sang into it, and did his parlor imitations of actors he had known, but when he began to dictate his life story he froze. "I was born on the fifteenth of January, 1897, in the town of High Ridge, Ohio. I was the youngest son of Mr. and Mrs. Daniel J. Connelley and I was named after my father. I attended the public school and graduated from high school in 1915." At that point he always stopped. It took him weeks to discover why he always stopped there: it was that the next autobiographical fact was his elopement, and speaking into the apparatus made him sound to himself like a boy telling his sins to a priest. That he would not do; he was not a boy, the apparatus was not a priest, and every time he approached the apparatus to begin again, Agnes Callaghan became more real and alive to him than she had been in almost fifty years. He could visualize her in her nun's habit; the face he had last seen in 1915, the features unchanged but the cheeks framed in white linen, the forehead almost hidden by white linen, and he could imagine her fingering a crucifix as he had seen other nuns do. Soon the apparatus was so inextricably identified with the calm face of a young girl that he did not like to go near it. He stayed away from it, until one night after some visitors went home he decided to exorcise the spirit of the apparatus, and he did so by turning on the microphone and speaking to it of women he had known. He had had more than his usual two cocktails and a brandy, and he described in detail their bodies and their passions. He played the recording back, and the nastiness of his performance so disgusted him that he pulled the tape from the spools and dropped the machine on the floor. He did not have it fixed. He put the broken apparatus in a closet and left it there. It is there now, much the worse for five years in the air that circulates over the Gulf of Mexico. The air is damp and salty, but the sun shines nearly every day and a man does not have to stay cooped up in a closet, like a broken tape recorder.

In the afternoon, after he has had his soup and pie, Dale Connell changes into cotton slacks and polo shirt and blue rope-soled espadrilles and goes to the beach. He takes a book with him, in case he sees no one he knows, but most days he is joined by some of his Glendale people, who love to hear him talk. "You must bear in mind," he says, "that anything can happen in the movie business, and anything can happen in Southern California. So when I tell you a story that sounds insane, just remember that combination."

"Tell us about the party at Lew Cody's," someone will say.

"The Lew Cody party? Well, he was having his house moved from Hollywood to Beverly. The men came to move the house, and Lew had a party going on. So he told them he didn't want to interrupt the party. Just disconnect the electricity and the water lines, he told them. And they put the house on rollers and moved it, but the party went right on, all the way out Wilshire Boulevard, for two days and nights. Lew, and Norman Kerry, and Fatty Arbuckle. Plenty of booze. A jazz band. Girls. Quite a party."

It is all new to his Glendale people, and when he has told them a story he makes a mental note to include it in his book. The trouble is there are so many stories. His Glendale people remember those stars, and they want to hear about their favorites. (Theda is just an anagram for death, Bara is Arab spelt backwards.) The Glendale people care not a whit about London or Paris or Rome and the people he knew during the frequent and sometimes lengthy sojourns he made in Europe. He wanted to say to his Glendale people, "You are missing a lot by not showing more interest in my European days." He has tried them out on stories of gambling in Monte Carlo, racing at

Cowes, horse races at Ascot, the extravagances of nobility when they are sowing their wild oats, the practical jokes and the freak bets in the London clubs. But he has noticed that the Glendale people have a way of looking at him, when he tells foreign stories, that is a mixture of polite skepticism and a lack of curiosity. Some of the stories are partially provable; he has trinkets to show for some of his adventures, a half-filled scrap-book—started late, neglected early—that would substantiate some others. Nevertheless the Glendale people do not encourage those overseas reminiscences, and at first he blamed their Middle Western isolationism. But it isn't that, really; not in the usual sense of corn-belt insularity. It is something more personal.

They like it when he talks about his Hollywood experiences, because they know he came from Ohio, and what happened to him in Hollywood could have happened to them. (Fat chance; but that's what they think.) He retains his Ohio twang, in spite of a few Englishisms (stick for cane, jacket for coat), and their ears tell them that he is one of them. It is stupid of them not to realize that what sets him apart from them is not his livingroom, or being a bachelor, or his manner of dress. In the matter of clothes, for instance, they see only a blazer, and everybody wears blazers today. If they had a little more curiosity they would examine the buttons on his blazer and he would gladly inform them that the crest was that of a dinner club he belonged to in London in the mid-Twenties: a duke was honorary secretary, a member of the royal family paid his three guineas annual dues, a theatrical producer, as famous abroad as Ziegfeld at home, was honorary steward. The Glendale people see only a cane, and some of the Glendale women as well as the men carry canes—could not take two steps without one. They never ask about his Malacca, and he has not created the opportunity to tell them that the lady who gave it to him was indeed a Lady. But they eat up everything he sees fit to tell them about Kitty Romaine. They all remember that Kitty Romaine was almost as famous as Pearl White.

Now and then Dale Connell begins to get a sensation of being overwhelmed by the Glendale people, of being irresistibly sucked back into the Middle West. He has never been back, he has had no communication with anyone in High Ridge since cabling the money for his mother's funeral in 1935. In 1934 he could not have sent the money; he was broke and in debt. In 1936 his sister would not have known how to reach him; he was in Calcutta, trying to promote a motion picture company. But in 1935 his sister telephoned a columnist on the Cleveland *Plain Dealer,* who obligingly gave her the address of Alexander Korda, Dale's most recent London employer. When Ursula Connelley died, in 1943, no one notified Dale. He could not have done much in any case; he was in Scotland in an O.S.S. film unit, with his major's pay and nothing more. Ursula was always a whiner, anyway, and in her rare letters to him through the years seemed compelled to say how awful his first wife looked, as though taking him to task for seducing a woman who in fact had seduced him. High Ridge, Ohio, was not small enough to be obliterated by progress, like the pretty little villages that are bulldozed out of existence to make way for super-highways, or inundated for the construction of dams. But there was nothing—and no one —in High Ridge that tugged at Dale Connell's heartstrings. Forty-five, almost fifty years, a long time, and in that time nothing that happened in High Ridge had happened to him. Nevertheless the town is still there, and in his moments of suspecting that his Glendale people have captured him, High Ridge becomes the Middle West, and he wonders if it has ever let him go.

So far there has been no one from High Ridge among the Glendale people. Roberta Wagner's granddaughter is a Pi Phi at State and has visited Tom Cookson's granddaughter in High Ridge. Dale Connell remembers Tom Cookson as an earnest boy who clerked in J. J. Cookson's grocery store and didn't get—or seem to want—much fun out of life. "We never knew each other very well," said Dale, when Roberta mentioned the Cooksons.

"They all remember you, though," said Roberta. "As Dan Connelley. All the girls were crazy about you, is what I hear."

"Now, now, Roberta. You only heard about one."

"Well—one was enough. Imagine running away with your music teacher. There was a case like that in Marion, Indiana, where I come from, only they stayed married. They moved away, but they kept on being married. It just goes to show, all that funny business isn't just confined to Hollywood."

Roberta's husband, Sam Wagner, is a mean little bastard. He has won the Senior Citizens' putting championship for three years running, and he is one of the few Glendale people to have a car. He has a way of listening during a conversation as though he were not listening, staring to his right for three or four minutes, then suddenly staring to his left for another three or four, and back again to his right, and then he will make some remark that shows he has not missed a word. "Dale, I can't figure you out," he once said.

"How's that, Sam?" said Dale.

"Well, I listen to these stories of yours, and I never been able to figure out where you been all the time. One minute it's Hollywood, California. Then the next minute you're in London, England."

"That's just about the way it was, too," said Dale.

"Writing scenarios. But didn't you tell us you wrote songs?"

"I wrote a lot of songs. Probably a hundred, but only a few of them got published, and only four made a hit. That's how I live. I get a little income from ASCAP. No income from the scenarios."

"Then why don't you knock out some more songs, if that's where the money is."

"Not my kind of songs, not today. 'Wackity-Doo.' 'Little Chapel on the Lake.' They don't go for my songs any more. 'Moana Moon.' 'Let's Tarry in Tallahassee.' "

"Jevver hear of those songs, Roberta?" said Sam.

"Oh, yes. I used to play 'Little Chapel on the Lake.' "

"That was my biggest hit," said Dale. "You still hear it once in a while on the radio. 'Wackity-Doo' when they revived the Charleston, although I wrote that before the Charleston was popular."

"What were you doing in Europe all that time?" said Sam.

"You name it. I wrote scenarios. Some songs. Acted in a couple of plays. Co-produced several shows on Broadway that I brought over from London."

"You certainly were a jack-of-all-trades, all right."

"I had fun," said Dale.

"Is that a picture of you?" said Sam. "You had a waxed moustache?"

"And a full head of hair. Yes, that's me."

"Look at that collar. It's a wonder it didn't choke you. It looks like it was cutting your ear lobes."

"We all wore them then."

"I didn't."

"That was London."

"You look to me like you had lipstick on," said Sam.

"I did. Theatrical makeup. The girl was Jocelyn Candee, a very big name in the London theater."

"Maybe in London, but they wouldn't have given her a second look in Hollywood," said Sam Wagner.

"No, but she managed to become Lady Medlock, the wife of one of the richest men in the United Kingdom. I visited their—"

"They always left me cold, Englishwomen. I couldn't understand half of what they were saying. We were there in '28, year before the crash. I said I was never going back there, and I never did. And the men were no better."

"Some of the men," said Roberta Wagner.

"Aah," said Sam Wagner. "You know what Napoleon Bonaparte called them, don't you? A nation of small shopkeepers."

"Pretty good shops, though," said Dale Connell.

"No. You order a suit there, and it takes a couple months to have it ready. But that's not what I object to. What I object to, they do everything on credit there, you see. Cons'quently, *you're* paying for the deadbeats. I'd rather do business on a cash basis and get what I pay for, not making up their losses on bad debts. You put that in your book, warn the American tourists what they're paying for."

"It won't be that kind of a book."

"Oh, you could put it in somewhere. Are you gonna have that picture in it?"

"I might."

"You better put some of the others in, too, or everybody'll

think you're a pansy. That lipstick. Boy! That oughta go big
in England. Is this you in the uniform? Doesn't look like the
same person."

"I've never been the same person I was in that picture,"
said Dale Connell.

"Do you think a person changes that much?" said Roberta.
"I think we stay the same."

"Of course we do," said her husband. "I'm the same,
you're the same, and Dale's the same. You know the old saying,
you can take the boy out of Ohio but you can't take Ohio out
of the boy."

Dale Connell shook his head. "That young fellow in the
Canadian uniform—I'd have nothing in common with him today."

"Don't you believe it," said Sam Wagner. "Our characters are formed by the time we're eighteen, and we stay that
way the rest of our lives."

"I'd hate to think so," said Dale Connell. "I certainly
don't want to believe that all the places I've been and the people I've met, the things I've done—all that had no effect on
me. I was twenty-one when that picture was taken. Now have a
look at this one, taken when I was about thirty-five. You don't
see any difference?"

"Of course there's a difference," said Sam Wagner. "In
this one you're wearing a gray high hat and a swallowtail, and
it looks to me like you have a waxed moustache. Field glasses.
Some race track in England, I imagine."

"Yes, and who do you think the other men are? Well,
this man on my right. You may not recognize him, but you'd
recognize his brother."

"I doubt it."

"His brother was the Prince of Wales. Now the Duke of
Windsor."

"Oh, let me see that," said Roberta.

"That may well be," said Sam Wagner. "All the same,
underneath the swallowtail and the high hat, it's still you."

"I don't even look the same," said Dale Connell. "Here,
do you recognize this man?"

"Sure, that's the writer—Ernest Hemingway. One writer

I would recognize. I'd know him, even without the gun. But what are you trying to prove? I admit you must have known all those people. But I can show you some pictures I have at home. One of me shaking hands with Bob Taft. I have one of me and Benny Oosterbaan. And Roberta has one of her congratulating Tommy Milton."

"It's lost," said Roberta. "I don't know what happened to it."

"You lost that picture of you and Tommy Milton? It must be somewhere, in storage."

"No, it's gone," said Roberta.

"Well, anyway, me, Sam Wagner, and my wife, Roberta, we had our pictures taken with famous people, but I don't claim that changed us. I claim just the opposite. Like that time I sat up and talked half the night, going East on the Broadway Limited, this fellow and I. He seemed familiar, but I couldn't place him and I couldn't place him. Turned out to be Al Jolson, only he didn't have his makeup on. Now there was a fellow I would of liked to get to know him."

"If you had, you would have changed. I knew Joley."

"I'll never forget him in *The Jazz Singer*," said Roberta. "Where did we see that, Sam?"

"You saw it twice. We saw it together in New York, but you saw it in Chicago when it played there."

"No, I think I saw it in Indianapolis. I went with Mary Jane Strohmyer. She didn't like it as much as I did. Al married a girl named Keller."

"Keeler. Ruby Keeler."

"Was it Keeler? I always pronounced it Keller, but you knew them. It's funny, I always pronounced her name Keller. Cute little thing. She used to do a tap dance with a cane. Keeler, huh?"

"But she wasn't in *The Jazz Singer*," said Sam.

"May McAvoy," said Dale Connell. "But I just happened to think, Roberta. Jolson's *first* wife was named Keller, although I don't know how you'd know that."

"I don't either. I'm not sure I did."

"Don't be so modest," said Sam Wagner. "You used to follow those movie stars. Probably know as much about them as

Dale does, without knowing them personally. You ask her something sometime."

"Oh, heavens, I have a terrible memory, and it's getting worse. I can remember what I wore to a party when I was fifteen, but don't ask me where I was last Thursday."

"Just for the hell of it, where were you last Thursday?" said Dale Connell.

"Thursday?" she said.

"That ought to be easy," said her husband.

"Is that a hint? Oh, I know. You were putting against Cy Runstadt."

"Bet your sweet life I was, and beating him three and two. See, you remembered."

Dale Connell has seen snapshots of Roberta in her girlhood, but they tell him very little, much less than he has been able to imagine from having seen her granddaughter in person. Although Roberta's hair is white, and she is rather tall for a woman, it is not impossible, from looking at her, to conjecture some similarities between her and the present Agnes, Mother Callaghan, of the Sacred Heart nuns, that do not depend on mere physical resemblance. It may come down to no resemblance at all, but rather a gentleness in common, and Dale Connell's strong belief that for the Wagners sexual activity is a thing of the past. He could be wrong about that; among his Glendale people he sees signs of erotic consciousness—fierce jealousies, hand-holding, flirtatiousness—but Sam Wagner is seventy, interested only in his capital and in beating other men on the putting green. He is generally disagreeable, and it is a commonplace among the Glendale people that Roberta is the only person in the world that could put up with him (although the principals in that commonplace are, so to speak, interchangeable; Sam Wagner says the same thing about his friends Cy and Lillian Runstadt). Roberta has the same sweetness that Agnes Callaghan would have today, and she is the first woman he has known in forty years that he likes to talk to—when he gets the chance—as he once talked to Agnes. In an odd way she is less sophisticated than Agnes. Simpler. During all those long conversations with Agnes he had never been given an inkling that she was mulling over in her mind a major problem, coming to a decision that would determine the course of her life. Roberta Wagner could not be so reticent. A certain kind of guile was essential to maintain that kind of reticence, and Agnes possessed it; Roberta said everything that came into her mind, and with an innocence that he had not discovered—or looked for—in any woman since those long conversations at the Callaghans' gate.

There is no manuscript of Dale Connell's memoirs, in the sense of a narrative that has continuity; there is only a stack of notes and a long list of names of once-famous actors and actresses, of big-game hunters and polo players, playwrights and theatrical managers, movie producers and directors, orchestra leaders and torch singers, restaurateurs and ballroom dancers, English novelists and American heiresses—and men like himself, who had minor talents in the arts or in sports, who had suites at Claridge's when they were in the money or stopped at the Cavendish when they were not. Carson Burroughs is quite right when he says that Dale Connell's memoirs would be a blockbuster, but it is a manuscript that Burroughs will never see. Dale Connell is trying to be conscientious. Every day he adds a name to his already long list; but he cannot bring himself to put down on paper the true stories of all those women. Once it was the face of Agnes Callaghan in a nun's habit, that made him smash a tape recorder. But now it is Roberta Wagner, a real presence, who intrudes. "I am dying to see your book," she says. But she would be repelled by the book he wants to write. She believes in Mary Miles Minter.

THE GOLDEN

The frolicking had been going on for about an 'hour. The Belgian Shepherd would chase the Golden Retriever around and around the box-hedge, and the Retriever would allow himself to be caught and the two dogs would spar with each other, mouths open, tongues hanging out. The Retriever, lying on the grass, would pretend to be vanquished, and then, for no discernible reason, the Shepherd would look away. Something he had heard, something he could catch the smell of, or mere boredom, would cause him to lose interest, and for perhaps half a minute he would behave as though the Retriever did not exist. He would trot away, and the Golden would follow him; then the Belgian would suddenly make a dash for nowhere and the chase was on again. So they played for about an hour, and Mary Calthorp, busy with her checkbook and bank statement, moderately enjoyed the distraction of the show they were putting on. She finished her chore, lit a cigarette, and stood at the window, trying to decide whether to slip into a coat and go for a walk, concurrently trying to decide to or not to engage the services of a topiary expert whose card had come in the day's mail.

She was not even conscious of watching the dogs, but she saw that they had reached the nipping stage. Then one dog's fang touched another dog's nerve, and in an instant both animals were making the horrible gurgling sound that meant a fight. Mary Calthorp snatched the brassbound broom from the fireside and ran out of the house. "Stop it! *Stop it!*" she cried. She poked the bristles of the broom into the Belgian's hide, and he looked up at her and skulked away. "Good dog," she said, and patted the Golden's head. She stooped over and examined her dog and found that his skin had not been broken. "Good dog, good-good dog," she said. He looked up at her and waited for more praise, but she returned to the house and left him on the terrace. She went back to her window, and saw the Golden trot off, following the direction the Belgian had taken. "Will I never learn? Will I never, never learn?" she said.

She waited, in case the Golden changed his mind, but he was gone and she knew he would be gone until his feeding time. "Oh, well," she said, and returned to her desk. From the large top drawer she took a long, glazed cardboard box, and from a pigeonhole a couple of sheets of foolscap that were rolled into a tube. She removed the lid from the box and rested the box inside the inverted lid. She unrolled the foolscap sheets and spread them singly on the desk and weighted them down with scissors and letter-openers to keep them flat. She put on her glasses, her Ben Franklins, and rubbed the ball-point pen until the ink came, and now she was ready to resume the addressing of Christmas cards. The little personal messages on each card would come later; first get the envelope addressed. Always get that part over with first; the little personal messages would come to her in the time between now and the fifteenth of December, her annual date for mailing the cards. She had a good two weeks in which to think up the personal messages, in which some ideas would come to her, and she would get out her cards and write the messages while the idea was fresh; but for some of the cards she would have to wait for ideas, sometimes until the very last minute, and she was not always pleased with the result. She hated to put things off until the last minute, but over the years she had found that with some friends' Christmas cards it was better to rely on last-minute inspiration than to try to think of something newsy or witty ahead of time. Allan Moffitt, for instance, was someone who had been on her Christmas-card list for at least thirty years, probably longer. How he had got there originally—well, he had sent her a card one year and she had put him on the list for the next year, and she had never taken him off it. From Christmas to Christmas he was not much in her thoughts, but somehow, at the very last minute, she could always come up with something to say, something that showed she remembered him as a person and not just a name on a list.

The list was getting quite long, possibly too long when it still included names like Allan Moffitt's. She would keep his name on it, because Allan's wife had died two years ago and he must be fairly close to sixty-five, and to drop him from the list without reason and when he probably needed little things like Christmas cards—that would be rather cruel. Especially since he had never failed to send her a card. Allan Moffitt. Allan A. Moffitt, what a strange, funny man he had been. Rather unpleasant, really, on that first meeting. Older than the rest of the people on that beach picnic, and there only because he was pursuing a girl named Amy Locke, from Providence, who did not have to be pursued. Who in all probability had been caught up with by Allan and was running away from him and was herself in pursuit of a boy named Charles Freel, a Dartmouth creature. "What are you doing here?" Allan Moffitt had said.

"What are *you?*" Mary had said.

"Oh, I should think that would be fairly obvious," said Allan.

"Yes, I guess it is."

"But you still haven't answered my question," said Allan.

"I don't know that I have to. Or that I'm going to."

"You're here because you've always been here, and these are your friends," he said. "Is that what your answer would be?"

"It should be enough of an answer."

"But it isn't. You could be with a lot more interesting people."

"More interesting than Amy Locke, for instance?"

"Much more interesting than Amy Locke. Amy's *my* problem, but she isn't very interesting. She's giving me the runaround, but that doesn't make her interesting. You go up and down the Atlantic coast, from here to Rehoboth, and everywhere some girl like Amy is giving someone the runaround."

"You keep coming back for more," she said.

"Yes, I do," he said. "But I've had enough. I've had enough of nothing."

"Well, you'll be better off."

"How? Why? Do you really think I couldn't win out over Mr. Freel?"

"No," she said.

"Why not?"

"Because you don't know Amy. She has you here, dancing attendance on her—"

"Dancing *attendance?* Did you get that one from your grandmother? Excuse me. She has me here, dancing attendance."

"Yes, and for all to see. While she gives you the runaround in favor of Charles Freel. If you had any gumption you'd have gone home Friday. Amy's as through with you as if you'd never been born."

"Maybe. But I wasn't quite through with her. I am now."

"Why? What made you see the light?"

"I didn't, exactly. I'm not really leaving on account of Amy. I'm leaving on account of you."

"What did I say, or do?"

"Nothing you said or did," he said. "I decided I find you more interesting, so I'm getting out of this atmosphere. I hope to see you soon again, but in entirely different surroundings."

"Oh, is that so?" she said.

"I get to Philadelphia pretty often. If Betty Sciberling asks you to dinner will you come?"

"I'm engaged to be married."

"I noticed your ring," he said. "Most people haven't got the money to buy that kind of ring nowadays. If it isn't an heirloom he must be very well fixed. Who is he?"

"His name is Francis Calthorp."

"Oh. *Well* fixed. And could be an heirloom, too. That explains why you have such a placid look. Your future all taken care of. So I guess it's back to Amy for me."

"And you'll get just what you deserve," she said.

He smiled. "I like you. I knew I would," he said.

He married Amy Locke, and every year Mary Calthorp got a Christmas card from him, not from him and Amy. And every year she sent a card to him, not to him and Amy. And always at the last minute she thought of something to say. The third year on his card he wrote, "I got just what I deserved," and it was her first news of his divorce. The twenty-fifth or twenty-sixth year, on his card he wrote, "If I had known, I would have written or come to see you," and from that she understood that he had learned belatedly of Francis Calthorp's death.

It was strange how big a thing Allan's cards had grown to be. Singly, they were inconsequential: an annual message, as succinct as a telegram, from a man whom she had never known well, who was not in her thoughts more than—at the most—a dozen quick times a year. And yet if she had saved his cards, and she wished now that she had, they would summarize the past thirty years in his life and hers as effectively as thirty diaries. Even during the war he remembered, and managed to get off a V-mail that took the place of a card. In 1944, for instance, he wrote: "It was my painful duty to welcome Lt Cmdr Chas Freel aboard my ship this year. The s. o. b. did not remember me!" A message like that, and then a year of silence. He always assumed that she would recognize old names and thirty-year-old references, and he was quite right. She did. He had not bothered to tell her that he had married twice, been divorced once, after his marriage to Amy Locke. He assumed, apparently, that such items would get to her by way of small talk or the society page. He was absolutely nothing in her life, and yet she was ashamed of her cold-blooded temptation to drop him from her list. She would *never* drop him from her list. In his way he was an old and dear friend, and he had never held it against her that she had said some rather rough things about Amy Locke, a short time before he married her. Some of her friends, the people in her immediate life, were constantly on the defensive against her forthrightness. How many times had they said to her, "Mary, you're a real bitch"? How often had someone said, "Mary, why don't you keep your nose out of it?" And there was the writer from New York, definitely not one of her friends but a man who kept popping up at weddings and funerals. Only a week ago, at the Johnson wedding, he had said to her, "Hello, Mary. Still exuding sweetness and light, taking charge as usual, I see." *Someone* had to, as he put it, take charge. The occasion was a large luncheon on the day of the wedding, and Mary Calthorp was not the hostess, but the host-

ess had done nothing at all about seating the guests, many of
them from out-of-town, and *someone* had to get the strangers
away from the buffet and put them at tables where they would
at least not be standing around like so many bumps on a log.

"You have it in for me, haven't you?" she asked the writer.
"Why? What have I ever done to you?"

"To me, nothing," he said. "But what could you?"

"Are you implying that I do things to people that I *can*
do things to?"

"So I've always understood," he said.

"Well, just for that crack I'm going to make you sit with
me."

"Sorry, Mary. I made other plans," he said.

"That's perfectly all right," she said. "I'm glad you could
find someone to sit with you."

"I did. Seven others," he said. And he had, and if there
could be said to be a cream of the crop at the luncheon, they
were at his table, having a better time than any other table.
The luncheon broke up fairly soon, to enable members of the
bridal party to change their clothes. She had had time to think,
and to regret having been as rude to him as he had been to
her. It was, after all, her territory and he was an outsider. She
went to him and put her hand on his arm, as friendly as
though nothing had happened. "Harry, I can give you a lift,"
she said. "Come see my new car."

"What have you got?" he said.

"A Mercedes-Benz. That gray one. I bought it second-
hand."

"It's beautiful," he said. "And thanks, but I have a car."

It was unintelligent to assume that he would not have
had transportation—the luncheon was at a house miles out in
the country—but now it was her turn to be hurt, and she was
hurt. She got in her car and drove home alone, getting very little satisfaction out of passing all the other cars on the way. She
changed her clothes, and she got back her confidence with the
knowledge that no woman in the church who was anywhere
near her age looked better or was better dressed. She sat on the
side of the friends of the bride, and this too helped restore her
confidence: she was only two pews behind immediate family,

and entirely surrounded by men and women who knew her faults but nevertheless were proud of her. But at the reception she was careful not to "take charge." Even when the bride said, "Aunt Mary, will I see you upstairs?"

"No, dear, I have these New York people. But much, much love and great, great happiness to you both." It was easy to slip out through a side door and away from all those young people doing the hully-gully. It was not so easy, at home and alone, to convince herself that Harry Barlow was merely an unpleasant man, ill-at-ease, out of his element, and completely unjustified in his snide criticism of her desire to help. It was not quite true, either, that he had as much of a reputation for his sarcasm as for his published works.

She put a check mark beside Allan Moffitt's name, although it was not the last of the M's and she had wanted to get halfway through the alphabet before evening. These lists, they came so soon, one upon another, as everything she did by the year was a too quick repetition of last year's doing. At first, when Frannie died, she had tried going abroad, but all too soon the annual trip became as much a part of the rapidly repetitious pattern as her Christmas-card list, her six dinner parties, Friday lunch at the Barclay and the Orchestra at two. And so she ticked a little *v* beside Allan Moffitt's name, to guide her when she took up the list again tomorrow. Actually she had done rather well to have got as far as Moffitt, Allan A. So many of her Philadelphia friends had names beginning with B and C that numerically she was more than half finished the task of addressing envelopes. She was not shirking, and if she kept on she would get eyestrain and one of her headaches. She put the lid back on the box, rolled the foolscap into a tube, clicked the ball-point pen, restored her Ben Franklins to their brocaded stand, and got up and stood at the window. The Golden was nowhere to be seen.

She turned when she heard the front door opened. It was a heavy door, three inches thick, slightly stuck and thus giving warning of a visitor. At this time of day a visitor who did not ring the doorbell would be a close friend or family. This visitor was her daughter, and she was not alone. "Mother? You in the library?"

"Yes," said Mary Calthorp.

"Oh, there you are," said Barbara Calthorp Conklin ("Change the name and not the letter—change for worse and not for better"). "Mother, this is Arthur Chapin. I said I was bringing him."

"Completely slipped my mind, I'm so sorry. How do you do, Mr. Chapin. Do you want to hang your coat in the closet? Barbara, you show him."

This was so much better than checkbooks and Christmas-card lists, her first look at her daughter's—according to the gossip—lover. Her very first look was reassuring: middle or late thirties, dark gray suit, polished shoes, striped necktie, and conventional good looks. All this she took in while he hung up his topcoat, and he had not yet spoken.

Now, free of hat and coat, he came forward and shook Mary Calthorp's hand, with an inclination of the head that was a vestigial bow, amusingly reminiscent of dancing-school manners. "Very nice to see you," he said. "I like your house."

"Thank you," said Mary Calthorp. "Barbara was born in the room directly above."

"I was born in a house, too. Most people are born in hospitals."

"Where was the house where you were born?" said Mary Calthorp.

"Upstate. Gibbsville," he said.

"Oh, I guess I knew your uncle. Did you have an uncle named Joe Chapin?"

"He was a cousin. I suppose you're referring to the lawyer. Was mixed up in politics? He had a son Joe, but I don't think you'd have known the son."

"The one I knew died ten or fifteen years ago, and I believe he *was* a lawyer. My husband was a lawyer, Barbara's father, and I think the two firms had business together. Are you a lawyer, Mr. Chapin?"

"No, I'm in the advertising business. I'm with a firm called —hold your breath—Mulligan, Orpen, Retlaff, Chaffee and Steen. With all those names I'm sure you never heard of any of them."

"Well, my husband's firm was—*you* hold *your* breath—

Dickinson, Godwin, Calthorp, Calthorp and Schmeltzer. And my husband was neither of the two Calthorps. Would you like to help yourself to a drink?"

"Thank you, but I'm that rarity in the advertising business. I don't drink, and I haven't got an ulcer. So far, at least. A year from now I may be a big lush or I may have a large-sized crater in my duodenum. But the business hasn't got me so far. Actually, I enjoy it."

"Prides himself on being very well adjusted," said Barbara. "Where's Rex?"

"Rex is my dog, a Golden Retriever," said Mary Calthorp. "Oh, he and the McGovern police dog are probably out chasing deer."

"You're ruining that dog, Mother," said Barbara. "She has this beautiful dog, the best papers you ever saw, and she's let him become nothing but a house pet."

"Well, I don't shoot any more, since your father died, and Rex is getting on, as dogs go. My husband got him as a puppy, and he *has* got good papers, but I don't think he minds being a house pet. Would you like a cup of tea, Mr. Chapin? Barbara, you would, I know."

"We had tea at Margery's. We stopped in there on the way," said Barbara. "My, she's disagreeable, that girl. But I suppose I would be too, cooped up with a broken leg."

"Hard to believe they're sisters," said Chapin. "They don't look the least bit alike."

"Oh, don't you think so?" said Mary Calthorp. "Their coloring is different, but as they get older I think they look more and more alike. Did you autograph her cast?"

Chapin laughed, and even before he spoke, Mary Calthorp disliked him for whatever he said that accompanied the laugh. "No, I didn't," he said. "She asked me to, and then changed her mind."

"Why not?" said Mary Calthorp.

"Oh, she said it wouldn't be discreet, to have his name on her silly cast. Good God, Lew knows about Arthur. I know about Rose Edwards, as who doesn't? And Lew knows about Arthur because I've *told* him. 'Wouldn't be discreet.' Really Mother, Margery is a stuffed shirt."

"Oh, I didn't mind," said Arthur Chapin.

"Well, maybe she has a point," said Mary Calthorp. "She's had a constant stream of visitors, and if people saw Mr. Chapin's name on her cast—"

"Who *cares* about people? I'll be so glad to get away from a place where a man's signature on a plaster cast . . ."

"You *are* getting away?" said Mary Calthorp.

"Well, Arthur has to get his divorce—"

"Won't be any trouble there, Mrs. Calthorp. The papers are all signed," said Chapin.

"But I didn't know you were that far along, Barbara. Or how far are you? This is all news to me."

"I'm not pregnant, Mother."

"I didn't say you were."

"But you said you didn't know I was that far along. That sounds like pregnancy talk," said Barbara.

"I didn't think of it that way. I'm sorry," she said. "Then you and Mr. Chapin are planning to get married? You realize, of course, that there may not be anything to this talk about Lew Conklin and Rose Edwards."

"Oh, Mother! Come off it!"

"We shouldn't have had this conversation in front of Mr. Chapin."

"Perfectly all right with me," said Chapin.

"But it isn't with me, Mr. Chapin. I wish Barbara and I could have had at least one thorough discussion by ourselves."

"Well, this isn't the way I planned it either, but maybe it's better this way," said Barbara. "Everything out in the open."

"I don't think it's a bit better," said Mary Calthorp. "But if you think so, if you want everything out in the open, as you say, then I have to tell you that I think you're making a terrible, enormous mistake."

"Meaning me, Mrs. Calthorp?"

"Perhaps. I don't know you at all. Naturally I've heard a few things about you and my daughter—"

" 'My daughter'!" said Barbara. "Gawd." She hurled her cigarette into the fireplace, missed her aim, and had to get up and pick the butt off the hearth rug.

"But all I really know about you is that you're in the advertising business, and apparently you and your wife are getting a divorce. I remember hearing a story about your cousin, that he drank himself to death over a young girl that was a friend of his daughter's. Not that I hold that against you, but it's practically all I know about you. And what do you really know about Barbara?"

"All I need to know, and that I'm in love with her."

"Well, let me tell you something about Barbara," said Mary Calthorp. "This is something you ought to know, Mr. Chapin."

"Mother? What are you going to say? Don't believe her, Arthur."

"It won't make the slightest difference," said Chapin.

"This might," said Mary Calthorp. "I want to tell you, Mr. Chapin, that Barbara's been married to Lew Conklin for over seven years, and during all those seven years she was as happy as anyone could be. Two darling children. And never the slightest bit of gossip about her. Then her husband, Lew, became attentive to a friend of Barbara's, this Rose Edwards. A very nice girl, by the way, and whether there was anything to the talk about Lew and Rose, but Barbara thought there was, and you came along."

"And I came along," said Chapin. "I don't see what you're getting at, Mrs. Calthorp."

"Don't you? Doesn't it occur to you that my daughter isn't so much in love with you as she is angry with her husband?"

"Except I happen to know better," said Chapin. "And I happen to be in love with Barbara."

"I see," said Mary Calthorp. "Well, then, there's the question of money. You may be rolling in wealth, I don't know. But Barbara is not. She has to wait until I die before—"

"All right," said Barbara. "We've had it. Come on, Arthur. Let's get out of *here*."

"Yes, the time has come, the walrus said," said Chapin.

Mary Calthorp could hear them muttering in the hallway, then came the groaning of the heavy front door as he opened it, and his first unsuccessful then successful attempts to close it. She did not hear his car, and she did not go to that side of the house to see if they had gone. She knew they had gone.

She stood at her window and looked out at the trees, their limbs bare, their trunks wrapped in burlap. A topiarist might help the box hedge; it was over thirty years old. But he might ruin it, too. She could not decide. She would have to talk to somebody about it. She picked up her blue leather address book and her Ben Franklins, and suddenly she was rushed by the Golden, his paws on her tweed skirt, his tail swinging and small joyful cries coming from him. She struck him hard with the address book, on the top of his head. "Where have you *been?*" she said.

HOW CAN I
TELL YOU?

A T-Bird and two Galaxies was very good for one day, especially as the T-Bird did not involve a trade-in. The woman who bought it, Mrs. Preston, had come in and asked for Mark McGranville and shown him a magazine ad. "Do you have one of these in stock, in red?" she said.

"Not on the floor, Mrs. Preston," he said. "But I can have one for you inside of two hours."

"You can? Brand-new?"

"Brand-new," he said.

"Red, like this?"

"The exact same color, the same body job, white walls, radio and heater. I could have it in front of your house inside of two hours. And if you were thinking of getting rid of your ranch wagon, I can allow you—well, let's see what the book says."

"Did I say I wanted to trade in my ranch wagon? I love it. I wouldn't think of getting rid of it. I want the Thunderbird for Buddy. He just passed all his exams and he's coming home for the weekend."

"Well, you know exactly what he wants, Mrs. Preston. Because he's been in here a couple times, looking at T-Birds. He's a very lucky boy."

"He's a good boy, Mark. Not a lucky boy."

"Yes, he's one of the best," said Mark McGranville.

"And you say you can have a car just like this in two hours? Where do you have to go for it?"

"Oh, all I have to do is pick up the phone, call the factory distributor, and tell him what I want."

"But how do you know he has what *I* want?"

"Because we dealers get a list of what was shipped to the factory distributor. I guarantee you I have just what you want. I'll bring it to your door this afternoon, personally, and be glad to take care of the registration, insurance, all the details. Would you want us to finance it for you?"

"I would not. You bring the car around and I'll give you a cheque for the whole thing, license and everything. I don't suppose you could have his initials put on today?"

"If you let me have the car overnight I can have his initials put on and bring it back to you before noon tomorrow. R. W. P.?"

"R. W. P. That's right. In yellow. Yellow would be better on red."

"About three quarters of an inch high? Or smaller? Maybe a half an inch. A half an inch in yellow shows up well. If he wants bigger initials later, that's easy to fix."

"I'll leave that to you, Mark. And you'll take care of everything? He gets home tomorrow afternoon."

"He couldn't have a nicer surprise. It is a surprise, isn't it?"

"It certainly is. It's a surprise to *me*. I wasn't going to buy him a car till he graduates. But he's been so good, and why not let him have the fun out of it?"

"You're right, Mrs. Preston."

"How's Jean? And the children?"

"They're fine, thank you. Very fine."

"You get credit for this sale, don't you?"

"You bet I do," he said. "Appreciate your asking for me."

"Well, you've always been a good boy, too, Mark. I'm sure your mother's very pleased with you."

"Thank you."

"Your mother's a fine woman, Mark. Any time she's thinking of going back to work again, I hope she lets me know first."

"She would, that's for sure. But I guess she likes keeping house for my sister. They have that little ranch-type out at Putnam Park, the two of them. Mary has her job at the Trust Company, and my mother has enough to keep her occupied."

"Very nice for both of them. Well, I mustn't keep you any longer. You have some telephoning to do."

"Thank you very much, Mrs. Preston," he said. He accompanied her to her ranch wagon, held the door open for her, and waited in the parking lot until she turned the corner.

The other transactions of the day were more typical, not sales that were dropped in his lap by a Mrs. Preston. But all three sales should have made him feel better than he felt on the way home, and he did not know why he should find himself wanting a drink and, what's more, heading for Ernie's to get it.

He locked his car and entered the taproom, hung his hat and coat on a clothestree, and took a seat in a booth. Ernie came to wait on him.

"Well, hi, stranger," said Ernie.

"Hello, Ernie," said Mark McGranville. "Quiet."

"Well, a little early. Never much action before six. The lunch trade till ha' past two, then maybe a few strays during the afternoon. How's it with you?"

"Not bad. Pretty good."

"Ed and Paul were in last night, them and their wives for dinner. Paul made a pretty good load. What's her name, his wife?"

"Charlotte."

"She snuck over and asked me to cut his drinks, but I couldn't do that. I said to her, what'd she want to do? Get me in trouble? You know Paul, he caught me watering his drinks and he'd have it all over town in no time. He's no bargain anyway, Paul."

"No, he's a noisy son of a bitch when he makes the load."

"But he's a friend of yours, though, isn't he?"

"I guess so," said Mark. "Let me have a bourbon and soda, will you, Ernie?"

"Why sure. Is there anything the matter, Mark?"

"No. Why?"

"I don't know. You want any particular bourbon?"

"I wouldn't be able to tell the difference. You know that."

"Okay, okay," said Ernie. He pantomimed getting a kick in the behind and went to the bar to get Mark's drink. He returned with a small round tray on which were a highball glass,

a shot glass with the bourbon, a small bottle of club soda.
"There you are. That's Old Gutburner, the bar bourbon."

"Old what?"

"Gutburner. Old Gutburner. That's what Paul calls the
bar bourbon. It ain't all that bad. You want some music?"

"Christ, no."

"You just want to sit here and nobody bother you. Okay,"
said Ernie. He walked away, spinning the inverted tray on his
forefinger, and Mark had a couple of sips of his drink. He
waited for some pleasant effect, and when none came, he finished the drink in a gulp. "Ernie? Bring me another shot, will
you?"

"Right," said Ernie. He served a second shot glass of the
bourbon. "You got enough soda there? Yeah, you got enough
soda."

"I don't want any soda. I'm drinking this straight."

"Yeah, bourbon ought to be drunk straight. Bourbon has
a flavor that if you ask me, you oughtn't to dilute it. That is, if
you happen to like the taste of bourbon in the first place. Personally, I don't. I'll take a drink of bourbon, like if I'm at a
football game to see the New York Giants. Or you take if I'm
out in the woods, looking for deer, I usely take a pint of rye
with me, or sometimes bourbon. It'll ward off the cold and the
taste lasts longer. But for all-day drinking, I stick to scatch.
You don't get tired of the taste of scatch. Your rye and your
bourbon, they're too sweet if you're gonna drink all day. You
know a funny thing about scatch, it's getting to be the most
popular drink in France and Japan. That was in an article I
read, this magazine I get. You know, in this business we get
these magazines. I guess you have them in the car business.
Trade publications, they're known as."

"Even the undertakers."

"Huh?"

"The undertakers have trade publications."

"They do, ah? Well, wuddia know. I guess every business
has them."

"Every business is the same, when you come right down to
it," said Mark McGranville.

"Well that's a new one on me. We're all in it for the money, but what's the same about selling cars and pushing Old Gut-burner?"

"What you just said," said Mark McGranville. "We're all in it for the money. You. Me. Undertakers."

"You're talking like an I-don't-know-what," said Ernie.

"I know I am. What do I owe you?"

"Be—nothing," said Ernie.

"On the house?"

"Come in again when you'll get some enjoyment out of it. I don't want to take your money under these conditions."

"You, Ernie?"

"Yeah, me. You got sumpn eatin' you, boy, whatever it is."

"I know I have," said Mark McGranville. "Maybe it's the weather. I don't know."

"Well, my booze won't do it any good, Mark. I get days like this myself, once in a great while. The women get them all the time, but that's different. Take in a show tonight. You know this English fellow, with the big gap in his teeth. Terry?"

"Terry-Thomas."

"He's at the Carteret. He's always good for a laugh. You're not a booze man, Mark. Some are, but not you. You were taking it like medicine, for God's sake. Castor oil or something."

"Yeah. Well, thanks, Ernie. See you," said Mark Mc-Granville.

He could not understand why he went through dinner and the entire evening without telling Jean about the T-Bird and the two Galaxies in one day. He knew that it was because he did not want to give her any good news; that much he understood. She would respond to the good news as she always did, enthusiastically and proudly, and he was in no mood to share her enthusiasm or accept the compliment of her pride in him. All that he understood, but he could not understand why he preferred to remain in this mood. She would cheer him up, and he did not want to be cheered up. He was perfunctory when the kids kissed him goodnight, and after the eleven o'clock news on the TV he rose, snapped the power dial, and went to the bedroom. He was in bed when Jean kissed him goodnight and turned out the light.

"Mark?" she said, from her bed.

"What?"

"Is there something the matter?"

"Nope."

"Goodnight," she said.

"Goodnight," said Mark McGranville.

Five, ten dark minutes passed.

"If you don't want to tell me," she said.

"How the hell can I tell you when I don't know myself?" he said.

"Oh," she said. "Shall I come over?"

"I just as soon you wouldn't," he said. "I don't know what it is."

"If I come over you'll sleep better," she said.

"Jean, please. It isn't that. Christ, I sold two Galaxies and a T-Bird today—"

"You *did?*"

"That ought to make me feel good, but I don't know what's the matter with me. I had a couple drinks at Ernie's, but nothing."

"I knew you had something to drink. It didn't show, but I could smell it."

"Oh, I'm not hiding anything."

"You hid it about the Galaxies and the T-Bird."

"I know I did. I'd have told you in the morning."

"All right. Goodnight."

"Goodnight," he said.

He thought his mind was busy, busy, busy, and that he had been unable to get to sleep, but at five minutes past two he looked at the radium hands of the alarm clock and realized that he must have slept for at least an hour, that some of the activity of his mind was actually dreams. They were not frightening dreams or lascivious ones; they were not much of anything but mental activity that had taken place while he thought he was awake but must have been asleep. Jean was asleep, breathing regularly. She made two musical notes in deep sleep, the first two notes of "Yes Sir That's My Baby"; the *yes* note as she exhaled, the *sir* as she drew breath. And yet he could tell, in spite of the dark, that she would be slightly frowning, dreaming or thinking, one or the other or both. He had so often watched her asleep, physically asleep, and making the musical notes of her regular breathing, but the slight frown revealing that her mind was at work, that her intelligence was functioning in ways that would always be kept secret from him, possibly even from herself. It was not that her sleeping face was a mask; far from it. The mask was her wakeful face, telling only her responses to things that happened and were said, the obvious responses to pleasant and unpleasant things in life. But in the frowning placidity of sleep her mind was naked. It did not matter that he could not read her thoughts; they were there, far more so than when she was awake.

He got out of bed and went to the warm livingroom and turned on one bulb in a table lamp. He lit a cigarette and took the first drag, but he let it go out. He was thirty years old, a good father, a good husband, and so well thought of that Mrs. Preston would make sure that he got credit for a sale. His sister had a good job, and his mother was taken care of. On the sales blackboard at the garage his name was always first or second, in two years had not been down to third. Nevertheless he went to the hall closet and got out his 20-gauge and broke it and inserted a shell.

He returned to his chair and re-lit the cigarette that had gone out, and this time he smoked rapidly. The shotgun rested with the butt on the floor, the barrel lying against his thigh, and he held the barrel loosely with the fingers of his left hand as he smoked. The cigarette was now down to an inch in length, and he crushed it carefully.

Her voice came softly. "Mark," she said.

He looked at the carpet. "What?" he said.

"Don't. Please?"

"I won't," he said.

I KNOW THAT, ROY

R. G. Hanwell carried a leathern shotgun case in each hand. He stood them against the wall in the front hallway. "We want to be careful of those," he said to his wife. "I don't think I'll put them in with the rest of the stuff. I don't want them to get banged around."

"Suit yourself," said Marian Hanwell. "All our china goes into barrels. The last time we moved, not a single thing was broken."

"Now that's not true, Marian," said R. G. Hanwell. "My class picture, the glass was smashed. And for some unknown reason they lost one golf shoe. One golf shoe. How the hell do they manage to lose one shoe and not both?"

"I really don't know," said Marian Hanwell. "But if you want to keep all your personal treasures separate, all right. We can put them all in the station wagon."

"Not everything, but there are some things I don't want to go in the van."

"All right," said Marian Hanwell. "Just so we have everything ready and not have to change things around at the last minute. The first van will be here at eight o'clock tomorrow morning."

"It's going to be strange, living in a small house, after this old barn," said R. G. Hanwell.

"It'll be strange, but I'll bet I won't take long getting used to it. You won't either, once we're settled."

"Oh, I'm not complaining, not a bit. I'm completely reconciled."

"Reconciled? I like *that* considering it was originally your idea."

"I know it was my idea," he said. "But I expected you to be a little more sentimental about leaving."

"Sorry, old boy, but I can't force a single tear. It was nice to have Susie married from this house. It was what she wanted. But she was too young to remember what I had to put up with during the war. All that rationing, half the time no servants, repairs. And I think of the money we sunk into this house. All right, we got it free, and your father and mother very nicely moved out. But they knew what they were doing, all right, moving to a hotel. Oh, boy, did they ever! For four years I had to cope, all that time you were in the Navy and—"

"All the same, Marian, we had a lot of good times here after the war. We couldn't have given a dance in a small house, we couldn't have had friends visit us. And Susie's friends. You enjoyed it, now don't tell me you didn't."

"It was just fine as long as we could get servants and we were young. But I don't get as much fun out of entertaining as I used to, and what's the use of spending all that money? For what it costs to heat this house I could have a new fur coat every year, if I happened to want a new fur coat every year, which I don't. All I say is, thank the good Lord for the Sisters of Christian Charity, or whatever their name is. Do you suppose they have to go around with incense and cast out devils before they move in?"

"I should imagine so," said R. G. Hanwell. "I can think of two or *three* people that didn't always stay in their own rooms when they visited us."

"Two or three," said Marian Hanwell. "Two or three indeed. If the holy nuns knew some of the things that went on in this house we never would have been able to sell it."

"It wasn't that bad. Don't pretend that you're any more tolerant of that sort of thing than I am. You think it's just as messy as I do."

"Yes, but there were times when I had to look the other way."

"Well, that won't be a problem in the new house," said R. G. Hanwell. "The problem there will be you and I getting in each other's way."

"Not really," she said. "Since Susie got married you and I have been living in just about the same number of rooms we'll have in the new house. She's coming over for a last look, by the way. And to pick up a few things she wants to keep that we won't need. Now would be a good time for you to finish up with the things you don't want to go in the van."

"All right, Madam," he said. "It won't take long."

He was in his room when his daughter arrived. He did not altogether approve of her driving a car and climbing stairs at this stage of her first pregnancy, but her mother had done the same things and probably more before Susie was born, without any ill effects.

"Hello, Pa," said Susie.

"Hello, Su," he said. "I missed you in church this morning."

She kissed his cheek. "We've almost given up church in favor of lying in bed. Four more months and Sunday'll be just like any other day to me."

"How are you feeling?"

"Fine. Oh, I know I'm carrying a child in my pouch, but it hasn't been too bad. How are you? Ma said you were getting a little of the old nostalgia."

"No, not really. That all started when I said I didn't want the movers to manhandle some of my things. She has complete confidence in them, but I remember when we first moved into this house. Just bringing our few possessions from our apartment in town, they smashed the glass on my class picture, and for some unknown reason they lost one shoe out of a pair of golf shoes. One shoe. Imagine losing one shoe. So I'm setting aside a few things I want to take in the stationwagon. There won't be room in the new house for everything I'd like to keep, so I'm being very ruthless in getting rid of stuff. This, for instance, this is an old cricket bat."

"When did you ever play cricket?"

"Well, I didn't much. When I was in college a bunch of us thought we'd try it. We had an Englishman, a sort of honorary member of our fraternity, and he tried to convert us. Didn't last. We bought caps and blazers, and that was the end of it. The strange thing is, I always thought this bat had the names of all the cricket players on it, but now I see there isn't a single name on it. My initials, R G H, and that's all. How did I ever get the idea that we'd all signed it? Well, out it goes."

"Save it. It doesn't take up much room."

"No, I haven't even looked at it for twenty years."

"What's this box?" said his daughter.

"This box? This contains, or at least it should contain, my Navy souvenirs, if they're still in it. Papers, fitness reports, some V-mail from your mother. Snapshots. Cat's eyes. A .45 that I surveyed out. I'm going by memory. I haven't opened that since about 1946. The last time I opened it was to get my Air Medal out of it, when I had my medals framed. You know, that box in the library."

"Do you mind if I looked inside?"

"Go ahead. You'll probably find some references to yourself in the letters. In fact I know you will. Amuse yourself while I start weeding out some old clothes. By Jove, the Salvation Army's going to do all right in this closet. Why did I keep this old dinner jacket? Was I hoping I'd regain my slim figure?"

He busied himself with mothproof suit bags while she sat on the floor, going through letters she took out of the black tin box. Once in a while she would mutter, "How sweet," or "That's *nice*," but he did not interrupt her; her comments were not intended to invite conversation. Then, after perhaps fifteen minutes, he was deep inside his clothes closet when he heard her shout, "Oh, no! Oh, *no-oh!*" followed by laughter.

"Daddy, is this you?"

In recent years she had taken to calling him Pa.

"What have you got there?" he said.

"Well, have a look," she said. She handed up a snapshot. "Is that you, second from the left? Why, Daddy. You *dog.*"

The snapshot was one that had circulated by the thousands in the Pacific Ocean Area. It showed five officers of the United States Navy standing close behind five young black women. The women were grinning, the men were laughing and each man had his arms around a woman. All the women were naked to the waist and the men were holding them so that the women's breasts were cupped in the men's hands.

"Those are NATS pilots," said R. G. Hanwell.

"The second from the left could be *you.*"

"It could not. I wasn't a pilot, I was an ACI officer. And I never would have posed for a picture like that. I don't know how that could have got in my box. That picture was all over the Pacific."

"What is a NATS pilot? Were they trying to get recruits?"

"Naval Air Transport Service. That man doesn't look a bit like me."

"I'm sorry, but he does, Pa."

"Somebody put that there. I never had a copy of that snapshot. I saw it, lots of times. The Navy was flooded with them, and pictures like it. But I never had one."

"They really had terrific shapes, those women. Look at those jugs. This man, the man on your right—"

"Don't say the man on *my* right."

"Let me see it again, to make sure," said Susie.

He handed her the snapshot.

"I'll ask Ma if this isn't you."

"Don't you show that picture to your mother."

"Oh, come on, Pa. Don't be so square," she said. She called out, "Ma? Ma? Will you come here a minute, please?"

The girl handed the snapshot to her mother. "See if you can pick out your husband," said the girl.

"Good Lord," said Marian Hanwell. "Second from the left."

"Damn it, that's not me."

"It certainly looks like you," said Marian Hanwell.

"It's not me at all, and it doesn't look like me. You need new glasses. Or a better memory."

"Now, Pa, your memory's not so perfect. Remember the cricket bat."

"*Is* it you, Roy?" said Marian Hanwell, smiling.

"I keep telling you. No, no, no. I don't know where the damn picture came from. Somebody put it in my box. They must have."

"You never saw this picture before?" said Marian Hanwell.

"Hundreds of times. Copies of it were all over the Pacific. It was supposed to be very funny."

"Well, it is rather funny," said Marian Hanwell.

"Some yeoman put it in my box, or some other officer. We had some practical jokers," said R. G. Hanwell.

"I don't know, Pa. Your story sounds very weak to me."

"I didn't ask you how it sounds, Susan. The fact remains that it's not me in that picture."

"Not that Ma would hold it against you at this late date, and I know months would go by without your ever seeing a woman," said the girl.

"Months? *Years!*" said R. G. Hanwell.

"Well—" the girl began, and was interrupted by her mother.

"Susie, that's enough now," said Marian Hanwell. "You go downstairs and I'll meet you in the diningroom. I put out the silver that I think you'll want."

"All right, but don't be harsh with him, Ma."

"Go on, I said," said Marian Hanwell. The girl obeyed, and her mother tossed the snapshot back into the open box.

"Marian, you don't believe that's me, do you?"

"No," said his wife.

"I couldn't stand it if you thought that was me," he said. "It was bad enough then, being away from you."

"I know," she said.

"And if you didn't know that all that time I never went *near* another woman."

"I know that, Roy," she said.

JOHN BARTON ROSEDALE, ACTORS' ACTOR

There is a lot of truculent style to John Barton Rosedale as he goes to his mailbox—never locked—and flips open the little brass door and slams it shut. He knows there will be nothing of importance in the box; he knows that the other actors, whom he has to pass on his way to the bank of mailboxes, know it too. Nevertheless he continues to make that defiant entrance every afternoon. He will not let those other actors keep him from observing this small ceremony. If he once gives in, if he once fails to *pretend* to pretend that he has good reason to expect to find some important communication in the box, he will be just like the rest of them.

He comes to the club every afternoon, timing his arrival so that the non-theatrical and semi-theatrical members will have gone back to their offices in Madison Avenue and Radio City. They know who he is. Even the younger ones, who may never have seen him on the stage, know who he is. Their connections with the theater, which justify their membership in the club, may be tenuous, but their interest in it, whether lifelong or recent, would almost make it mandatory that they know who John Barton Rosedale is, or was. His name is a mouthful and not liable to be forgotten; and if they really know, have taken the trouble to learn, a little about the theater, they associate his name with those of the venerable stars and the prominent managers and the deceased playwrights who were so busy and successful between 1910 and 1930. The young fellows look at him now, and not many of them stop to think that in, say, 1925 John Barton Rosedale was younger than they are today. "Don't ask me if I ever knew Clyde Fitch," he has been known to say. "And for Christ's sake, no! I didn't play with the divine Sarah." But he has also been known to say, to one of the Madison Avenue-Radio City boys, "Who did you say? Terence Rattigan? Is he one of the Abbey crowd? I knew Barry Fitzgerald. Real name Shields. But I never heard of Rattigan." In truth he has heard of Rattigan and of everyone else of any consequence in the New York and London theater; was, in fact, extremely critical of Lunt's performance in *O Mistress Mine*. But he will concede nothing to these smarties from the ad agencies and the television studios. If they want to talk theater with him, let them talk business first, and stop giving all the parts to Cedric Hardwicke and Nehemiah Persoff. "*I* can play a Chinese general," he says. "I'd be wasted, but I could play one if the money was right. If I can play an Irish priest, I can damn sure make up to play a Chinese general. But the money'd have to be right." These Madison Avenue-Radio City boys have never done a thing for him, and now that he has told off so many of them, they probably never will. But they know who he is. He is John Barton Rosedale, never a bad performance, never a really bad notice, an actors' actor. "And I'm not broke, either," he has said; a boast that is literally but only literally true.

After he pays his ceremonial visit to the mailboxes, he goes to the bar and orders a half-Scotch. He drinks it alone, and it is his only drink in the clubhouse. He declines invitations to join other actors at the bar, and when he has had his drink he says to the bartender, "My people here yet?"

"In the cardroom. Mr. Dowell, Mr. Ruber, and I just saw Mr. Hafey on his way up."

In a sudden hurry John Barton Rosedale will scribble his last name on the chit and be off to the cardroom. He does not like to be late, but he likes to be last, and he always is.

The others, his people, are in the cardroom, sitting near but not at the bridge table. "Hello, Rosey," they say.

"The ever punctual Rosedale," he says. "Always just under the wire. Shall we cut?"

They cut for partners and deal, the game begins, and they play until five o'clock. It is quiet, serious bridge. The players understand each other's game so well that instead of a lengthy post-mortem, it is only necessary for one player to say, "Harry's spade lead did it," and the others will nod, and they will use the time between hands to make brief exchanges of conversation that are cut short at the conclusion of the deal. The four men are not close friends. Their congeniality, such as it is, has been achieved as a result of weeding out players in the past who played badly or much too well, and who by temperament revealed characteristics that were unsuitable to the atmosphere toward which this table was headed. In the beginning it had been John Barton Rosedale and Harry Hafey. Judd Ruber and George Dowell joined the table after other players were left out because they were too argumentative, played too slowly, drank too much, did not bathe often enough, could not be counted on to appear every day, or—in one case—wanted to talk about his troubles with his wife. For six years now the table has been made up of the same four players, who meet every day except matinee days when one or more of the four are working. They all have been actors, but Rosedale and Hafey have remained actors while Dowell makes his living as a free-lance writer, and Ruber is a staff announcer at a radio station. In six years Hafey has been in four flops, and Rosedale has been in one play that ran seven months on Broadway and five weeks on the road. Consequently the rule concerning matinee days has seldom been invoked. It was agreed at the start that no substitute would be invited to sit in for an absent player.

The four men, though not deliberately avoiding each other, make no effort to continue their companionship away from the bridge table. Hafey and his wife live in a theatrical hotel in the West Forties; Dowell, a widower, lives at the club; Ruber, a homosexual, shares an apartment with a friend in West Fifty-eighth near Fifth Avenue; and Rosedale and his wife live in London Terrace. It is a question whether Hafey, who worked regularly for good salaries in the days before heavy taxes, or Ruber, who is highly paid at present, is the best fixed financially. Hafey has an annuity; that much is known. He has one son a lieutenant colonel in the Air Force and another a dentist in Manhasset, Long Island, and both seem to be self-sufficient. Ruber wears a star sapphire ring and has a large collection of oversize cuff links, and he has at least twenty suits that he rotates, a Patek Philippe wristwatch, and a golden dollar-sign money clip which he displays when the day's bridge score is totted up. He is the youngest member of the foursome—fiftyish —and he was not even a featured player in the days before the income tax became confiscatory. George Dowell, who no longer receives royalty payments for a radio serial based upon his most successful comedy, writes little pieces for the magazine sections of the Sunday newspapers, and is believed to pick up fifty dollars here and there for one-liners he sells to television comedians. He has eighteen thousand dollars in compound interest accounts that he opened when his wife's estate was settled, and he is writing a book of reminiscences that eventually will appear as the autobiography of a quite well-known actress. She has already paid him more than five thousand dollars for his work, and she now wants to start it all over again, this time without the reticence that she imposed upon herself while her third husband was still alive. Dowell is confident that he will get at least another year's work out of it and that the book, in its new conception, will be a best-seller.

The four men avoid the topic of their personal finances. Hafey and Ruber, the well-heeled, may now and then exchange more or less general comments on the state of the stock market, but if the money talk continues overlong, they run the risk of another recital by John Barton Rosedale on the subject of his experiences with Goldman, Sachs and Aviation Corporation in the early Thirties. He can be very angry about having been a near-millionaire, and they have heard it all before. "Everything went," he says. "Everything. The house in Great Neck. My thirty-eight-foot cruiser. I had to resign from North Hempstead, and haven't been on a golf course since. I had to start all over again, just when I thought I'd never have to worry again about money. But luckily I was in my early thirties and in demand. I was absolutely smashed, financially, but do you know that for the next three years I was never out of work? And I went from a thousand a week to eighteen hundred in the *theater* before Hollywood beckoned. *They* started me at twenty-five hundred, and I got all the way up to five thousand before they decided I was too difficult. But I learned one lesson—stay out of the stock market, and don't put your money in express cruisers. It couldn't have happened to me at a better time. I suppose nothing would have stopped me from spending my money the way I did when I was in my twenties, but you can be damned sure I was more careful thereafter. You see, by that time I was old enough to get a little sense in me, and I said to Millicent, 'This time we're going to put it away.' No more cruisers and fancy cars—we had a big Lincoln convertible a block long. And no more houses in the suburbs. Or for that matter, apartments on Park Avenue. I know fellows, actors that weren't making half what I was making, and they loved to give that Park Avenue address. But after I was burnt the first time Millicent and I've *never* had an apartment bigger than four or five rooms. What would we do with one of those large apartments? Millicent does very little entertaining. Mostly the opera crowd for little informal suppers. Spaghetti and red wine, and Millicent loves to cook. I just sit back and relax while they all tell these fascinating stories about grand opera. You think there's bitchery in the theater? You ought to hear what goes on up at the Met. Stories about Jeritza, and Scotti, and all those people, and going back to Caruso and Tetrazzini. Millicent of course gave it all up when we got married, but she knows the racket inside and out, and they all like to come to our place for our little informal parties. Six, eight people at the most, so it doesn't get unwieldy. And it's quite something, you know, to see one of your big opera stars put on an apron and help with the dishes. They love Millicent. I, of course, I'm only that actor fellow that seduced Millicent away from grand opera and made her give up her own career. I didn't, but that's what they say, and they really don't hold it against me. On an opening night I get almost as many wires from Millicent's opera crowd as I do from show people. They're very loyal to Millicent. Confide in her, ask her advice. And all they really care about Rosedale is that I'm her husband and apparently made her happy. Oh, I take second billing there, all right, but I don't mind a bit. It does any actor a world of good to get around in other circles outside of our own profession. And these are talented people, don't forget. They're real artists. God knows they're lousy actors, that I can't deny. Once in a while I'll put on my white tie and tails and take Millicent to hear some newcomer that's been recommended to

her, and as far as the singing is concerned, I take my cue from
Millicent. If she says a soprano is good, then I know she's good.
But while they're about it, learning all the various languages
and vocalizing and all that, it beats me why they don't spend a
few hundred dollars on a dramatic coach. I wouldn't want the
job myself, but occasionally I've made a few suggestions. I
don't know whether they ever took them or not. The last thing
I'd ever want to do would be to try to teach anybody to act.
Hell, I took fencing lessons for two years when I was starting
out, and I'm sure they taught me how to move about. But I
didn't believe then and I don't believe now that you can be
taught how to act. The tricks, yes. But not what has to come
from down here and up here. The old ticker and the old gray
matter, that's the combination. Plus the dedication, the pride,
the love of the whole stinking God damn racket, regardless of
the cheap sons of bitches that run things today."

"You're absolutely right, Rosey," says Hafey.

"Where is there a man like Hoppy today?" says John Barton Rosedale.

"You don't mean the billiard player?" says Ruber.

"Arthur Hopkins," says George Dowell.

"Of course! I thought of Willie Hoppe because he came on
a show I was announcing, oh, several years ago."

"Shall we cut? I didn't mean to get launched on that subject," says John Barton Rosedale. "How did I get started? We
were talking about Wall Street, for Christ's sake. Well, it's lucky
we got away from that. I have the nine of clubs. George, it looks
like you and me start."

"And I believe it's my deal, with the diamond king," says
Harry Hafey.

John Barton Rosedale is an honest sixty-seven now, and
when five o'clock comes and the day's last rubber has been
scored, he goes downstairs and has a cup of free tea and the free
Lorna Doones and Hydroxes that are served with it. He is at
home with a cup of tea; it has been a prop of his in three or four
plays, and nowadays he gets a lift from the brew itself. He needs
that lift; the bridge game could go on for many more hours and
so long as he was playing he would not notice how tired he was
getting. But at five o'clock or thereabouts he is ready to quit; his

body and his brain are ready to quit. His long legs have been too long in a fixed, sitting position, and he has learned to get slowly to his feet, to move about slowly while Harry Hafey is totting up the day's score.

"I have this damned sacroiliac," says Judd Ruber, the youngest of the players. "I think it must have something to do with my weight. I ought to take off thirty pounds. But I can't resist starchy foods. As Alec Woollcott said, everything I like is either illegal, immoral, or fattening."

"I think G. K. Chesterton said it first," says George Dowell.

"Well, whoever said it, it applies to me," says Judd Ruber. "Rosey, how do you keep in such good shape? Do you do exercise?"

"Exercise? Yes. I stand up while I'm shaving. That's my exercise," says John Barton Rosedale. But he is pleased that no one has noticed that he has been hesitant about getting to his feet. "I don't believe my weight has varied five pounds since I was a young fellow in my twenties. This jacket and waistcoat—"

"I was about to ask you," says Ruber. "You had them made in England?"

"In London in 1930. English friend of mine sent me to Jason Driggs, just off Savile Row, and being flush at the time, I ordered four lounge suits, a dinner jacket, and a suit of tails. I've still got them all. This suit, the trousers have gone, but I rather like it with slacks."

"It's very country, the black and white check, but *you* can wear that and get away with it," says Ruber.

"Well, I don't know about that," says John Barton Rosedale. "That is, I don't know whether I do get away with it or not, but I know damn well there isn't a better-made suit in the club, and I've always been whatever the opposite is to a slave of fashion. I wear what I think is right for me, not for Jack Paar, or Douglas Fairbanks Junior. I have that other Driggs suit that I wear with slacks. The plaid?"

"Doesn't have quite the same snap, the same dash as this one," says Ruber.

"Well, this is a check, and the other's a Glen plaid. But do you know what these suits would cost me to duplicate today?"

"I certainly do. Not less than two-fifty apiece at any half-way decent tailor's," says Ruber.

"Two seventy-five, the fellow I go to," says Rosedale. "I can't see myself paying that much for a suit."

"Well, you could probably go to Brooks and get something off the rack and look well in it," says Ruber.

"Thank you, Judd. If the part called for it, that's what I'd do. Last year I read for a part, a university president. A good part. But I wouldn't work for the money they were paying, so we never did get together. However, for that part I most likely would have gone to Brooks, got one off the rack." They say their farewells and go their separate ways, John Barton Rosedale to his cup of tea and Lorna Doones.

He does not stay long. It is now the time that the Madison Avenue-Radio City types begin to drift in for cocktails. "Why do they want to come here?" he asks, when there is an actor friend to listen. "They have their own places. The Advertising Club is where they belong, not here. But no, they have to come here because they want to be part of show business. Show biz, I hear them call it. Show biz. But do they do anything for any of us?"

"Well, you know they do, Rosey, once in a while. Paul Ingles."

"Paul Ingles. Every time I ask that question I always get Paul Ingles for an answer. Now let me tell you about Paul Ingles. In the first place, Paul Ingles is a toady, a sycophant. He got a job on a radio serial, ten years ago, and he's the one brought these radio and television people into the club. They know he's on their side, so they always see to it that he gets a job. Where else could he? I recognized his voice the other day on a ʳadio commercial. For dog food. That's Paul Ingles, and that's the man that's supposed to be the great example of how those people help us. Not that it makes any difference to me personally. I'm not *quite* reduced to doing dog food commercials or any other commercials. And I'd never be a toady for anyone. But you look around here any afternoon and you'll see half a dozen good actors that come here hoping one of those outsiders will give them a television job. It's enough to break your heart, seeing fellows like Earl Stafford hamming it up for one of these hucksters. 'I don't believe we've met,' he said to one of them the other day. 'I'm Earl Stafford, welcome to the club.' And buying drinks for them. They have expense accounts, but has Earl Stafford got an expense account? I happen to know that Earl is supported by a group of members that work in Hollywood. And how much longer will that last, with Hollywood the way it is now? Earl Stafford, this is. Not one of your Ed Minzers. Poor Ed was always one jump ahead of the sheriff, but Earl knew the time when he could practically command his own price. He was a *draw*. But now he feels he has to buy drinks for advertising hucksters, and what does it get him? Maybe you'd better not be seen talking to me. They know how *I* feel about them."

And they do know. They know who he is, and they know how he feels about them. They would be extremely obtuse not to know. In times past John Barton Rosedale, making use of his professional reputation and of the energy available to him in his thirties, could be enormously persuasive in club affairs. He led the demand for better food and more efficient operation of the telephone switchboard, and his electioneering defeated Earl Stafford for a fifth term as club president. John Barton Rosedale denied having anything personal against Earl Stafford, but he argued that Earl had been in office too long and would be fifty on his next birthday. High time, in other words, for Earl to make way for younger blood.

In times more recent, John Barton Rosedale has not been in the diningroom and he rarely receives telephone calls. But he has tried to interest his friends in a tightening of the eligibility rules that will keep out people like Norman Bahs. He had paid no attention when Norman Bahs's name appeared on the list of candidates for membership. Later he vaguely recalled having seen the name, the designation "theatrical manager," and the names of two actors as proposer and seconder. Six months passed, and Bahs's name now appeared among the list of the elected.

John Barton Rosedale was introduced to Bahs at the bar. He was a bright-eyed, tooth-flashing, fat little man in a blue serge suit, white shirt, and plain blue silk tie with a Windsor knot. "I've always wanted to meet John Barton Rosedale," said Bahs.

"Well, he's usually around here somewhere. I'll see if I can arrange it," said John Barton Rosedale.

Bahs laughed. "Say, you're quick, Mr. Rosedale. Somehow I always thought of you as—I don't know. More like the parts you play."

"This is one place where we let down our hair. Impossible to maintain one's dignity among these ruffians. Look at some of these scoundrels. Ed Minzer. Harry Hafey. A den of thieves if ever I saw one. Let me buy you a drink, Mr. Bahs."

"I'd consider it an honor and a pleasure," said Bahs.

"And well you might. What will you have?"

"Same thing. Bourbon on the rocks," said Bahs. "Do you mind if I ask, are you reading any plays for next season, Mr. Rosedale?"

"What a question to put to an actor. Of course I am. Why? Have you got one you'd like me to read?"

"Yes I have."

"Then why haven't you sent it to me?"

"I did, but I never got any answer."

"What was the play?" said John Barton Rosedale.

"It's a play called *Perihelion*, by an unknown. I guess you never got around to reading it."

"Tell me a little bit about it," said Rosedale. "Maybe it will refresh my memory. I have a stack of plays I've been meaning to send back to my agent."

"It's modern. Time, the present. This young fellow has come back from the war. World War Two. Switches around from job to job and doesn't find anything to interest him. Then he meets this Japanese girl—"

"She was in one of those internment camps during the war. I remember that much of the play. I thought it was sent to me by mistake. Nothing in it for me. I have as much vanity as any middle-aged actor on Broadway, but I didn't see myself playing a twenty-five-year-old veteran. I'd have to stretch my imagination *and* my skin."

"Oh, you didn't read the second act?"

"As far as I know, there is no second act. No, when the curtain falls for the end of the first act, that's as far as I got. Don't tell me there's a fat juicy walk-on in Act Two for a man in my age bracket."

"Well—you don't know about the judge?"

"The judge? He's mentioned in the first act. That one?"

"Yes sir."

"Yes, I could see that coming. When you've read as many plays as I have you can spot a planted character immediately. Your judge is going to be very intolerant of the young Japanese girl. Am I right?"

"That's one way to put it."

"Is there any other way? Yes, I could see that coming. But why did you send *me* that play? Do you need backing?"

"The money is raised, Mr. Rosedale."

"Sometimes—too many times—a manager will send me a play and then put out an announcement that I'm reading it. That's in the hope of raising money."

"I don't operate that way, Mr. Rosedale. I have the backers for my next two plays."

"Have you indeed?"

"I wish you'd read the second act before you send it back."

"What for? I can guess what's going to happen. You admit that yourself."

"I said the judge is intolerant, yes. But there's a lot more to it than that. This play could do a lot of good for an actor like yourself, Mr. Rosedale."

"How?"

"Well, it's a strong dramatic role."

"That's a matter of opinion, too, isn't it? And you still don't answer my question. How would it do a lot of good for an actor like me, as you put it?"

"It just would. Any good part is good for an actor."

"That's a very sweeping statement, isn't it? But let's pass it for the moment," said John Barton Rosedale. "Roughly, what sort of money were you thinking of offering me?"

"Seven-fifty. I know it'd be no use trying to get you for less."

"You never said a truer word. Do you realize that what you're offering me is less than a hundred dollars a performance?"

"Well, I could go to eight."

"My dear fellow, you can go to *hell*. What do you *mean* by coming to this club and using your brand-new membership to chisel on actors' salaries? Is that why you joined? I'm going to find out who put you up, and have a little talk with them."

"I'm sorry you feel that way about it, Mr. Rosedale."

"I've never done this before, but I'm going to let it get around how much you offered *me,* and then everybody will have a pretty good idea what you're paying the poor slob that takes the part. You may have a hard time getting a three-hundred-dollar actor."

"No I won't," said Bahs. "But don't you start fouling up my business, Mr. Rosedale. Don't you *do* that. Maybe I'm not big yet, but I had as good actors as you in a couple my plays. Don't you start fouling *me* up."

"If you're threatening me, that's a chance I'm going to have to take."

"You're the one that threatened. You threatened me."

"Oh, you're tiresome, really you are, old boy," said John Barton Rosedale.

He went home that day—it was easily ten years ago— and was so unaffected by the encounter with Bahs that he neglected to give a report of it to Millicent. She was in the midst of preparing onion soup, which took a while the way she made it, and until eight o'clock he occupied himself with his wardrobe, rehanging his suits so that they would not get that closet look; polishing his shoes, which he called boots; inspecting his shirts for signs of fraying. Millicent, in and out of the kitchen, had the radio tuned in on an FM symphony program. Both of them were looking forward to eight o'clock and dinner, and conversation was not necessary or even especially desirable, since she enjoyed her cooking to a musical accompaniment, and he liked fussing around with his clothes, every item of which was associated with starring roles in plays that had paid him well.

It was a little past eight when they sat down in the dining alcove, with the entire meal on the table and Millicent's candles the only light. The onion soup and scallopini were kept warm in glazed earthenware containers; the Rosedales owned sets of Limoges and Meissen china and an assortment of solid silver, and the only concession they made to modern living was in the use of paper napkins, and even that was elaborately justified by pointing to the work it saved Millicent and the avoidance of

wear and tear on the good napery. They had a bottle of wine—
the musical friends of Millicent always brought more wine than
they drank, and tonight's bottle from the surplus was a Riesling
that went well with the veal.

"Who did this come from?" said John Barton Rosedale.

"This was from Lenny Giordano. He brought three bottles
that night and we didn't open a one. But this is the last, isn't it?"

"Yes. The last of the Riesling. We're getting low on wine.
Maybe we ought to have another party soon."

"All right. I'm willing. I want to try out some new recipes.
Eddie Petruccini found me an old Italian cookbook, in Milano
last summer."

"Mee-*lann*-no! Fee-*renn*-zeh! Love to hear old Eddie pro-
nounce those Italian names. Mee-*lah*-no! And he sure does love
to eat."

"So do you. I just wish I could eat what you eat and stay
thin."

"Baby, you're going to eat, so why torture yourself about
it."

"I know, but to think that when I was twenty years old I
only weighed a hundred and thirty. And five feet seven and a
half."

"Well, you're still five-seven-and-a-half."

"It was Zumbach that made me eat. Eat, eat, eat, he used
to tell me. You'll sing it off in one performance, he'd say. And
sometimes I did. But you, you bastard, you let me go on eating.
You should have stopped me."

"Don't blame it on me, baby. You were a food addict before I came along."

"I know, but you could have made me stop."

"Well, you were a nice bed-full. I'd had enough of
scrawny dames, onstage and off. In bed and out. My mother,
my sisters, my first wife, and Diana. All built like boys."

"Diana wasn't built like a boy."

"Pretty near. You ready for espresso? I want to take a
look at a TV show. Jack Masters particularly asked me to watch
a show he's on. It goes on at nine o'clock, Channel Two."

They cleared the table and left the dishes in the sink, and
were seated comfortably with a bottle of grappa when the tele-

vision program began. "I have no idea what Jack's doing," said John Barton Rosedale. "I don't even know when he comes on. But he particularly asked me to watch this show, so he must be good in it."

The first twenty minutes passed and Jack Masters had not yet made his appearance, but during the commercial interval John Barton Rosedale had little to say.

"What do you think of it so far?" said Millicent.

"Good," he said. "The sets are awful, and the lighting is something fierce. Did you notice those shadows in the hospital room? Somebody ought to be shot for that. But the play's all right—if they can keep it up. This is only the first act."

Halfway during the second twenty minutes Jack Masters came on the screen. He played the proprietor of a Mexican cantina.

"Good heavens," said Millicent. "Jack's as fat as I am."

"Sh-h-h."

At the end of the second act John Barton Rosedale refilled his glass. "Now I know why he wanted me to watch," he said.

"Yes. He's good," said Millicent.

"He's better than good, baby. This is the best he's ever been. Jack Masters, Jake Moscowitz, playing a Mexican saloonkeeper. I wonder how much the Hollywood people watch these things? They pretend they don't, you know, but I hope for Jack's sake they're watching tonight. I wonder if Bogey ever watches these things?"

"Which Bogey? Humphrey?"

"Naturally. He has his own company now, and he used to be a friend of Jack's. The play isn't holding up very well, but they sure are getting a performance out of old Jack."

The play resumed, and they remained silent through the third act, to the very end. "Shall I turn it off?" said Millicent.

"Wait a second, I want to see the credits. This is what they call the crawl, or the crawler, I'm not sure which. Sometimes the names go slow, sometimes fast, depending on how much time they have left. There we are. Pedro Gomez, Jack Masters. Now let's see who directed it. That usually comes last on a movie. Here we are. Produced by—Norman Bahs. For Christ's sake. Directed by—Norman Bahs! No! I don't believe it."

"Who is that? I never heard of him."

"Oh, I'll tell you about him later. Now I have to call Jack and congratulate him." John Barton Rosedale telephoned the broadcasting company, asked for the studio, and learned that the play he had just seen was on tape. "I'll call him at his house," he said, and did so.

The line was busy.

"You were going to tell me about the director. I've forgotten his name already."

"Producer and director. His name is Norman Bahs. Over there in the light blue envelope on my desk is a play he wanted me to do. I just got finished telling him to go to hell."

"Oh, Rosey. Again?"

"What do you mean again? I only met him this afternoon."

"You know what I mean. Was it money again? What did he offer you?"

"He offered me seven-fifty. That's not even a hundred dollars a performance. Then he said he might go to eight, and I said he might go to hell, too. And don't you start on seven-fifty is better than nothing."

"It is, though. It's seven hundred and fifty dollars a week better than nothing, I know that much. What's better? Waiting a year for a thousand and then maybe working four or five weeks, or getting seven-fifty while we're waiting?"

"I'm not broke. We have enought to eat—even enough for you."

She had her glass in her hand. She looked at it, quickly raised it to her lips and drank, and got to her feet and went to the kitchen. He waited for her to turn on the FM radio, with one of her musical programs, but the only sounds that came out of the kitchen were the small noises of china on china, water running out of the sink, closet doors closing. Then the barely audible click of the light switch.

She walked through the livingroom. "Goodnight," she said, as she passed him. He could tell by the later sounds that she was preparing to sleep in the guest room, and then he heard the guest room door pulled to.

THE LOCOMOBILE

Shortly after getting out of the army in 1919, George Denison gave—*gave*—his mother's Locomobile limousine to Arthur Gow, who had been the lady's chauffeur. The car was a beauty, purer in line than the Pierce-Arrows and Packards that were generally chosen by women like Mrs. Denison. It was painted Brewster green, and it was the only one of its kind in the county. It had less that 15,000 miles on the odometer, six new Pennsylvania Vacuum Cups to replace the original tires, and it would have fetched five thousand dollars in a trade-in if George Denison had wanted to bargain. But his mother had neglected to mention Arthur Gow in her will—she had never got around to it in the years since the will had been drawn up—and George Denison wanted to do something for Arthur. Mrs. Denison's personal maid, Agnes, was left five thousand dollars, the cook, Margaret, a more recent addition to the Denison establishment than Arthur Gow, got two thousand dollars. Something had to be done for Arthur, whose nose was a little out of joint at not being included among the beneficiaries, but who had stayed on, taking care of the limousine and George's phaeton and doing odd jobs about the house and grounds, until George's return to civilian life. Arthur did not exactly say so in so many words, but he *as much as* told Agnes and Margaret that he would not quit the job until George had had a chance to do what was right and fair. George would surely do the right thing. He was a young fellow, George, but very fair, and when he had had time to study the whole situation would realize that the missus —well, it wasn't only the money. All those nights sitting outside somebody's house while the missus was at a dinner. Up at six o'clock every morning and sometimes not getting to bed again till after midnight. Supposed to have one day off a week, but how many times did she ask him to change to another day, so that he never knew for sure whether he could go fishing or plan a picnic with his wife and kids. And if it came to money, how much money he had saved the family by cleaning the spark plugs and vulcanizing inner tubes and things like that that other drivers, *some* other drivers, would take to a garage. The Winton salesman, the Cadillac salesman, the Peerless salesman had all approached him to use his influence with Mrs. Denison and he had turned them down flat, although some other women's drivers had used *their* influence and collected a nice cut. Could anyone say that there was a car anywhere in the whole county that was better taken care of than the Denisons' two Locomobiles? In all kinds of weather Arthur put on his gum boots and washed and polished those cars and caught many a cold doing it. Was *her* car, the limousine, ever once pulled up at the portecochere without fresh flowers in the cutglass vases? Didn't he always warm the laprobe in front of the carriage-house stove so she wouldn't have a cold cover over her knees? And who was it saw to it that the car never left the carriage-house without her little flask of brandy where she knew it would be?

George Denison knew most of these things about Arthur Gow and his diligence, his pride in his work. True, George took a lot for granted, as you do take a lot for granted in a good servant such as Arthur and Agnes and Margaret; but having so recently got out of the army, with its blundering and inefficiency in spite of the disciplined atmosphere, George was more inclined to observe and appreciate the quiet smoothness of a wellrun household and of the persons responsible for it. "I want to do something for Arthur Gow," he told the family lawyer, Arthur McHenry, himself just returned from overseas.

"I had another look at that will," said McHenry. "I helped your mother with it, and I remember at the time thinking it was strange she didn't mention Arthur. But I didn't say anything. You know how your mother was. She came in here one day and had a batch of notes on how she wanted everything disposed of, right down to who was to get your father's cuff links. The diamond ones." He smiled.

"Who did get them? I forget," said George Denison.

"Nobody," said the lawyer. "Originally she was going to leave them to me, but I persuaded her not to. As her lawyer I didn't want to figure as a beneficiary. Somewhere you'll come across a letter suggesting that you give them to me, but it's not in the will itself."

"Well, I haven't taken a good look at her jewelry. It's all in one box," said George Denison. "I'll have another look and if they're there, I'll bring them down to you."

"No hurry," said the lawyer. "And I never saw the letter. But she told me she was going to write it, and when she said she'd do a thing she usually did it. So it's somewhere around."

"Yes. Mother had two desks, one in the library and the other upstairs in her sewingroom. I haven't even attempted to go through the stuff in the sewingroom."

"Well, it's around somewhere, you may be sure. And incidentally, when you come across it you may find some suggestion as to what to do about Arthur Gow. Although I'm inclined to doubt that. She was so explicit about the bequests to the cook and the maid, I think she had very positive feelings about leaving him out. I thought at the time, well, she might have lent him money, for instance, and had some understanding with him that she would forgive the debt."

"Oh, no, Arthur," said George Denison. "I doubt that very much. Unless it was a small sum, fifty dollars or something like that. But not anything like a thousand or two thousand. Mother liked to live well and she spent money with a fairly free hand, but she always considered that money as mine. That is to say, eventually mine, and from the time Father died, when I was eighteen, she always made quite a point of telling me how the money was going out. She didn't ask my permission, of course, but things like—oh, taking the cobblestones out of the carriage-house and putting down a concrete floor. When we got rid of the horses and turned the carriage-house into a garage, she showed me all the bills. And if she gave money to Farmington or the Children's Home, she was always careful to let me know how much and where and so forth. She wouldn't have lent Arthur Gow any considerable amount without telling me. And she wouldn't have forgiven the debt without asking me. Of that I'm sure. Also, Arthur never needed money. He was very stingy

with his money. If I wanted a nickel or a dime outside my allowance, I could get it from Margaret or Agnes—although it was
much easier to get it from Margaret than Agnes. But Arthur
was hopeless. 'You're not supposed to ask me for money,' he
used to say."

"I'm surprised that you have such charitable feelings for
him now, considering," said the lawyer.

"Not charitable, Arthur," said George Denison. "I just
don't want him thinking my mother was as stingy as he was."

"Oh, I understand," said the lawyer. "Discriminated
against. Just what I thought when we were working on the will.
But knowing your mother, I don't think it was an oversight."

"No, it couldn't have been an oversight. After all, Arthur
drove her down here to this office, and he was sitting in the car
downstairs while she was talking to you. It wasn't an oversight.
But it was and is a good excuse for someone to have unkind
thoughts about Mother, and she was too good for that . . .
There's another thing."

"What's that?" said the lawyer.

"I'm going to let him go."

"Fire him?"

"Terminate his employment. I don't intend to stay in
Gibbsville. You know that."

"Well, I guess you've thought that all out. You and Pammie. It's probably not very stimulating here."

"I want to be near the water, somewhere where I can go
sailing every good day. And these past ten years, prep school,
college, and the army, I've made different friends than those I
grew up with."

"You've got the Gibbsville doldrums, and you want to get
out. Well, why not? And if you don't do it pretty soon, you
never will."

"That's exactly what Pammie says. I'm fond of my old
friends, but I like my new ones, too. And since I can't afford to
move Long Island Sound to Lantenengo County, we'll move to
Long Island Sound."

"And you're not going to need Arthur Gow."

"What I thought I'd do—I don't want to give him any actual cash. Mother saw fit not to, so I won't. But there's that

Locomobile limousine. It's probably worth at least as much as Mother gave Agnes, and if he wants to sell it, fine. That way everybody should be satisfied. I haven't gone against Mother's wishes, but he has no cause to complain."

"Certainly no cause to complain," said the lawyer. "I think it's the handsomest car in the county. He shouldn't have any trouble selling it in Philadelphia."

"Then you approve?"

"I have one slight reservation—that your mother knew exactly what she was doing, and *she* might not approve. But as you said a minute ago, she always considered that the money was yours. And I never knew her to really go against your wishes."

"No, not after I began to make some sense," said George Denison. "Whenever that was."

"Seems to me you've always made pretty good sense, George," said the lawyer.

George Denison found Arthur Gow in the carriage-house (which, from habit, they had not learned to call the garage). Appropriately, Arthur was giving the limousine windows a polish. "You like that car, don't you?"

"I do," said Arthur Gow. "That I do. You can have all your Pierce-Arrows and Packards—"

"And Rolls-Royces?"

"Well, I don't know as I'd go that far. The Rolls-Royce is in a class by itself. But it ain't only the make of car I was thinking of. It's this here car, this particular one, I have a fondness for. I guess if I put in the same hours on a Scripps-Booth I'd feel the same way. Only I never would—put in the same hours on a Scripps-Booth, I mean. I took a liking to this car the minute I saw it. Now for instance Mrs. Hofman has that Pierce, and you know what we call it? The drivers? We call it her china-closet. This ain't no china-closet."

"How would you like to own this car?" said George Denison.

"Yes, well if a man owned a car like this he could consider himself—he could consider himself very fortunate. I guess there ain't but two or three hundred like it in the whole country, if that. A car like this don't wear out, and you never get tired of looking at it. The Pierce-Arrow people are improving the looks of their new models, but they have a long way to go before they catch up to this one. You'll have this car another five years, at least."

"No, I've decided to give it away."

"Give it away? If you give this car away, I'll quit."

"Well, that's all right, Arthur. Because I'm going to give it to you. As a sort of a farewell present."

Arthur Gow went to the car and rubbed the door-window with his chamois. He was thinking. "I heard talk you were leaving town," he said. Even his incredulity was slow, as slow as belief might have been in a less cautious man. "Somebody said you were putting the house up for sale."

"Putting everything up for sale, except the closed car. I'm going to give you that."

Arthur Gow stopped polishing the glass. "You're in earnest?"

"Positively in earnest. Go down to Mr. McHenry's office, tomorrow morning if you like. He's making out the bill of sale."

"Sale?"

"To make it legal, I'm selling it to you for one dollar. But you can owe me the dollar."

"What do you want me to do with the car when I own it?"

"When you own it you can do whatever you please. You can keep it, you can sell it, you can fill it full of Singer's Midgets and go all over the country in it. What would you *like* to do with it?"

"What would I like to do with it? I'd like to ride in the back seat, from here to Reading and back. Just to see how it feels. Then when I got that out of my system—are you giving me my walking papers?"

"Yes, if you put it that way. I'd like you to stay on till Mrs. Denison and I leave for good. That'll be the first of June, we've rented a house in Connecticut. Mrs. Denison is giving the women notice today."

"Margaret not going with you? Or Agnes?"

"No. We have a couple, a man and wife, that go with the house in Connecticut. You don't seem very surprised at any of this."

"Well, there was talk around that you and your missus

were moving away. Everything gets around in Gibbsville."

"Yes. What will you do? Take a vacation? I'm sure you've been thinking about this."

"I've been thinking. I'll get offers. There's always a couple ladies wants me to drive for them. When you were away in the army I had a couple offers. But I didn't know you were thinking of giving me this car."

"Does that change your plans?"

"To some extent. To *some* extent, it changes them. To some extent it don't change them at all."

"I see—although I don't see," said George Denison.

"What I mean is, George, I don't want to drive for nobody else. I want me own hours. And I got a little money put away. I was thinking of going in business for myself, driving for hire. There's a lot of ladies in town, widows and old maids, that your mother used to lend them the car with me driving. Most of them I got tips from. But now I can charge them all, like so much a head to drive two-three-four of them to the golf club. Reading. Philadelphia. Card parties. Evening parties, but double for parties after ten o'clock."

"You *have* given it some thought."

"There's a lot of these ladies, they got the money but they don't want to go to the expense of a car and a garage and a driver. They all know me, and they all rode in this car, most of them. It'll be the same as living retired but making money at the same time."

"You wouldn't like to work for whoever buys the house?"

"No more driving private, George," said Arthur Gow. He faintly, almost indiscernibly smiled. "When you come back for a visit you can ride in this car, and I won't charge you."

"Well, thank you," said George Denison. (Later he was able to recall that his was the only word of thanks offered during the conversation.) "You go see Mr. McHenry tomorrow."

"What would be a good time to go?" said Arthur.

"Oh, any time after ten o'clock, I should think."

"Yes, I guess there won't be much to it, just a bill of sale," said Arthur.

"Well, go on with your work, Arthur. I don't want to interrupt you."

"That's all right," said Arthur Gow, and resumed his task.

George Denison found his wife in his mother's sewing-room. "Well, I just got rid of one Locomobile and one Arthur Gow," he said.

"That's good. I was never very fond of either," she said. "I don't look well in green, and as for that pickle-face Arthur, dignity is all right but he carries it too far. Before we were married I used to see him, chauffeuring your mother around, and from his expression he seemed to say, 'Look what I've got in the back seat.' Not in a complimentary way, either."

"Well, after the first of June," said George Denison.

"Yes," she said. "What do you want me to do with all these letters and little scraps of paper? Can I throw them away? Your mother was very efficient, but she kept everything. Every letter you ever wrote, from the time you were visiting your Uncle Joe and Aunt Something, I can't decipher her name."

"Not a real uncle and aunt. He was my godfather. Joe Riddle, friend of my father's. Aunt Sophie. They're both dead."

"Ah, you poor little orphan, let me give you a nice pat on the head. Go away. Now what *about* these things? I'm in favor of holding on to your letters and things like that, but here is a whole stack of miscellaneous. Reminders that your mother wrote to herself."

"Did you by any chance come across anything about Arthur Gow?"

"Arthur Gow? I'll say I did. A whole stack."

"Are they all together in one stack?"

"No, they're all mixed up in the miscellaneous. Do you want me to separate them? Some are from him to her, and some are memorandums she wrote herself."

"Memoranda."

"Memoranda sounds like a pancake flour," said Pammie Denison. "If you want me to go through this whole accumulation, I will, but having gone through it once I can assure you there's nothing worth saving. Unless you suspect your mother of carrying on a romance with Arthur Gow."

"Somehow, *somehow,* I have my doubts about that. Mother liked men, all right, but if she was ever going to have a romantic attachment it wouldn't be Arthur Gow. If she'd had some dashing French chauffeur—but not Arthur. Mother was more like you in that respect. Very impatient with dull men. Luckily you have me."

"Uh-huh. And if I should happen to forget how lucky I am, I have you to remind me."

"Yes, isn't that splendid? Very few wives——"

"Never mind. Just tell me what you want me to do with this junk. Your letters and other family letters are all tied together, but the rest of this hodge-podge, you'll have to decide. I mean I'm certainly not going to go through it all over again. So shall I leave it all here and you go through it? I warn you, you're in for a very dull three or four hours."

"I'll get to it after dinner," he said.

The miscellany turned out to be full of items that were easily discarded. They went back to his father's death six years earlier, at which time Mrs. Denison apparently instituted the practice of jotting down notes that covered repairs and changes in the house and grounds, wedding presents to be purchased, social engagements, books to be read, letters to be written, telephone calls to be made. All these notes were written on paper of uniform size and texture which bore the initials A.S.D. in the upper left-hand corner. Here and there would be an item of simple arithmetic—addition, subtraction, multiplication, short and long division—that indicated her attempts to estimate her income and expenses. Here George Denison was going in for guesswork, since the items were not identified by words or names; but he recognized figures that represented his recollection of her income for various years, which she seemed to have divided by twelve. Conversely, he found notes in which certain repeated figures were multiplied by twelve, indicating her attempts to arrive at a year's outlay on wages and other fixed expenses.

"This is rather fun," he said to his wife.

"Why?" said Pammie Denison.

"Well, for several reasons. First of all, I didn't realize that Mother didn't trust her memory. I wish I knew whether she kept notes before Father died. I doubt it. I think he did all this while he was alive, and she only started after he was dead. She wasn't very good at long division."

"Another thing she and I had in common," said Pammie.

"But I'll say this for her. When she did a problem in long division, she'd prove it."

"You multiply the thing on the right and the thing on the left, and it's supposed to come out the thing in the middle."

"Oh, you do know how," he said. "My compliments."

"Of course I know how. It's just those damn subtrahends that confused me. Those names for things. I have a very good mind for figures."

"Yes, as a matter of fact, you have," he said. "Ah, here's something I'm glad I came across. 'A. McH., C. Links.' "

"Oh, boy!"

"Well, it's important. It means that she really wanted Arthur McHenry to have my father's diamond cuff links."

"Good."

"I'm sorry. Am I distracting you? What are you reading?"

"It's called *The Magnificent Ambersons*, by Booth Tarkington," she said. "He's the one that wrote those Penrod stories, but you wouldn't guess it from this book."

"Princeton man," said George Denison.

"Oh, *well.*"

"Class of—I'm not sure. I think he went to Exeter, too. Ivy Club."

"Naturally," she said.

"When you get finished with his book I'd like to read it."

"If you ever get finished with that stuff," she said. "At the rate you're going, checking your mother's long division."

"I'm almost finished that part, and practically all of it goes in the trash basket."

For an hour or so she went on reading, while he continued with his chore, and there was no conversation. But she chanced to look across the room at him twice in a five-minute period, and she saw that both times he was sitting back in his chair, his legs stretched out, a piece of paper in his hand, and he had hardly changed his position. He was no longer reading the notes, but he was deep in thought.

"Have you discovered something?" she said.

"I don't know," he said. "See what you make of it." He handed her not one but two sheets of the notepaper.

On one sheet she read: "Send A.G. away."

On the second sheet: "See A. McH—advice about A.G.!!! Afraid!!!"

"Well?" said George Denison. "Does it make any sense to you?"

"Does it to you?" she said. "You've been brooding over it for the last ten minutes."

"I've been letting my imagination run riot. She obviously never did see Arthur McHenry about Arthur Gow, or he would have told me so when I spoke to him about giving Gow the car. But she must have been afraid of Gow. Can you read any other interpretation into it?"

"No. I never realized it till now, but he does give me the creeps."

"I'm a little sorry now that I promised to give him the car."

"You can get out of that easily enough."

"Not so damn easily. What excuse can I give? What have I got to go on?"

"Go see Arthur McHenry first thing in the morning, and take these notes with you. What about the notes from Arthur Gow to her? Is there anything in them?"

"Not a thing. I've got them all here, but they don't tell anything. Here he wants a new hose. Here he wants a new nozzle for the hose. Here's one that asks for a new storage battery for the car. This one is a request for three days off, 'next week,' whenever that was. This one—a long one with a list of things he's ordering at the hardware store. Chamois. Bon-Ami. Brass polish. Whisk broom. You saw all this, and there isn't a thing in it that gives any clue."

She was silent.

"Are you still with me?" he said.

"I'm thinking," she said. "Let me see his notes to her."

He handed her the sheaf of notes, and she quickly went through them, one by one. "I wonder," she said. "But I think I'm on to something."

"Like what?"

"In all the years he worked for us, Jim McGroarty, our chauffeur, never wrote a note to Mother or Daddy. They may have written notes to him, or left messages in the kitchen.

'Please have car to take me to eight-thirty-five train.' Things like that. But I don't even remember that. The point is, all these things that Arthur Gow asked for in his notes, he could have much more easily asked her in person. Do you see what I'm getting at? Why write these things out, when all he had to do was say, 'Mrs. Denison, can I buy a chamois and charge it?' Do you see what I mean? They didn't speak to each other, he and your mother. At least any more than was absolutely necessary. For five or six years, ever since your father died, she's avoided conversation by having him put everything on paper."

"So that she wouldn't forget anything."

"No! Because she was afraid of him," said Pammie Denison.

"You're basing that on that one note, the one about seeing Arthur McHenry. Afraid."

"No I'm not. I'm basing it on instinct. Intuition. And common sense. Here you have dozens of notes from Gow to your mother, dozens of them, and it must have been a nuisance for him, writing notes every time he wanted to buy a feather duster. But she made him do it, and why? Because she couldn't bear to talk to him, or more likely have him talk to her."

"Why didn't she fire him, if she felt that way?"

"Because she had no good reason to, that's why. I'm sure he never said anything, or did anything, that would give her grounds to fire him. But she had an instinctive feeling—yes, like me. And she was *fair,* your mother. She wasn't going to discharge a servant because he gave her the creeps, not as long as his work was all right. I couldn't have discharged him, either, not without reason, but I'm awfully glad he isn't going with us to Connecticut."

"And she left him out of her will," he said. "He was honest, sober, reliable, a very thorough worker. What do you suppose happened?"

"Nothing, I tell you," said Pammie. "But I swear to you, she was afraid something would happen, or could happen, or might happen. I know exactly how she felt, and you never will, because you're not a woman."

"I may be making a big mistake, giving him the car," he said.

"Possibly, but now you can't go back on your word, any

more than your mother could discharge him without grounds. Let him have the car, and let's forget about him."

"If we can," he said. "From now on I'll always think of my mother, the last six years of her life, intimidated by a perfect servant."

"I agree with you, because that's the way I think it was."

"There's one thing that does worry me, a little," he said. "Maybe it shouldn't, but it does."

"What's that?"

"Oh—thinking of those old ladies, those friends of Mother's, that he's going to have for customers. Are they my responsibility?"

"No, George," said his wife. "You can stop being a captain."

"I suppose so," he said. "I suppose I should."

THE MANAGER

The Wilburs always arrived at the Inn a little before or a little after the summer season. True, in recent years, with the popularity of skiing, the Inn enjoyed two seasons, but a very different sort patronized the place when the snow was on the ground. The Wilburs were quite definitely not of the skiing crowd.

There had been a time when the Wilburs were summer regulars, with their same room and their same table year after year, and paying the summer rates. But after thirty seasons they came only in the spring and the fall, when reduced rates were in effect, and these visits were shorter. "We don't like to let a year go by without a week or so at the Inn," said Mrs. Wilbur. "But now you have to charge almost as much for a single day as we used to pay for a week. Oh, we understand why. But it *is* a shame, isn't it?"

"It is indeed," said Mr. Greene, the proprietor. "We've lost some of our summer people on account of it. But there always seem to be others to take their places."

"Where do you suppose they get the money?" said Mrs. Wilbur. "I know that's a foolish question, but these younger people. I mean the ones in their forties. They can't possibly get away with deducting the cost as a business expense."

"Well, naturally I don't inquire into where they get it, as long as they do. But they seem to have it. Your room goes for twelve hundred for the month of August. A thousand for the month of July. And next year I don't know what it'll be. Won't be any less, that's for sure." Once, and only once, Mr. Greene had had to tell Mrs. Wilbur that much as he would like to give old patrons a special rate, the fact was that he could not make an exception for anyone. Not anyone. Not Colonel and Mrs. Broadbill. Not the Reverend and Mrs. George W. T. Magee. Not Miss Polly Woodward, whose father and mother had been the second couple to sign the registry in 1894. Mrs. Wilbur— and Mr. Greene knew it—was not so much advocating a special rate for the Broadbills and the Magees and Polly Woodward as trying to learn whether they got one. Mr. Greene was too polite to say it, but the stern fact was that even at the full rate the Inn was not making much money off the Broadbills and those others. They spent no money in the Colonial Taproom. Colonel and Mrs. Broadbill had their nip of bourbon before coming down to dinner; the others did not drink at all. And it was not only a question of the money they did not spend; there was their appearance, which was noticeably inhibiting on the younger guests, those couples in their forties who had cocktails before every meal and liqueurs in the Taproom every evening after dinner. As for the Wilburs, Mr. Wilbur was afflicted with some liver ailment that made him appear to be sunburnt in patches on his forehead and cheeks. Young children stared at him, and several young wives had asked to have their table changed so that they would not have to look at him. He was a perfectly nice man, a gentleman, well dressed and neatly groomed; but as one young woman said, very unappetizing. One child of ten had asked him, "Were you *burned?*" and Mr. Wilbur had replied, "In a manner of speaking, yes." The child's mother was infuriated, embarrassed by her daughter's forwardness, but far more annoyed that someone like Mr. Wilbur was there to provoke the child's rude curiosity. Mr. Greene heard all about that. He did nothing, since there was nothing he could do; but he was greatly relieved when the Wilburs advised him that the next year, 1959, they would not be needing their old room in August. They were going to be traveling—they did not say where—and hoped they would be able to stop at the Inn for a week or so in late September. Mr. Greene in his reply expressed regret untinged with sorrow, and advised the Wilburs that he would be unable to guarantee their getting their old room back in 1960 if they relinquished it in '59. Another couple—perhaps the Wilburs remembered them, the Lamports, from Toledo, Ohio—had applied for the Wilburs' room for '59 and subsequent years and Mr. Greene, or the Inn, was redecorating to suit Mrs. Lamport. He was sure the Wilburs would understand. They did.

But they kept coming back. In '59 they stayed two weeks in the latter half of September; in '60, a week in May; in '61 they came for the first week in October. In '62 they arrived in time for lunch Friday and left after breakfast on Monday of the first weekend in October. Mr. Greene was not unhappy to see them go. He liked Mr. Wilbur, but he hoped the Wilburs would never come back, because on the Sunday evening during dinner, with the diningroom and the Taproom filled almost to capacity, Mr. Wilbur suddenly rose, with a napkin to his mouth, and hurried out of the diningroom, fighting back a vomiting spell and barely making the men's room in the lobby.

Mr. Greene, from his position behind the main desk, saw it all happen. It was distressing to see the immediate effect on the men and women in the diningroom—and not many had failed to see Mr. Wilbur, with the napkin at his mouth, staggering out toward the lobby. Nevertheless Mr. Greene obeyed the impulse to follow Mr. Wilbur, and in the men's room he found Mr. Wilbur lying on the floor, hemorrhaging from the mouth. Mr. Wilbur looked up at Mr. Greene with the eyes of a dog pleading not to be shot, then fainted away. Two young doctors, who were dining with their wives, entered the men's room. "Get him to a hospital," said one doctor. "I'll stay with him till the ambulance comes." There was nothing more Mr. Greene could do after sending for the ambulance, and he went looking for Mrs. Wilbur. In time he found her, sitting in the lobby with Colonel and Mrs. Broadbill.

"Oh, Mr. Greene, I didn't think it was right to go into the men's room. How is he?"

"There are two doctors in there with him, I guess they're doing all they can till the ambulance gets here."

"The hospital? Did they say he had to go to the hospital?"

"Now don't you worry, Edwina," said Colonel Broadbill. "I had the same thing happen to me six years ago."

"They'll want to give him transfusions, most likely," said Mrs. Broadbill. "They did with Clement."

"They sure did," said Colonel Broadbill. "Whole bunch of fellows from the Army and Navy Club volunteered, but there weren't but two had my type of blood. Mike—"

"Do you think I ought to go in there now, I mean the men's room?" said Mrs. Wilbur.

"Oh, that part'll be all right, Mrs. Wilbur. Yes, I'd go in if I were you," said Mr. Greene.

"Good Lord, Edwina, you don't have to stand on ceremony at a time like this," said the colonel. "You go right in there and pay no attention."

"Would you like me to go with you?" said Mrs. Broadbill. "Goodness me, the places I've been. I'll go in with you."

"I'd appreciate it if you would, Lillian."

"Mr. Greene and I will look out for everything," said the colonel.

Mr. Greene did not quite know what the colonel had in mind, but he was already uncomprehending of Mrs. Wilbur's ability to sit in the lobby while her husband could be bleeding to death a few feet away, behind a door marked Gentlemen.

"Hit him all of a sudden," said Colonel Broadbill. "We just finished our dinner and I was here having my cigar. Mizz Broadbill won't let me smoke one of these Castro cigars in the bedroom, she calls them. Ever since Castro we haven't been able to get any good Havana leaf, and I must say I go along with Mizz Broadbill. But I do like a cigar after dinner, good or bad. Mrs. Wilbur said he ate too much of the paté. He ate his and then he ate hers, and it was just too rich for him. You set too good a table, Mr. Greene. That hard sauce you give us with the Brown Betty, I have to order seconds on it every time. Now that I don't have to worry about my teeth any more, I eat those things like your hard sauce as if I were a schoolboy. Sweets. I eat too many sweets."

Mr. Greene wanted to get in a denial that the liver paté had had anything to do with Mr. Wilbur's attack, but the colonel had raised so many points that called for denials that Mr. Greene ignored them all. "How long did they keep you in the hospital, Colonel?" he said.

"How long did they keep me in the hospital?"

"Roughly. Approximately," said Mr. Greene.

"Roughly a week."

"I suppose that means they'll keep Mr. Wilbur that long," said Mr. Greene.

As it turned out, he was wrong. By the time the ambulance arrived Mr. Wilbur was up on his feet, and he stubbornly —for him, angrily—refused to leave the Inn. The doctors said they would not be responsible; Mr. Wilbur said he would absolve them of any responsibility. The ambulance driver said there would still be a charge of thirty dollars, and Mr. Greene paid that and said he would put it on Mr. Wilbur's bill.

Mr. Greene saw the Wilburs off in the morning. They had a well-kept Dodge station wagon, six or seven years old. Mrs. Wilbur was doing the driving, as she always did nowadays, but they had a long ride ahead and Mr. Greene, taking a good look at Mr. Wilbur, was convinced he would never see him again. Mr. Wilbur was all bundled up in his old polo coat and a thick woollen scarf, and a robe over his legs; the brim of his hat turned down all around, and a large area of his face hidden by his sun glasses. He was a pitiful sight. Mrs. Wilbur, however, sitting back confidently, with her hands resting on the steering-wheel, seemed capable of driving the car as far as San Francisco.

"I'd rest easier if you phoned me when you get home," said Mr. Greene. "Reverse the charges, of course."

"Oh, now, Mr. Greene, that's very nice of you, but I'm all right. We'll be home before dark," said Mr. Wilbur.

"Not before dark, Lewis, but not long after," said Mrs. Wilbur. "It gets dark earlier now."

They lived in a place called Uniontown, Pennsylvania, and that evening, while he was having his dinner, Mr. Greene was called to the telephone. The Wilburs had had a pleasant trip, stopping for lunch at a very nice motel near Scranton, PA. Mr. Wilbur had not eaten very much for lunch; milk toast, as a matter of fact. Then they had stopped again for a cup of tea at a Howard Johnson on the Pennsylvania Turnpike. A cup of tea with lemon and a little nibble of toast was as much as he wanted. He was in bed now, and the family doctor was coming in to see him later in the evening. Mr. Wilbur had insisted on her making the call, and he wanted to thank Mr. Greene for taking an interest, and to tell him how sorry he was to have caused such a disturbance the night before. He was still weak, naturally, and Mrs. Wilbur had put him right to bed when they got home; but there was nothing to worry about. She had not even bothered to telephone their daughter, who lived in Pittsburgh, but Mr. Wilbur had insisted on her telephoning Mr. Greene. They hoped to be back in the spring, and Mr. Greene said he hoped they would be back. Mrs. Wilbur said she thought their three minutes was up, so she rung off.

Now and then, through the winter months, Mr. Greene would give a thought to the Wilburs, not of the Wilburs independently but as typical of the older crowd, who hung on and hung on in spite of the high rates (which did not affect them all), and the younger summer crowd and their children, who were now the favorite guests of the Inn. If the Wilburs and the Broadbills, people like that, ever had a good look at the skiing crowd, sitting on the floor in their stretch pants, they would not recognize the place. And Mr. Greene wished the old-timers could have a look at the ski crowd; it would tell the old-timers most effectively that the Inn was going along with the times. It would remind them that they had always been given good value at the Inn (and why else would they have come back year after year?); that he had worked hard to make them comfortable; that their steady patronage did not really entitle them to any special rights—or rates.

Mr. Greene liked the new young faces and figures of the ski crowd. They were such a welcome relief from the Wilburs and the Broadbills and the Polly Woodwards. The older ones would come back to the Inn, having been absent eight or ten months, which was just long enough for the passage of time to make those depressing changes in their countenances and in their figures and their gait. Miss Polly Woodward was almost blind, and only in 1962 had she at last begun to carry a cane. Colonel Broadbill had a breath that would knock you over, and it was not from alcohol. Mrs. Broadbill's stockings were always falling down, and when they were not falling down they clung so loosely to her skinny legs that they looked like long underwear. He could not complain about Mrs. Wilbur's appearance; too many of the other guests had been saying for years that *there* was a handsome woman, a woman who aged gracefully. But he had never liked Mrs. Wilbur. Let something, anything, go wrong, and Mrs. Wilbur noticed it, whether it was a malfunction of the plumbing or an erroneous item on the bill. And who else would have complained that the liver paté was so rich that it had made her husband sick? Mr. Greene hoped that he would never have to see Mrs. Wilbur again.

His wish was gratified.

One afternoon in May he was standing in the driveway, having a look at the newly painted shutters on the upper stories, when a station wagon drew up slowly. It came to a stop directly behind him, and as he was not expecting any arrivals that day, and as it was an expensive English car, he assumed it was bringing some drop-in trade for the Taproom.

"Hello there, Mr. Greene!"

Mr. Greene had a better look, and now he saw Mr. Wilbur on the front seat, but the woman at the wheel was not Mrs. Wilbur. "Why, it's Mr. Wilbur. This is a nice surprise."

Mr. Wilbur, in his same old polo coat but wearing a tweed cap that had a little strap in the back, got out of the car and shook hands with Mr. Greene. He looked extremely well for a man who had gone through so many ailments. "I don't see Mrs. Wilbur," said Mr. Greene.

"No, I'm afraid Mrs. Wilbur passed away during the winter. Heart. We'd never known anything about it. At least she'd never mentioned it to me. Halfway up the stairs one morning, she collapsed and that was the end."

"I'm very sorry to hear that," said Mr. Greene. "But you're looking well."

"Well, thank you. I had quite a siege myself. They took out over half of my stomach. I was just beginning to get around a bit when Mrs. Wilbur had her attack. The young lady with me is my nurse. Do you suppose you could put us up, two nice single rooms not too far apart?"

"Why yes. I can give you adjoining. Twelve and Fourteen are vacant. You know them, there on the east side where you get the morning sun."

The nurse had parked the car and now joined them. "Miss Buckley, this is Mr. Greene, our famous host. Mr. Greene, my nurse, Miss Buckley."

"I'm very pleased to meet you. Mr. Wilbur speaks very highly of you."

"Pleased to meet you," said Mr. Greene. "Mr. Wilbur's

one of our most valued guests. Has been for a good many years."

"Well, the Inn has always been one of my favorite institutions in *my* life. And thanks largely to Mr. Greene, I might add."

"How long will you be with us, you and Miss Buckley?" said Mr. Greene.

"Till Monday at least, maybe a few days longer if you still have room for us."

"I may have to move you out of Twelve and Fourteen, but we'll find something."

"Miss Buckley doesn't mind sharing a bathroom with me," said Mr. Wilbur. "So if you have rooms with an adjoining bath, that'd be all right. I've been a patient of hers for so long now."

"Aaw, now, don't make it sound too long," said Miss Buckley. "He'll think you want to get rid of me."

"Now you know better than that, Miss Buckley," said Mr. Wilbur. "Well, shall we go in and register?"

"I'll send Chester out for your luggage," said Mr. Greene.

"Oh, I'm glad you still have Chester," said Mr. Wilbur. "He's in his sixties, but strong as an ox."

"Age doesn't make that much difference," said Miss Buckley. "If a man takes proper care of himself."

"That doesn't account for Chester. I have to fire him every so often, when he gets to thinking he owns what's in the cellar."

"Well, maybe if he didn't do that he'd get all tensed up," said Miss Buckley. "This man has three ounces of bourbon every night preceding dinner, and I see that he gets it. The best thing in the world for him."

"I'd miss it, no doubt about it," said Mr. Wilbur. "I'm getting to be a drinker in my old age."

"*Stop* with that talk about old age," said Miss Buckley. "I almost wasn't going to let him come here when he started talking about the good times he had here. You'd think he wanted to come here to be buried."

"That was at first. I haven't been talking that way lately, have I?"

"No, I'll admit that, or I wouldn't have let you come," said Miss Buckley.

"Mr. Greene remembers one unfortunate episode."

"Oh, think nothing of it, Mr. Wilbur."

. . . Mr. Greene knew perfectly well what went on among the ski crowd. It would have taken an army of Pinkertons to do an hourly bed-check, and as long as order was maintained in the Taproom and the bedrooms were not occupied by more guests than were on the registry, Mr. Greene was not going to try to be everywhere at once. They were young, healthy, vigorous people, with large appetites in every sense of the word. To try to police their behavior would be like going against nature and the times. But if he was willing to overlook certain things with the ski crowd, he had never relaxed his vigilance where the summer people were concerned. Through the years the Inn had acquired a reputation for respectability that was second to none. (Some of the ski crowd had told Mr. Greene that they had heard about that respectability from their parents and grandparents, and that because of it the younger ones were felt to be in safe hands.) A newcomer to the Inn was always asked who had recommended the place, and a letter would go off to the referred-to party so that the reference would be made to feel some sense of responsibility for the newcomer. Mr. Greene had never tolerated any funny business, no matter what or who. A British lord once showed up with a young American woman who obviously was not his lady, and when Mr. Greene saw the young woman he looked the Englishman straight in the eye and told him that there had been some mixup in his reservations and that he was afraid he could not accommodate them. He suggested they try a hotel in a city fifty miles away. His lordship knew better than to risk a scene, and out he went, followed by the young woman and Chester with their luggage. In a sense they were also followed—by a sharp letter from Mr. Greene to the travel agency employed by the Englishman.

The principal stockholders of the Inn, a well-to-do group of men in the insurance business in Hartford, and women, widows, who lived in the Hartford-Springfield area, had complete confidence in Mr. Greene's discretion, integrity, and acumen, and gave him what amounted to carte-blanche. They, too, were well aware of the greater freedom accorded the ski crowd, but they relied on Mr. Greene to keep it well in hand . . .

It was not so much that Mr. Wilbur was a problem. Mr.

Wilbur had been coming to the Inn too long not to be thoroughly indoctrinated in the policies maintained by Mr. Greene. And Mr. Wilbur was not a young man. Mr. Wilbur was an *old* man. But during the few minutes in the driveway Mr. Greene had formed an impression of Miss Buckley that was decidedly not in her favor. The late Mrs. Wilbur, whatever else she was, was a lady, and that much could not be said for Miss Buckley. Mr. Greene resented personally her saying "this man" has three ounces of bourbon, or whatever it was; he resented her saying that *she* was almost not going to let Mr. Wilbur come here. No doubt Mr. Wilbur had been so completely dominated by Mrs. Wilbur that her passing gave him a sense of relief; he certainly had not looked so well, so relaxed, in many years. But Mr. Greene wanted better things for Mr. Wilbur; most of all he wanted Mr. Wilbur to live out his remaining years without loss of the dignity that was perhaps his outstanding characteristic, that indeed had made the episode of the hemorrhage so distressing for Mr. Wilbur and all those who admired him. To be referred to to his face as "this man" was an affront to Mr. Wilbur's dignity, even though *he* might not yet regard it as such.

Mr. Wilbur was not a problem, and yet he was a problem for Mr. Greene. Mr. Greene usually designated as problems the men who got noisy-drunk in the Taproom, guests who antagonized the help, women who had dogs or cats. Mr. Wilbur, by appearing with this Miss Buckley, became a problem for Mr. Greene that was of a different nature from any he had dealt with as manager of the Inn. Mr. Wilbur was a good fifteen— well, a good ten—years older than Mr. Greene, and he needed protection. It came down simply to that: Mr. Wilbur needed protection.

There was a daughter living in Pittsburgh, but Mr. Greene remembered her only as a child and a young girl who was a bit of a scamp. She was not an evil girl, but she had started smoking in the lobby at a too early age, and several of the older women had spoken to Mr. Greene about the shorts she wore. The Wilburs' daughter had never appeared at the Inn after her marriage, and that was twenty years ago. In any event from what he knew of her she was not likely to concern herself much with her father's undeniable willingness to submit to a

Miss Buckley, and Mr. Greene was unhappy. Long ago, as a
bellhop and assistant manager, he had learned that old men
and old women did not automatically become sexless when
youth was gone. He had seen things that were hard to believe,
but he had seen them: old women murderously jealous over an
old man; lovemaking that belied all the jokes about age and im-
potence. Twice as a very young man with curly hair and the
face of an acolyte he had been propositioned by older people,
one of them not a woman. A bellhop of his acquaintance had
wheedled a Packard roadster out of one old woman, and was
contemptuous of the young Greene for passing up equal opportunities. Dignity therefore meant more than a dignified manner
to Mr. Greene; dignity of the right kind was often the only protection the old people had. Lose your dignity, and you are putty
in the hands of a Miss Buckley.

Mr. Greene was too fond of Mr. Wilbur to assign to one
of the help the task of watching out for any funny business
with the nurse. Saying nothing to anyone, he took on the job
himself. With his reputation for attention to small details he
was more or less expected to pop up here, there, and everywhere in the hotel and on the grounds, a fact which made it
easier to keep an eye on Mr. Wilbur and the nurse. Rooms
Twelve and Fourteen, though adjoining, were separated by a
locked door, and on the morning after Mr. Wilbur's arrival Mr.
Greene satisfied himself that both beds had been slept in, and
not merely rumpled for show. Throughout the second day Mr.
Greene kept tabs on Mr. Wilbur and the nurse. Mr. Wilbur
apparently had a routine; a walk after breakfast; a nap after
lunch; a game of gin rummy with Miss Buckley, followed by a
perfectly legitimate massage for which Miss Buckley had re-
quested a table. Mr. Wilbur then had his bath, dressed, and
came down to the Taproom for his three ounces of bourbon
before dinner. In the evening they played gin rummy again,
watched the eleven o'clock news on the television set in the
lobby, and went up to their rooms. In the course of the day
Mr. Greene had spoken to them three or four times, not at any
great length but in his offhand, casual, managerial way. Mr.
Wilbur made some favorable comments on the dogwood, Miss
Buckley admired the abundance of brass trinkets and won-

dered how they were kept so bright and shiny in these days of irresponsible help. Even in her own profession, the nurses they turned out these days . . .

Mr. Wilbur and the nurse said goodnight to Mr. Greene as they made their way to the elevator. Mr. Greene had never called a man's face beautiful, but there was a serenity in Mr. Wilbur's half-realized smile that was close to beautiful, and that in spite of the lines and discolorations. Mr. Greene mentally absolved Mr. Wilbur of all wrongdoing, and was chiding himself for suspiciousness. But just as the elevator door was closing Mr. Greene heard Mr. Wilbur laugh in a way that was different from any laugh that had ever come out of Mr. Wilbur. It had almost a cackle to it, that laugh, and Mr. Greene wondered what Miss Buckley had said to provoke it. In an instant Mr. Greene's suspicions all returned. Indeed, the laugh practically confirmed his suspicions of Miss Buckley as a woman who practiced some seductive power over Mr. Wilbur. The elevator was a self-service one, and in Mr. Greene's imagination Miss Buckley had said something to the old man that she would not have said in front of anyone else. The cackling laugh was so horrible that it provided a test of Mr. Greene's fondness for Mr. Wilbur.

The Taproom closed at midnight, and in the more than half empty Inn all was quiet by a quarter past twelve. Mr. Greene made his final rounds of the Taproom, the lobby and the other rooms on the main floor. Walter Downs, the night watchman, was on his patrol. No one else was to be seen. Ordinarily it would have been the time of day Mr. Greene liked best, when his work was finished and his guests all safe for the night. But now his job was not enjoyable and his immediate task was unpleasant, as unpleasant as the inferences he had drawn from that laugh of Mr. Wilbur's. He was certain now that Mr. Wilbur, under the influence of Miss Buckley, had turned into a nasty old man.

"Everything in order, Walter?" said Mr. Greene.

"Everything," said Walter Downs.

"You might have a look around out back, make sure the painters didn't leave any ladders lying around," said Mr. Greene.

"I will. I'll do that after I eat my lunch," said Walter.

"No hurry," said Mr. Greene. He wanted to make sure that Walter would be out of the way for a while. "They're forgetful sometimes. They leave those ladders any place. Person could stumble on them in the dark and we'd have a lawsuit."

"Want me to do it now?"

"No, you go eat your lunch and then do it," said Mr. Greene. "I'll say goodnight to you."

"Goodnight," said Walter Downs, heading for the kitchen.

Mr. Greene took the elevator to the third floor, got out, and walked down to the second floor. It was possible to hear the elevator from Twelve and Fourteen, to judge where it was stopping. He walked down the hall past Twelve and Fourteen, the sound of his steps deadened by the carpeting. The light was on in Fourteen, Miss Buckley's room. It showed in the transom. Twelve was dark. He listened outside Fourteen; Miss Buckley had the radio going softly. Mr. Greene decided that if there was any funny business between Mr. Wilbur and Miss Buckley, it had already been finished for the night. He was somewhat relieved, although he was only postponing the moment when he would catch them together.

He now walked to the end of the hall and pushed the button for the elevator. He heard the machinery go into operation and was waiting for the elevator's slow descent when Miss Buckley's door was opened. He only chanced to see the light from her room suddenly falling like a square on the carpet. Miss Buckley came out of her room in a hurry and went quickly to Mr. Wilbur's door and opened it with a key. She went inside, closing his door behind her. She had never once looked in Mr. Greene's direction.

Mr. Greene in his anger nearly lost control of himself, but he waited a full minute, then went back to Twelve, inserted his passkey, and flung open the door. Miss Buckley was sitting on the bed, holding Mr. Wilbur and rocking from side to side, muttering to him. Mr. Wilbur was babbling words that Mr. Greene could not make out, staring at the foot of the bed.

Miss Buckley looked at Mr. Greene and went on holding Mr. Wilbur in her arms. "He gets these nightmares," she said.

THE MAN ON
THE TRACTOR

They were the fabulous Denisons, Pammie and George.

There was a time when Booth Tarkington and Louis Brom-field, who had never met the Denisons, were called upon to admit or deny that they had used the Denison family in certain novels. By letter and in person the novelists tried to make it clear that they had relied on invention, and though coming so close to the facts of the Denison family, they had not been assisted by a knowledge of the Denison history, past or present. A letter from a Gibbsville lady to F. Scott Fitzgerald went unanswered, and the lady and her friends agreed that Fitzgerald did not dare deny that the automobile accident in *This Side of Paradise* was right out of life. Why, even the car was the same as George Denison's old Locomobile. True, George Denison had run over a man on the Boston Post Road, but obviously Fitzgerald had made that change to confuse people. And if Daisy in *The Great Gatsby* was not patterned after Pammie Stribling Denison, the lady from Gibbsville would eat your hat. For instance, Pammie Stribling, as everyone knew, had been madly infatuated with Johnny Gruber, the qualified assistant pharmacist at Hudson's drugstore. Same initials as Jay Gatsby's; and wasn't Gatsby somehow mixed up in patent medicines or something? Fitzgerald would not have had a leg to stand on, and he was pretty smart not to answer those letters. He wouldn't have had a leg to stand on. How absurd of Booth Tarkington to pretend he had not patterned the Ambersons after the Denisons; how ridiculous of Louis Bromfield to protest that the Shaynes were not more or less based on the Denisons.

Regardless of the denials and the non-denial, the legend

of the Denisons as literary source material went into the Gibbsville lore, along with the firmly held belief that Lichtenwalner's
ice cream was famous the world over and that the town was
the richest per capita of all third-class cities east of the Missis-
sippi. As it happens, Lichtenwalner's has gone out of business,
and little is said these days of per capita wealth in Gibbsville;
but due in part to the Fitzgerald revival the Denison legend
has persisted. Men and women of a certain age have told their
children that not only Fitzgerald, but Booth Tarkington and
Louis Bromfield too, wrote stories about the Denisons. It has
been denied that Scott and Zelda ever visited Gibbsville, but the
denials have grown weaker, and it is certainly true that Pammie
and George did once have as house guests a screwy couple
with an Irish name who could very well have been the Fitzgeralds. The man was short and good-looking and insisted on
playing the drums at a club dance; the woman stayed in her
room all the time she was at the Denisons'. Walter Spiker, the
Denisons' best friend, would have been able to say for sure
whether it had been the Fitzgeralds, but Walter, alas, was
dead. Long dead, and during the last five years of his life had
lost the power of speech. If Walter had had any literary ability
he could have written about the Denisons—and how! He knew
more about the Denisons than the Tarkingtons and Bromfields
and Fitzgeralds all put together, and he would have got it right.

Pammie and George were in town not long ago, stopping
at the John Gibb Hotel, but they saw only a very few people.
Their reservation at the hotel was handled by a clerk who
wrote out a slip for M & M Geo. Dennison; the name meant
nothing to him, but the request for the reservation had come
from a reputable travel agency in New York. When Mr. and
Mrs. Denison arrived at the hotel the clerk saw only a man and
woman who were pretty sure of themselves in a hotel lobby,
with four pieces of expensive foreign luggage; the woman in a
tweed suit with a little cape on the shoulders, the man in a
striped gray flannel suit and a reversible tweed-and-gab topcoat
over his arm. "Check-out time is three P.M.," said the clerk.

"Is it indeed?" said the man, signing the registration card.

"But an extra hour, I guess we won't charge you a full
day," said the clerk.

"I'm sure of it," said Denison. "Maybe even two hours."

"I don't know about *two* hours. It's our—"

"*I* do," said Denison. "Will you see that my car's washed and serviced, high-test gas, and back here in an hour, please? It's the green Bentley. The bellboy knows. But I want *you* to see that I have it back in an hour."

"I'll try," said the clerk.

"You do a little better than try, won't you?" said Denison.

"Let's find out if there's a hairdresser in the hotel," said his wife.

"Is there?" said Denison.

"No sir, not in the hotel. There's one around the corner to the right, three doors to the right. Our switchboard will connect you."

"Dear, it's twenty of three," said Denison to his wife. "You go on upstairs. I'm going over and see Andy Stokes before the bank closes. I'll only be a few minutes, but I don't want to miss him."

The mention of the name Stokes had as much impact on the clerk as the name Bentley. "If there's anything I can do, sir."

"There is. Will you send up a bottle of Scotch, any good Scotch that you have, and a bottle of sherry. Bristol Cream. And the Gibbsville papers."

"There's only the one paper in the afternoon."

A man had come up behind Denison during the exchange with the clerk. The man fully recognized Denison, but he allowed himself the protection of a feigned uncertainty. "Isn't this George Denison?" said the man.

Denison turned. "Yes it is," said Denison.

"George, you don't remember me, it's such a long time and all," said the man. "Karl Isaminger? Used to drive for your Aunt Augusta, Mrs. Hamilton?"

"Why, I *didn't* recognize you, Karl," said Denison.

"Hello, Karl," said Pammie Denison.

"Hello, Mrs. Denison."

"What are you doing now, Karl?" said Denison.

"Oh, I'm the night man at Coleman's Garage."

"Coleman's? I don't know that name."

"Used to be Jimmy Brady's that had the Studebaker agency."

"Uh-huh. Aren't you up rather early for a night watchman?"

"Oh—I can't stay in bed more'n six hours at the most. I had this operation three years ago the twentieth of May. You remember Doc Robbins, or was he since you left town?"

"Must have been after my time. You living here at the hotel, Karl?"

"Ah, you, George. Living *here?* No, I come in here to buy a magazine. Gives me something to read at work, and when I get finished with it the wife likes to look through it. The print's a little small for her, but she says her glasses gives her a headache. Won't *wear* glasses. I said to her—"

"Dear, if you're going to get to the bank before it closes, I hate to interrupt but—" said Pammie Denison.

"Oh, ixcuse me, I didn't—"

"That's all right, Karl," said George Denison. "You can walk to the bank with me, if you like."

"No, I wouldn't do that, George. I just wanted to come up and say hello to you and Mrs. You're both looking fine. I'd of known you anywhere. Remember the old Pierce-Arrow, Mrs. Denison? 'Karl, go fetch Pammie Stribling,' Mrs. Hamilton used to say. Remember when you used to come and play the piano for the old lady? Rainy days, she used to like you to come play the piano for her."

"Oh, do I? Shades of 'Country Gardens.' Dum-dum tee dum-dum, dum-dum tee dum. But always followed by hot chocolate and *sand* tarts."

"*I* remember them sand tarts," said Karl Isaminger.

"So do I," said George Denison. "Mrs. Hamilton used to send them to me at school. But this isn't getting to the bank. Karl, nice to see you. Remember me to your wife. Dear, I'll see you in about an hour or less."

"Don't hurry, George," said Pammie.

"The sand tarts had little pieces of citron in the middle," said George Denison. "Some had pecans, but I preferred the citron." He left them.

Andy Stokes was expecting him. They had had correspondence over the years, and Andy Stokes was one of the few Gibbsville citizens who occasionally saw the Denisons. When the pleasantries were over Stokes rang for his secretary. "Miss Arbogast, will you bring me the papers on the Denison sale?" said Stokes.

"Certainly," said Miss Arbogast. She smiled at George Denison, who had already greeted her in the outer office.

Andy Stokes sat back in his chair. "It's kind of sad, George," he said. "I don't mean how little you're getting for the property. I guess your tax man has that all figured out for you. But this land is your last link with Gibbsville."

"Except for my stock in this bank," said George Denison.

"Well, that, of course. I hope you never part with that," said Stokes. "But that's not the same as actual land. That land's been in the Denison family close to a hundred years. I had a look at the title search, naturally, but I hadn't realized how long you'd held it. Do you know what I wish?"

"What do you wish, Andy?"

"Well, I wish you and your tax man could figure out some way to donate the land for a playground, a park, something on that order. And continue the Denison name."

"My tax man would much rather have me take the money," said George Denison.

Miss Arbogast came in with the papers, laid them on Stokes's desk, smiled again at Denison without looking at him, and departed.

"Yes, I suppose he would. That was just a sentimental thought I had," said Stokes. "Considering how little you're getting for the land. If it was a big deal I never would have thought of it, but what's eighteen thousand to you?"

"I don't know, but my tax man does. He said to unload it, and I'm unloading it."

"Well, I wouldn't give *him* an argument. From the correspondence I've had with him, I'd say he was as smart as a tack. Doesn't miss a trick."

"He's kept me out of prison, that's as much as *I* know," said George Denison.

"Okay, George. All you have to do now is sign your name on these papers, where you see the check-mark. Miss Arbogast will notarize them and I'll have one of our people witness them. Here's your cheque. It's made out to the Denison Land Company. Want me to forward that to Longstreet?"

"Yes, will you please?" said Denison, busy with Stokes's desk pen.

"The last transaction of the Denison Land Company," said Stokes. "In the old days an occasion like this would call for some kind of a celebration."

"Well, we're not exactly celebrating, Pammie and I, but we decided to make the trip. They sure have done a lot of things to the roads around here. The town is practically by-passed. What ever happened to South Main Street? We never did get on South Main. And these God damn one-way streets. I almost got a ticket. If I hadn't had a Connecticut license, the cop at Main and Scandinavian was going to slap me with a summons."

"That was Paul Keppler. He's tough."

"Oh, God, is that who that was? The big fat baby-faced guy? That would have been appropriate. His father arrested me back in 1920 or thereabouts. But he took a look at my driver's license and let me go. He never said who he was, or pretended to know me. 'Just watch the signs,' he said, and waved me on."

"You can be damn sure he knew who you were, though. We think he's the best cop on the force. He graduated from the FBI school, and he's the only one the kids pay any attention to."

"There," said George Denison, laying down the pen. "I guess that does it." He picked up the cheque, read it, and put it back on Andy Stokes's blotter. He found that Stokes was looking at him, half smiling, trying to read his mind. George Denison smiled back and shook his head. "No, Andy, I'm not going to cry," said George Denison.

"Maybe not, but for just a few seconds it hit you," said Andy Stokes.

"I suppose so," said George Denison.

"I'll tell you who we're having tonight," said Stokes. "Out of deference to your wishes we kept it small. We couldn't get Joe and Verna. Joe's in Philadelphia, having a big operation. Cancer. It doesn't sound so good, either. Verna told Alice that we might as well be prepared for the worst. So they're out. But we did get Stubby and Jean."

"That's good."

"Stubby and Jean. Bob Rothermel and Cynthia. That's two, four, six, eight. And Henry and Ad. There won't be much drinking with that group. Stubby's been on the wagon five or six years. Henry is AA, very active in it. Bob still likes to put it away, but Cynthia only drinks a little wine at dinner. Alice never did drink, as you know, and I limit myself to two before dinner, usually a bourbon on the rocks."

"What about Ad, and what about Jean?"

"Ad is AA, too. Jean is unpredictable. She's on and off the wagon from one month to the next. She may arrive tonight with the blind staggers. On the other hand, she may not take a drink. It all depends. You knew their daughter had to be put away?"

"No, I didn't. Was that Barbara?"

"Barbara, yes. Bobbie. Oh, yeah. It was a tragic thing. She cut her wrists, and another time an overdose of sleeping pills. Some guy in Wilkes-Barre she was crazy about, so they said. Stubby went on the wagon, but Jean still ties one on. They sold their house, and then Stub was out of a job for over a year. He's got something now, Henry gave him a job at the brewery as a sort of a coordinator with the advertising agency."

"Stubby? He's a civil engineer."

"He's not the only guy with a Lehigh degree that's doing something altogether different. Do you remember Chuck Rainsford?"

"Sure. General superintendent of the Dilworth Collieries. I used to play golf with Chuck."

"Not any more. I'm afraid he's come down in the world. He gives a course in geology at the adult education setup we have here. Two nights a week. They pay him something like a hundred and fifty dollars a term, and he tells me he's glad to get the money."

"I've seen him bet that much on a single putt," said George Denison. "Haven't you any *good* news, Andy?"

"Well, you know how it is. The good news is always less spectacular. Let me think. Of those coming tonight? Henry and Ad's oldest grandson ran for the state legislature and nosed out the Democrat."

"That's always good to hear," said George Denison.

"Well, it's a start," said Stokes. "Let me think, now. Cynthia's taken up painting, but I don't know whether you'd classify that as good news, exactly. It's what she calls non-representational. In other words, not supposed to represent anything—and believe me, as far as I'm concerned, it doesn't. Both their kids have moved away. Young Bobby is a test pilot for one of the big aviation companies in California. The daughter married a fellow from Chicago and they're living out there. The husband is with Continental, the bank. There's no money here, George. Not the way we knew it. We're losing population, a thousand a year. The town is back to where it was in the 1910 census, and no new industries coming in. These people that are buying your land, they'll put up a supermarket and a big parking lot, but sure as hell that's going to be the end of some more of the smaller stores. And if they lease the rest of the land to a drive-in movie, which is what I understand, that'll close down one of our movie theaters. Banking isn't much fun any more, the hard luck stories I have to listen to. When I first started working here I used to hear a lot of crazy schemes that we had to turn down, but at least there was some imagination at work. Not any more. It's the fast buck, the quick turnover, build as cheaply as possible, take your profits and get out. Some of our people drive as much as fifty miles to work and fifty back. Car pools. Our biggest cash depositor, week to week, used to be the old Stewart department store. Now do you know what it is? The numbers racket. A few of our old friends have made some money in the stock market, but that's not here. That's New York and Philadelphia, and representing industries as far away as California."

"That's enough good news for one day," said George Denison.

"I know, and I have to live with it three hundred and sixty-five days a year. If there was only some way we could reduce the population and become a small town, with enough work for everybody. I wouldn't mind being a small town again. But I'm a banker, and I have to keep up this pretense, like a booster. Well, in three more years I retire. A banquet at the hotel, a silver cigarette box, and the responsibility passes on to one of those young fellows you see out there. He's welcome to it."

"I've been away too long, you've stayed here too long," said George Denison.

"That's about the size of it, I guess," said Stokes. "Yes, I guess that's just about the size of it."

"I must be going, Andy. I'll see you a little later."

"Mike will let you out. You remember Mike Kelly? If you don't, he'll remember you. Used to pitch in the Twilight League, and was on the police force. About our age. He'll appreciate it if you remember him—and so will I."

Mike Kelly was waiting to unlock the heavy plate-glass door. His eagerness to be recognized was almost a supplication.

"Hello, Mike," said George Denison.

Mike Kelly put the door key in his left hand and shook hands with George Denison. "George, it's mighty good to see you. You're looking great, George. Great."

"Well, you might be able to go nine innings yourself," said George Denison.

"You remember those days? You used to play under the name of—what was the name?"

"George Denny."

"George Denny," said Mike Kelly. "So you wouldn't lose your amateur standing. You could hit. You were a good hitter, George. There was a couple times there where you threw to the wrong base—"

"Never. I never threw to the wrong base in my life."

"Now you know you did, George. But when it come to hitting that apple, you had the power. There was only one pitcher could get you out. Marty Boxmyer, pitched for the Knights of Pythias. Marty was such a little guy and he had so much steam that you never knew where the ball was coming from. But outside of Marty, you could hit any pitcher in our league."

"Yes, I could even hit you, Mike."

"I'll admit it. I wasn't the greatest pitcher in the league. But there was very few could get a long ball off of me, when my sinker was going right. How long you gonna be in town, George?"

"Just overnight."

"Living in Connecticut, I hear. How's your missus?"

"Fine thank you. And yours?"

"Passed away, George. I buried her two years ago the sixth day of May. But I have eight grandchildren. Five boys to carry on the name. One of them at Villanova was scouted by a couple of major league clubs. He has three one-hitters to his credit, one of them against your old college alma mater. A two-to-one win against a good Princeton team. Pardon my ignorance, George, but you didn't have a son if I recollect."

"Two daughters, but one of the grandsons is on the Harvard crew."

"Well, that's good, George. You could of been a great athlete if it wasn't for that one thing. You know what I mean. I don't have to say it."

"I guess you must be referring to the suds," said George Denison.

"Not the suds. It was the hard stuff."

"I don't think it made much difference, Mike. I wouldn't have been much better, and I wouldn't have had as much fun."

"I used to try to lecture you," said Mike Kelly.

"Yes you did. Mike, it's nice to see you, and maybe I'll see you again before I leave. If not—keep the faith."

"You remember that, huh? Keep the faith. So long, George. Glad we run into one another."

Back at the hotel George Denison found his wife standing at the window, looking down at the traffic on Main Street. "I was watching you," she said. "You came all the way from the bank without being recognized. I was trying to remember the stores between here and Scandinavian Street. Do you realize there's not a one that used to be here that's still here? Not a one, in the same place. There may be some that moved."

"They didn't move. They closed. At least that's what I gather from Andy. Did you get an appointment with the hairdresser?"

"No. They wouldn't take me before tomorrow."

"Then let's go for a ride," said George Denison.

"Where to?"

"Oh—wherever old Dobbin takes us. I'll just wrap the reins around the buggy-whip."

"What's this quaintness, all of a sudden? Old Dobbin? Did you ever know anyone that had a horse called Dobbin?"

"I knew a girl that had a dog called Dobbin," said George Denison.

"She must have been terribly affected. I suppose she had a horse called Rover."

"Towser," said George Denison.

"Frankly, I don't believe it," said Pammie Denison.

"Come on, put your coat on while there's still daylight," he said.

She put on her coat and hat. "Did you really know a girl that had a dog called Dobbin?" she said in the elevator.

"I really did," he said.

"When?"

"During what we sometimes refer to as the Tommy Williams Period."

"Oh," she said, and in the presence of the elevator boy said no more.

The green car was at the door. They got in and he drove south on Main Street. "Who *was* the girl that had—"

"With a dog called Dobbin? What difference does that make now? She was never as important to me as Tommy Williams was to you."

"All right. I was just wondering whether she was one that I knew about or one that you never mentioned. Where are we headed for?"

"You'll soon see," he said.

"Oh, then I guess I know," she said.

"Right," he said.

After a while he drove off the main highway and up into the hills, and presently he stopped the car on a township road, midway between two farmhouses. "Are you going to kiss me?" she said.

"Don't you think I ought to?"

"Yes I do," she said.

He kissed her on the lips, and when he drew away she was looking down at the floor, vaguely smiling. "That was very nice of you," she said.

"I feel rather self-conscious about it," he said. "But it's just about the only chance we'll get."

"Do you know something, George?"

"What?"

"After twenty-five years, twenty-seven, whatever it is, this is the first time I've really felt that you've forgiven me for Tommy Williams."

"Really? Well, maybe it is the first time. I don't know."

"I forgave myself a long time ago," she said.

He laughed. "I'm sure you did."

"Oh, it wasn't as easy as all that. A girl that's made a damn fool of herself—first she has to justify herself. Then she has to forget all about that and start being honest with herself —if she can. And I did. And that was when I was harder on myself than you ever were. It was at least a year before I could forgive myself for what I did to you and to myself."

"I didn't realize it'd taken you that long," he said.

"I know you didn't. That's why today, just now, is the first time I feel that you've really forgiven me. All those years in between, you took me back and we've been nice to each other, but there's always been something missing. Why is that?"

"I don't know," he said. "I've had it in my mind that I wanted to come here, to this very spot where I first kissed you over forty years ago. And I planned to kiss you. Then on the way to Gibbsville I more or less gave up the idea. Oversentimental. Forced. Awkward. But then I saw old Karl Isaminger. Then I had a long talk with Andy and heard what's happened to people we used to love. To this town. Life has been awful to them, Pam, the town and the people, and it hasn't been nearly as bad to you and me. Not yet, anyway. But our luck will start running out. We're getting there. And I wanted to bring you here and tell you that I've always loved you. Here, where I told you the first time."

"Then what I felt was right," she said.

"Yes," he said.

"From now on I guess we have to be ready for anything," she said.

"Yes," he said. With the tips of his fingers he caressed the back of her neck. "And don't be depressed by what we see tonight, at Alice and Andy's."

"Thank you," she said. "I won't. Now."

"Here comes a man on a tractor," he said. "He thinks we're lost."

THE MAYOR

Yock Schindle usually opened up around nine-thirty, to be ready for the first customers of the day. The first hour's customers were always the same men, each one had the same thing every morning, each stayed about the same length of time every morning. Most of the men would have a Coca-Cola with a squirt of lemon or lime, a few would have a glass of milk flavored with chocolate syrup, there were three or four who would take nothing to drink but would buy a cigar or two. At about ten-fifteen every morning Yock's place would contain as many as fifteen customers, all in the front room. Yock had no actual rule against their playing pool at that time of day, but the back room, with its four pool tables, would be empty of customers, the overhead lights were dark, the tables covered with black oilcloth. Once in a great while a man would say to a friend, "We have time for twenty-five points," and they would play, but it was not customary, and it was not encouraged by Yock, who was kept busy behind the tiny soda fountain (no ice cream, no sundaes). The cigar smokers would help themselves out of the case on the opposite side of the front room, and would put the money for their purchases on the soda fountain. Six days a week Yock's ten o'clock trade did not vary as much as fifty cents from day to day, and nearly every man who belonged to the ten o'clock trade would also drop in again later in the day, in the middle of the afternoon or after work.

Yock got the most enjoyment out of the ten o'clock trade because it was as good as reading a newspaper. Better, really, because he heard things that the newspapers could not print.

The mayor was a ten o'clock customer, and he usually had just
come from sitting as a magistrate in police court. Two doctors
and three lawyers were among the ten-o'clockers, as were a reporter from each of the two newspapers, a couple of insurance
men, a jeweler, the proprietor of a ladies' specialty shop, a private detective, and a couple of professional politicians who
were perennial office-holders. The men who owned the town
seldom or never patronized Yock's place, but there was no other
group who knew more than Yock's crowd about what was going
on. Up to a point they trusted each other, and the morning conversations at Yock's were considered confidential at least to the
extent that if you repeated something you heard at Yock's you
were discreet about attributing the source of your information.
The politicians were the only ones who used Yock's as a place to
start rumors, and they were the only ones whom the others did
not always believe.

The mayor was not a professional politician—dependent,
that is, on public office or graft for his living. He was mayor
because he wanted to be mayor and considered the office good
publicity for his business, which was an already prosperous,
second-generation shoe store. He was a Shriner and an Elk, a
Lutheran, a former president of the Merchants' Association, a
founding member of Rotary, a one-time captain of the Gibbsville High basketball team and currently a captain of one of
the senior league teams at the Y.M.C.A. There were also *non*-
memberships in certain organizations and institutions that were
in his favor: he did *not* belong to the country club or the Gibbsville Club, the Catholic Church or the Ku Klux Klan. He lived
on Market Street, in a house that was three stories high and had
a marble stoop in front and a well-kept yard that went back to
the next street, but it was on Market Street, and as long as a
man continued to live on Market he remained a man of the
people. The people, who voted for him in large numbers, were
quite proud of the fact that he could buy and sell some of the
upper-class aristocrats of Lantenengo Street. His money did not
count against him. Saturday night you could still go to Lester
Flickinger's store and be waited on by the mayor of the town.
If you were buying a pair of shoes for your kid and Lester did
not happen to be waiting on you, it was still Lester who came

and handed you a scout knife (unofficial) or a school companion for your kid, depending on whether it was a boy or a girl.

Les Flickinger was such a natural for the office of mayor
that the talk around town was that he got the nomination for
five thousand dollars, then told the professional politicians that
he saw no reason why he should spend any more of his own
money to get elected. This did not sit too well with the politicians, but he had the Republican nomination ("Tantamount,"
the newspapers always said, "to election") and they could blame
only themselves for not having put a bigger bite on Les in the
beginning. As a consequence of their short-sightedness they
were compelled to get money elsewhere, and to do so they had
to make commitments that resulted in one of the most graft-
ridden administrations in the town's history. The town coun-
cil approved contracts for the paving of roads in outlying areas
that were not yet cleared for the construction of houses; and
the street railway company was once again threatened with a
municipally owned bus system. But no one could say that Les
Flickinger took a dirty dollar. He put through an appropriation
for a car for the police chief, which he may have used more frequently than the chief. He took trips to Philadelphia and the
state capital and other cities in the Commonwealth, extolling
the virtues of his town and thereby justifying the expense accounts he submitted for these trips. No one seemed to care, or
to notice, that those trips also coincided with lodge conventions
and sporting events. He was the town's biggest booster, and
whatever the cynical may have thought and said about those
paving contracts for undeveloped areas, they doubted that Les
Flickinger was getting anything out of it.

When Les turned up at Yock Schindle's for morning
prayers, as someone called the ten o'clock gatherings, he often
had some amusing or scandalous or pathetic story direct from
police court. His magisterial powers were limited, and most of
the prisoners brought before him were d. and d.'s—drunk and
disorderly. The usual sentence was ten dollars or ten days.
Not more than half the culprits had ten dollars cash on them,
and Mayor Flickinger would suspend sentence and let the man
off with a warning. Habitual offenders could be sentenced to
thirty days in the county jail, and with the coming of cold

weather there were some regulars who would request a sixty- or even a ninety-day sentence to the stony lonesome. The mayor never denied such requests: any man who would willingly prefer the county jail to freedom was on his last legs, and if he froze to death or got run over by a switching engine, the cost of burying him had to be borne by the municipal government. If he died in jail, the county had to take care of it. For the mayor it was a strange experience to be thanked for sending a man to prison, and especially to a prison that offered almost nothing but shelter from the elements. At Thanksgiving and Christmas the newspapers reported that the "guests of the county" would be served a turkey dinner, but the oldest con had never seen a scrap of white meat, for the reason that the prison cook carved the breast and sold it to the local restaurants. "When I think of those poor souls up there," said Les Flickinger one day.

"Makes you want to stay honest, eh, Les?" said Arnold Goble, one of the professional politicians.

"Sure makes you want to stay honest, all right," said Les. "But then on the other hand you have the ones that are the scum of the earth. I mean that. The scum of the earth. You wouldn't believe it possible in this day and age, how low some men can get. And women. They brought in Jenny Faust again last night. She kept everybody awake all night, yelling and screaming."

"What did Jenny do this time?" someone asked.

"Well, I guess Jenny always does the same thing, if you get the drift. But this time she set up business down in the lower yards, down near the Pennsy freight station. I mean the Reading freight station. I ought to know the difference between those two. Anyway, there she was and half a dozen men waiting in line when they arrested her. A woman like that, there ought to be some way to put her away for good."

"Well, I see the A's won," said Charley Dewey, another politician. "Al Simmons got a hold of one with the bases loaded. It must of been some poke, over four hundred foot. It's 468 foot from home plate to the center-field fence. If that fellow was with a better team you'd never hear of Ruth."

"Ah, nuts. They're both hitting the same pitching, practically," said someone. "You guys that root for the A's, what did

Mack ever do for you? Connie Mack is in it for the money, and as long as you got him running the A's—"

"Aah, shut up. Connie Mack knows more baseball in his little finger than your Hugginses and the rest of them ever *will* know," said someone else.

"I agree with you on that," said Charley Dewey. He had a hard, loud voice, and when he wanted to take over a conversation he could do so. It was not until a little while later that he revealed to Les Flickinger that that had been his purpose.

He followed Les out into the street. "You know why I interrupted you in there?"

"Oh, you did it on purpose?" said Les Flickinger.

"Sure I did," said Charley. "What's the use of you making an enemy when you don't have to? Don't you know about Jenny Faust and Yock?"

"Jenny Faust and *Yock?* Yock Schindle? I never heard him so much as mention her name."

"You never will, either. You know, Les, there's a lot of things in this town you don't know. Being from well-to-do parents and a graduate of Lebanon Valley and all that, there's some things you're not familiar with, and you oughta ask me. Not that you could of asked me in this particular case, but hereafter, be a little more careful."

"Never mind about that, Charley. Don't start issuing orders to me, you know. But what about Yock and Jenny Faust?"

"What I ought to do is leave you flat, right here in the middle of the sidewalk, and let you go on making mistakes, but I got the party to consider. So this time I'll tell you for your own good, *and* the good of the party organization. I'm not just some guy that a year from now's getting out of politics."

"Maybe I'm not either, but what is it you want to tell me?"

"I want to tell you this, Les. You don't make enemies out of a fellow like Yock Schindle, and if I didn't interrupt you back there, that's what you were doing. Yock Schindle, Jacob W. Schindle, is responsible for Jenny Faust being a fifty-cent hooker. Now how do you like *them* for apples?"

"Well, how do I like them? I think you're crazy with the heat. I remember Yock's father and mother, lived over on South Canal Street. I waited on them in the store many a time, and Martin Schindle was a brakeman on the Reading. Martin L. Schindle. His wife came from near Swedish Haven, on a farm. There was I think one other brother and two sisters in addition to Yock. I waited on all of them. They had good credit and they were a very strict family. The father didn't say much, but you could tell."

"Uh-huh. Now tell me all you know about Jenny Faust."

"Jenny Faust? Well, I don't know which Faust she was. I don't remember her coming in the store when I was a young fellow, and I wouldn't *let* her in now. There was one Faust family up on North Second, and another 'way out Market. Then there were Fausts lived out there near the packing-houses."

"Well, you missed one family. Jenny's family. They lived down at the end of South Canal. There was the mother and two daughters. The old man was dead, and the mother took in washing. The two daughters used to carry the baskets with the wash, Jenny and her sister Lizzie. They used to go call for the wash and then lug it back when it was done. That was all they had to live on till the girls got big enough to get work. Lizzie got a job in the silk mill, and Jenny got a lot of jobs. I remember she had a paper route, and then she got work in the hospital for a while, and I guess when she was around fifteen or sixteen years of age she got a job in the silk mill with Lizzie."

"Where does Yock come in?"

"Then. Right about then. Yock was a call-boy for the Reading, through his old man being a brakeman. Yock was waiting to be notified that he could take the examination for brakeman, but they passed him over for bad eyesight and he got transferred to the weighmaster's office. He could never be a railroader, with bad eyesight, not on a train crew anyhow. But they fixed him up with a job in the weighmaster's office just about the time his old man took the examination for fireman."

"How do you know all this?"

"I lived on South Canal then. I'm only about four or five years younger than Yock. He just looks older. Them thick glasses he wears."

"And then what?" said Les Flickinger.

"Well, Yock took a liking to Jenny, only his parents put a

stop to it. No son of theirs was getting mixed up with anybody as poor as that. They were poor, all right. The girls used to when they were kids walk the tracks to pick coal. We all did, but not our sisters. Only the boys did, except the Faust girls. They had to have a lot of hot water for the old lady to do her washing."

"Uh-huh, uh-huh."

"So one day Mrs. Faust knocked on their door and Yock's mother wasn't going to let her in, but she pushed right past her and back to the kitchen to the old man having his supper. Either Yock was going to marry Jenny right away, or she was going to the squire's office and swear out a warrant. Old Man Schindle got up and threw her out by the kitchen door, and then he went to work and beat Yock insensible. He didn't ask nobody no questions. Yes, no, or amen. He just threw her out, and then went to work beating up his son."

"How old was Yock?"

"Eighteen. Maybe nineteen by then."

"And what happened to Jenny? Did she have the baby?"

"Some say she did and some say she didn't. Some say she had it and got rid of it, and others said it was stillborn."

"You mean she may have had a live baby and killed it?"

"Who knows? Jenny knows, but her old lady kicked her out, just like Old Man Schindle done to the old lady."

"But that's, uh, homicide. It comes under the head of homicide. Manslaughter, maybe."

"Yeah, but who was going to take the trouble to find out? Jenny's old lady? And not Yock's parents."

"Where did she have the baby?"

"You ask these questions that all these things happened thirty years ago, and nobody knew the answer then. Now I doubt if Jenny herself could give you the answer. It was damn near thirty years ago. All she had to do was wrap it in a burlap bag and weight it with some ballast off the tracks, and drop it in the canal. One kid more or less on South Canal Street—especially down there at the lower end."

"Even so, human life—"

Charley's voice was harder than ever. "Come on, Les. Come on," he said.

"Don't talk to me in that tone of voice," said Les.

"Yeah? Well, I'll bet old Yock was glad to hear my tone of voice this morning."

"Yock Schindle," said Les. "And Jenny Faust. Yock Schindle and Jenny Faust. She's being held in the county jail for the next term of court. I could have made it harder for her, but I guess I'm just as glad I didn't."

"Yeah. Uh-huh."

NINETY MINUTES AWAY

It was a very cold night in February. More snow was expected, but apparently it was waiting for the temperature to go up a little. In the streets the going was rough; snow piled high in the gutters, ruts in the roadway frozen solid, and the sidewalks were hazardous with patches of ice. Not many people were to be seen on the streets of South Taqua, although it was the night before Washington's Birthday and the mines would be idle the next day. The people who had gone in to Taqua to see a movie were already home. The store window lights were out. The only illumination was from overhead arc-lights at three inter- sections, and from the Athens, the all-night restaurant. A few cars were parked near the Athens, as near as they could get.

Harvey Hunt paid his check at the Athens, folded his muffler over his chest, turned up his overcoat collar, put on his hat and went out. He took a few steps on the sidewalk, and someone called to him from the doorway of the Athens. "Hey, Harve, you forgot your arctics."

"I'll be back for them later," said Harvey Hunt. "But thanks."

He resumed his walk to the borough hall, a block away, sliding where there was enough ice, walking flatfooted where the ice was patchy. Halfway to borough hall he covered his nose with the muffler; the wind was strong and cold and made breathing difficult.

He entered the borough hall though the side door marked Police. The room he entered was warm, small, and crowded with desks, chairs, filing-cases, fire extinguishers, assorted traffic

signs and stanchions, a gun closet, a small telephone switchboard, a couple of rubber tires, an oxygen tank, new and old
first-aid kits, clothestrees, several pairs of hip boots. There was
only one human being in the room, sitting at the desk near the
switchboard. He was a rather handsome man who was getting
thick through the middle. He wore a dark blue woollen shirt with
sergeant's chevrons and a silver-plated shield. In one hip pocket
was a .38 revolver, encased in a pocket holster. In his shirt
pockets were three or four fountain pens and pencils. "Shut the
door, shut the door," he said.

"Let me get inside first," said Harvey Hunt. "What's doing, Ken?"

"You'll find out soon enough," said the sergeant.

Harvey Hunt took off his overcoat and hat and hung them
on a clothestree. "All right, what's doing?"

"Nothing, yet, but there will be," said Ken. "Just keep your
shirt on. I wouldn't get you here on a false alarm."

"What kind of a story is it?"

The policeman looked up at the wall clock. "It's a raid."

"A Prohibition raid?"

"I wouldn't get you down here on a Prohibition raid," said
Ken.

"I noticed you looking at the clock. Is the raid going on
now?"

"Yes. I wouldn't of told you that much if it wasn't."

"Are you afraid I'd have tipped off somebody?"

"Not intentionally. But by accident you could have."

"The raid was supposed to start at eleven o'clock?"

"Five after eleven. Eleven-five," said Ken. "They'll be
coming in pretty soon."

"Then tell me what it's all about."

"All right, I guess it's all right now," said Ken. "You know
Buddy Spangler's place, out there by the freight yards."

"Sure. I know every saloon in the county. I haven't been
to Spangler's much, but I know the place. It's back off the main
road."

The cop nodded. "That's where the raid is."

"Who's raiding it? Not just your fellows."

"All our fellows are in it, but the raid was partly our fellows, partly the state cops. The orders came from the county attorney's office. They didn't tell us anything about it till around nine o'clock. They didn't want any leak. There isn't any of our fellows would spill the beans, but the county attorney wanted to make sure."

"Now maybe you're ready to tell me what *kind* of a raid it is."

"It's a dirty show. Spangler imported in some women from Allentown and Bethlehem, and they're putting on a dirty show. Spangler didn't invite any of the local men, or anyway only two or three. He's charging five dollars a head admission. Men from Gibbsville and Reading, Hazleton. Business men. Sports. Somebody tipped off the county attorney, and he notified the state cops. They got here around nine o'clock and told us about it so we wouldn't look bad. McCumber, Jefferson, O'Dwyer, and Snyder. Those are our men. The state cops are some in uniform and some in plain clothes."

"Who will they arrest? Spangler and the women. But those business men, they won't arrest them."

"No, they won't arrest them. But the county attorney, Millner, he's there and he'll recognize them, most of them, anyway."

"How nice for Millner. He's going to run for judge this year."

"You don't have to look at it that way. Millner's doing his job. And he could of left us out in the cold. We get just as much credit as anybody else. Millner's all right."

"Well, this won't do him any harm. Raiding a dirty show, and getting something on all those business men. They'll shell out when he starts running for judge."

"Why shouldn't they? You always take the opposite side. You don't believe any cop is honest. Or politician."

"As far as I know, *you're* honest, Ken."

"I'm pretty honest. And I don't like dirty shows in this town. McCumber don't either. This is a pretty clean town, considering. We got a lot of church people here."

"You don't have to tell me," said Harvey Hunt. "Are they bringing them in here, the prisoners?"

"Bringing them here, then we gotta wake up Squire Palsgrove if he's home asleep. They'll get a hearing, and I guess most likely keep them here overnight. Take them to the county jail tomorrow. It depends on if they get somebody to go their bail tonight."

"Depends on how high the bail is."

"It'll be as high as Squire Palsgrove can make it. That you can be sure of."

"You say the women came from Allentown?"

"Allentown and Bethlehem, according to what I heard. Three of them and their pimp. They're supposed to come from Allentown, but who knows where they come from originally? Allentown is what they say, Allentown and Bethlehem. But they might as well come from New York City."

"Or South Taqua," said Harvey.

"There you go again, always taking the opposite side."

"I was just kidding you, Ken."

"I don't say we don't have some immoral women in South Taqua. That wouldn't be true. You'll come across immoral women everywhere you go, I guess. That's been my experience. But we never had a whorehouse in South Taqua since Mc-Cumber was chief of police. McCumber won't tolerate it, and I won't either. The people don't want a whorehouse in this town."

"It would save some of the men a trip to Taqua."

"Taqua and South Taqua are a very different thing. They got three times our population in Taqua. Maybe we get a black eye for having this raid in South Taqua, but it'll be worth it to get rid of Buddy Spangler. He don't care anything about the reputation of this town, or else he wouldn't let them put on a dirty show in his place."

"What kind of a dirty show is it?"

"How should I know what kind? They're all the same, aren't they?"

"Did you ever see one?" said Harvey.

Ken paused. "Yes, I saw one."

"Not here in town, though."

"No, not here in town. Wilkes-Barre, when I was a young fellow. Before I was a police officer. Some little town outside of Wilkes-Barre. There was things went on you wouldn't believe if you didn't see them with your own eyes. You'd wonder how a woman could stoop so low. I was around nineteen or twenty at the time, and I never forgot it."

"What were *you* doing there?"

"What was I doing? You mean why did I go? Well, in those days I wasn't married, and just like all the young fellows my age I was after all I could get. We all went after as much as we could get. I had a friend of mine had an auto. It was a big old second-hand Chandler. We used to drive around every Sunday afternoon, him and I. Half of those girls never had a ride in an automobile, and all we had to do was open the door and they'd get in. I used to raise a lot of hell in those days."

"And you were a good-looking fellow before you began to put on that weight."

"I sowed my wild oats. But as soon as I got married I settled down. With some fellows it's just the opposite. They get married, and they're no sooner married than they start chasing after other women. I don't believe in that. You marry a woman, you ought to settle down. Unless *she* won't settle down. But that don't often happen . . . Car outside. I guess that's them."

The office door opened and the newcomers streamed in. There were three women, each carrying a small overnight bag and keeping close to each other; there were five men. It was easy to tell which man was Spangler, and which was Millner, the county attorney. Spangler was wearing a suede windbreaker and a hunting cap. He was dissolute-looking and harassed, and except for Millner the other men pushed him around. Millner was very much in charge, better dressed than the others, who were police officers in plain clothes.

"Here they are, Sergeant," said Millner. "Will you call up Squire Palsgrove? I'd like to get them committed as soon as possible."

"Snyder, you call the squire. I want to book these people. Your name?" said Ken.

"You know my name."

"Come on, Spangler. Answer my questions. I don't know your first name."

"Marvin J. Spangler."

"Age?"

"Thirty-seven."

"Occupation?"

"Hotelkeeper."

"You don't have a license to run a hotel."

"Then put down—restaurant proprietor."

"Rest. Prop.," Ken wrote in the book. "Address?"

"You know that. Washington Street."

"You ever been arrested before?"

"Plenty."

"What's the charge, Mr. Millner?" said Ken.

"Chief, do you want to make the charges?" said Millner.

"Conspiring to give an indecent performance," said Mc-Cumber. "Disorderly conduct. Resisting arrest. Illegal possession of firearms. Selling intoxicating liquor without a license. Lewd and immoral conduct. Running a bawdyhouse. We got him on about ten counts. Lock him up, Snyder."

Snyder, one of the plainclothes policemen, took Spangler's arm and led him out of the office to a cell.

"All right, young woman," said Ken. "Your name."

"Gloria Swanson."

"Don't get fresh here. I said your name."

"Mary Smith."

"Mary Smith, huh," said Ken. "Age?"

"Twenty," said Mary Smith. The others laughed.

"You must of had a hard life," said Ken. "Occupation?"

"Manicurist," said Mary Smith.

"She really is, too," said one of the other women.

"I didn't ask you," said Ken. "Address?"

"Bellyvue Stratford Hotel, Philadelphia. Bellyvue. Get it?" The men and women laughed.

"Ever been arrested before?" said Ken.

"Never," said Mary Smith, and the women laughed.

"How many times you been arrested before, Mary Smith?" said Ken.

"I don't know. I didn't keep a diary."

"What's the charge, Chief?" said Ken.

"Against all three of these women, indecent performance, indecent exposure, soliciting, illegal possession of narcotics. No, strike that out. We only found narcotics on this one. Jefferson, take her back and put her in Cell Two."

"You're not gonna put me in a cell with that Spangler gorilla," said Mary Smith.

"You'll be with the other women," said McCumber. He nodded to Jefferson, who led her out.

A second woman now stood before Ken. "My name is Jane Doe, age twenty, address Seventh and Hamilton, Allentown, PA. Occupation, artist's model. No previous arrests. And did anybody ever tell you you look like Bryant Washburn, because you do?"

"Seventh and Hamilton?" said Ken. "That's where the monument is."

"I know. I live up there on top of the monument."

"Cut the comedy," said Ken. "Snyder, put her in with the other one, Cell Two."

"Do I get anything to eat here? I'm hungry. If I pay for it myself can I send out for something to eat?" said Jane Doe.

"What do you want?" said Ken.

"Steak tartare with a raw egg on top. Here's a buck, that oughta take care of it. And tea with lemon and sugar."

"We'll see. Go on, beat it," said Ken. "Chief, I understood they had a pimp with them."

"He got away," said McCumber. "We don't know how he got away, but he got away all right. He won't get far, the state police'll pick him up."

"All right, you, young woman," said Ken. "Your name."

"Jean Latour."

"How do you spell that?" said Ken.

"J, e a, n, capital L, a t, o, u, r."

"Age what?"

"Seventeen."

Ken looked at her. "I almost believe you. How old *are* you?"

"I'll be eighteen on my next birthday."

"You're starting early," said Ken.

"Huh. I started before this."

"How many arrests?"

"None. I was never arrested before."

"Where do you live? On top of the monument with that Smith woman?"

"That was Jane, that lived on top of the monument. Mary lives at the Bellyvue. Bellyvue. Funny." She giggled.

"We book this one on the same charges, Chief?" said Ken.

"This one was the worst," said McCumber.

"The best, you mean. I get the most pay," said Jean.

"You'll need it," said Ken. "What occupation?"

"Dancer and actress. And *singer,*" said Jean.

"Put down prostitute for this one," said McCumber.

"All right, put down prostitute. I don't give a damn. Put down whore if you want to."

"The youngest, and the worst," said McCumber.

"Give me a cigarette, somebody," said Jean.

Harvey offered her his pack, as the others remained still. "You don't look like a cop. What are you, a lawyer?"

"I'm a reporter."

"Oh, are you gonna take my picture?"

"No."

"Then give me a good writeup, if you're not gonna take my picture. What paper is it gonna be in?"

"The Taqua *Chronicle.*"

"The what?"

"The Taqua *Chronicle.*"

"I never heard of it," she said. "Is that just local?"

"That's all," said Harvey.

"Oh, *well.* The hell with *that.* I thought maybe you were on some big paper, from Philly. But you're just a hick reporter, like these hick cops." She spat the smoke out of her lungs. "I have a proposition. You're the chief, huh?"

"I'm the chief," said McCumber.

"But he's higher than you," said Jean, pointing the cigarette at Millner. "Who do I have to talk to to get out of this?"

"Save your breath," said Millner.

"I don't want to spend the night with those other girls. I never saw them before tonight. How about if you get me a room in the hotel? I don't care which one of you. I'll give you a good time."

McCumber and Millner were silent, but she did not give up.

"All right. I tell you what I'll do. Get me a room in the hotel, and whatever I make I'll split with you, fifty-fifty."

Millner and McCumber were still silent.

"Then how about this? You can have all I make over ten dollars."

The silence continued.

"What's the *matter* with you? Don't you have any manhood? You? Reporter? Will you help me out?"

"I don't have the say," said Harvey.

"Take her back and put her in a cell," said Ken.

The telephone rang, and Ken answered it. "Police headquarters, Sergeant Dunlop. Yeah. Yeah. Oh. All right, Mrs. Palsgrove." He hung up. "That was Mrs. Palsgrove. Squire couldn't get his car started, and she don't want him out in this cold. He won't be here tonight. Now what do we do, Chief?"

"Up to Mr. Millner," said McCumber.

"Nothing we can do. Leave these people here tonight and give them a preliminary hearing in the morning. We can hold the women for a medical examination anyway, that's the law. We'll take all four of them to Gibbsville tomorrow and put them in the county jail."

"You're not gonna put me in any jail," said Jean. "I want a lawyer."

"You can get one tomorrow, but you're still going to jail. You admit you're a prostitute," said Millner.

"You can't prove it. I was never arrested before in my whole life, you dirty son of a bitch," said Jean. "You. Reporter. You put it in the paper that I asked for a lawyer, and they wouldn't let me have one. You didn't arrest any of those johns. Who was that hot-pants funnyman that got up on the stage, that respectable business man? He was as much in the act as anybody. But I don't see *him* here. You let him put his clothes on and get away, but he was as much in it as we were."

"Who was it, Millner?" said Harvey, grinning.

"Never you mind, Hunt," said Millner. "Don't you start poking your nose in where it doesn't belong."

"That's what I do for a living, Millner," said Hunt. "If this broad finds out who the business man was, she could subpoena him when she goes to trial."

"Who's going to help her find out? You?" said Millner.

"Well, I could," said Harvey.

"Yes, I suppose you could," said Millner.

"And you don't want that, do you?" said Harvey. "If this kid gets herself a smart lawyer, somebody like Bob Dockstader, Dockstader could subpoena your business man and maybe he could even subpoena some of the other sports, the ones you didn't arrest."

"Say, Hunt, are you a reporter or what are you?" said Millner. He turned to McCumber. "What about this fellow, Chief? Is he in some kind of a racket?"

"Not that I know of, but he's very contrary," said McCumber.

"He's against everything," said Ken. "If you're *for* something, he'll be against it. He's an againster."

"Oh, one of those," said Millner. "Well, Hunt, what is it you want? Not that I couldn't get you fired in one phone call. Your boss is a man I know better than you do."

"You could get me fired, all right. But if you did, then believe me I'd go right to Bob Dockstader, and the two of us would have a lot of fun with you when you get into court. You just threatened me, Millner, so now I'm not on your side at all. Maybe I was before, but I'm not now."

"I didn't threaten you. I said I *could* get you fired, but I never said I was going to," said Millner.

"Nuts. I know what you're thinking, Millner. You're thinking this kid and Spangler and the others will plead guilty and there won't be any trial. That's the way it always works in these cases. But you respectable lawyers don't think much of Dockstader, and he doesn't like you either. Dockstader would plead them all not guilty just for the fun of it."

"Everybody knows what Dockstader is," said Millner. "These are the kind of people he has for clients. What I want to know is, what do you want? Speak up. You want something."

"Let this kid off," said Hunt.

"Let her off? You're crazy. She was the worst of all four of them," said Millner.

"That's right, there were four. The pimp you let get away. All these South Taqua cops and the state police, but the pimp eluded your grasp. The pimp and your business man were the only ones that got away. Can you imagine Dockstader when he gets you all in court. I can just see it. The courtroom'll be crowded. Probably Number Three Courtroom. And Dock-stader starts asking a lot of embarrassing questions. The whole thing will be embarrassing anyway. Millner, you taking charge of the raid personally, and Dockstader will want to know why. Chief, you letting the pimp get away. And all these prominent guys under subpoena."

"What are you trying to do, Hunt?" said Millner.

"I don't know. But I never like it when some politician says he'll get me fired. Oh, I know I'll be out of a job tomorrow, but I've been out of work before."

"Just out of curiosity, why do you want me to go easy on this Latour woman?" said Millner.

"I didn't say I wanted you to go easy on her. I said let her go."

"Why? What's she to you?" said Millner.

"Yeah, I don't understand it myself," said Jean Latour. "I never saw him before I came in here."

"Because she's pretty, and I like pretty dames," said Harvey.

"That's not your reason," said Millner.

"Then you tell me what my reason is. I don't know. She said she was never arrested before, and I believe her. Maybe that's the reason."

"Maybe she was never arrested before, although I doubt that. But if you could have seen her an hour ago you wouldn't worry so much about whether she was arrested or not. Ask any of these police officers. This young woman has absolutely no morals. In all my—"

"That's a speech you can save till you take her to court," said Harvey.

"You didn't even pay your way in, did you, Mister?" said Jean. "What are you squawking about? The johns that were there all paid to get in. And it was private."

"Hunt, even you can see that this young woman has no morals. The only thing that counts with her is money. No guilty feelings, no regrets. Only money."

"You know, Millner, you put your finger on it. I've been trying to dope out why I'm on her side, and you found the reason for me. She has no morals."

"Then what are you defending her for?" said Millner.

"Because I never saw anybody like her before. She isn't like those other dames. She doesn't even look like them. She's a very unusual dame. But if you throw her in the clink, she'll be just like all the others."

"I told you," said Ken to Millner. "He likes to be different. Always different. He comes in here every day and there's hardly a day he don't come out with some new idea. Wants to be different. I think he's a Socialist, into the bargain."

"The hell I am," said Harvey. "But different, yes. Come to think of it, I voted for you, Millner. Because it didn't look like you had a chance."

"Appreciate that, I'm sure," said Millner.

"That's all right. I won't vote for you for judge."

"Hunt, we've had enough talk from you. You're only a reporter, and you wouldn't be here if you didn't work for the *Chronicle*. So shut up. You have your story, so shut up and get out." The speaker was McCumber, the police chief.

"Okay," said Harvey. "But Millner knows where I'm going tomorrow morning, first thing. I know I won't have a job tomorrow, but I'm sure as hell going to call on the Honorable Mr. Dockstader. Then we'll watch the fur fly."

Millner was frowning, deep in thought and trying to make a decision. "Chief," he said to McCumber. "We have Spangler and those two women in there. I'll let them plead guilty and go to prison. But if this fellow and Dockstader get together, there'll be a court trial and a lot of pretty well-known men will have to appear. You know what Dockstader is like when he gets somebody on the stand, and a lot of reputations will be ruined. If this goes to trial there'll be no stopping Dockstader, you know that."

"That shyster lawyer," said McCumber. "He ought to be disbarred."

"And some day maybe he will be. I'd like to help bring that about," said Millner.

"And I'll tell him you said that in front of five police officers, Millner," said Harvey. "I just want to remind you, Millner. Dockstader has never been up on charges before the Bar Association, but you and the chief have been making statements about him, *in front of witnesses,* that he could sue you for. These cops are officers of the law, and they won't all perjure themselves to protect you and McCumber."

Millner realized he had made a mistake. "I'd be glad to take my chances if Dockstader wanted to sue."

"You're bluffing. These are good cops, and they won't lie on the stand to save your neck. Also, Millner, you're from Gibbsville, not South Taqua. Here they don't like Gibbsville people very much. But you were saying something to the chief, and I don't want to interrupt that."

"I'd like to give you a punch in the nose, but I'll deny myself that luxury," said Millner. "Chief, if you have no serious objection, I'm willing to let this Latour woman go. Provided that she leaves here tonight, right away, and this fellow Hunt goes with her."

"Hey, Reporter! You got me off," said Jean Latour. "Do you have a car?"

"Not so fast," said Harvey.

"Now what do you want?" said Millner.

"Two weeks' pay, at thirty-five dollars a week. That's what the paper would give me if they fired me. I've been with them three years."

Millner took a roll of bills from his pants pocket. "Here's your seventy dollars. On your way."

"And don't come back," said McCumber. "You or the woman. Snyder, you go with them and see that they leave town."

"I want to go to the boarding-house and get my other suit."

"See that he packs his suitcase and is out of town in a half an hour," said McCumber. "Go on, get them all out of here." McCumber was displeased with Millner's deal. He hardly looked at Millner.

"You gotta give me more than a half an hour, McCumber," said Hunt. "I have to stop and get my arctics at the Athens, and I don't know how long it'll take me to get my car started."

"Go on, get out. Just get out," said McCumber.

"Well, Miss Latour," said Harvey. "Fate has thrown us together."

"Yeah," she said. "Well, goodbye, boys, no hard feelings."

"Goodbye, you guys," said Harvey.

The cops did not respond, vocally or otherwise.

"Come on, little one," said Harvey.

"One thing," said Jean to the men. "I still never been in jail."

Snyder gave Jean and Harvey a couple of hard nudges, and all three left the room. "Wow, is it always as cold as this?" said Jean.

"I have to stop and get my arctics," said Harvey.

"I oughta brought along a pair of arctics," said Jean. "What kind of a car do you have? I hope it's a closed car."

"It's a Ford coop."

"Does it have a heater in it? Where we going?"

"Where do you want to go?"

"I got a friend of mine I can stay with her, in Allentown."

"Where do *you* live? Where is home base for you?" said Harvey.

"You mean where do I keep my wardrobe?" she said. "I got most of it in my room, in Philly. I got a room in a hotel there. I didn't bring much tonight. You don't need much on this kind of a job."

"No, I guess not." They were outside the Athens. "Here's where I left my arctics. Do you want a cup of coffee? Snyder, how about you? You want a cup of coffee?"

"My orders are to—"

"Aw, come off it, Snyder. Have a cup of coffee with us," said Harvey.

"Listen, you," said Snyder. "Quit stalling around. Get your arctics and then we go to your boarding-house, and you get the hell out of town."

"What are *you* so sore about all of a sudden?" said Harvey.

"This here little tramp ought to be run out of town on a rail, and you're no better. I should of known all along what you were. A lousy pimp."

"I'll be right out," said Harvey. He entered the Athens, put on his arctics, and returned to the sidewalk, where the girl and the policeman were staring at each other.

The cold wind discouraged conversation during the three-block walk to Harvey's boarding-house. "If you're in such a hurry, Snyder, you can see if you can get my car started. The key's in it. Kid, you can sit in the car with him while he warms up the engine."

"She don't sit in any car with me," said Snyder. "She can wait inside with you. And you be out in ten minutes or I'll come and get you."

In about fifteen minutes Jean and Harvey were ready to drive away. "Well, Snyder, South Taqua is safe once more. No more sin in South Taqua."

"Birds of a feather flock together," said Snyder.

"Goodbye, copper. Keep your knees together," said Jean.

"Get outa here, you little bum."

"We're off!" said Harvey. "Off in a cloud of dust."

"Where to?" said the girl.

"Well, we'll try Allentown first. Maybe if the roads aren't too bad we can make Philly tonight."

"Let's try to get to Philly," she said.

It was about thirty-five miles to Allentown and the road was sometimes blown clean by the valley winds, sometimes they had to proceed in low gear through snow and ice. The girl fell asleep ten minutes out of South Taqua and stayed asleep until Harvey found a garage in Allentown that was still open. Drowsy, the girl said she wanted to continue to Philadelphia, and almost immediately fell asleep again.

On North Broad Street, when they were getting closer to City Hall, Harvey shook her knee until she came awake. This time she was fully awake. "Why look where we are. Old Willie Penn. Boy, I'm glad I'm not sitting up there with him, like Jane. What's on top of the monument in Allentown?"

"Do you want to go back and look?" said Harvey. "Where is this hotel you stay at?"

"You go around City Hall and then on Market Street I'll show you," said Jean Latour. "They'll be surprised to see *me*."

"They may be surprised to see me, too," said Harvey.

"Not as much," she said.

It was not a hotel of faded elegance; it was an establishment that had never had any grandeur, built and furnished for the brief accommodation of transients. The atmosphere, and the night clerk, proclaimed the motto: No questions asked.

"Hello, Jean," said the night clerk. "Back already?"

"I couldn't stay away from you," she said. "You know that, Albert. Any messages for me?"

"Not since I came on. I'll look in your box. No. Nothing there. Do you have your key?"

"I got my key."

"The elevator's out of order again. You'll have to walk up," said Albert. "Your friend gonna register?"

"No, he's with me," said Jean.

"That'll be one dollar," said Albert.

"If you don't register you have to give Albert a dollar," said Jean.

"Either that or I have to charge her the double rate," said Albert.

"But this goes into your pocket," said Harvey.

"Yeah, I get a dollar. The other way, she has to pay the double rate, or else I have to register you and charge you for a single."

"Oh, I don't mind paying the buck. I just didn't understand the racket, but now I do," said Harvey.

"Where's Henry?" said Jean. "He ought to be here to carry our baggage upstairs. I give him enough tips."

"I sent him home early. He was coughing, coughing, coughing, and I didn't want to catch his God damn cold."

"All right, we'll carry our own."

Her room was three flights up but they were not long flights. Above the main floor the rooms were low-ceilinged. In Jean's room there was a double brass bed. Harvey looked at the bed and said, "What's this going to cost me?"

"Well, I know you only have around seventy dollars on you," she said.

"Not only *on* me, but that's my entire bankroll. I have to get a job quick, and probably sell my car."

"What would you say to five dollars? I usually get more. Twenty-five I been getting. I only take a few regulars."

"Five is all right," he said. "Maybe if I get a job in Philly I'll get to be one of your regulars."

"Maybe, who knows?" she said.

"At least it's warm here," he said. "This is where you make your headquarters?"

"It's one of the places. Why, because you don't see my wardrobe?"

"Not only that. It doesn't look as if you spent much time here."

"You're very observing," she said. "All right, I'll tell you. I got a keeper, an old guy around fifty years of age. He has an apartment. That is, I have, and he pays for it. That's where I live, mostly."

"Where is he now?"

"In Florida. Palm Beach, Florida. But I couldn't bring you to the apartment. I don't trust the elevator man. He spies on me."

"How can you take a chance on lousing up that arrangement?"

"You mean like working for Spengler, or Spangler, or whatever his name is? How much do you think I got tonight? Well, I'll tell you. I got a hundred dollars from Spengler-Spangler, and if it wasn't for those cops I would have picked up easily another hundred. Easily. There was one guy there tonight, I think he was a bootlegger. I could of got a hundred from just him. He was flashing money around there like it was going out of style. He gave Mary ten dollars just to sit on one guy's lap. He wanted to see what the guy would do if he got a naked girl on his lap."

"What did he do?"

"Oh—started to wrestle around with her. This bootlegger wanted me to go back to Griggsville with him."

"Gibbsville."

"Yeah. He had some scheme. I don't know what."

"But you were taking a big chance, going up to South Taqua. As it was, you got pinched."

"I know. But *you* sit around doing nothing, going to the movies, and the elevator man spying on you. See how long before *you* went crazy. I heard about this chance to make a few dollars and have a little fun, and Spangler guaranteed me there wouldn't be any trouble. That Spangler, I shoulda known he was a small-time smallie. I hope they give him ten years. Do you know what he got those other girls for? Twenty-five apiece. And what will they get out of it? What kind of a rap will they get, do you know?"

"Oh—six months, maybe. They'll plead guilty and get off pretty light."

"Six months! You call that light?"

"They could get more, if Millner wanted to get tough with them. But he's only after two things. He wants to put Spangler away, and he wants to have this hanging over some of those men that were there. He's going to run for county judge, and that costs money in Lantenengo County. Every little bit helps."

"I didn't trust him either. All that time he was calling me names, if there was nobody else there I could tell by the way he was looking at me."

"I'm not so sure. Millner's supposed to be a family man. In politics he's a double-crosser and everything else. But I never heard about him and the women."

"You make me laugh," she said. "You stood up for me, but I know why and so do you. There's only the two kinds of men. The real queers, that get sick if a woman touches them. They can't help it, they were born that way, and I'm afraid of some of *them*. But the others, I don't care if they're a family man or a priest or what, if they can like one woman they can like them all. And if they don't like me, believe me, I know what they are. All those cops tonight, I could of got a week's pay out of all of them. Even the old chief, he was afraid to look at me."

"What about the fellow behind the desk? The sergeant?"

"Him? Oh, boy. He was kind of handsome-looking, too. I bet I could have got him to let me go before the night was over."

"Where did you get all this information? When did you start finding out so much about men?"

She laughed. "They always want to know that. Simple. When I was a kid, one of the towns where I lived there was a man there that if I put my hand in his pocket he let me keep what I found. The son of a bitch, he used to put five or ten pennies there ahead of time, never anything big like a quarter.

Cheap thrill for him, but I didn't care. I used to pester him to let me put my hand in his pocket. It's a wonder I have any teeth left, I used to eat so much candy."

"Did you know what he was doing?"

"What he was doing, or what I was doing? Sure. How could I help it? The penny game. I knew what was there besides those pennies. It wasn't his *coat* pocket, for God's sake. I probably would have got him up to a dollar bill, most likely, but we had to move to another town. Otherwise I probably wouldn't have a tooth left in my head. I used to eat those penny creams, and do you remember those peanut-butter bolsters, all covered with chocolate? Every day after school. One day I ate ten of those penny creams and I got sick, and that took away my taste for creams. But carmels I liked. I guess they were good for my teeth, you had to chew carmels. Look. See my teeth? I have these two fillings and that's all."

"And what did you do in the next town?"

"The next town? You mean when we moved from Pittsburgh?"

"Wherever the guy was that you played the penny game with."

"That was Pittsburgh. Then we moved to Buffalo, New York, but we didn't stay there very long. My old man worked on the railroad and he got his leg cut off."

"Did he lose his job?"

"His job? He got killed."

"How old were you?"

"When my old man got killed? Search me. Ten? Eleven? I don't remember."

"Who took the place of the guy that gave you the candy money?"

"Where did I get money from? Why do you want to know that for?"

"Don't tell me if you don't feel like it," said Harvey.

"Oh, well, I might as well tell you. You couldn't report me to the police for that. I used to steal. Some boy I knew, the two of us used to go around and steal stuff. We used to steal things out of cars, and off of clotheslines. The five-and-dime. The most we ever got was five dollars, a fur neckpiece we swiped off a clothesline. The other kid used to take the stuff to some hockshop near where the boats came in. We never got what the stuff was worth. I'll bet you that fur neckpiece was worth a hundred dollars. Maybe more. But we only got five for it. Or that was what he said, the other kid. Maybe he was holding out on me. But we didn't stay there very long. My mother divided us up. I and my two older sisters went to live with my aunt and uncle. Paterson, New Jersey. And the three youngest to another aunt and uncle in Cleveland, Ohio."

"Where did your mother go?"

"Oh, she got sick. Consumption. She died, too. That was after I ran away. They wouldn't give us any money, and my two older sisters went to work in the mills. But I knew where he hid his money, my uncle, and I took a hundred and fifteen dollars and went to New York. He kept his money in a cigar box under the bathtub. I had a hard time finding it, but I knew it was somewhere in that house, so I used to search every room when they were out. They used to go to the eight o'clock Mass every Sunday, and I went to the nine. The children's Mass. So while they were out I gave that house a good going-over till I found out where he kept the money. There was over three hundred dollars in the box, but I only took a hundred and fifteen."

"Why a hundred and fifteen?"

"It was five twenties and three fives. Eight bills. In case he got back early from Mass I didn't want him to notice that some of it was gone. You know, if he took a quick look, he wouldn't notice only eight bills were gone. Unless he counted. If he counted, I was licked. But he came home from Mass, and I started out for the nine, only I never went to the church. I rode on a couple of trolleys and got to Newark and took the Tube to New York and went to the movies. The Rivoli. I sat in the back till my eyes got used to the dark and I could see better. Then I waited a while till I picked out some john that was there alone, and I got up and sat next to him."

"And then you were on your way," said Harvey.

"Not with the first one. He got up and changed his seat. But the next one I didn't have to do anything. He started on me, the second one. He sure did. He was a john, all right."

She laughed. "He took me to some hotel, a dump like this, and around ten o'clock that night I cried and said I was afraid to go home. My father would kill me. Kill him, too. I said I was gonna give myself up to the police. Well, we argued back and forth till finally he gave me all he had on him, sixty or seventy dollars, and said I was to stay there till Tuesday and he'd come and take me away. To Florida. I knew he was never coming back, the son of a bitch, and I didn't care. I had about a hundred and eighty dollars, and I wasn't worried."

"Then what happened?"

"Well, the fellow that ran the hotel came to the room the next day. He said I had to get out, and I said the john was coming to get me the next day. The manager knew damn well he wasn't, but he said he'd give me till the next day. Well, about a half an hour later this woman came in my room. She pretended to feel sorry for me and all, but she was just sizing me up. Finally she said to me, she said she knew I was a little hooker and if I wanted to do business I had to do business with her. I swore up and down I didn't know what she was talking about, and I didn't know very much, to tell the truth. I could tell she wasn't sure whether I was telling the truth or not. She just couldn't figure me out. Then I said to her, I wasn't what she thought I was, but I ran away from home and the police would be looking for me. I said I had to stay there for a while and I had thirty dollars that the john gave me. I said I was a virgin, but if there was no other way to make money, I'd work for her. She fell for it. She said I didn't exactly have to work for her, but some johns liked it if a young girl was there to watch. And that was how I really got started."

"How long did you work there?"

"A week. She paid me fifty dollars for the week and my room rent, and at the end of the week I went down to Florida with her boy friend. He and I got married down there. He ran a clip-joint in Miami, and that was where I started singing."

"Oh, you sing?"

"You heard me tell those cops I was a singer. I sing as good as anybody around. I ought to be getting a thousand dollars a week. I can sing rings around Ruth Etting, *or* Helen Morgan. I traveled all over the country with a couple bands. Teddy Bryer. You ever hear of Teddy Bryer?"

"Yes, I heard of him."

"He came in the joint one night and heard me sing. Came back every night for a week, and when the band was going north I went with them."

"What about your husband?"

"Him. I walked out on him. He wanted Teddy to buy up my contract, a thousand dollars. Teddy hit him so hard I thought he killed him. Teddy knew I didn't have any contract. You don't know Teddy, I can see that. He punches first and argues after. He gets in trouble with everybody. The union. The dance-hall managers. He'll go right down in the crowd, come down off the bandstand, and punch some stranger and you won't ever know what Teddy had against him. That's what finally broke up the band, his bad temper. He beat up the piano player for making a play for me, and they took it up with the union. Teddy was fined and he refused to pay the fine."

"So that's what happened to Teddy Bryer. He used to play at the parks, near the place where you were tonight."

"Then I went with Bobby Beach and the Beach Boys. I made two records with them. I did the vocal on one and the other was a duet with Bobby. I did the vocal on 'Sunny Side of the Street.' The trouble with that was we made it for one of the small companies, and it was a lousy arrangement. Bobby wouldn't spend money for an arranger. He'd take the stock arrangements and fool around with them himself, to save a dollar. If I could have stayed with Teddy six more months he was just beginning to get in good with Victor again. He had some fight with them, too. He fought with everybody."

"Well, you're a girl of many talents," said Harvey.

"You think you're sarcastic, but I do have one talent, and that's singing. I know what you had reference to, but some day you can forget all about that. You and everybody else. Because I'll tell you something, boy. The way those cops looked at me tonight, and you saw them. That's the way the people look at me when I sing, even with a lousy band like Bobby Beach behind me. You ask the musicians. What girl singer is the best? They'll name off Ruth Etting, Helen Morgan, Lee Wiley, half a dozen others. But the musicians that heard me, they'll tell you. And they know."

"Well, you're still young."

"You bet I am. Some day you'll be bragging that you laid Jean Latour. And people won't believe you."

"Well, so far I don't believe it myself. And you know what, kid? I'm dead tired."

"You mean you just want to sleep?"

"You had a nap in the car."

"Yes, I'm ready to go. I can stay up the rest of the night."

"How about if I grab about an hour? What will you do?"

"I'll take a bath," she said.

"Just give me about an hour," he said. The long day, the cold drive, the warmth of the room made sleep, just a little sleep, more desirable than the girl. There was, in fact, and considering the girl's build, a strange absence of urgency in his desire for her. He had not yet touched her body, although he had every intention of doing so. He was not going to leave this room unsatisfied, and his willingness to postpone his pleasure with her now, in favor of sleep, was so that when he awoke he would be strong and virile.

"I'm gonna turn on the water in the bathtub," she said. "Will it keep you awake?"

"Nothing'll keep me awake, now," he said. He got out of his suit and shirt and lay on the bed in his B. V. D.'s. He heard the water plunging into the tub, and in two minutes he was dead asleep.

When his sleep was over, that first heavy sleep, the room was dark, but he was a man who had slept in many places and at odd times of day and night, and he awoke knowing exactly where he was. He looked at his wristwatch, glowing in the dark, and guessed that he had been unconscious about two hours. His next conscious thought was the irritating observation that he was alone in the bed. He would have liked to wake up with her beside him and to give her a good lay, perhaps even before she was fully awake. He fumbled around for a match or a light switch. He could find neither, and he got out of bed and by following the length of the bed went straight to the hall door, and now he found the light switch in the wall. He went to the window and pulled the shade aside. First light had come. Now he had a look in the bathroom and saw that there were still a couple of inches of water in the tub and it did not appear to be water that anyone had used for a bath. No human body had been in that water, and the soap in the dish was dry and hard, the rubber sponge was brittle.

Little by little he began to realize that when she left the room she had taken away everything that belonged to her. There were some cigarette butts in the ash trays, and in the bathroom a small bottle containing a couple of powdery aspirins. But everything else was gone, and he remembered now that there never had been much of hers in the room. Immediately he made a couple of quick steps to his suit, which lay on an easy chair. As he knew it would be, his wallet was empty of money; in his pants pockets she had left a five-dollar bill and eighty-four cents in coins.

"Not even rolled," he said aloud. He laughed angrily at himself. "Not even rolled, not even laid, not even got a hangover." He took the receiver off the hook and waited for the switchboard to respond. He waited and waited before he got a response.

"Hello?"

"Hello, Albert. Did I interrupt your sleep?"

"No, I had the buzzer off. I didn't take notice to the light flashing," said Albert.

"Did our young lady leave any message for me?"

"No, she didn't say anything. I got her a taxi and she left here about an hour ago, I guess it was."

"Do you know where she went? Not that you'd tell me."

"Well, I don't know for sure *where* she went."

"But you have a pretty good idea," said Harvey.

"I guess that's right."

"But you wouldn't tell *me*," said Harvey.

"No."

"Why did she take all her stuff with her? I understood she had this room on a permanent basis."

"All her stuff? She didn't have much stuff. She paid up for the last couple days and checked out. You can stay there till tonight if you want to. The room's paid for till six o'clock tonight."

"She walked off with my bankroll, but you don't know anything about that, do you?"

"No, but what the hell? You weren't born yesterday. You

didn't look to me like some college kid. You been around, I
could see that."

"I'd like to get that money back, or some of it. I'll give
you ten bucks for her address and phone number."

"You don't *have* ten bucks, you just said. No, I don't know
her phone number, so I couldn't give you that if I wanted to.
And I wouldn't give you her address. Not for ten bucks, anyway."

"Did you ever lay her, Albert?"

"Why?"

"I just wondered whether it was because you liked her
personally, or the little tips you get."

"Oh, well I guess it's both. I laid her one time."

"Only once? Wouldn't you like to again?"

"Well, she's pretty. She sure is built. But I could get fired
if I let her stay here free."

"She's too expensive for you," said Harvey. "When do
you guess she'll be back here again?"

"I wouldn't want to make a guess on that. She comes and
goes. Like maybe I won't see her for weeks at a time, then
she'll have the room for a whole week. She had some piano
player here for over a week one time. He was a piano player in
some orchestra down on South Broad Street. A baldheaded
fellow. He'd roll in here drunk every night, and she'd be here
all day, till it was time for him to go to work. I'd come on
about my usual time, eight o'clock, and they'd just be leaving."

"I understand she's a pretty good singer," said Harvey.

"That's the first I ever heard of it, but that wouldn't prove
anything. I only know her from coming in here. She has some
rich guy, but she sure is the little two-timer."

"And yet I like her, don't you?"

"Well, yes, I guess so, and she's only a kid. But when it
comes to money—oh, boy. They ought to have her over at the
Bourse."

"Well, I guess you're not going to help me out with her address," said Harvey.

"No. You gotta find that out for yourself, but this is a big
city. If I was you, buddy, the best thing is to forget about it.
You got taken. Too bad. But look at me. I got asthma. I think
I get it from the soap they use here, scrubbing the floors."

"If I get my money back I'll buy you a bottle of cologne," said Harvey. "It's all right for me to leave my suitcase here?"

"Till six o'clock tonight. If you want a cheaper room, I got one for a dollar and a half a night. It's an inside room, quiet. And the weekly rate is nine dollars, the same as if you were getting one night free. You share a toilet and a shower with another guy, but he's away a good deal of the time. He's a salesman, an elderly bachelor or maybe a widower, I don't know which. That's as good as you'll find anywhere in town."

"And I may run into Jean if she comes back here. I'll let you know tonight," said Harvey.

As a reporter he was pleased with the information he had extracted from Albert, and reasonably confident that in one or two further conversations he would be successful in his attempt to learn Jean Latour's address. He went back to bed and slept until ten o'clock. He shaved and dressed and went out and had a good breakfast; fried eggs, French fries, toast and coffee. He was going to need all his strength.

He first went to the garage where he had left his car, and asked for the boss. "How much will you give me for the Ford coop?" said Harvey.

"I wouldn't give you five dollars for it," said the manager. "I can't use it."

"I paid six hundred for it a year ago, and it's in pretty good condition. Give me four hundred for it."

"No sale."

"Look at the rubber. Those are all new, all four."

"I can see that, but I'm not buying."

"Give me two hundred for it," said Harvey. "You can make yourself a quick hundred and a half on that. You know you can. I think you could probably get five hundred dollars for this car."

"Then you get it."

"Make me an offer. I need money quick. Or how much would you *lend* me on it?"

"I wouldn't lend you a nickel on a Lincoln phaeton," said the manager. "I'll give you seventy-five dollars for the car."

"Make it an even hundred."

"You got the papers on it?"

"I have the bill of sale, the registration, and my driver's

license. I'm a newspaper reporter, and I just lost my job. Will you give me a hundred?"

"All right, I'll give you a hundred dollars," said the manager. The papers were signed, the money handed over.

"I'll be interested to see what price you put on it," said Harvey.

"I'll show you," said the manager. He took a piece of soap and wrote on the windshield: "For Quick Sale—$495."

"Nice going," said Harvey.

"What the hell, you would of taken seventy-five," said the manager. "You got no kick coming."

"Only one thing more. Will you kiss me? I like to be kissed when I'm getting screwed," said Harvey.

"So long, buddy, I'm a busy man," said the manager.

Harvey returned to the hotel and paid a week's rent on the $1.50 room, commencing that night after six. He then went to Jean's room and made half a dozen telephone calls to newspaper offices. He had some luck. A day rewrite man on the *Public Ledger* agreed to meet him for a drink late in the afternoon; a copyreader on the *Inquirer* said he would nose around and see if there might be a job for him; a sportswriter on the *Evening Ledger* invited him to go to the fights that night and have drinks later with a fight promoter who was a soft touch for newspaper men. All at once Philadelphia was a warm and friendly town. At least it was a town of *brotherly* love, he told himself.

In a few days he had a job as a rewrite man on the morning *Ledger*. It paid forty dollars a week. It was not exactly what he wanted; he preferred to be a leg man, but he did not know Philadelphia too well; his personal acquaintance with the geography of the city was only less limited than his contacts with the police and other such news sources. But rewrite was a job he could hold down, and live on, while he was getting better acquainted in the city. Accidentally Jean Latour had done him a couple of favors by getting him out of South Taqua and by stealing his money, but they were not favors he would have to return.

In the succeeding weeks he could find no one among his newspaper acquaintances who had ever heard of the girl, and he guessed that Albert had tipped her off that he was living at the Royal, which was the uninspired name of the hotel. Another guess that concerned Albert was a wrong one; Albert kept the secret of Jean's address, and with the occupational suspiciousness of a night clerk he refused to be drawn into conversation about the girl. Often at night Harvey would stop for a chat with Albert before going upstairs to bed. The Royal had no kitchen, and Albert brought his own lunch, to be eaten at midnight. Henry was always sent out to get hot coffee, and Harvey would sometimes order a container for himself. He had begun to like the Royal; it was certainly a more inviting place than the rooming-house in South Taqua, a cheerless room in a cheerless house, that he had gone to only for sleep. The Royal had the smell that went with the unending war against vermin, but it had the fascinatingly unwholesome human traffic of its lobby and elevator and halls. The majority of the male guests were horse-players, including two men who worked in bookmaking establishments. The women were anybody's women, trying not to think of the day when nobody would want them. It was an orderly place; the police had their instructions from the ward leaders, who got their own instructions from the landowners' representatives at district headquarters. Out in Chestnut Hill the real owners of the Royal were pleased with any property that paid its own way and showed a little profit; over on the Main Line it might not have pleased Mr. Gaston Pennington to learn that indirectly he was a minor contributor to the income of his cousins who owned the Royal. Gaston Pennington was the gentleman who supported Jean Latour.

For Harvey Hunt this was a period of contentment. The three years in South Taqua had been easy and not unpleasant, and should have provided contentment but had actually been a period of unrest. In South Taqua he did his work, the pay was not bad; he was given passes to the movie theater in Taqua and small discounts at the store where he bought his clothes. The business department helped him to buy a car. He was rewarded for small favors with the small graft that was a perquisite of small-town newspaper reporting. He gave the name and address of Levy's store when writing that Levy's daughter had won a mathematics prize at State, and Levy would pay for the puff with a free pair of shoes, Bostonians worth ten dollars a pair, retail. Harvey got a complimentary weekly five-dollar meal ticket at the Exchange Hotel for remembering to mention the hotel in his accounts of Rotary luncheons. He was not much of a drinker, but he would run up a bill for pints of whiskey at Mac McDonald's Pharmacy, and McDonald would forgive the debt in appreciation of an occasional news item that tied in with a paid advertisement of a shipment of exotic French perfumes and Eastman Kodaks.

Literary brilliance would have been wasted in the columns of the *Chronicle,* and Harvey Hunt was not the man who could supply it. He had not gone into the game as a trainee in belles-lettres. Until senior year in high school he had more or less wanted to try for an appointment to West Point or Annapolis, but his Congressman lived in the next county, and neither Harvey nor his father or mother knew exactly how to go about getting the appointment. It had not been a burning desire in any case. Harvey's father was station agent for the New York Central at Elk City in one of the sparsely populated northern counties of Pennsylvania, and he had wanted Harvey to learn a trade, but Harvey's mother had insisted on the boy's finishing high school.

The Hunts lived in an apartment on the second story of the Elk City railway station, and Mrs. Hunt earned three dollars a week on the local paper by reporting the comings and goings of her fellow citizens. It had not occurred to her that there might be a future in journalism for her son, but when Harvey wrote an account of an accident to a circus train a couple of miles down the track, she brought the article with her to the newspaper office. It was printed in its entirety, and the publisher of the paper said that Harvey had a real knack. Harvey received no payment for the article, but he was given his first byline, and his fate was sealed. At the end of high school he became a reporter at double his mother's salary.

The paper died three years later. It was not a paper that was much better or much worse than many others. It had been publishing for forty years, into the second generation of the family that founded it. It had never known any extensive prosperity. It had served the community reasonably well, but only as a convenience. There had rarely been any reason for a citizen to read the paper unless he were personally involved in the content, and between such personal involvements the citizen would lose interest in the paper. It made no difference to him whether the paper came out or not, and when finally publication was suspended no one asked, "What will we ever do without the *Constitution?*" The *Constitution* would be missed, they said, but there was no sense of emergency, no dramatic effort to revive the paper while there was still a chance. The publisher wept privately, settled with his creditors for fifteen cents on the dollar, and took a job in the county office of the Sealer of Weights and Measures. Only then did he realize that for fifteen years he had neglected to send away copies of his paper to be bound.

Paper by paper Harvey Hunt made his way southward through the Commonwealth, making friends with other newspaper men, but acquiring no other assets. On one paper he received pay for one week out of five; on another he was fired for using the publisher's office for a rendezvous with a young woman; on another paper he quit because he was not given a single day off during a twenty-one-day stretch. In Reading he was fired for lying about his salary on his previous job; in Allentown he was offered a five-dollar raise by the publisher of the Taqua *Chronicle,* who liked a story he wrote about a South Taqua mining disaster. There had never been any complaints about his work as such, and during his time in South Taqua he was given good reason to believe that he could stay there forever, eventually to take over as the publisher retired.

The publisher was a man who had other and more profitable interests than the *Chronicle:* a stone quarry, the gas company, half a block of business properties, and, through his wife's inheritance, a nice income from electric power and light. John Barringer was the *owner* of the *Chronicle,* and he made it pay. His interest in the paper was in making it pay, just as he made his stone quarry and his real estate pay, and if he was only vaguely aware of the existence of Munsey and Ochs, Pulitzer and Northcliffe, he was even less aware of the Kents and Chapins and Wattersons and Whites. He was an owner-publisher and not an editor-publisher. Nevertheless he ran a successful paper, because he published the kind of paper he liked to read and his preferences reflected the tastes of most of the solvent readers of his paper. To that extent he was a good editor by accident. When by accident something got into the *Chronicle* that he did not like, he nearly always learned next day that his readers had not liked it either. The *Chronicle* seldom carried a story longer than one column, and almost never was there a story that was given a two-column headline.

For Harvey Hunt that meant a lot of work; many news stories rather than one or two big ones. It was the best sort of training. Because he was under restrictions of space, he was prevented from acquiring bad stylistic habits. Because he was expected to bring in quantities of items, he learned not to waste time in useless questions. John Barringer, who literally could not have named the capital of Maryland and had never heard of Bonar Law, described Harvey Hunt as the best reporter he had ever known, and from time to time he would drop a clumsy hint that Harvey ought to settle down with a nice local girl and get ready to take over the managing of the *Chronicle*. Barringer was a man of his word, and Harvey Hunt knew that if he stayed on in South Taqua, Barringer would make it easy for him to buy the *Chronicle*. But Harvey grew restive under the gentle pressure from John Barringer. Without knowing what it was, without trying very hard to understand it, there was something about the life he led in South Taqua that was worse than being broke and jobless, and he never experienced the slightest regret either for leaving South Taqua or for the manner of his leaving. John Barringer would not have fired him for quarreling with Millner, but John Barringer would not have been able to help him understand why he wanted to come to the defense of a girl like Jean Latour. An older man ought to be able to understand such things, but John Barringer only understood that it was time to settle down with a nice local girl as a step toward taking over the *Chronicle*.

In Philadelphia, sitting behind the switchboard with Albert and listening to the horse-players' lies, Harvey Hunt was more truly at home than he had ever been. The Market Street trolleys did not have to make so much of a clangor, but at least they made it all the time, all through the night, so that you needed nothing else to tell you that South Taqua was past and gone. You could wake up in the dark of four A.M. and some angry motorman would stomp his bell for you, and you would go back to sleep. In a big city like Philadelphia there was always enough news to fill the paper. You did not have to worry about the news supply, as you did on a small-town paper. Harvey Hunt was appalled at the waste of news by the big city papers. In Philadelphia they had a Chinatown that should have provided hundreds of fascinating news items but was practically ignored; the city was a seaport, with ships arriving and sailing for places all over the world, but nobody ever did a story on the seaport. There was surely one good news story a day in each of the big department stores; stories in the theaters, among the highbrow musicians, in the fancy hotels. You simply could not have two million persons living together without creating the frictions that result in news items. To a man who had worked in the small towns of eastern Pennsylvania the city was inexhaustibly rich with unwritten columns of wonderful, exciting stuff. To Harvey Hunt, blasé was a word that went with long cigarette holders and the magazine *Vanity Fair,* and in the excitement of his first year in a big city he felt the need to live forever.

He saw a tall man in a brown broadcloth greatcoat with a fur collar, brown spats, brown Homburg, waxed moustache, and monocle. He saw the man again, and noticed that in the band of the Homburg, the man wore a tiny feather. He had never seen any such man in Allentown, but he saw him half a dozen times, and as the weather improved the man was in different costume but always had the glass in his eye or dangling from a thin cord. There was an elderly lady who rode around in a baby Renault towncar, which had a chauffeur and footman. There was no such turnout in Reading or Bethlehem. In the dead of winter he saw young men carrying oddly shaped tennis racquets, escorting young women carrying similar racquets. He had never seen any such racquets in Scranton or Wilkes-Barre. He had never seen a Negro policeman, or a Boy Scout wearing bare-kneed shorts, a subway or an "L" train, a fire-fighting water tower, an eight-oar shell or a single sculler, four Japanese couples in evening dress at a theater together, a department store with its own bugle corps, a house of prostitution where men went to meet other men, a butler in knee breeches (perhaps the father of one of those Boy Scouts?). He had never seen so many rich people, so many poor people, so many people, and he wanted to know all about all of them.

He began with the obvious ones, the men and women who worked on the paper with him. He had heard of them because of their bylines—the general news reporters, the political reporters, and the sports writers. They never looked the way he expected them to. Walter J. Bright, who covered major crimes of violence, should not have looked like a policeman but he might at least have looked like a private detective. Instead he was a short stout man who wore a slouch hat in and out of the office and believed that every man and woman was guilty as charged, should be sent to the electric chair, and would be so if it were not for the bungling and venality of the prosecutors. He was married and had a homely daughter who worked in the classified-ad department.

Theodore N. Kruger, the top political writer, was thin to the point of emaciation, and owed at least part of his success to his ability to sit up all night, drinking whiskey with the politicians and remembering what they told him when they, but not he, got drunk. He had a modest fortune, acquired by being let in on state and municipal real-estate deals. He would buy a piece of property, sell it to the city, and divide his profits with the proper officials, whose names were kept out of the original transactions. He was a Swarthmore graduate and eventually the one to enlighten Harvey Hunt on the oddly shaped tennis racquets.

Martha Swanson came as a surprise to Harvey Hunt. The stories he read under her byline were so completely unadorned with feminine touches—they were, in fact, stories that would not ordinarily have been assigned to a woman—that during his first weeks in the office he had her confused with Miss Pitney, a secretary in the financial department who affected Eton collars and Windsor ties, and wore rimless pince-nezs. Martha Swanson, although she usually wore tailored suits, was abundantly feminine. She wore single-pearl earrings and a seed-pearl necklace, and whether she had on one of her cashmere pull-

overs or a shirtwaist, her bosom was distracting. Between assignments she would sit at her desk, bent over a Modern
Library volume, chain-smoking, not taking off her hat, always
at the ready, so to speak. She was a trifle overweight, completely
at home in her surroundings, and Harvey Hunt guessed that all
romantic notions between her and the men on the staff were a
thing of the past. They referred to her as Swanson behind her
back, and she was always good for a five- or ten-dollar
touch. She appeared to be lazy, but when she went out on a
story she worked hard and efficiently. In time Harvey Hunt
learned that she was the daughter and only child of O. C.
Swanson, a San Francisco newspaper man and magazine writer
who was a friend of Herbert Hoover's *and* Woodrow Wilson's.
She was divorced from Don Bushmiller, the one-time Stanford
football and track star, and when Harvey Hunt asked her to
have dinner with him she smiled and said, "I don't see why
not."

They went to a more or less open speakeasy in an alley,
where the steaks and chops were reasonably priced and the
liquor was safe. She knew the waiters by name, and they
knew her tastes in food and drink. "You come here often?"
he said.

"Force of habit," she said. "It was the first place I went
to when I started working in Philly."

They had visitors from other tables, and the bill came to
fourteen dollars. "Have you got enough?" she said. "I have
some money, and there's no reason why you should buy drinks
for my friends."

"I can swing it," he said.

"Well, if you're sure. The next time we'll go Dutch. I make
more money than you do, and it isn't fair to have you pay for
those extra drinks. I mean it. Here, why don't we start now?
I'll pay half."

"All right, if you insist."

"You have to watch out for that Morton fellow. He'll sit all
night and never pay for a drink. He's that kind."

They walked to her flat—in another alley—and he was
overwhelmed by the presence of her books. From floor to ceiling three walls were covered with filled shelves. "They're not all

mine," she said. "Some of them were my father's. I got rid of a
lot when I left San Francisco, but they're beginning to pile up
again. I hate to part with a single one of them, but I have no
room for my pictures." In her bedroom the wall space was
taken by a profusion of Japanese prints and American mod-
erns. "All from San Francisco. The prints are good. They were
my father's and he knew what he was doing. The others are
mine, and it's too soon to say whether they'll stand the test of
time. I'm beginning to get tired of some of them. The ones I
liked the most when I bought them, I bought them for their
colors, but they're going to be the first to go the next time I
move. Do you care anything about pictures?"

"Not very much," he said.

"If you want to use the bathroom, there it is. Would you
like a drink? I have some gin and some rye. I'm going to have a
rye and ginger ale. You?"

"Okay," he said.

While he was in the bathroom she stood behind a screen
and changed into a pajama suit. "Your drink is on the brass
tray. I'll be with you in a minute."

She rejoined him presently and sat with her legs folded
under her on a studio couch.

"Do you mind if I ask, is that a picture of you in the bathroom?"

"The nude, you mean? Yes, that's me. As I was six years
ago. Seven."

"Who painted it?"

"People always ask that. It was painted by a man that
didn't like women, obviously, but I think it's pretty good."

"Why would you pose for a man that didn't like women?"

"Oh, he wasn't the only one I posed for. Wouldn't you
pose if someone asked you to?"

"I'd never pose for a woman that didn't like men," he said.

"Very few women artists that don't like men. That is,
women artists that would ask a man to pose in the nude."

"I never thought of that," he said.

"There's always sex in it when a woman asks a man to
pose, at least I think there is. No matter what they say. But men
and women can have a woman pose without sex entering into
it."

"Do you think so?" he said.

"I know so. I used to pose for just about anybody and everybody that asked me to."

"I'll never be an artist," he said. "I couldn't keep my hand steady if I had a naked girl in the same room with me."

"Well, then, don't be an artist."

"I couldn't be anyway," he said. "I have no talent for it."

"Are you writing a novel?"

"Hell, no. I have no talent for that either. I'd never have the patience to write fiction. Are you writing one?"

"Oh, I've written two. Neither one published. One I wouldn't even show to anyone. Some day, when I have enough money, I'm going to take a year off and write one good novel. Just one. I'll publish it under an assumed name and then go back to the newspaper business. I couldn't publish it under my own name because I'd never have any peace. I could never cover another story without having all the other reporters saying I was the one that wrote that novel. But I know I can write one good novel. Just one."

"About your own life?"

"Well, mostly."

"Then wouldn't people recognize it anyway, even if you used a phony byline?"

"Some people would recognize themselves, but they'd keep quiet about it. They wouldn't brag about being in it. What I wouldn't like would be every reporter and rewrite man trying to go on the make for me because I wrote the book. That would get to be a bore, and I like this business. I expect to stay in it all my life."

"You don't intend to get married again?"

"Later on, maybe. When I'm thirty-five or forty I might marry a newspaper man and the two of us can settle down with a small paper somewhere."

"Where have I heard *that* before?" he said.

"You probably heard yourself say it."

"Not me. No more small-town papers for me," he said. "From here I go to New York, get a job on the *News*. The big money."

"And then what?"

"Oh, I don't know. By the time I'm forty I'll be ready to

take over as managing editor. I'll either stay with Patterson, or Hearst will make me an offer."

"How can you be so sure of yourself?"

"I never was till I came to Philly, but I'm a city man. I wasn't here two days before I knew that. I was a different person. It was as different as day and night, working upstate and working in the city. You wouldn't understand that, coming from San Francisco, and your father a big shot."

"Oh, it isn't hard to understand," she said. "I'm not over-awed by Philly, but it's the East, and I guess I was a little nervous about that. In San Francisco everybody knew who my father was, even people he'd never met. But here the only people that knew of him were a few newspaper men and some of the big politicians. So his reputation didn't help me much here. San Francisco is a real newspaper town. Philly isn't."

"Why?"

"Well just tell me one newspaper man in Philly that has the same standing my father had. Don't waste your time. There isn't any. What have they got here that corresponds to the Bohemian Club? Certainly not the Union League, and certainly not The Rabbit or the Fish House. Or the Philadelphia Club. My father belonged to the Pacific Union, which corresponds to the Philadelphia Club, but what newspaper man could ever get in the Philadelphia Club?"

"I'm not much for clubs. I've never belonged to one and never wanted to."

"You'll change your mind about that when you start making big money."

"I doubt it."

"What's the most you ever earned?"

"What I'm getting now. Fifty."

"Then you haven't started making real money. And incidentally, you're getting forty, not fifty. They don't pay fifty for your job, and you won't get fifty till you've been on the paper five years. If then. You're wise to think ahead. New York. You could probably start at seventy-five on the *News*, but wait a while and start at a hundred. I could get a hundred on the *News*, but I'd hate the kind of assignments they'd give me. I don't want to cover those love-nest stories, but that's what I'd get on the *News*. One of the reasons why I stay here is because they let me do general assignments."

"You're trying to be your father all over again."

"Not a chance. But at least I'm covering stories they don't usually give to women. I showed them I could in San Francisco, and when they took me on here they knew I could."

"Yes, you're good," said Harvey Hunt. "You're as good as any of the men."

"I'm better than most of them. I'd had several offers from magazines. *Collier's. Cosmo.* But they offer me two or three hundred for pieces they'd pay a man five hundred or a thousand. And I told them so. When they pay me men's prices, I'll write for them, but not before."

"It's nice to be able to afford your independence."

"Yes, my father took care of that. Insurance, and some stocks and bonds. I could have got alimony, too. Don's family have money. But I'm against alimony for women that have no children."

"Why did you break up?"

"None of your business."

"The only way to find out is to ask questions."

"You're not on a story now," she said.

"Not for the *Ledger,* but for my own curiosity. I never knew anybody like you before."

"What's so different about me?"

"Damn near everything. The way you think. Your independence."

"I think it's time for you to go home now, Hunt."

"I was thinking just the opposite."

"I know you were. That's why I'm sending you home."

He got up and sat beside her, but she would not put down her highball. "You're going to spill my drink," she said.

"Then let me put it somewhere out of the way."

"Why? I'm not going to go to bed with you."

"Why not? Because you make sixty-five a week and I make forty?"

"Partly that, I guess."

"Put the God damn drink away and give it a chance," he said.

She smiled, then placed the drink on the floor. "All right," she said. "Now show me how irresistible you can be."

"No I won't," he said. "If you don't want it, I don't want it either. You're so God damn independent, you ought to know that much."

"Well, you're not as sure of yourself as I thought you were."

"I'm sure of myself, but now I'm not so damn sure of you. You like wearing pants because it comes natural to you. Goodnight, Swanson old boy."

"Goodnight," she said. She was angry. She remained immobile until he had closed the door behind him.

He did not see her during the next three days. She was in Atlantic City on a bankers' convention, a "must" story that even she could not make readable. On the third day she returned to Philadelphia on an early afternoon train. He saw her come in the office, have a few minutes' chat with the city desk, collect her mail, go to her desk, toss her hat on the desk and run her fingers through her hair to fluff it up. She lit a cigarette and examined her mail, half of which she dropped into the wastebasket unopened. So far she had not looked in his direction. She read her letters, and apparently answered one immediately, or so he judged by the fact that she put some notepaper in her typewriter, tapped out a few lines, and copied the address before signing and sealing the letter. Now she looked around the room, and he averted his gaze just a fraction of a second before her eyes fixed on him. He could see her slowly get up and slowly make her way to his desk.

"Hello," she said.

"Oh, hello. When did you get back from the shore?"

"Just now. I'm going to cash an expense-account cheque. Do you want to have dinner?"

"I can't leave here before nine, nine-thirty."

"That's all right. I have a lot of little things to do. Will you stop for me when you can get away, or would you rather meet me at Kessler's."

"Kessler's, a little after half-past nine."

"I brought you some salt-water taffy."

"You did?"

"Of course not. I've had the most boring three days—but I won't inflict that on you. Nine-thirty, then?"

She was at the restaurant when he arrived. She was wearing a light blue bouclé dress, as simple in design as all her clothes, but made more feminine by the color and the material. "Well, sorehead, what have you been doing for excitement?" she said.

"Reading those stories of yours from the convention."

"Never mind," she said. "It's a front-office must, and the first time they ever let a woman cover it."

"How did the bankers feel about *that?*"

"One or two of them thought it was a great idea."

"Those were the ones that didn't bring their wives."

"None of them brought their wives, not while the convention was on. Some of the wives began showing up this morning."

"A good time for you to get out of town," he said.

"Aren't you going to say you missed me? Try to say something nice, can't you? After all, I invited you to dinner. I have my expense-account cheque—and this."

"What's that?"

"A twenty-five-dollar bonus, from upstairs."

"You don't deserve it."

"You don't think so, but the convention chairman did. He called the paper to say so, hence the bonus."

"Then you'll be getting a lot of bankers' conventions from now on."

"Not if I can help it," she said. "Let's order. Anything but seafood in any form. Let's have something like Wiener schnitzel. Or spaghetti. Just so it doesn't come out of the ocean."

They arrived at steaks and beer, and when she finished her tenderloin she said, "As a matter of fact I had a steak yesterday, but no matter what I ate in Atlantic City it all seemed like lobster Newburg."

"I went there for a week when I was a kid. My old man was a station agent and we used to get passes. We went to quite a few places that way, but we never had enough dough to stay very long. We stayed at a hotel on South Carolina Avenue, all three of us in the same room. We didn't have as much privacy as we did at home, and I always liked my privacy, even when I was little."

"So did I," she said. "I still do. Don never understood that. My husband. He wanted to do everything together, and I *mean* everything. He wanted our house to be like a locker-room, and it was."

"Is that why you broke up?"

"No. Although that may have been at the base of it. We had a good-sized house down on the Peninsula, and it wasn't a question of being in cramped quarters."

"I spent eleven years in a sort of an apartment on the second story of a railroad station, but I always had my own room."

"How could you sleep, with those trains going by at all hours?"

"I never heard them. That is—I knew when they were late, so I heard them that much. But the noise didn't bother me. It's a funny thing. I like my privacy, but I don't mind noises. Where I live now is about as noisy as any place in the city—except maybe the Baldwin Locomotive Works. But noises mean people, and I like to be near people. With my privacy, but knowing that people are somewhere around. I'd go crazy on a farm. I never wanted to be a cowboy, not after I found out how much time they spend miles away from anybody."

"I'm the same way, I guess. I don't mix much with people, but I like being in the midst of them, where things are going on. Then I like to go home to my flat and be alone. But not really alone. I just want to be able to shut people out when I feel like it. I suppose everybody is more or less the same way, really. Although I'm not so sure about that. My father wasn't. He was really gregarious, always on the go, loved his clubs. He would even have had a good time at that convention. And they would have loved him. He would have come away from there with a hundred new friends."

"Did you?"

"Me? I have no friends."

"I don't have so many myself."

"Everybody has a best friend, some people have two or three best friends, but not me. I was a terrrible pain to the girls in my sorority. They were to me, too. But they used to give me

lectures on the subject of cooperation, and friendship and loyalty. I had nothing against loyalty, but cooperation meant practically nothing to me. And as for friendship—I was bid to four
sororities, and I know exactly why. They were the best. The
richest and the most social. But I was bid because everybody
knew who my father was. Friend of Mr. Hoover's and Woodrow Wilson's. Pictures in the paper with Lloyd George and
Clemenceau. I didn't have to be rich. The rich people cultivated my father. It was a mark of being somebody to say you
were a friend of O. C. Swanson. Not only on the Coast, either.
He went to New York and Washington two or three times a
year, and to Europe on assignments, and when he came home
he'd have all sorts of offers to move back East. But he had
California all to himself, and if he'd gone back East he would
have lost some of his individuality. So when O. C. Swanson's
daughter went to Stanford the parents and the alumni saw to it
that I was rushed."

"Did you know that was why it was?"

"Of course. I'd known it all my life, practically. It wasn't
only because my father was a famous reporter. Even before he
won the Pulitzer prize or was given the Legion of Honor, my
father attracted people by sheer force of personality. When we
were still living at a small hotel we always had famous visitors,
every Sunday night. Opera singers. Politicians. Writers. Stage
people. When I was about eight years old I played a duet with
Paderewski. He was there on a concert tour, and I had no idea
who he was. Madame Schumann-Heink always had supper at
our apartment, whenever she was in San Francisco. They all
could have gone anywhere they liked, but they came to our
apartment in the Belvedere."

"Was your mother artistic or anything like that?"

"My mother? No, not a bit. She was educated, the University of Minnesota. Her father was a dairy farmer, Swedish.
But she stayed in the background. Nothing to contribute. Well
—*contribute?* They used to quarrel about money, how much
those parties used to cost, and all he had was his reporter's pay
till the paper began to realize that Mr. Hearst had his eye on
him. That was when Daddy's boss, Mr. Stewart, invited Margaret Anglin to his house for supper and Anglin said she was
having supper with us. Made it a rule whenever she came to

San Francisco. A *rule*. They gave my father a raise and something extra for the parties. But I'll say this for my father. He
never invited Mr. and Mrs. Stewart to our parties, and he never
went to the Stewarts'. When Daddy was put up for the Bohemian
Club he never even asked Mr. Stewart for a letter. Got in without
him. If you want to know where I got my so-called independence, it was from him. Then that wonderful day when Daddy
went to see Mr. Stewart about a raise, and Mr. Stewart said he
thought Daddy was entitled to more money and offered him
two hundred a week. 'I thought that was about as high as
you'd go,' Daddy said, and walked out without another word.
That same day he signed his first big contract with *Collier's*.
When Mr. Stewart heard about it he was wild. Came to see
my father and accused him of all sorts of ingratitude and so
forth. 'You'll see how far you get without the paper,' said Mr.
Stewart. And Daddy said, 'So will you, Charlie, you tight-fisted
bastard.' Mr. Stewart tried to keep Daddy out of the Pacific
Union, but he didn't get very far with that. The men that put
my father up were much more important than Mr. Stewart ever
was and he just didn't have the nerve to go against them. And
Daddy *looked* more like a Pacific Union member than Mr.
Stewart. He was six-foot-one and never an ounce of fat. Spent
a lot of money on clothes. You should have seen him all dressed
up for some big banquet. Full dress, of course, and he had a
medal that hung around his neck and the Legion of Honor badge.
It was no wonder the women fell for him."

"I was going to ask you about that."

"Well, he couldn't help it. My mother should have made
more of an effort, but she was really a farm girl. If she'd had her
way—I can remember her trying to persuade him. 'Olaf, let's
go back to Minney-*saw*-ta! Minney-*saw*-ta. My grandfather
wanted Daddy to take over the farms. My mother's father, that
is. My paternal grandfather was a carpenter, nicely fixed but
nowhere near as much money as my mother's family. When
they had those spats over how much the Sunday night suppers
were costing, my mother would threaten to leave him. She complained that she was paying for the parties, which I guess was
true, but all she ever did was threaten him. And she didn't
really like it when he began making more money. She didn't have
that hold over him any more."

"He liked the ladies," said Harvey.

"The *ladies* liked *him*. Even when I was a little girl I could see that, and that was behind my mother's bickering about money. He'd go on those long trips, especially when *Collier's* used to send him abroad, and when he got home you'd think she'd be glad to see him but instead of that they hardly spoke for several days. I know why, now. She was accusing him of having other women, and I suppose he didn't deny it. But she didn't make any effort to live up to what *he* was. She was pretty, and she spoke three languages. English, French, and Swedish. She played the piano and the organ. She could have been more of a help to him, and I'm sure *Collier's* would have been glad if they'd moved to New York and did a lot of entertaining. But Daddy didn't really want to live in New York, and Mama didn't even want to live in San Francisco."

"Well, if your old man was running around with other women, he was smart to keep your mother in San Francisco."

"That isn't why he wanted to stay there. I told you before, he had California all to himself."

"Sure. But he was away on trips a good deal of the time."

"You've got it all wrong. If she'd made the effort to keep up with him—but she wouldn't."

"Didn't she ever try to get a divorce?" said Harvey.

"What?"

"Why didn't she divorce him? All those women, she could have taken him for plenty, and she certainly would have got custody of you."

"Don't you know? I thought you knew."

"Knew what? She *did* divorce him?"

"She committed suicide," said Martha Swanson.

The casualness of her statement made it no less abrupt. "No, I didn't know that. How would I have known it?"

"I guess I thought everybody knew it. I've always thought everybody knew everything about my father."

"He was a big name to me, but I never knew much about his personal life," he said. "O. C. Swanson, on the cover of *Collier's,* and you always see his name with Richard Harding Davis, Frank Ward O'Malley, Irvin S. Cobb. And I've seen pictures of him. But I never knew anything about his family life. Now I think of it, I sort of had the idea he was a bachelor."

"He was no bachelor. He was a wonderful father," she said. "He came home that day, late in the afternoon, and the maid said my mother left word she didn't want to be disturbed, not even for lunch. She was going to stay in bed all day. She did that sometimes, and the maid knew why. So did my father. So did I."

"Hitting the booze?"

"Yes," said Martha Swanson. "She'd do it for two or three days at a time, pretending to have a sick headache but actually just locking herself up with a bottle. She'd been doing that for a couple of years, every few weeks. Their friends didn't know it, but Daddy did, and I did, and the maid was a Swedish woman that they got from one of my grandfather's farms. Practically a member of the family. So my father went to their room and he found her there, hanging from the big four-poster. She'd been dead six or seven hours, maybe a little longer."

"Any letters or anything like that?"

"No," said Martha Swanson. "So my father cut her down and phoned the police, and said he wouldn't be there when they got there. They ordered him to stay, but he said he'd be back around eight o'clock. They asked him where he was going but he wouldn't tell them, and hung up on them. He went out and got in his car and drove as fast as he could to Stanford. I was a junior. He wanted to get there and tell me before anyone else did."

"How far was it?"

"Oh, under thirty miles. I'd just finished supper and was listening to some records. He came in and beckoned to me. The other girls started making a fuss over him, the way they always did, but he told them they'd have to excuse him. I don't know *what* he told them, but they knew something was up and they behaved I will say very sensibly. He took me to the car and we drove away, and then he stopped the car and told me what'd happened. He said there were only the two of us now, and that whenever I got over the shock he'd let me do whatever I liked. Stay in school, or quit, or go abroad. But I wasn't shocked. My first reaction, to tell you the truth, was anger."

"Angry with him, or with your mother?" he said.

"With her. It was like publicly blaming him for all her own

deficiencies. That's really what it was, too. Have you covered many suicides?"

"A few," he said.

"Isn't that what most of them are? Blaming the world, or some individual? Getting even with somebody?"

"I guess some of them are," he said.

"Most of them," she said. "And the way she did it. Taking all her clothes off and hanging herself to the bed. She knew that's how he'd find her, and she made sure Minnie wouldn't be the one to find her."

"Strange she didn't leave a note," he said.

"That was part of it. People could make up their own stories, and you can be damn sure they did. Horrible stories. And you can imagine Stewart had a field day. Don't think he'd miss a chance like that. 'The nude body of Mrs. O. C. Swanson,' up in the lead. The other papers were bad enough, but Stewart was awful. You know how they can tell you to play up a story, play down certain angles and so forth. Stewart must have stood over the rewrite man and made sure my father got all the worst of it. A lot of people stopped speaking to Stewart, but of course there were some jealous ones that relished every minute of it."

"What happened to you? Did you stay in school?"

"I never went back. I didn't even go back to get my clothes. I had another girl bring them to my house. If my mother'd lived I'd have stayed to graduate, but only because I didn't want to be at home with her. I'd had a few dates with Don before my mother committed suicide, and he came to see me during the notoriety. He graduated that year, and he was so nice and easygoing that I married him. Worse luck for both of us."

"Why?"

"He was a wild bull. Do you remember the Wild Bull of the Pampas?"

"Luis Angel Firpo," said Harvey Hunt. "The Argentine boxer."

"Yes," she said. "Don was known as the Wild Bull of the Campus, but he'd never been that way when I went out with him. Quite the opposite, in fact. Maybe because I wouldn't neck

with him, not at all. Other girls would come back from dates
with him and tell these awful stories, but I'd go out with him
and there'd be nothing like that. It wasn't only that I wasn't a
necker. It was Don himself, and he worshiped my father. He
was always disappointed if my father wasn't home when he
came to our house. Don was a famous athlete, but he wanted
people to think he had brains, and most of all he wanted Daddy
to think he wasn't just a big football hero. 'What did your
father say about me?' he used to ask. He'd read Daddy's pieces
in *Collier's* and bore the hell out of Daddy, trying to discuss
inflation in Germany and things like the trouble between Peru
and Chile. Way over his head. But Daddy treated him as
though he were the Secretary of State. Nobody ever knew it
when they bored Daddy. He used to say to me, 'You'll never
know when some dull bastard's going to turn out to be very
useful.' "

"And so you married the dull bastard."

"Well, he was better than that. For one thing, he was a
beautiful specimen of manhood, whether he was in a track suit
or a Tux. He was almost as striking-looking as Daddy, although in a different way, and girls made fools of themselves
over him. And he knew it. He knew he had that power over
women. Animal magnetism."

"But not over you."

"Yes he had. But I'd met a lot of famous people for a girl
of my age, and a Stanford athlete didn't turn my head the way
it did some girls. I never have been one to show what's going
on inside of me. Also, I knew my father expected a great deal
of me. When I asked him for permission to marry Don he said
he considered Don a fine boy, good family, well off financially,
popular. The only thing he wanted to be sure of was that I'd
seen enough of the world to be sure I was ready to settle down
to being Don's wife. What a wonderful man! He was trying to
tell me that he understood me better than I understood myself,
but at the same time he didn't want to frighten me off marriage.
So we were married, quietly, because of my mother. And on my
wedding night I wanted to run away."

"You were a virgin?"

"Of course. Not a dumb virgin. I knew what it was all
about. But I'd married a man that had had dozens of affairs, if

not hundreds, and he expected me to be as sophisticated as he was. Well, I just wasn't. In the first place, his uncle had lent us his yacht for our wedding trip. Well, even if it was a big yacht, I was the only female aboard and there was a crew of four or maybe five. It was like being in a hospital for an operation, with all those men knowing we were just married and staring at me. The yacht would slow down for meals, so's not to spill things, I guess, but I wanted to stop completely so I could go for a swim. I just felt that if I could put on a bathing suit and dive into the ocean I'd feel better. But Don said we'd have plenty of time for swimming when we got to Honolulu. That was one small thing, and I couldn't explain it to him without sounding ridiculous, so I went without my swim. And felt dirty all the way to the Islands. In Honolulu I insisted on staying at a hotel. Anything to get away from that boat. If there had only been one other woman aboard, a maid, they'd have had someone else to stare at. I tried to persuade Don to come back on a steamship, and he thought I was crazy. I should have pretended I got seasick, but I couldn't have got away with it. If anything I was a better sailor than Don, having sailed small boats most of my life. So we didn't exactly get off to a good start. And then before we had our first wedding anniversary I had a stupid affair with an artist and Don found out about it. That gave him all the excuse he needed, and that was the story of our marriage. *Well!* Did you ask me the story of my marriage? You got it anyway."

"And what ever happened to Don?"

"Why, he's happy as a clam. He has two five-handicaps, one at golf and one at polo. Trying to raise the one and lower the other, and he will, make sure of that. And he has a five-year-old son."

"Five seems to be his lucky number."

"Exactly. No doubt he has five girl friends, too. He married a dumb little girl from Santa Barbara, with all the money in the world, and he doesn't have to pretend any more that his brains are going to waste. I hear from him now and then."

"Do you ever see him?"

"What you really want to know—yes. After we were divorced, and I'd had one or two affairs of my own. That was what finally made me quit my job in San Francisco. I wasn't very proud of myself, listening to him tell me how much he loved me when I knew his dumb little wife was having a baby. He was telling the same thing to other women, and really believing it."

"But *you* didn't love *him*."

"Of course not. But I never refused to see him, and as long as I stayed in San Francisco that's the way it was going to be. When my father died the only person I could bear to talk to was Don. The only living human being I wanted to be with. The night of the funeral I went away with Don. We drove to Elko, Nevada, and stayed two days. If we could have stayed in Elko, who knows? I might have been there yet. No, that's silly. But I was happier those two days with Don than I've ever been with anyone. I'm a Swede. We like a little misery with our pleasure."

"I guess I do too, and I'm Scotch-Irish," he said.

"There was a fascinating little tramp in Atlantic City. I couldn't figure out who she was with, because I never saw her with any of the bankers. They all wore badges with their names on them. She was there with one of them, I'm sure of that, but she never appeared in public with him. Whenever I saw her she was alone, riding on the Boardwalk in a wheel chair, and I saw her several times in the elevator. She must have been staying at the Marlborough, where I was."

"Why was she so fascinating?"

"Because I think she just this minute came in with that big fellow. Do you know Gaspar Pennington? Does that name mean anything to you? It isn't Gaspar, it's Gaston. Gaston Pennington."

"Yes, I've seen the name and I've written it in some connection or other," said Harvey Hunt.

"Old Philadelphia, Main Line."

"Oh—the fellow with the monocle? Standing at the bar between us and the girl?"

"Yes, you can't see her till he gets out of the way."

"I've seen him around, and wondered who he was," said Harvey.

"Gaston Pennington. One of the few loafers in Philadelphia. Most of them have jobs, but Pennington keeps busy doing nothing. He knew my father *and* my ex-husband."

"Have you ever been out with him?"

"No, he steers clear of the press. You can be sure he didn't come here because he wanted to. The girl must have brought him."

"How did you meet him?"

"I never have met him, actually. He called me up one day at the office, four or five years ago. Said he'd been to San Francisco and someone had told him to look me up. He'd been there a lot, to play polo at Burlingame, and had met my father and Don. He was leaving for Florida the next day, but he'd like to take me to lunch when he got back. That was the last I ever heard from him. That's a great custom in Philadelphia, in case you haven't run into it yourself. They invite you, but they don't say when, and they feel they've done their duty. So Pennington hasn't the least idea what I look like."

"You're right about the dame. She's a tramp," said Harvey Hunt. "Her name is Jean Latour."

"She could have been more imaginative than that. You know her?"

"Yes."

"You've had business dealings with her?"

He laughed. "Wasn't for her I wouldn't be sitting here tonight."

The room was dark enough for anyone who wanted to pretend not to see anyone else to pretend to blame it on the dim lighting. Jean Latour now did just that. She recognized Harvey Hunt, but gave no sign.

"Did you see that?" said Martha Swanson. "Either she's very near-sighted or she doesn't want to have any more dealings with you. Tell me about her. I gave you *my* life history."

"Let's watch and see what she does," he said.

Pennington, standing behind Jean Latour, leaned down to hear what she was saying. Obviously he was protesting, then he shrugged his shoulders in controlled exasperation, dropped some money on the bar, and followed the girl to the door. Kessler, the proprietor, hurried to them, concerned by their sudden decision to leave.

"Kessler doesn't often get a Gaston Pennington in his place," said Martha Swanson.

Kessler, giving up, went back to the bar and questioned

the bartender, who was very busy and impatient with Kessler's agitated interrogation.

"Kessler doesn't know who to blame," said Martha Swanson. "If he knew it was you, you'd most likely get a Mickey Finn. *After* he found out what you had to do with it. On second thought, maybe he *wouldn't* give you a Mickey. He'd wonder what you knew that could upset Pennington, or the girl, and no matter what you told him, he wouldn't believe you. He'd always think you were holding out on him. *I'm* pretty curious *myself.*"

"You sure have made a study of Kessler," said Harvey Hunt.

"He's one of the biggest phonies I've ever known. He doesn't give a damn about us. It's the people we bring in that count with him. The sports writers bring the prizefighters and baseball players, the rest of us bring the politicians. It was the same in San Francisco. The newspaper people find a place they like and can afford, and pretty soon the place is popular and the prices go up, and the newspaper crowd can't go there any more."

"We're here now."

"We're not here every night, not any more," she said. "Get back to your friend with the phony French name. She looks to me like a Polish girl from the coal regions. Is that where you knew her? She's awfully young, but then most of them are, and anyway you wouldn't mind that, would you?"

"She claims to be seventeen."

"I don't think she *is* much more," said Martha Swanson. "But why are you stalling me off? Where do you fit in?"

"I never did fit in, if you know what I mean," he said.

"I'd have to be stupid *not* to know what you mean," said Martha Swanson. *"At all?* Why did she look at you that way?"

"It's a long story," said Harvey Hunt.

"Well tell it, for heaven's sake. Kessler stays open till four."

He told his story of Jean Latour as fully as it came to him, and Martha Swanson was so quiet that he needed her interruptions—to reorder a drink, to light a cigarette—to reassure him of her attention. Her interruptions were never in the form of questions, and when he finished the story she remained silent. Her silence made him uneasy.

"Are you still awake?" he said.

"Yes, I'm awake," she said.

"I thought maybe you'd fallen asleep."

"No, I didn't fall asleep," she said.

"You sure seemed it," he said.

"Well, that was because right at the beginning I wanted to ask you a question, but I didn't like to interrupt."

"What was the question?" he said.

"The question was, why did you want to play a sort of Sir Galahad for this girl? Why did you want to go to bat for her?"

"I honestly don't know. I've had almost a year to figure that out, and I still don't know."

"Just obeyed an impulse," she said.

"She wasn't an ordinary, banged-up whore," he said. "And she wasn't the usual run of sixteen-seventeen-year-old tarts. I've seen plenty of them, plenty. You do, in the places where I've worked. The coal towns, where the girls quit school at thirteen or fourteen and get work in the stocking factories. And places like Reading and Allentown, they get jobs in the silk mills and so forth, and they have to bring home all their pay. If they hold out a buck or two they get hell beaten out of them, and they soon find out that there're other ways of making a little money on the side. Some of them run away, some of them are sent to the Catholic Protectory. This kid didn't happen to come from the anthracite region, but the background was the same. But *she* wasn't the same. She was worse—but she was better."

"You didn't know all that when the police brought her in."

"No. But if she wanted to stay out of jail, I wanted to help *keep* her out. I don't *know* why. Maybe just because it was what she wanted."

"In other words, you fell for her," said Martha Swanson.

"That's just it. I don't think I did. But maybe I did."

"Well, you did a nice thing—"

"And I got what I deserved," said Harvey Hunt.

"She's sorry, though. She has it on her conscience. I saw her look at you."

"I'd hate to bet on that."

"But you wish it were so," said Martha Swanson. "Let's ask Kessler what he knows about her."

Kessler, when questioned, became suspicious. "Why do you want to know about *her?*"

"Now, Kessler, you know better than that," said Martha. "If you have nothing to say, all right."

"Oh, I got no objections," said Kessler. He plainly could not bear to be left out of things, even to be left out by his own doing. "Martha, you can always wheedle me around your little finger. Lemme sit down a minute here. Now, you want to know who she is and all? Too much I can't tell you because there's a lot I don't know. She showed up around town a couple years ago, not in my place so much but I seen her around. First with guys from dance orchesters. Then lo and behold she stard once in a while I seen her with Gaston Pennington. Pretty big stuff for her. Then the next I heard he was paying the rent. A lotta little girls would give their eyeteeth to have Gaston Pennington pay the rent, but there's one thing with Gat. That's what they call him. Gat. A girl that he pays the rent, she gotta be there, at his beck and call. He's not an every-night guy, but they gotta be there. He don't come in here much because he don't like the newspaper reporters, so she come in here with other guys, and I said to myself I bet her days are numbered because she's two-timing Gat, and one of these nights she won't be there when he wants her. But I guess she was lucky so far. He's always going away some place, but she don't know when he'll be back. Gat's a very close-lipped guy. What I call very close-lipped."

"Why did they suddenly leave here tonight?" said Martha.

"Oh, you know. Gat's the kind of a guy, he's changeable. Very changeable. I seen him order a whole meal and send it all back because he decide he wanted something else. He'll pay for it. No trouble about paying. But very, very changeable. Very changeable. You take now tonight, maybe he decide he didn't want to eat with her. And I gotta yumor him or he could raise my rent. He owns all the way to Spruce Street."

"Does he own the building where she lives?" said Harvey Hunt.

"That I'd have to guess, because I don't know where she lives. I asked her, but she clammed up on me."

"You could follow her home," said Harvey.

"Yes, I could. And I could not only get my rent raised, but he could refuse to renew my lease. And it ain't like I could move next door or across the street. She's a nice little dish, but first I gotta think of my business. No broad is worth that much to me, not with what I got coming in here from all the shows. Not to mention I'm a married man and Miss Latour looks at all the angles. All the angles, that kid." He looked to the right, to the left, and behind him, leaned forward and lowered his voice. "I could ask where was she yesterday and the day before and I *know* where she was and who with. But I don't want her sore at me. Not her. You know, some day she's liable to turn up with somebody I don't want to tangle with. I don't mean like Gat Pennington. I mean—well, shall be nameless."

"You mean one of the big boys in the racket?" said Martha Swanson.

"Draw your own conclusions," said Kessler.

"Oh, don't be so mysterious," said Martha Swanson. "If you mean Choo-Choo Klein why don't you say so? Is that who she was with in Atlantic City?"

"Wuddia wanta know all this for, Martha? You starting a big expos*é?*"

"You hit it," she said. "We just discovered that the Wanamaker Bugle Corps are taking over South Philly. It's going to mean a new gang war."

Kessler looked at her without changing his frozen half smile. He tapped the table with his fingertips. "Martha, where you from originally?"

"San Francisco," she said. "Why?"

"Oh, yeah. They got a big Chinese population out there. Bigger than here."

"Yes, why?"

"Did you ever cover a story where a man got his head cut off? Did you ever *see* a man with his head cut off?"

"No."

"Well, I did. Don't kid around about gang wars, Martha. Just don't kid around."

"Or I'm liable to get hurt?" she said.

"If it was you I wouldn't give a damn," said Kessler. "I

don't care what happens to you. But I care what happens to me. Just don't kid around about gang wars, and keep your nose out of where it don't belong. You're liable to say the wrong thing and it wouldn't be *you* that got hurt."

"I'm sorry, Kessler," she said. "But you're not going to get hurt over anything I say."

"As usual, you don't know a God damn thing. Even the cops know more than you newspaper reporters. I had one of the owners of a paper in here one night and he stard shooting off his mouth about Choo-Choo Klein. And all the time you know who was sitting at the next table? Choo-Choo Klein. Choo-Choo knew who *he* was, but the newspaper fellow didn't know Klein when he saw him. Would you know Choo-Choo?"

"Of course."

"How about you, Hunt? Would you reccanize him?"

"I met him the second night I was in Philly. Sure I'd know him. That's not saying he'd know me."

"Would you know his brother? Either one of you?" said Kessler.

"I didn't know he had a brother," said Martha Swanson.

"Well, he has a brother. He has a brother is a respectable business man. But the brother that's a respectable business man, *he* has Choo-Choo Klein for his brother, if you follow me." Kessler was in a conflict between the urge to shut up and the compulsion to talk. "Martha, you was down't the shore? Then did you happen to see a fellow there looked like Choo-Choo only heavier set and darker complected?"

"I didn't happen to notice. But that was Choo-Choo's brother?"

"Draw your own conclusions. I din tell you nothing. Have a drink on the house." He stood up and left them.

"I've found him very unreliable. He never knows as much as he likes you to think he knows, but in this case he produced a few facts. Very interesting, your little tramp two-timing Gaston Pennington with the gangster's brother. When I go home tonight I'm going to go through the handouts from the convention, see if I can find Choo-Choo Klein's respectable brother."

"It must be pretty well known that he has a brother."

"Yes, but I didn't know it, and neither did you. Shall we

wait for the free drink or would you like to go home and listen to some records?"

They went to her apartment. "I have all of Art Hickman and the early Whiteman records. Whenever I get homesick for San Francisco I play them. Well, not all of them, that'd take all night. But they were both friends of Daddy's. I'll see if I can find the dope on Klein. Meanwhile, help yourself to a drink, and fix me a rye and soda, please?"

He prepared the drinks, and she found a publicity sheet from the convention. "Uh-huh," she said. "M. A. Klein, president, Barnegat Bank and Trust Company, Hamilton Bays, New Jersey. That must be near Atlantic City, Barnegat."

"Say any more about him?"

"No, this is just a list of the men attending the convention, and where they were staying. But M. A. Klein doesn't give a hotel address."

"Why are we so interested in M. A. Klein?"

"I thought you'd be," said Martha Swanson.

"Do you know what I think? I think you're interested in Gaston Pennington."

"And why do you say that?" she said.

"A hunch."

She took a long, deep breath. "That's twice tonight you surprised me. First when you told me about your reaction on seeing that girl in the police station. And now, Gaston Pennington. If you surprise me one more time I'm going to have to change my impression of you."

"What's your impression of me?"

"That you were just another newspaper man on the make."

"Maybe that's all I am, but what's wrong with that? I don't pretend to be an O. C. Swanson. I'm a fast, accurate rewrite man, without any flowers, or I'm a damn good reporter. If I can get off rewrite I'll show this town what a good reporter I am. In fact, I'd like to go out on a story against you, Martha. I'd come back with stuff you never thought of."

"Maybe you would. I don't feel like arguing. Play 'Rose Room,' and imagine yourself in San Francisco."

"It makes me think of Joe Nesbitt at Harveys Lake."

"All right. I'll think of San Francisco, you think of Harveys Lake, whatever that is. But don't let's argue."

When the record was finished she asked him to play it over again, and the second time it was finished he looked at her, implying the question, did she want it again? She shook her head. He sat beside her and took her in his arms and kissed her, and she was acquiescent. With their faces close together she looked at him. "I don't know," she said.

"What don't you know?" he said.

"Why I like you. But I do. Will it be all over the city room tomorrow?"

"No."

"I'd hate that. They've all tried, and got nowhere. A year from now you can talk, but don't for a while, will you please?"

"I won't."

"You've been pretty lonely, too. God knows *I* have. God *knows* I have."

There were three weeks, nearly four, of their well-kept secret, achieved by their meeting only in her apartment and staying apart when they were in the office. When they made love they spoke of love, but they avoided the committal declarations and plans. There was a continuing passion that carried them from day to day and that enabled them to postpone the calmer declarations and long-range plans. His hours were later than hers, and he would go to the flat and eat her dinner and stay until she had left in the morning. At the Royal the change in his routine had been noticed by a vaguely resentful Albert. "Don't see as much of you these last couple nights," said Albert.

"Well, as long as I pay my rent," said Harvey Hunt.

"Oh, I wasn't thinking about the rent," said Albert. "Y'aren't the only one keeps their room and don't sleep in it, much."

"I know. I remember. She been in lately?"

"Yesterday. And asked about you," said Albert.

"Asked about me? She didn't leave an envelope with seventy bucks in it, did she?"

"Not with me. And there's nothing in your box that I can see, so I guess she didn't. I thought maybe you run across her somewhere."

"No."

"That's what I thought, though. Something she said made me almost positive, like as if she was expecting to see you. Maybe she was just looking for you."

"She wouldn't be looking for me, Albert. And I'm not looking for her. Only the seventy bucks she swiped, that's all I ever want from Miss Latour."

"Yesterday was the first time she was here since you checked in. Well, maybe not the first. But not more than twice or three times since you checked in. Other times she didn't want to run into you, but yesterday she particularly asked for you. Maybe she had the seventy on her and wanted to pay you back, I don't know."

"As much chance of that as a celluloid cat in hell," said Harvey. "Just tell her to leave the money in an envelope, and I'll give you ten of it."

"Ten dollars, or ten percent?"

"Dollars, Albert."

"Didn't run across her anywhere, hey?"

"And don't want to," said Harvey. "I'll have some laundry I want done."

"You can leave it here on your way out and it'll be taken care of."

"Thanks, Albert," said Harvey Hunt.

He did not always see Albert when he went to the Royal to change his linen. On some mornings he slept past Albert's time to leave. On one such morning it was close to ten o'clock before he got to the room at the Royal, and when he let himself in, she was there.

"Kind of late," she said.

"Well, so are you. Damn near a year. Have you got seventy dollars that belongs to me?"

"Right there it is, on the dresser. Seven tens. Count them to make sure."

"Thank you. Anything else you want?"

"You don't have a cigarette on you? I smoked all mine, waiting for you to show up."

"If you want a Fatima."

"Yeah, for a change. Beggars can't be choosers. And a light, please?"

"Take the pack and the matches."

"Trying to get rid of me?"

"I want to change my clothes and go to work."

"You don't have to be bashful with me. I've seen everything you have."

"So you have. All the same, I'd just as soon you let me have some privacy."

"Don't be such an old maid," she said. "I'll go as soon as I finish my cigarette. For seventy bucks I'm entitled to that."

"All right, if you put it that way."

"Why didn't you give me a tumble at Kessler's that night?"

"It seemed to me, you got the hell out of there fast when you saw me."

"I tried to say hello to you."

"No you didn't."

"I did so, but you were sneaking a feel with that dame, I guess. Is that who you're getting it from that you're so bashful? I didn't think much of her. Big tits, that's all. Probably hangers, too. Takes off her brazeer and *blump,* down they go. Is that what you like?"

"Smoke your cigarette."

"Don't hurry me. I don't like to be hurried. I like to take it slow—and easy. Slow—and easy."

He laughed. "I was just thinking of you and your dude with the monocle. That must be a funny sight."

"That dude could buy and sell you *and* your paper. You know Kessler's? He owns all that land. He happens to be one of the richest men in Philly."

"I know all about him. And M. A. Klein, too, for that matter."

She was startled. "Who did you say?"

"You heard me, you're not handcuffed. I said M. A. Klein, the president of the Barnegat Trust Company. Whose brother—"

"Where did you get all that? From Kessler? That son of a bitch Kessler. He talks too much." She was confused by fear. "You got it from Kessler, didn't you? Listen, please tell me. I gotta know, for certain reasons I gotta know. I'll do anything you want, but only tell me, was it Kessler?"

"I won't tell you anything. You're a two-timing, triple-timing little bitch, and—"

"I know, but this is different. Harvey, I'll get in that bed and give you the biggest thrill you ever got from any woman. You want a thrill, and you like me. I know you do, the minute you saw me. You gave up your job for me. And I like you, too, even if I did steal a few dollars from you. Honey, let me show you how I can give you a thrill. Will you let me show you?"

"No."

"You're sore at me, that's it." She looked about her from place to place, then rushed to him and pulled his belt out of the loops and handed it to him. "Beat me. You want to beat me. Look, I'll take everything off and you can hit me with your belt. I'll like it if you do, Harvey."

"Stop! Cut it out!"

She sat wearily on the edge of the bed. "A fellow wanted to give me a thousand dollars if I let him, and I wouldn't. A thousand dollars. I don't know what else I can offer you, Harvey. If I give you this ring will you tell me?"

"Why do you want to know that so much? What difference does it make who told me?"

"Oh, if you only knew," she said. "Please tell me if it was Kessler."

"First you tell me why it's so important to know where I found out."

"I can't, I can't, I can't. I can't tell you anything. Don't you see I'm scared?"

"Look, you're not going to get anything out of me. And I have to go to work, so beat it. What the hell did you come here for?"

"I don't even remember that," she said. "Oh, I remember all right. I came here to pay you back the money, and then we could be friends again."

"We never were friends," he said.

"Yes, you liked me. There was something going, don't deny that."

"Well, it didn't last very long."

"No. I always louse things up. But that's all I came here for, I swear to God."

"You're a natural-born liar."

"I know," she said. Behind the conversation it was apparent that she was thinking of something else. "But this is one time I'm going to tell you the truth. This part will be the truth. Will you believe me?"

"I doubt it, but go ahead and try."

She waited, and in her manner and appearance there was so much defeat, so complete a lack of her young arrogance— the kind that had made her so defiant in the South Taqua police station—that she was half convincing even before she began to speak. "You know how I got started and all that, way back. You know all about me, or a hell of a lot. And I never claimed to be a Sodality girl. And you know I got this Pennington fellow keeping me, and I cheat on him. I admit all that, and why shouldn't I? Who do I have anything to hide from? Even Pennington isn't that much of a chump that he thinks I sit home all the time, waiting for him to get horny. We have a kind of an understanding, where he don't ask me questions because he knows I'll just fill him full of lies. Oh, he's all right, Pennington."

"Gat," said Harvey Hunt.

"That's what they call him," she said. "Then I don't know, several months ago I met a fellow and I didn't know very much about him except he had money and he lived out of town. How I happened to meet him was Pennington took me to New York and then he went to Boston and I was on the train back to Philly and I saw this fellow. He rode with me as far as Broad Street Station and I gave him my phone number. He said his name was Mr. Little. The *L* didn't go with the initials on his suitcase, but I didn't think I was ever gunna see him again, but I did. A week or so and he called me up and I went out with him in his car. We had dinner out near Paoli, out in that direction, and I liked him and we went to some apartment of a friend of his. That's the way it was for a couple months. Then one day I was home and the doorbell rang and this stranger came in and asked me if I knew him. I said I didn't. I didn't know him, and why should I? He said he was Max Klein's brother and I said I didn't know any Max Klein and to get the hell out or I'd call the cops. He laughed at that. Well, he called me a lot of names till I finally convinced him I didn't know any Max Klein, but from the description I figured out he was talking about my friend Little. This took about an hour, I guess, and it finally dawned on me who this fellow was. 'Are you *Choo-Choo* Klein?' And he said he was. Well, *then* I knew who he was all right. I said I was pleased to meet him and he got friendlier. No pass, but flattered me a little. He said he could easily understand how his brother could go for me and all that. Then came the payoff, why he was there. The brother was legitimate, ran a bank down at the shore, and had a wife and kids and all. I was to give him up. Give him up? Outside of a few meals and maybe two or three hundred dollars for presents I didn't have anything to give up. Little was nothing in my young life. Two or three hundred bucks and a couple bottles of per-*fume*. Choo-Choo peeled off four hundred-dollar bills. 'For your trouble,' he said. The next time the brother called I was to brush him off and make it stick. Then Choo-Choo got a little nasty again, just a little but enough so I remembered who I was talking to. He said if I did see his brother again a lot of things could go wrong for me. Like I could get in a taxi some night and it'd be a long time before I got home again. He wanted that brother respectable, he wanted that bank respectable. He didn't want his brother playing around and getting talked about. On the other hand, if I was a nice kid and did what he said, I'd get a little bonus at Christmas when he handed around his other bonuses. I said I didn't want a bonus, but maybe he could fix it so I could sing in a club. I was fed up with hanging around with nothing to occupy my time. He said that could be arranged."

"You always land on both feet, don't you?" said Harvey Hunt.

"The next time Little phoned I said I was all sewed up. I couldn't give him any more time. He knew about Pennington and he said he'd top what Pennington was giving me, but I said it wasn't only the money. I made up a story that Pennington wanted to marry me, and Little said he'd match that offer too. He'd marry me. I said Pennington's both offers were better than his, and all bets were off. I hung up, but a couple days later he was on the phone again and I almost told him to go talk to his brother, but I didn't. I hung up on him that time and the next, but then I realized he was hanging around Philly getting drunk, and what good was that doing me? So I said I'd see him once more, and I did. That was when I told him about Choo-Choo coming to see me, and believe me, that scared him. He told me Choo-Choo didn't give a damn about him, but wanted him respectable to please their mother. Choo-Choo worshiped the old lady, even if she treated him like dirt. She called Choo-Choo a gunsel and some other Jewish name, but Max was a good boy. So I said I didn't want to get my little ass in a sling because of some old lady I never even heard of. Well, he didn't want any trouble with Choo-Choo either. He went home the next day and I thought that would be the last of him, but no.

"I had guys stuck on me before, carrying the torch. But Max Klein was different. Why different? Well in some ways they're all different and in some ways they're all the same, only Max was more different than anybody. He'd sit and look at me and say did I realize what we were? According to him we were a tragedy. A tragedy? I didn't want to be any tragedy. He said we were doomed, and I didn't want to be doomed. This guy ran a little bank down at the shore and he had a brother the top guy in the mob. I didn't get it, this tragedy, this doomed. I was just a girl trying to get along, and I didn't want any of this Shakespeare. He said we were invented by Shakespeare, and I'm lucky I even heard of Shakespeare. But he must of appealed to me, because otherwise why would I take all those chances? I always said I wouldn't see him again, but he could always talk me into it. And God knows there was nothing in it for me. A fifty-dollar bill once in a while. And as far as being the great lover, this guy was on a par with—well—"

"Albert, at the Royal?"

"All right, Albert. To tell you the truth, Albert was better. At least with Albert he didn't kid around. I wouldn't have him again, but he can satisfy a woman, and that's more than you can say for most of them. Albert told you, hey?"

"Sure."

"Well, all right, if he wants to brag about it. If I said he was a liar nobody'd believe him, so I don't worry about Albert ruining my reputation."

"Go on about Klein," said Harvey Hunt.

"Nobody caught on, because I made him go on the wagon and pay attention to his bank. He had to do that or I'd get in trouble with Choo-Choo, and so would he, and if he didn't I wouldn't meet him. We never went to the same place twice, in case Choo-Choo was suspicious. We went to Trenton, Baltimore, Wilmington, Reading. A different hotel every time, and only for the one night. It was costing him money, but it was costing me almost as much. Why did I want to take all these chances with a guy that was a lousy lay. He was, he was a lousy lay. And all he could talk about was the sword of democracy hanging over us. Jesus! I don't know. Did I get a kick out of taking the chances? I must of. I don't know what else. What the hell was in it for me, I'll never know. Oh, maybe I got a kick out of outsmarting Choo-Choo. I guess there was that. I guess so. I don't like to take orders from anybody, whether he's a big-shot racket guy or a wealthy millionaire, I don't like to take orders. And Choo-Choo never got wise. Every so often I'd be out with Pennington and I'd see Choo-Choo and he'd just give me a little tumble, just enough to get it across to me that I was doing great. Then like a stupid dumbbell I said I'd meet Max at that convention down at the shore. There was three or four hundred guys there and I could of been with any one of them, the way Max figured it, and that made it safe, according to him. But safe? You know about it, that broad knows about it, and who else? If Choo-Choo Klein finds out, me there with his brother and all those bankers, in one of the big Boardwalk hotels—I'm finished. I'd be afraid to take a taxi, I'd be afraid to walk on Walnut Street in broad daylight. And if you found out from Kessler, that's as good as Choo-Choo finding out, because Kessler made a play for me and I said I'd rather get in bed with his busboy." She had come to the end of her speech, and she was now in an attitude of waiting.

"It was Kessler," said Harvey Hunt.

"Yes, I guess I knew it all along," she said. "If it was anything else I could go to Pennington. He very seldom turns me down when I ask him something. But I can't ask him to get me out of this."

"Probably not," said Harvey Hunt.

"Ten o'clock in the morning and I'm afraid to go out on the street," she said. "All of a sudden I don't have any place to go."

"Do you think it's as bad as all that?"

"Yes. The minute Kessler opens his mouth, and maybe he opened it last night."

"How do you think Kessler found out?"

"What's the difference, how? Maybe it was something that broad said that was with you. Maybe he saw us in Baltimore a month ago and we didn't see him. Kessler's like an old-maid gossip. He hears plenty, and he has to be in on everything. What he don't know he makes guesses at."

"Well, what do you do next? I mean today."

She opened her purse, turned it upside down to dump the contents in her lap. "A hundred and forty-two dollars, and some cents," she said.

"Plus seventy."

"No, you keep that. It won't do me much good. This ring. My pin. The earrings. I got about six hundred dollars in the bank. Will you do me a favor?"

"If I can," he said.

"Will you put me on the train? Go all the way with me to the seat in the coach, and stay with me till the train leaves?"

"I never went all the way with you, and I never stayed with you," he said. "All right."

"I owe you that, don't I? Well, I made you a good offer and you turned me down."

"What happens when you get to New York?"

"New York? Don't you remember me telling how I started out in New York? New York's easy, and don't forget I learned a few things since the first time I went there."

"Well, be sure and let me know how you make out."

"Let you know? Read the papers. Or I know. I got a better idea. You come with me."

"Sure. Great," he said.

"Listen, I'm gonna need a press agent. Don't get stuck here all your life. You're still young."

"A minute ago you were shaking."

"I know I was, but all of a sudden I can hardly wait to hit the big town again. Harvey, this is a chance for you, too. We just pull out of here and get a whole new start. Will you do it? Harvey, I know I'm right. I go by feelings, and I got a feeling. This is the exact minute for both of us."

"For you, not for me. Or maybe for me, too, but I don't have the same feeling."

"Oh, I see. You know what's gonna happen to you, don't you? You'll end up marrying that dame and living out in West Philly, and five years from now I'll come here with some big show and you'll wish you went with me today."

"It's a possibility," he said.

OUR FRIEND THE SEA

On the second day out Donald Fisher finished his work, the daily task he had assigned himself, by eleven o'clock. It could hardly be called work, since it consisted largely of reading more or less confidential biographical sketches of the men and women he would be associated with in the London branch. The sketches were easy to read, having been prepared by some anonymous individual in Personnel who had a lighter touch than the Bank usually permitted itself, and the confidential nature of the write-ups gave the author some leeway. "McPherson," according to one sketch, "has made himself agreeable to our English friends with his fund of slightly risqué stories. He is in great demand as an after-dinner speaker." Donald Fisher was not sure he would like McPherson. On the other hand he looked forward to meeting Rathbun, whom he knew only through office correspondence. Rathbun, according to his sketch, had stayed in England after the war. He was Harvard '16 and had gone up to Oxford for a year, taking advantage of the opportunity offered to American officers, and had joined the Bank in 1920. Rathbun was a member of Sunningdale and played golf in the high seventies. Married. Four sons. Somewhat of an expert in *arbitrage,* which Donald Fisher already knew. Rathbun sounded like his kind of man.

"Don't try to read these all at once," the Boss had said. "Two a day should be enough, and then you won't get them all mixed up in your mind. And there *are* only ten men you'll have to know about, to start with. They're the ones you'll be seeing the most of." It was interesting to find that on his first day's reading he had formed a favorable impression of one man and an unfavorable impression of another. It would be even more interesting a year from now to find out how these first impressions held up. He wished he knew what *really* made the Bank decide to send him to London. He had never been abroad, anywhere, and as far as he knew he had no living relatives in the British Isles. Nevertheless the Bank had chosen him over two other men, and the Bank usually knew what it was doing. "We would like you to stay at a hotel for two or three weeks, and *then* send for your wife," the Boss had said. "Get acquainted with the men at the Bank, the different routines, and learn a little bit about London. The time will pass very quickly, you'll find, and we've learned that it's better all around if a man doesn't try to do too much all at once. First few weeks in a new town. And especially since neither you nor Mrs. Fisher knows London."

That was perfectly all right; although he had not informed the Bank, his wife was four months pregnant, and he *wanted* to spare her at least some of the chore of looking for an apartment, which he must remember to call a flat. Moreover, at this particular stage of her pregnancy—it was her first —Madeleine, to put it mildly, did not need him around. She was peevish and bilious, and spent a great deal of time apologizing for her physical and mental state. This would pass, she assured him, and by the time he was ready for her to come to London, she would be more like her real self; her mother said so, and all her married friends had said so. It was just that at this particular time she felt unattractive and could not bear to have him touch her, or even to be sympathetic. *"Don't* keep saying you understand," she said, the night before he sailed. "How could you possibly understand? I feel awful and I look awful. I've never had a hickey in my life before, and now look at my chin. *Two* hickeys and another one coming."

"I should have told the Bank," he had said. "They *might* have postponed my transfer."

"I don't want them to. I want you to go to London and be away from me for that long, and then we'll be glad to see each other again and I'll be out of this slough of despond. And I want the baby to be born in London."

"Why?"

"Oh, it's silly, but a girl I went to school with was born in Mexico City. She was an American, but it always seemed rather chic to be able to say you were born in some foreign country."

"And you won't miss Dr. Lane?"

"I love Dr. Lane, but truthfully I'd rather have a total stranger there at the final moment. Dr. Lane would be like having my uncle there."

"Well, I'm sure there are lots of good doctors on Harley Street."

"London is the largest city in the world, so I guess they must know how to deliver a baby. *I'm* going to be all right, Don. Stop fussing over me."

Her sourness at least had had an effect that a more pleasant leavetaking might not have achieved. She not only didn't mind his going away; she desired it. Consequently he was able to enjoy his first voyage in a big ocean liner, unharassed by twinges of conscience. He had had breakfast in his stateroom, and in a little while he would take his place at the purser's table for his first official meal. So far he had not seen anyone he had ever met before, and he now set forth on a brisk walk around the promenade deck.

On someone's advice he booked a deck chair on the starboard side, but for the present he was more interested in having a look around the ship, and after three or four turns about the prom deck, he ascended to the boat deck, port side. There he found a place between lifeboats that he liked, and he stood at the rail and watched the sea flowing past.

He was there he knew not how long before he had a thought of himself, and when the thought came it was that he was alone and at peace, that there was nothing between him and the North Pole but all that restless water. Just below him the water streamed by, and lulled him to a wakeful sleep; and if he looked out beyond the racing stream, he saw the beginning of the vastness that lay between him and the top of the world. Behind him was the superstructure of the ship, and inside the ship were two thousand men and women; but he could not see them or hear them, and for as long as he gazed out on the sea, they did not exist. No one existed. He could not remember another time when he had had such a sense of being alone on the planet and feeling neither sorrow nor joy. Beyond the ship-made stream of the ocean the sea was quiet and not watery; more like a purple-black mass of sticky stuff for a Peter to walk on. And it was all there was between him and the top of the world—where there was no one either.

He felt a drowsiness that was unrelated to the pull of sleep, and he moved away from the rail and sat on a large box marked Life Preservers. He lit a cigarette and tried to get free of the desire to return to the rail and renew the experience of aloneness. It was wrong, against everything he felt and believed, to want nothing but emptiness when his life had been so full. It was wrong and dangerous now, when he had started a new life that was no longer his after it passed from his body into the body of the woman he loved, and yet was his because it had once been his. It was wrong and ungrateful to want that aloneness when he had been honored with the confidence of good men. He dropped his cigarette on the planking and rubbed it with the sole of his shoe until it was no longer recognizable as anything but a few shreds of tobacco and a tiny scrap of paper. The wind came and blew it all away.

And now he turned his head because something had happened far to the right of him that immediately and completely banished his aloneness. What had happened was that nothing had happened, but far to the right, toward the bow of the ship, a woman's white skirt had been fluttered by the breeze, and the white movement had caught his eye.

She was leaning against the rail, as he had been, but she was standing with her head back on her shoulders, accepting the breeze and the noonday sun, and he knew without confirmation that her eyes would be closed and that she was sure she was alone. She had not been there when he came up to the boat deck, and he was certain she had not passed behind him on her way to the spot where she now stood. She was wearing one of those little French hats they called a beret, a blue jacket, the white skirt, black silk stockings, and black-and-white saddle shoes. And now he saw that there was a book under her arm. She slowly raised her right hand and slowly slipped the beret back and off her head, and the wind took hold of her hair but she did not move. Her hair was blond and short, and she was young.

He watched her with an odd sense of deity, as God might watch her, and as though she were playing with the wind and the sun as her personal playmates. He had not yet seen her face, but she had grace. Then suddenly the wrath of God came down on him and on her—or so it seemed for one full second: the ship's whistle blasted forth. The girl—or woman—was startled and jumped back from the rail. Amidst the shock of the whistle blast a ship's bell had begun to strike, pairs of sounds that Donald Fisher took to be eight bells. Noon. He looked at his watch, and he saw that at the same moment the girl was looking at hers. Her game with the wind and sun was over. She bent over, smoothed back her hair and put on her beret, turned, and now she was coming toward him and inevitably would have to pass him.

He was awkward, embarrassed, and trapped, as though he had been apprehended in the act of peeping at her through a bathroom window. She was halfway toward him before she saw him, and he knew that for her it was like having been the victim of the peeper through the bathroom window. He could see her drawing her teeth back over her lower lip, and then abruptly she turned around and walked toward the bow, unwilling or unable to come any closer to him. He had violated her solitude.

Her name was Miss Constance Shelber, a simple deduction arrived at by reading the names of the passengers at Table 4. She was certainly not Mr. or Mrs. Jack Rappaport, Sir John or Lady Castlemund, Dr. or Mrs. John J. O'Keefe, Prof. or Mrs. Otto H. Von Riegenbusch. Or J. B. L. Hantlee, the medical officer. Miss Constance Shelber, of Rochester, N. Y., she had to be, and was. She came down to lunch in a different costume from the blue and white she had worn on the boat deck. She threaded her way among the tables until she reached Table 4. The men all rose, the ship's doctor introduced her to the other passengers, and she took the last vacant seat. It was then that Donald Fisher was able to guess her identity.

"Very attractive young lady," said Mrs. Harris, on his

right. "Oh, I saw you perk up and look, Mr. Fisher. Well, I can tell you who she is, if you haven't guessed. Her name is Constance Shelber, and she comes from Syracuse. *Not* Syracuse. *Rochester.* Upstate New York."

"Oh, you know her?" he said.

"She sat with us last evening at dinner, before the seatings were announced. Maybe a handsome young man like yourself could draw her out. We couldn't. She told us her name, but that's all she volunteered. Mr. Harris had to ask a separate question for everything else. Where she came from, where she's going. I asked her what she was going to do abroad—not curiosity, just polite conversation. And she said one word. 'Hide.' Well, ordinarily the next question would be what was she going to hide from, but she looked at me as much as to say she dared me to ask it, probably so she could give me some impertinent answer. But I fooled her. I didn't ask her, and what's more I didn't pay any attention to her for the rest of the meal. But she's attractive. Or maybe *unusual.* Unusual would be the better word for her. She doesn't do anything to attract, so I won't call her attractive. And yet she does attract, so maybe attractive is the right word after all, but not in the usual sense." Mrs. Harris paused. "She certainly does attract *you,* Mr. Fisher. You haven't taken your eyes off her."

"I was listening," he said.

No matter how hard he tried, he could not look at anyone at his own table without then turning to look at Constance Shelber. It was a kind of trade: a look at Mr. Harris or the purser and convention, in exchange for a look at a girl who had already begun to crowd his wife and his job out of his life. And he barely knew her name.

She finished her meal and left the table, and on her way out she nodded to Mrs. Harris, and during that momentary delay of her exit she saw, merely saw, Donald Fisher. He was ready to nod at her, but her eyes traveled past him. "Miss Shelber! Miss Shell-berr," said Mrs. Harris.

The girl halted.

"Would you care to join us for coffee? In the smoke room? This is Mr. Fisher, Miss Shelber."

"Oh, thank you, but I have to write some letters," said the

girl. "But thank you." She resumed her exit, not once having looked at Donald Fisher, even to acknowledge the single intro-duction.

"Well, I did my little bit," said Mrs. Harris. "Now you've been formally introduced."

"Thanks, but she doesn't think so. Anyway, Mrs. Harris, I'm a married man."

"Shipboard," said Mrs. Harris. "And you two are bound to get together as sure as God made little green apples."

"Well, you know what little green apples can do to you," said Donald Fisher.

"Oh—now that's a pretty wise statement for a young man your age," said Mrs. Harris. "If you're as wise as that then I didn't do any harm introducing you."

He declined Mrs. Harris's invitation to coffee in the smoke room. "I have a lot of letters to write, and I really have," he said. He also knew now where the Harrises would be and where Constance Shelber would not be—the smoke room. He went everywhere else he thought she might be that was available to him, and he had abandoned his search when he saw her stretched out on a deck chair, with a writing tablet lying on her rug. Inadvertently he had passed in front of her twice without seeing her. Now he sat on the chair next to hers and faced her.

"That wasn't my doing, that introduction," he said.

"Wasn't it? I was almost sure it was," she said.

"Well, it wasn't," he said.

"Then what are you doing here now?"

"Do you want me to go away?"

She shrugged her shoulders. "You're sitting in someone else's chair."

"Goldilocks. Me, not you," he said. "I'm sitting in some-one else's chair."

"I got the point," she said.

"Let's be friends, Miss Shelber. I'm not a tea-fighter, a lounge lizard. A snake."

"Anyone can see that," she said. "You're an up-and-coming young business man. Probably a member of Skull and Bones."

"Not even the right college. I went to Hamilton, and I know you heard of it because you're from Rochester."

"Not only heard of it, I've *been* there."

"Did you like it?"

"What are you trying to do, prolong this conversation? I suppose Mrs. Harris told you I wanted to hide. Well, that's what I told her. Do you expect me to tell you anything different?"

"No. I discovered this morning that I like to be alone, too. And I guess that's hiding."

"Then you ought to understand it in someone else."

"All right, I give up. But I'm not going to give up the boat deck, Miss Shelber. I was there first."

"I was there first, I was there first. You really sound like a ten-year-old boy. All right, I'll stay on the other side, if I disturb you. And you stay on your side."

"And you sound like a disagreeable little girl. It's a shame, too, because you and I are the logical ones on this boat to be friends."

"Why?"

"Well, for the same reason that the ship's doctor had you put at his table. But that's only one of the obvious reasons. The others I don't care to talk about. And so, suiting the action to the word, he went to his side of the boat deck. Nice to've seen you, Miss Shelber."

There were some clouds now, between him and the North Pole, and although it was only a few minutes past three o'clock, the evening had begun. The daylight was there, but daytime had gone. All that vastness was getting ready for the night—if night made any difference to the vastness. And why should it, apart from the sun sucking water out of the sea, the moon doing its mysterious things to the tides? The clouds would break and the water would be returned to the sea; the moon would go away—hide?—and the sea would rest. Donald Fisher was back where he wanted to be, untroubled now by thoughts of wrong or right, of his spent seed in the womb of his wife, of the trust of good men. All the way to the North Pole, if he did not look too far to right or left, he was alone in the world, had always been alone and would always be. Nothing had ever happened to him, nothing ever would. *Cogito, ergo sum?* Well, he had begun to doubt even that.

Because he felt rather sad for the ocean, getting ready for

the night, he knew that he existed and that the ocean existed. *Cogito, ergo sum.* This vastness, millions of square miles, was his friend.

Then she was there beside him, standing so close to him that her arm was pressed against his. "Is there room for me, too?" she said.

"Yes," he said.

"Do you love it as much as I do?" she said.

"I don't know. I was just thinking it's my friend."

"Oh, I never thought of it that way."

"I've never really seen it till today," he said.

The space at the rail was small, between two stacks of lifeboats and the stanchions that held the lifeboats. He put his arm around her shoulders, and he knew that she understood he was merely making room for her. They looked out at the sea for a while, and then she turned her face to his and he kissed her once on the mouth. There was only the one kiss and she turned away and looked out at the sea again.

"You ought to have a coat," she said.

"I'm all right," he said.

"If you want to go down and get a coat, I'll wait for you," she said.

"I wouldn't think of leaving you, not now."

"That's good," she said. She turned her face again to him to be kissed, and he kissed her. "Are you happy?"

"You know I am," he said.

"Mm-hmm." Her assenting murmur was gentle and old, like the echo of some grandmother, and unlike anything he had noticed about her.

"How old are you?" he said.

"Twenty-two," she said. "How old are you?"

"Twenty-seven," he said.

"Why isn't your wife with you?"

"How do you know I have a wife?"

"I don't, but you are married, aren't you?"

"Yes. Married two years. I'm going to London on a new job. Same firm, but a new job. She's coming over later. You guessed that I was married, I'd guess that you're not."

"No, I'm not," she said.

"You're Miss on the passenger list, but I would have guessed it anyway. I think you're getting away from some man. Is that what you meant by hiding?"

"Yes. Partly. But the man is dead," she said. "I'm not a very nice girl."

"Who said so?"

"I say so. He was married, and he killed himself."

"On account of you?"

"Yes, I'll take the blame. His wife wouldn't give him a divorce, but I'm the guilty party. So it seems, at least."

"Was he a lot older?"

"Twelve years. He was thirty-four."

"Were you in love with him?"

"At first. Very much so."

"And then what?"

"And then I wasn't in love with him, but that didn't seem to make much difference. To him, or to anybody. He wouldn't let *me* go. His wife wouldn't let *him* go. I would have had to marry him if she had, and that would have been almost as bad as this. *This,* meaning that I'll never be able to live in Rochester again. *Not* you and me. So I'm not a nice girl, Donald Fisher."

"He couldn't have been much of a fellow," he said.

"He wasn't. He really wasn't. But I wasn't any judge of that. I was nineteen years old, and going to house-parties at Hamilton and Cornell. All of a sudden I was a dangerous woman, carrying on an affair with a married man. I wish I loved him. It wouldn't have been so bad if I'd gone on loving him, especially now. But he's going to be with me the rest of my life, and I don't love him. I don't even feel very sorry for him. The only one I feel sorry for is his daughter, nine years old. She was crazy about her father, and every year, little by little, she's going to hate me more and more. That's a terrible way for a child to grow up."

"What are you going to do?"

She smiled. "You mean hide? Not really, just stay out of the way of Rochester people. My father and mother are coming over this summer and we're motoring through France, Germany, Switzerland. They're going back in August, and I'll stay

on somewhere. Paris, most likely. I have friends there, quite a
few, actually. Eventually I suppose I'll marry some foreigner."

"Why a foreigner?"

"Oh, because an American would like to go home, and I
just couldn't go through all that hell, when his family and
friends find out about my Rochester past. And they would. No
matter where I went in the United States, it'd all come out
again. In Europe I don't think it would matter so much. I'll
have quite a lot of money some day, and European men take
that into consideration."

"Won't you miss Rochester? Your friends there?"

"Oh, sure. Not that I have so many friends there at the
moment. But I like it there. I ride, and sail, and if you like
music, Rochester is getting to be quite a place to be. It was
my *home.*"

. . . A man had chosen death to life without her, and
Donald Fisher could understand that. That other man had no
doubt kissed her one day for just a kiss, and you could not kiss
this girl and let it go at that. You could not look at her and let
it go at that. Donald Fisher reminded himself that he had fallen
in love with her before even seeing her face. Was it her grace?
Yes, but not that entirely. Her figure? Her figure was no better
than Madeleine's . . .

"I'll be getting off at Cherbourg," she said. "You go on to
Southampton."

"Yes, it seems strange to stop at France first and then
come back to England."

"Not if you look at the map," she said.

"I confess I haven't looked at the map."

"I feel robbed already," she said. "They're sending me
away from you before the trip is over."

"Well, we have four more days," he said.

"Have you any friends aboard?"

"Not a soul I ever saw before."

"Neither have I," she said. "The sweetest thing is the way
we take so much for granted. We haven't had to say much,
either. I told you about me, and I can guess about you."

"There isn't much to tell about me," he said.

"I didn't mean your background, who your wife was,

where you live. I meant a man who could think of the ocean as his friend. I understand that much better than if you explained it. It's why I went looking for you."

"But you didn't know that when you went looking for me."

"Yes I did. Not that one thing, but I knew there'd be something like it. I knew you were that kind of man."

"*I* didn't," he said.

"Then maybe you never were until today. Or maybe you just don't know much about yourself."

"That's the truth. I don't know much about myself. I never thought there was very much to know."

"That's *good,*" she said. "You see, I know all about *my*self. Past, present, and future. And God! what a future. A selfish man shot himself, and because of that I can see my whole life, every day of it. A nine-year-old girl growing up to hate me, hate me, hate me. A nasty Rumanian marrying me for my money. And me going off on little trips with other nasty Rumanians. And two trips to Rochester, one when my father dies and the other when my mother dies. But I'll remember you, Donald Fisher, because you're the only nice thing that's happened to me in two years. And maybe the last nice thing that ever will happen to me."

"I love you," he said.

"Stop there," she said. "Don't say any more. I know you love me, and I love you. But let's not say any more. I've been through all the rest of it. I know every word of it, and I don't want to hear the same words from you. Will you come up here every day?"

"I'm planning to. Aren't you?"

She turned and looked up at him with a smile. "I *had* planned to," she said.

"Good," he said.

"Now I am going down and write some letters," she said.

"Will you have a cocktail with me before dinner? How about seven-thirty in that Terrace Room, whatever they call it."

She kissed him lightly on the cheek, and left him.

That much had happened and been said, and how right she was to let him say no more. He was experiencing automatic love, a different thing from love at first sight. He wished he could tell his new friend, the sea, why it was different; instead he could tell himself that he had not had to wait for first sight, a look at her face. The moment his eye caught the flicker of her white skirt, even before he saw the rest of her, her welcome to the wind and the sun, her hair—a sound that was neither a bell nor a pistol shot announced to him that she had arrived and love had begun. None of the things that matter to people who have just discovered each other had mattered to him—or to her. She snubbed him, repulsed him, and then she had gone looking for him. And when she found him he was not surprised. It was easy to believe that he had been expecting her all his life, and he believed it.

He would have a cocktail with her, he would meet her after dinner, he would get a small table where they could talk while the other passengers danced. He would begin to tell her that her life was not going to be a succession of Rumanians and flights from Rochester, of an embittered nine-year-old girl's growing hatred and of the untold miseries she was foreseeing. She would not have to remember him; he would be there. To-night he would go slowly, because the things he would begin to tell her would have to be in the same words that she had heard before. But haste was not on their side anyway; it would be a year before he could leave Madeleine. And there was the Bank. As he thought of the Bank he recalled a remark of the Boss's that gave a clue to the choice of him over the other two candidates for the London job. It was six months ago, but they must have been already deciding on the man. "Don, we like the way you make up your mind and stick to it," the Boss had said. Well, the Bank would find that his mind was made up about Constance.

Constance. The first time he had thought of her by name. It was a strange name on his tongue, and as a name it was not yet in his heart. But to her he was Donald-Fisher, the full name. Everything was new, and haste was not on their side. So much was it not on their side that he had not noticed the passing time or the darkling of the vastness. But the vastness was not the same as it had been. The sea was still his friend, but he was no longer alone. He thanked the sea for having been his friend, but he would never really need that friendship again.

He went to his stateroom and was pleased to see that the steward had laid out his evening clothes. It reminded him of the weekend at the Boss's country place, when he knew he was being looked over for the London job. This was the second time in his life that clothes had been laid out for him. Oh, there would be a lot of new things from now on. He went to the bathroom to run a tub, and found that it had already been run for him. Razor, shaving brush, shaving stick on the lavatory, all ready for him, but he could do without a second shave. He took off his clothes and got into the tub, and the water was just warm enough. He lathered himself with the English soap, and when he had rinsed off the foam he lay back in a state of relaxation that was better than sleep.

In that state he did not immediately notice that the water in the tub had become completely still, as though he were in a tub on *terra firma*. He followed this discovery with the realization that all was quiet, that what was missing was the vibrant drone of the engines. And then he knew that the ship had stopped.

He got out of the tub and rang for the steward. Now that he was out of the bathroom he could hear people in the passageway outside the stateroom. They were all talking, but he could not make out what they said as they hurried past his room. He rang again for the steward, and in a minute or two there was a knock on his door and the stewardess entered. "No cause for alarm, sir," she said.

"But the engines are stopped," he said.

"Yes sir. They're lowering a boat, sir," she said.

"Lowering a boat? What is it, some kind of a drill?"

"No, sir. I'm sorry to say, sir, a passenger seems to have jumped overboard. That's all I can tell you, sir. I wouldn't give much for his chances in the dark. I mean to say, there's no moon, is there?"

"His chances? It was a man?"

"Well, now you ask, I don't know as it is, sir. I really don't know very much about it. Just what I was told, sir. *Is* there anything else, sir?"

"No, that's all, thanks," he said.

Some poor son of a bitch, he thought, and went on dressing. He was torn between going to the Terrace Bar and going to watch the rescue operations. The Terrace Bar won out; she would need him now, with her own experience of suicide.

The Bar was completely deserted of passengers. "A bit of excitement, sir. Not every day in the week they stop this 'ere ship. May I serve you, sir?"

"A dry Martini, I think I'll have," he said.

"Dry Martini. Very good, sir. The gentleman wouldn't by any chance be Mr. Donald Fisher, sir?"

"Yes, that's me."

"Oh, well now I've been asked to deliver this note to the gentleman. One of the stewards left it here about an hour ago, sir. To be handed to Mr. Donald Fisher, sir."

"Thank you. I'll have my drink at the table," he said.

He sat down and lit a cigarette, and waited for the steward to serve his cocktail before opening her letter.

It was not a letter. It was a piece of the ship's notepaper, and all that was written on it was the bare sentence: "The sea is a friend of mine, too."

He returned the notepaper to the envelope and put it in his pocket. He took a sip of his cocktail.

"Oh, there's Mr. Fisher!" It was the voice of Mrs. Harris. "You're a very clever young man, Mr. Fisher. Why do you suppose she did it?"

"I have no idea, unless she meant what she said to you."

"Said to me? What did she say to me?" said Mrs. Harris.

"That she wanted to hide."

"Of course! Of *course!*" Mrs. Harris said more, but her words were overwhelmed by the wrathful blast of the ship's whistle.

"Means we're getting under way," said the steward. "Giving up the search."

"Well, you couldn't see anything out there anyway," said Mrs. Harris. "She came from Rochester, New York. I must try to think of who I know there."

"Oh, why bother, Mrs. Harris?" said Donald Fisher.

"Perhaps you're right," she said. "You know, you impress me. Mr. Fisher. What's the *name* of that bank you work for?"

THE PUBLIC DOROTHY

It had never been like this before, never as bad, never as arid. He watched her put all the things back in her purse that she had taken out and laid on the table in her careful search for one scrap of paper. "It was here, I know it was here," she said. "I know because as I was leaving the house this morning I made sure."

"It was in your purse then?" he said.

"Of course. No question about it."

"You *saw* it in your purse?" he said.

"I didn't *see* it in my purse. Not *then,* darling. Not at that exact moment. I didn't stop on the porch and take everything out the way I've just been doing. I didn't have to, because less than a half an hour earlier it was there on my dressing-table with all the other things, all this stuff. I have this little sort of bin, where I keep all my purses and handbags. I have all the nice ones, the beaded ones and the brocaded ones, all wrapped in tissue paper. But of course I wasn't going to carry one of those today. They're mostly for evening. The leather ones and the cloth ones, like this one, they're all arranged in little piles, according to color. This one, I have seven or eight black ones, cloth *and* leather, and this one was at the bottom of the pile of black, but I wanted to take this with me today because it goes better with this dress. You probably wouldn't notice, but this is grosgrain and it almost matches the material in my dress. Not on close inspection, of course. They don't exactly match. I wouldn't want them to, exactly. But they go well together. In fact—this may sound crazy—but the first thing that came to my

mind when I saw this dress—I had a purse to match it! I don't
ordinarily buy a dress that way. Usually the other way around.
It wouldn't be very sensible to pay that much for a dress because it matches one of your handbags."

"You had no occasion to take the clipping out of your
purse on the train?"

"Why should I? I had my round-trip ticket in this little
pocket, and when the conductor came I handed him the ticket
—see, here's the other half of the ticket."

"In the ladies' room, when you took out your lipstick," he
said.

She shook her head. "I can't imagine what's become of it.
I don't usually lose things. I know *this* isn't lost. It'll turn up in
some perfectly logical place. But it's annoying to have this happen."

"You might as well tell me what it said."

"Well, it certainly isn't worth making all this fuss about.
The only thing was, you had to read the whole thing to get the
humor of it."

"What *kind* of thing was it?"

"It was an account of a wedding. It was in yesterday's
Times, on the society page. I didn't know either of the families, but I usually skim through to see if any of the bridesmaids are friends of Meg's, or sometimes the ushers. *You* know.
Big weddings there's always *someone* you know, and this one
had about ten bridesmaids and ten or more ushers. One of the
ushers was the brother of a girl that's in school with Meg, so it
had some personal interest for me. Anyway, this boy and girl
that were getting married, it told all about her family. Grandfather was a Supreme Court judge in Kentucky or Tennessee,
and descended from somebody a member of some august body
in Virginia."

"The House of Burgesses?"

"Probably. And father was president of some company
that I didn't recognize. And where she went to school. Fox-
croft, and one of the junior colleges and some place abroad. And
then the boy. All about his grandparents and great-grand-
parents, who *they* were. You could almost hear the one family
say, well if *they* were going to brag about *their* ancestry, we'd

do a little bragging of our own. And it was all there. Signer of the Declaration of Independence. Founder of some little college I never heard of. And then a list of the boy's clubs. The Racquet. Seawanhaka. Piping Rock. Some club in London. Porcellian. It was all there. Oh, and of course St. Paul's and Harvard, and Buckley. Then at the very end, where they were going to live. An apartment house that I happen to know is cooperative, no apartment in the building worth less than a quarter of a million. We looked at it several years ago, but it was far beyond us. The smallest apartment in the building was ten rooms, so you can imagine."

"Yes," he said.

"Then—I'm sure it was completely by accident—but in the very next line, no separation of any kind, but as if it belonged in the article, this one line. 'Give to the Hundred Neediest Cases.' When I saw that I just burst out laughing. I'm sure it wasn't intentional, but it made the whole article seem so ridiculous. It just struck my sense of humor, and I cut it out purposely to show you. And now I can't find the damn thing. So irritating, because it's one of those things you have to *see*."

"It is very funny," he said.

"Well, if you happen to have that kind of a sense of humor. I knew *you'd* appreciate it," she said. She put her hand on his knee. "Darling?"

"What?"

"I have some bad news for you, for both of us."

"What?"

"I can't see you this afternoon."

"What's the trouble?" he said, but what he almost said was, "You brought me all the way uptown to show me a clipping that you can't even find?" He was so close to saying it that for one second he was not sure it had not slipped out.

"I called your office, but you'd already started uptown. Mother asked me to go with her to the hospital. She's going in for a checkup and I'm meeting her at half past two."

"I suppose that takes precedence," he said.

"There'll be other times," she said. "She doesn't ask me to do very much, and the fact that she asked me to go with her this time shows she must be worried. She's seventy-four. It's her heart. I have to stop and pick up a bedjacket I ordered for her, so if you'll get the check—or maybe you'd rather stay and have a drink with Larry Campbell. I saw him wave to you."

"I think I will stay, if you don't mind," he said. "I'm sorry about your mother. I hope it turns out all right."

She squeezed his knee in farewell, and left him, and on the way out she waved to Larry Campbell at the bar. Campbell immediately joined him.

"Hello, Roger," said Campbell. "Why is Dorothy in such a rush?"

"Taking her mother to the hospital for a checkup. If you're going to have a drink with me you'd better make it quick. I have to get back to the office."

"Don't flatter yourself, old boy. All I want from you is your table. I've been standing there over a half an hour."

"Well, you can have the table. You can have the check, too, if you like. It'll be about fourteen dollars, without tips. How've you been?"

"Okay. Doing as well as I have any right to expect, I guess. You know I was thinking, standing at the bar, that Dorothy is really a remarkable woman. How many of the girls we used to know have held up as well as she has? She's a good forty-five. I know that for a fact. She's three years younger than Edwina, but she doesn't look forty. She doesn't look any age. I suppose if I weren't such a tactful fellow I'd have to give you some of the credit."

"Yeah, you're noted for your tact, Larry."

"Well, what the hell? How many guys with an office downtown will take time out to come all the way up here for lunch? You and I don't have to make a big thing of it, and as far as that goes, you and Dorothy don't go out of your way to make a secret of it. You never have. After all these years you're practically an institution, you two."

"Isn't that nice?"

"*I* think it is. Some people don't, but you and Dorothy are a lot more honest than some of those that take a high and mighty view of it."

"Did I hear you say you *were* going to pay this check, or are you getting my table for nothing?"

"What'd you say it was? Fourteen dollars? All right, I'll

take care of it. It's a pleasure to pay for Dorothy's lunch, and I hope you remember to tell her. *When* you *see* her, of course."

"So long, Larry," said Roger.

He had, accidentally, a free afternoon, so completely free that he could think of nothing more original to do than to sink into a chair in the club library, where he was not likely to be bothered. As always, when he was meeting Dorothy, he had so carefully arranged things at the office that to show up now would be to create some doubt when he made such arrangements in the future. And already it had been a trying day.

It was quieter than a church in the club library. The librarian moved about, but the high-pile carpeting muffled his steps, and Roger was not acquainted with the other two members in the room, one at a writing desk, the other taking a nap. Roger had almost forgotten that there could be such quiet, such peace, in the middle of the city.

It had been a trying day, she had been at her worst, and at one point during her chatter he had been tempted to say, "Will you for God's sake shut up." Lunch in a public restaurant was a part of their meetings that she had insisted upon from the very beginning. ("We can always say we were having lunch, and it will be the truth.") A secondary part of their lunches was that they must always be seen saying goodbye in the restaurant, and she looked upon it as a piece of luck when someone like Larry Campbell could join Roger after she left. It was up to him to manage to shake free of people like Larry. He had willingly cooperated in all these ritualistic deceptions, but for a year now her chatter had been barely endurable. It had never been scintillating, stimulating. It had always belonged with the public Dorothy, the girl and then the woman who had gone from pretty girl to beautiful woman and in looks was the gainer. But there had been no major change in the thoughts she uttered. He had never known a time when she said anything worth repeating, worth remembering. It was a child's mind she had, and his desire for her had begun as a simple and fierce admiration of her face and body. Whatever he had to give up to get her, he was willing to give up—and then it turned out that he had to give up almost nothing. She, it turned out, loved him as well, and did not wish to love anyone else.

He remembered, he would never be able to forget, their

first time together. He took her in his arms and kissed her, and the frankness of her embrace was so true that he waited for her to say something childish, coquettish. It was what he expected, and his right to be annoyed was one of the things he had been prepared to give up. But she had not been childish or coquettish. None of that was present that day or ever during the thousand times they had made love. In those moments she was womanly proud, of her body, of her beauty, and of being loved by the man she loved. These were her moments of peace and calm, and they were what he remembered between one meeting and the next. He longed for her now, and he would always long for her, no matter what.

He went to a writing desk and took out a sheet of club stationery, and wrote the first thing that came to his mind: "I love you, Dorothy. Please forgive me." It did not matter that she would never see what he had written. He had written it, and he felt forgiven, and there would be other times.

THE RIDE FROM MAUCH CHUNK

One evening ever so long ago Maudie McWilliams was waiting at the Mauch Chunk station to take the train to New York. The train, as was not infrequently the case, was late and she had sent the family chauffeur home. It was a cold evening, but she remained outdoors, knowing that the Pullman, once it arrived, would be very warm and this would be her last chance to get some fresh air until the ferry ride at the end of the rail journey.

Presently a car drew up, and after a moment or two a young man got out. He stood bareheaded until the car drove away, then he allowed the lone porter to take his suitcase to the platform. The young man and the porter took a position not far from where Maudie McWilliams stood; close enough so that she could hear their conversation. At first the porter was content to comment on the lateness of the train and the likelihood of snow, but soon in a different tone of voice he said to the young man, "You work for the Lehigh Valley?"

"No, why?" said the young man.

"Your valise. I seen them letters on your valise. L-V, L-V. Thought they stood for Lehigh Valley."

"Oh, I see. No, I don't work for the Lehigh Valley. No."

"Well, you know, them initials. Around here, you know. The Lehigh Valley."

"No, as a matter of fact, it's a funny coincidence, but the initials are V. L."

"Oh, V. L. I got the cart before the horse. V. L."

"Yes. I, uh, I'm a musician. I work with an orchestra. Maybe you heard of us. Vincent Lopez?"

"Vincent Lopez. Oh, well I should say I did hear of him. On the radio. Lopez spee-king. So you're on radio? Do you mind telling me what instrument you play? The wife'll want to know that."

"What instrument? I play the sax."

"The sax, huh? That's the saxophone, eh? The wife listens all the time, every night. We live up the hill there, and our reception, we get Kansas City, Atlanta-Georgia. My missus'll sit up till one, two o'clock in the morning. She says the static ain't as bad then. Oh, sure, I heard of Vincent Lopez. *You're* not Vincent Lopez, are you?"

"Oh, no. No, I'm only one of the musicians. We all get these bags when we sign up with Vince. It's good advertising, you know."

"All having the same baggage, yes. Were you just playing, somewhere near?"

"No, I took a little time off. Visiting my uncle in Gibbs-ville."

"The party that you just got out of their car?"

"Uh-huh. He's a saxophone player, too."

"And with a Packard. I guess I should of took up some instrument when I was young. I got a brother that can't read a note, but he can sit down and play a tune on the pyanna. But I never had the knack. Well, here she comes. Twenty-two minutes late, but you'll make up most of it. You just leave your valise here and I'll see it gets on board all right. I got this other young lady, she's in the chair car too."

"What young lady? Oh, I see. Here you are, never mind my bag."

"Thank you, thank you, sir," said the porter, identifying the quarter tip without looking at it.

The young man stood aside to let Maudie McWilliams precede him into the Pullman car and, she guessed, to get a better look at her. A few minutes later, when the second call for the diner was announced, he followed her, as she knew he would, and permitted the steward to guess that they were traveling together and put them at the same table. The steward was embarrassed when Maudie McWilliams asked for separate checks. "Excuse me, would you care to sit by yourself, ma'am?"

"No, this'll be all right," she said. She saw that the steward glared at the young man, and it was not hard to guess that the young man had somehow created the impression that he was traveling with her. The steward took her order and pointedly let the young man wait.

There was no one else at their table. He was tall and very blond, wore a white button-down shirt and a black knit tie. She could see a fraternity pin on his vest, but it could have been Deke or Psi U or any of a number of diamond-shaped badges. "Will it bother you if I smoke?"

"No, go ahead," she said.

"Will you have one?"

"No thanks," she said.

"I didn't see you at the wedding," he said.

"What wedding?"

"That was just a shot in the dark," he said. "I just came from a wedding, and I thought you might have been there too."

"No," she said.

"Now I'm not so sure you *weren't* there," he said.

"Well, I wasn't, so you're wrong."

"As a matter of fact you *were* there. I saw you there. Do you solemnly swear that you didn't go to a wedding yesterday? To wit, Joan Barnes's wedding in Gibbsville? Reception at a country club with a jawbreaker of a name?"

"Oh, yes, I was at that wedding. But I didn't think you could have been there."

"Why not?"

"Because they had Markel's orchestra."

"What's that got to do with it?" he said.

"Don't you play for Vincent Lopez?"

He laughed. "Oh, for God's sake. You heard all that?"

She smiled. "Yes. You know, my brother has a Louis Vuitton bag, and he makes jokes about its belonging to the Lehigh Valley, but I never heard anyone say anything about Vincent Lopez. That was clever, although taking advantage of that poor old porter."

"I made it up on the spur of the moment."

"Oh, you admit you're clever. Oh, dear me."

"I don't have to admit it. Everybody admits it *for* me.

And you, naturally I deduce that you're on your way back to some institution of learning."

"I am, yes."

"You're going to make me guess which one? Smith?"

"No."

"Wellesley?"

"No."

"Radcliffe? No, I take back Radcliffe. Is it a college, or are you still at boarding-school? You're a little old for boarding-school."

"It's college."

"Oh, of course! Vassar. I should have thought of Vassar first. *Is* it Vassar?"

"Yes."

"And who do I ask for, the next time I go up to Vassar?"

"Go right on asking for the same people you always ask for," said Maudie McWilliams.

"All right, I will. And I'll ask *them* to tell me, who is a disagreeable young woman from the Pennsylvania coal mines. Blue eyes, blond hair, about five foot five. A hundred and twenty pounds. Having a violent love affair with an Alpha Delt from Wesleyan."

"Oh, the pin," she said. "No, you're wrong about Wesleyan."

"Yeah, I'm wrong about the violent love affair, too. All the A.D.'s I ever knew were too insipid to do anything violent, let alone have a violent love affair. How come you weren't a bridesmaid for Joan Barnes?"

"She didn't ask me."

"Are you too rich?"

"Too poor."

"The hell you are. You said your brother has a Vuitton bag. Poor boys don't have Vuitton bags."

"Then *you* must be rich, you have one."

"Mine was my uncle's. I'm not rich yet. I won't be rich till I'm thirty, but then watch it roll in."

"How nice to be so sure of yourself," she said.

"I told you before, you think I'm egotistical, but I'm only admitting what everyone else says. I can't go against public opinion."

"Oh, dear. It's so refreshing to meet someone so modest. Not like most of the college boys these days."

"Careful. I'm a college *graduate.*"

"How long did it take you? Two years?"

"No, I stayed the full four years. I probably could have got out in three, but I had a scholarship that was good for four."

"Strange, I don't see a Phi Beta Kappa key."

Without a word he lifted his watch and chain out of his vest pockets and laid them on the tablecloth. At one end of the chain were a gold ball, a medal for track, and a Phi Beta key. "Take a closer look, if you like. It's the real thing, not Kappa Bete," he said.

"I'm crushed," she said.

"When I toot my own horn I can always back it up," he said. "Tilden himself said I could have been Davis Cup material, if I'd been more serious about my tennis."

"And what's the other medal?"

"High hurdles. I was on the Cornell-Princeton team against Oxford-Cambridge. What's your *name?*"

"Maude McWilliams."

"Jarvis Brittingham," he said.

The waiter served her jelly omelette.

"I'll have the same thing," said Jarvis Brittingham. "And a glass of milk, please."

"I hope you don't mind if I go ahead," she said.

"I eat fast. I'll probably be finished before you are," he said. "Everything fast. That's where I got my nickname. Speed."

"What they call a fast worker," she said.

"You mean picking you up?"

"You haven't quite picked me up yet, have you?"

"I have your name, and where you go to college, haven't I? As a matter of fact, not very fast. I remember seeing you at the reception, but as an usher I had certain obligations. This fellow that gave you his pin, was he at the wedding?"

"No. He comes from a different part of the country."

"Is he still in college?"

"Yes."

"What is he going to do when he gets out?"

"He hasn't decided."

Jarvis Brittingham tapped his fingertips on the tablecloth.

"Probably go work for Pop. The usual thing. I knew what *I* was going to be when I was fourteen years old. We had two literary societies, and I was assigned to debate the question, 'Resolved: that the South was justified in seceding from the Union.' We took the positive side, and we won. That was the first time the positive side ever won, and I was against it too, but we won. Then and there I decided to become a lawyer. I'm at Columbia Law School. I have one more year. I could have been a Rhodes Scholar, but I didn't put in for it. I have to start making some money. I could marry a rich girl, and I probably will, but first I have to make some of my own so that I don't have to take any guff from her family. I wouldn't marry a girl that *didn't* have *some* money. After all, she ought to have something more to offer than just the fair white body."

"And love, and brains, and a nice disposition."

"All right, what *about* love and brains and a nice disposition? I have brains and a pretty good disposition, and I'm going to make a lot of money. As far as love is concerned, every divorce started originally with two people thinking they were in love, and boy, look at how many divorces there are. My father and mother are divorced. My uncle and aunt. One of my best friends in college got married the day after he graduated, and he's getting a divorce already. And that's not taking into consideration how many married couples would get divorces if they could."

"I don't see why you get married at all, feeling that way about it," she said.

"Well, one thing you can be sure of, and that is I'm going to take my time. Aha! Jelly omelette. Looks pretty good, too. I hear people complain about the food on dining-cars, but I don't think it's so bad." He commenced to eat, and she watched him fascinatedly. His hands and even his arms never stopped moving. He would put a forkful of omelette in his mouth, lay down the fork and pick up the knife and a piece of toast, butter the toast, take a large bite of it, put it down, take another forkful of the omelette. He drank his glass of milk in three mouthfuls and ordered a second glass. The omelette, toast, and milk were consumed in three minutes, and he had finished ahead of her. He looked down at his vest, used the fingers of both hands as a whisk broom to brush away imaginary crumbs, and after a deep breath he lit another cigarette. "Are you having dessert?"

"No," said Maudie McWilliams.

"No, I don't think I will either. You know what I like on a Pullman diner that I never get anywhere else. Figs, with that rich syrup. But there was a lot of jelly in that omelette, so I guess I'll pass up the figs. Are you having coffee? Have some, why don't you?"

"Yes, I'm going to," she said.

"They give you black looks if you sit here and don't order something—no pun intended," he said. "We can stay here for an hour or so, then I have to crack the books. Can you study on a train?"

"Sure," she said.

"The whole secret is to study when you feel like it. Never drive yourself to it. I got plastered to the hat at that reception, but nobody knew it. I pride myself in holding my liquor. That can be a big attribute for a lawyer. You see, I'm going into politics. Get myself a reputation in criminal law. Then the district attorney's office, then back into private practice where the money is. Then I'll run for district attorney. Governor. United States Senate. About three quarters of the men in the Senate are lawyers, you know. Once you've been in the Senate your name alone is worth a hell of a lot in a law firm. What does your father do?"

"He's dead. He was in the coal business."

"Just you and your mother and one brother?"

"And a sister."

"Your brother in the coal business too?"

"Yes. In West Virginia."

"Smart, to get out of Pennsylvania. No matter how good he was they'd still say he owed everything to your father. I suppose you'll finish college and then marry your Alpha Delt, or someone like him."

"Very likely."

"That's probably the best thing. A lot of girls get out of college and think they ought to get jobs, do something. Welfare workers. Comparison shoppers at Macy's. But a girl like you, I've been studying you, and I've come to the conclusion that you'd make an ideal wife for some young guy just starting out. You'll have an education, some money, and I wouldn't be surprised if you made a very good mother."

"All cut and dried, my life all mapped out for me," she said.

"Just about. But I didn't plan it. Neither did you. I'm just telling you what I see. Are you going to let me buy your supper?"

"No. Why should you?"

"I'm not that broke. I got out of college ahead of the game, financially. Come on, let me pay for your omelette."

"All right, thanks."

"I wish I would have had more time at the wedding, or if you'd have been a bridesmaid."

"You mean you'd have given me a rush?"

"You're damn right I would. But now the chances are I'll never see you again."

"I thought you were coming to Vassar and so forth."

"I changed my mind after talking to you. The girls I know at Vassar—I don't think they'd be friends of yours."

"Obviously they're not, or I probably would have met you, or heard about you."

"Listen, you know what I'm driving at."

"Well, I don't think it's a very nice thing to say."

"I didn't *have* to say very much, but you got my meaning. So don't go too innocent on me. Waiter, can I have the check please? Both checks."

"Thank you for my supper."

"Pleasure was all mine, Maude."

"Goodnight," she said.

That was all, all she ever saw of Jarvis Brittingham. By accident or otherwise they stayed apart throughout the remainder of the journey. On the New York side of the river she took a taxi to Grand Central and the train to Poughkeepsie. In her room at last and tired, and through changes of scene and the distance, she was far removed from Jarvis Brittingham and his strange mind and his vitality. And yet she found the time and the wish to write to the boy whose pin she wore and tell him proudly that she had missed him terribly, every minute. "Darling Phil—I so envy Joan," she wrote. "I know now that my whole life is mapped out for me. It will be with you."

And so, indeed, it was.

She was sorry, truly sorry, to read in the paper that Jarvis Brittingham, former district attorney of some upstate New York county and frequently mentioned as a potential candidate for the Republican gubernatorial nomination, had been sentenced to prison. It was a complicated thing to someone living in Pennsylvania and not up on her New York State politics, but it had to do with some sort of bribery of a member of the legislature. In pronouncing sentence the judge declared that Mr. Brittingham had known exactly what he was doing, and that he therefore was imposing the maximum penalty that the law allowed. The severity of the sentence, the judge hoped, would serve to remind the general public that the vast majority of lawyers looked upon their profession as a sacred trust, that the oath they took as officers of the court was no mere formality, and that Mr. Brittingham had betrayed his trust and violated his oath with full knowledge of the fact that he was bringing discredit on himself and his fellow members of the bar. The newspaper article reported that Mr. Brittingham heard the sentence with no show of emotion.

"I guess that was just the trouble," said Maudie.

SATURDAY LUNCH

As soon as it became known that Jud and Carol Ferguson were in the market for a larger house the real-estate agents were on the phone or dropping in. "They seemed to know it before we knew it ourselves," said Carol Ferguson.

"Oh, you probably said *something*," said Judson Ferguson.

"I didn't, I positively didn't. I didn't say a word to anyone, not a soul."

"Your bridge club," said her husband.

"Why does it have to be me? It could just as easily have been you, a casual remark on the train."

"All my remarks on the train are casual, believe me. But buying a new house isn't a casual matter, not with me."

"Well, me either," said Carol. "And I never opened my trap. On the other hand, I've known you, when you take the late train, you've arrived here so high that you could have *bought* a house and not remembered it. You can't deny that."

"And how many times have I taken the late train? Maybe four times in three years."

"Well, anyway, we got a call today from a Mr. Ebberly, Duncan Ebberly. He's with Rawlins and Clark. They're the ones that have their office in the little miniature Cape Cod house, up the street from the station. He asked if he could come and see us, and I said yes."

"When?"

"Tomorrow, before lunch. I said about twelve o'clock. We can get rid of him by saying we're having people for lunch. And we are. Joe and Alice are coming. Is that okay with you?"

"Sure," said Jud Ferguson. "The more agents get into the act, the better for us. At least I hope so."

The next day, a Saturday, brought rain and a cold wind, and the man who introduced himself as Duncan Ebberly inspired immediate pity. "Come in, come in," said Carol Ferguson. "You can hang your raincoat right there, to your right."

"I should have taken a taxi, but I thought it was clearing up. Shall I leave my rubbers—I'll leave them here. I hope I don't forget them. That's what I do. I've lost three pairs since last fall."

"Just put them on the floor under your raincoat and you won't forget them."

"Oh, you don't know *me*," said Duncan Ebberly.

She preceded him into the livingroom, and he waited until she was seated and indicated a chair for him. "My husband will be down in a minute. He had to change because we're expecting some people for lunch."

"Oh, yes. Saturday lunch all the young people seem to entertain. It's a very nice custom, I think. Especially nowadays, when buffet is so popular." He wore a neutral gray suit, small-figured four-in-hand, and a button-down white shirt. His shoes were black, plain-toe bluchers, exactly like some that Jud Ferguson had worn during his hitch in the Navy. Carol Ferguson got the impression that he dressed as well as he could on a limited budget; the style of dress was one thing, the quality of the clothing was something else again. On an impulse that was contrary to her plan she said, "Can I get you a cup of coffee? It's made."

"No, no thank you," said Duncan Ebberly. "Very nice of you, but I'm only going to take up a minute of your time. I'm not, uh, I'm not a, uh, salesman. By that I mean, Frank, Frank Rawlins, he's your man. I'm only here because he had to drive to York to go to a funeral. An aunt of his passed away quite suddenly or he'd have been in touch with you. I'm only, uh, I more or less take charge of the office, but I don't do the actual selling. Frank heard you were interested in buying a house, and he suggested I get in touch with you. I brought some of our listings with me, that he thought might be of interest to you and your husband. Here we have a list of the houses Frank understood you—well, anyway, here's the list. All of these houses except this one, the fieldstone. Perhaps I'd better put a checkmark beside that, or, no, I'll just cross it off. I'll run a line through that. That was sold the day before yesterday, to a party from Camden. Young couple are coming to live here, the husband is changing his job, I believe. Ah, here's Mr. Ferguson, I should imagine."

"Dear, this is Mr. Ebberly, from Rawlins and Clark."

"How do you do," said Judson Ferguson. "Has my wife bought anything yet?"

"That's a good one. No, I was just saying to her, before you came in, I'm not one of the sales staff. I, uh, handle things at the office."

"Mr. Rawlins had to go to a funeral in Lancaster. No, York," said Carol Ferguson.

"York, that's right. They're very close together, the two. As I was saying, Frank asked me to bring you this list. All except this one house, the fieldstone. That was, uh, closed Thursday."

"Quarantined?" said Jud Ferguson.

"No. No, the deal was closed. Uh, uh, finalized. A young man about your age, coming here from Camden. He bought it. So I'm crossing it off the list. But all the others are for sale. Going pretty well, too. By that I mean we have to change our list every week. Various listings in the different price classes. That's my job, you know, keeping the listings up to date. Not all I do, of course, but this is by far, by *far* the most active of our price classes. Yes."

"How about a cup of coffee?" said Jud Ferguson.

"I asked him, he said no."

"Mrs. Ferguson very kindly. I know you're expecting guests for lunch, and I won't take up your time, but I just wanted to make sure you got our listings. Oftentimes people don't pay any attention to listings we put in the mail, and that's why Frank asked me to get over here today. He'll be back late this afternoon, and I imagine he'll phone you tomorrow to find out whether he can show you any of these properties. All except the fieldstone."

"Well, we won't have time to look at the list now. We're having some people for lunch."

"Yes, I know. Mrs. Ferguson told me. So, if you have no questions, I'll be getting along. Is there anything you wanted to ask me?"

"Yeah, when is this damn rain going to stop?" said Jud Ferguson.

"Oh, can we call you a taxi, Mr. Ebberly?" said Carol Ferguson.

"Well—no, I don't think so, thank you. I might as well brave the elements once again."

"Or I could drive you back to your office. Why don't I do that? Yes. Just let me go upstairs and change my shoes—"

"I wouldn't *think* of it. Good heavens, no," said Duncan Ebberly.

"But I insist," said Carol Ferguson.

"And when she insists, my advice is don't cross her."

"Well—it *is* over a mile, and it looks as if it was coming down harder. Are you sure?"

"You start putting your things on, and I'll be with you in a minute," said Carol Ferguson.

"It's such an impo*sition,*" said Duncan Ebberly.

In the car, on the way to the office of Rawlins and Clark, Carol Ferguson made no effort to maintain a conversation; the weather, and the Saturday noon-hour traffic, made driving something less than a pleasure, and the man at her right, sitting with his hands folded in his lap, participated in the driving to the extent that at Stop signs he would lean forward and look to the right and then to the left and sit back again when the road was clear.

"It's the white house in the middle of the next block," he said.

"The little miniature Cape Cod," said Carol.

"That's correct," said Duncan Ebberly. "It's a pre-fab, you know. Frank is talking about putting it on a truck and moving it to a different location. This land around here is too valuable for just a little office. Taxes. But I'll be sorry to move. I like the hustle and bustle, especially around train time. Well, here we are. I can't begin to thank you enough."

"It was no trouble, really," said Carol.

"Do you know what I'm going to do?"

"No, what?"

"I'm going to give you a little kiss."

"You what?" said Carol.

He was smiling at her, in a way that was intended to express without words a secret mutual understanding. "Just a little kiss, you won't mind."

"Don't be ridiculous," she said.

"Now," he said, rather angrily. "Don't make a fuss." He leaned toward her and put his face close to hers. She drew back, and for a split second she was not conscious of his hand on her leg.

"What are you, some kind of a nut or something?" she said.

"I wouldn't say things like that if I were you," he said.

"Oh, get out before I push you out."

He looked at her with blank, dull hatred, and got out of the car. He entered the office without turning back, and she drove away quickly. "The miserable creep," she said.

What with the traffic and the rain it was a good ten-minute drive back to her house, and she could now see—second-guessing—that he had been an object of her pity because he had *made* himself an object of pity. The self-effacing humility was calculated, as much so as the diversionary tactic of the attempted kiss to draw her attention away from the hand on her leg. There was, moreover, the element of surprise; passes had been made at her many times, by friends and by strangers, but never by a man whose initial effect on her had been to invoke pity. She rejected the thought that anything she had said or done invited the pass. The little creep had interpreted kindness as weakness.

"Back again, safe and sound!" said Joe Reeves.

"Hello, Joe. Alice," said Carol Ferguson.

"Or *is* she safe and sound? That's the question," said Joe Reeves.

"What do you mean by *that* remark?" said Carol Ferguson. She was hanging up her raincoat.

"Well, you have to watch out for old Duncan Ebberly," said Joe Reeves.

"You shouldn't say things like that," said Alice Reeves. "You know, a crack like that could get around, and hurt him in a business way."

"What are you talking about?" said Carol.

"Listen, any crack I'd make about Duncan Ebberly is mild, compared to the things they used to say," said Joe Reeves.

"Used to, maybe, but give the poor old thing a break," said Alice Reeves.

"They've been speculating over whether you'd be all right, driving around with Ebberly," said Jud Ferguson.

"Not they—just Joe," said Alice Reeves.

"All right. Joe," said Jud Ferguson. "You want a scoop?"

"Yes. Bring me a bourbon. I'll be in the kitchen."

"Can I help?" said Alice Reeves.

"You can keep me company in the kitchen while these two lap it up," said Carol Ferguson. "Are we still going to play bridge?"

"It's a good day for it," said Jud Ferguson.

"Well, then just remember, we're having wine with lunch, so don't think you have to finish the whole bottle of bourbon. You have a tendency to overbid when you've been imbibing too freely."

"The only way to take any money from these people is to overbid. Reeves doesn't like to see anyone else play a hand."

"That's quite true," said Joe Reeves. "But who took the money the last time we played? We did."

"Come on, Alice. I can see what kind of an afternoon this is going to be," said Carol Ferguson.

"Here's your drink," said Jud Ferguson.

The casserole was in the oven. "I'll give it ten more minutes," said Carol Ferguson. "Sit down, Alice. Nothing to do till then."

Alice sat at the kitchen table, sipping her drink and smoking a cigarette. "I hope Joe didn't embarrass you."

"Embarrass me? Oh, about Mr. Ebberly."

"There's some truth to it. I mean, when we first came here one of the first stories we heard was about Duncan Ebberly. Not a story, exactly. Just that he was pointed out to us as one of the town characters. He belongs to one of the oldest families, the kind of person they're always finding jobs for, but it's a well-known secret that Duncan had hand trouble, if you know what I mean."

"Oh, sure. Is he married?"

"He was. But his wife left him a long time ago, even before we moved here. Whether that was the cause of it or not, I mean whether that was why she left him, I don't know. Personally, I always thought he was kind of a nothing, and if the stories were true, I never knew anyone he made a pass at. So I'm going to give Joe hell. *You* know. Like supposing you decide to buy your new house through Frank Rawlins, Frank's completely trustworthy and as good a real-estate agent as we have in town. But after what Joe's been saying you wouldn't want to have anything to do with Duncan Ebberly."

"Well, I wouldn't have to, would I? He told us he wasn't the salesman."

"No, but there are some women in town that wouldn't *think* of being alone with Duncan, for a minute. If they saw you giving him a ride in the rain they'll think you've gone out of your mind. Or asking for it."

"Why does Rawlins keep him?"

"What I just said. Duncan is one of those people they find jobs for. And there's some family connection. I think Frank is Duncan's nephew by marriage, something like that. Did you get a chance to look at Frank's listings? The Martin house is for sale. That's the fieldstone on Walnut Lane, near Carteret Road. I understand they're asking sixty-five, but you could probably get it for sixty thousand."

"It's gone. That's the only one I know about."

"Too bad. I know that house, and you'd have liked it. Isn't it something, the prices they're getting these days?"

Alice Reeves had no curiosity about the ride taken by Carol Ferguson, therefore no suspicion, and Carol had to be content with the information Alice volunteered. But in the middle of lunch Joe Reeves reopened the subject. "I want to say something, if I may," he announced.

"Nobody's been able to stop you," said his wife.

"No, now Alice, you keep quiet. This is serious, it really is. And the Fergusons are friends of ours, or ordinarily I wouldn't say anything. But Carol, *and* Jud, this concerns you as much as it does Carol—don't have anything more to do with Duncan Ebberly."

"Oh, we're back on that again," said his wife.

"Alice, I don't want you to interrupt. I'm going to say something that I never even told you, because I was sworn to secrecy. I happened to be the lawyer for a woman named Constance Parlow. Mrs. E. L. Parlow. You may have met her, or you may have seen her around town. She's a woman now in her fifties, although she looks a lot older and she walks with a decided limp. Carries a cane."

"I've seen her, lots of times," said Carol Ferguson. "She usually has someone with her, a nurse or some kind of a companion. She has to be helped in and out of her car."

"I'm sorry I took these drinks, because you're going to think the liquor has loosened my tongue. But the fact of the matter is, I'm very fond of you two, and when I arrived here today and was told that Carol was giving Duncan Ebberly a ride in her car, I had all I could do to keep from going right out and getting in my car and looking for you, Carol. I don't know if you noticed. Probably not. But when you got back I said something about you being safe and sound. I wanted to sound humorous, but to be absolutely candid with you, that was an expression of relief. I was worried every minute, and I even thought of calling police headquarters, but I didn't want to worry Jud. Enough having one person worry. Me. The cops know about Duncan Ebberly."

"Tell us about Mrs. Parlow," said Carol Ferguson.

"Constance Parlow ten years ago was a young middle-aged widow, whose husband was killed in the war. She had two children, both away at boarding-school, and she'd come into quite a lot of money. She was an attractive woman, and I guess it was no secret that she had a couple of boy friends that wanted to marry her. One from New York and one from Philadelphia, and it's reasonable to suppose that when they came to visit her, she probably went to bed with them. Why not? Definitely the New York fellow did. Whether the other one did too, I don't know, but I would guess so. She was a damn attractive woman, Alice will bear me out."

"Yes, she certainly was. And terribly friendly. *You* know. When she went shopping, or at church, she'd always stop and say hello. Remembered children's names, of the people in the post office, ex cetera."

"Right," said Joe Reeves. "And that, in a way, was her downfall. Because one of the people she was nice to was Duncan Ebberly, that half the women in town would barely speak to, or not at all. Well, one night her New York boy friend had been there for dinner and left early, about nine o'clock or so, to drive back to New York, and Constance locked up and went to her room, took a bath, and was in bed, reading, and suddenly there was Duncan Ebberly. Standing in the middle of the room. How he got there we were never quite sure, but obviously he'd been there in the house for several hours, before she locked up. Naturally she was frightened, and it was obvious what he was there for, but she didn't lose her head. He started making passes at her, but she got away from him and out of bed and kept trying to reason with him. She got out in the hall and called for help, trying to rouse the servants, and he struggled with her trying to shut her up, and somehow or other he pushed her or she fell down a flight of stairs. Broke her hip and one arm, and lay there unconscious. He of course got away."

"But she knew who he was," said Carol Ferguson.

Joe Reeves nodded. "Yes. She knew. But when the police came she gave a phony description of the intruder. She'd never seen him before. He wore a mask over his face, and so on. The cops brought a couple of suspects to the hospital for her to identify, but naturally she said they were the wrong ones."

"What about the New York boy friend? Was he brought into it?" said Jud Ferguson.

"He appeared voluntarily. He was completely in the clear. The servants had seen him leave. The maid saw Constance kiss him goodbye. Oh, he was all right. Except that he passed out of her life, as did the Philadelphia guy. She was in and out of the hospital for over a year, a series of operations. That pin thing they do for a broken hip. She had a hell of a bad time."

"When did you find out about Duncan?" said Alice Reeves.

"The cops decided she wasn't telling the truth, her phony

description. Norman Hackett, he was then chief of police, had a talk with her and told her frankly he didn't believe her story, and from what they knew about Duncan Ebberly they had a pretty strong suspicion that he might be the guy. That's when she sent for us, and I was assigned to handle the case. I went along with Norm Hackett. They'd never had enough on Duncan to make an actual arrest, but cops hear things and they knew he was a bad actor in that department, and they were anxious to put him away. So I tried to persuade her to tell us the truth, and she *did*. She told *me*. But she also told me she wouldn't sign a complaint or do anything else, and if she ever had to testify against Duncan she'd swear he wasn't the man."

"Why?" said Jud Ferguson.

"Well, Duncan's mother was still living then and there was a family connection. And in addition to that, Constance had these misguided notions about the humanitarian thing to do. She had some twisted notion that she might have accidentally, unintentionally, given Duncan some reason to think that she was flirting with him. I tried to argue with her that the real humanitarian thing would be to put him away where he could get psychiatric treatment. At least get him out of the way before he killed somebody, maybe a child. But I got absolutely nowhere."

"There should have been some way to make her testify," said Jud Ferguson.

"You haven't got much of a case if your plaintiff swears the defendant is the wrong man," said Joe Reeves. He turned to Carol Ferguson. "So you see, Carol, I really was worried about you."

"I never heard any of this before," said Alice Reeves. "I said to Carol in the kitchen, I always considered Duncan a kind of a nothing."

"You all understand, of course, that this is top secret. I only told you because I wanted to warn Carol, just in case he misinterprets her doing him a favor. Constance Parlow only spoke to him, but that was all he needed. She spoke to him when other women gave him the cold shoulder."

"Well, if he ever forces his attentions on my little treasure, I'll take care of him," said Jud Ferguson.

"How will you know? I don't tell you everything," said Carol Ferguson.

"Any more than I tell Joe everything," said Alice Reeves.

There was in her tone—or was there?—something that made Carol look quickly at her, and she found that Alice was ready, waiting for that look.

"Is anybody cold here?" said Carol Ferguson. "Jud, will you go back and see if the kitchen door blew open?"

"I wasn't going to say anything," said Alice Reeves. "But I think there must be a door open somewhere."

"So delicate," said her husband.

"Christ, aren't they?" said Jud Ferguson.

TEDDY AND
THE SPECIAL FRIENDS

They could be organized into The Special Friends of Teddy
Morris, and if ever they should be, the organization would be
as far-flung as the American Express Company, on a not considerably smaller scale. But it is unlikely that any effort will be
made to formalize the band of men and women who are united
in a common concern for the welfare and happiness of Edlon
Warford Morris and for exchanges of information regarding his
activities. The special friends already feel, and rightly, that
there is something arcane and distinguished about being an acquaintance of Teddy's; and to create an organization that
would have a name would be to run the risk of having people
apply for membership, and if that should happen, it would not
be possible, as it is now, for each of Teddy's friends to decide for
himself who is and who is not one of the specials. All over the
world there are men and women who have met Teddy Morris,
and there are many, many more who have heard of him, but it
is certainly more deliciously exciting to think that Teddy himself
does not write his outrageously insulting letters to anyone and
everyone, and that friendship with him demands a special toler-
ance that the run of men and women are not equal to. To be a
special friend of Teddy's requires special qualities that distin-
guish each friend as a rather special person. And it is more
than an acquired taste.

Teddy, of course, is a Philadelphian, and in spite of his
prolonged absences from that city, he is loyal to it. But notwith-
standing the fact that some of the special friends are also Philadelphians, it would be a great mistake to look for Philadelphia

characteristics (whatever they may be) in the unorganized band of his special friends. Teddy is also a Harvard man, but again it would be a mistake to look for Harvard characteristics (whatever *they* may be). He is knowledgeable about painting and music, food and wine, the race of Frenchmen, the Christian martyrs (he was a convert to and for many years a devout communicant of the Roman Catholic Church), six-day bicycle riding in the Twenties, the Scottish crofters, and the Basque tongue, among his countless interests and hobbies. But he has special friends who would not know the difference between Letourner and de Latour, between Milhaud and Millet, the Fly Club and The Rabbit, the Wharf Rats and the Fish House. He has special friends who would not recognize any of those names, as well as a few who could identify them all.

He is Teddy, and to the special ones the only Teddy who needs no more explicit identification. Such an episode as this, for instance, has happened: Louis Cathcart, having a drink at a bar in Nairobi, was accosted by a German woman who had been left behind while her husband went shooting. "You are Louis Cathcart, no?"

"Yes, I am. How do you do?"

"How do I do? How do I do what? You don't care how I do. I don't care how you do. But you will have a drink with me and I will have ten drinks with you. Shall I tell you why? Because we are friends of Teddy's."

"Oh, do you know Teddy? Of *course* I'll have a drink with you. When did you last see Teddy?"

"When? In 1939. He will not speak to my husband ever again, but no matter. When did you last see Teddy?"

"A month ago. I had dinner with him, as a matter of fact."

"Let's drink to Teddy. I miss him, but he will not speak to my husband ever again. My husband was a Nazi, but some Nazis Teddy will speak to, some he will not. To my husband, no. Don't ask me why that is so. I don't know. But Teddy always has reasons for everything."

"And usually pretty good ones, although I don't *always* think so."

"Usually pretty good ones, I think so. My name is Herta Schlageman. My husband is Willy Schlageman."

"Means nothing to me, if you expected it to. But I have no list of the good Nazis and the bad ones."

"Teddy has his own list."

"I'll just bet he has," said Cathcart.

"Louis Cathcart. Once when you were a young man you and Teddy rode bicycles together. Three weeks? Four weeks? The chateau country."

"Think of your remembering that. We were gone a month. I was twenty-two, and that's quite a long time ago."

"You speak German? You know *rote Ruhr?*"

"No."

She laughed. "You got it on the bicycle trip."

He laughed. "Well, I just learned the German for dysentery," he said. "Wait a minute. *I* know who you are. You say your name is Schlageman, but what was it before that? Herta— Herta—don't make me guess."

She smiled. "I make you guess."

"You were a skater! Herta—von—von—Weil. Herta von Weil!"

She nodded.

"The Olympics, at Garmisch," he went on.

She smiled and shook her head. "No. Before Garmisch. But must you att four years to my age?"

"And to my own, for that matter," said Cathcart. "You— let me see now—you were at school at Lausanne when you met Teddy. Or you'd just finished your schooling, right?"

"Finished," she said.

"He told me that you were the most exquisite creature he'd ever seen."

"On skates. You must remember to att that—on skates. Off the ice I was a shy, neurotic dumbbell. An American boy called me a dumbbell. I cried, and Teddy came to my rescue. He danced with me and zent me flowers. My mother didn't like it, Mr. Morris dancing with me and zenting me flowers. My mother didn't like the friends of Mr. Morris. The riffraff. His friends, perhaps, but not Mr. Morris. Mr. Morris, my father said, was a friend of Mr. Dawes, the vice-president of the United States, and Mr. Dawes was a friend of my father. Did you know Mr. Dawes?"

"Well—slightly. I worked for him, in an extremely minor capacity. He used to go to Teddy's flat in Paris to relax. He played the piano, and Teddy had two very good pianos. Mr. Dawes was a composer, too, you know."

"Mr. Dawes? A composer? No, I did not know. But I did not meet Mr. Dawes. He was not with Teddy when I met Teddy."

"Who *were* with Teddy then?"

"Then? Oh—I think you know them. Maggie Vollmer. You remember Maggie Vollmer?"

"Sure. That married the Peruvian."

"He was with her, but they were not married. He wanted to sleep with me—"

"So did she, I imagine."

"You are correct. But they never looked at me before Teddy was nice to me, and I had no liking for them."

"Who else was in the entourage?"

"Nicky Pelascu. He wanted me to pose for him."

"Too bad you didn't. At least from the artistic standpoint. He was a pretty good portraitist, you know. But I'm afraid your mother was right. From a mother's point of view, they were riffraff. Who else?"

"Pat Sweeney."

"There's a name out of the past! Pat Sweeney. I guess he was the original free-loader of all time."

"Free-loader?"

"American slang for a man that sponges off everybody."

"Sponges off? . . . Oh, I remember that now. My English is rusty. The Americans and the English go to see my husband at the Works, but he does not bring them home so much."

"What did you think of Pat Sweeney?"

"He was a beautiful tennis player. He could do all sports well."

"What else?"

"What else was there? He drank whiskey day and night. Even on the tennis court he drink whiskey-sodas."

"Desmond Patrick Francis Xavier Sweeney. Teddy used to call him the director of athletics."

"He was sad."

"Sad? Yes, I guess he was."

"If he was not playing a game, he was sad," she said. "He had to do some sports, or if he did not do some sports he had to drink whiskey-sodas. And if he did not do sports or have whiskey-sodas he would think about his life, and that was not very nice."

"No, I guess it wasn't. But how very astute of you to have noticed that."

"Astute?"

"Clever. Observant," said Cathcart.

"Oh, no. It was the same with me," she said.

"Except for the whiskey-soda."

"That came later," she said. "Pat was a dumbbell, too, and I was a dumbbell. Teddy put us together and we fell in love."

"And you still love Pat?"

"No. Only when we were with Teddy. He thought we would be nice together, and so we were, but that was because Teddy wanted us to be together, to be nice together and in love."

"Yes, I see what you mean. Teddy was always finding people for people. We all did what Teddy thought we ought to do. Amazing how often he was right. Teddy introduced me to my first wife, and as long as we were where Teddy could keep an eye on us, we made an ideal couple. The trouble was, Teddy arranged so many lives that he couldn't keep an eye on all of them, and we couldn't live up to his expectations when we were left on our own."

"Do you know why?"

"No."

"I do, I think. I think it was because that is the kind of people we were. We had to have Teddy show us what to do. We were nothing very much without Teddy. All of us, all over the world, for thirty years, forty years."

"Yes," said Cathcart.

"Teddy was Reverend Mother. At school I adored Reverend Mother. I was good because she wanted me to be good, but when I was away from school I did not have Reverend Mother to make me want to be good."

"But what about your skating? You were good at that."

"Oh, that," she said. "That was me. I didn't need Reverend Mother for that. I could do something better than anyone else could do it. Some girls could sing, some girls could flirt. I could skate. No one ever had to make me practice. I was good, I wanted to be the best."

"And you were."

"But when I became the best an American boy called me a dumbbell. A stupid boy, cruel, but he made me realize that life is not skating. Skating is not life, I should say. It is not life to put on skates and go out on the ice all by oneself. After one has given a beautiful performance, one leaves the ice and takes off one's skates, and an American boy calls one a dumbbell and one cries. Then I met Teddy, and he thought Pat Sweeney and I would be nice together. Teddy knew that Pat and I were very much alike."

"Possibly you should have married Pat."

"You did not know my parents, or you would not say that," she said. "They wanted me to marry Schlageman, and there was nothing else for me to do. Well, I am still the wife of Schlageman. I would not be still the wife of Pat Sweeney."

"No, the Luftwaffe took care of that. Sweeney was killed the first time he flew combat."

"He was lucky," she said.

"Why do you say that?"

"Don't be angry. Wasn't it better to be killed the first time than to fly many times and suffer in between? He would have suffered. I told you, when he was not doing sports he was sad. It would have been the same between one mission and the next. But worse, because that was war and not tennis. And he was going to be killed. Those early pilots were killed quickly, R.A.F. and Luftwaffe. So he was lucky."

"Why are you here and not out shooting?"

"Schlageman does not like me to shoot."

"Then why do you come here?"

"Schlageman wants me to be here."

"And that settles it?"

"Yes."

"You always do everything that Schlageman wants?"

"Yes."

"Would you have done everything that Pat Sweeney wanted?"

"Oh, no."

"We're both friends of Teddy's, and that makes us sort of members of the same club. So do you mind if I ask you—did you have an affair with Pat?"

"Yes. He was my first."

"Was that because you thought Teddy wanted you to?"

"Of course. You did the same thing with your first wife."

"Quite right. I did. And for the same reason, I suppose. And you think it's because we're all the kind of people we are?"

"Yes. We all need Teddy, and we're all terrified that he will disapprove."

"That's true, but how do you know that? You haven't seen Teddy since 1939."

"One doesn't forget Teddy. One still needs Teddy, and is terrified of his disapproval."

"But in your case not enough to make you want to leave Schlageman."

"Ah, but Teddy would not want me to leave Schlageman. Teddy does not need me. Or you. Or anyone."

"You're right. He needs us all, but not any one of us. Will you have dinner with me?"

"No. Schlageman would not like it."

"And therefore you dine alone. But you drink with me."

"It is not the same, drinking at a bar, and dining at a table. But thank you for asking me, Cathcart. And give my love to our Teddy. Tell him I think of him every day of my life. And I do."

They all do, the special friends of Teddy Morris. In New York two of the special friends are Mary Whiting and Andy McCullen, who never see each other; but a year ago Andy was called to the telephone in his shop on Second Avenue. "Big deal," his partner said, handing him the phone. "It's Mrs. Arthur Whiting. Maybe we could unload the marble top on her."

"No big deal," said Andy McCullen, taking the phone. "I know why she's calling. *Hello?*"

"Andy, it's Mary Whiting. I just had a letter from Teddy."

"I was just thinking of him. Where is he?"

"This was written from London, three days ago. It's odd,

because I was thinking of him the morning he wrote it."

"E.S.P., dear. Extra-sensory perception. What does he have to say, and why don't you ever come in my shop?"

"I've been in your shop, and you have nothing there I want to buy."

"You sound just like Teddy," said Andy McCullen. "Does he mention me in the letter?"

"No, not by name, but I know he must have been thinking of you because he goes on at great length about his new flat. Did you know he's taken a flat in Chelsea?"

"I knew he was thinking about it."

"Shall I read you his letter? Have you got time?"

"Not now, but why don't you drop in and bring the letter? I'll give you a sherry or a cup of tea, and you can have a look around. We have a lot of things you haven't seen. I really have to buzz off now, Mary. I have a customer."

He hung up and faced his partner.

"Is that the way to treat fifty million dollars?" said the partner.

"The only way to treat this fifty million dollars," said Andy. "You see I had a letter from Teddy, too, and I know what's in his letter to her. She lied. He did mention me by name. He told her that if she wanted to give him a present for the new flat, to go have a look at our stuff."

"Then why didn't she just come in and *have* a look?"

"Not Mary. First she had to find out whether I'd heard from Teddy. She never would have come in if we knew Teddy'd sent her. Oh, Teddy knows that one, all right. He knows us all."

"Maybe we *can* unload the marble top," said the partner.

"Not on Teddy. It's not good enough for him, and you know it."

"No I don't, but I don't know Teddy. Why are you all so sweet on Teddy?"

"You've just seen one reason why. He understands us all, and there's no one kinder. I wouldn't be at all surprised if Teddy knew we haven't sold an ash tray this month. I'm going to make her buy the sewing box."

"The sewing box? That's only four hundred."

"That's the only thing we have that Teddy would like. Teddy trusts me."

"The marble top is eighteen hundred. Make her buy it for herself."

"Not this time. I'll let her pay six hundred for the sewing box, but I positively won't let her buy the marble top for Teddy. And if you try to sell her anything while I'm out, I'll give you the worst slap I ever gave you. Now you remember that, do you hear?"

"Teddy, Teddy, Teddy," said the partner.

When a special friend and a new acquaintance of Teddy's get together the outcome is not inevitably happy, despite their joint and several favorable opinions of the man. For instance in Hobe Sound last winter Caspar and Eve Ellington, from St. Louis, were asked by the Walter Newcombs to provide a room for their friend Gertrude Dinsmore, who had arrived a day sooner than she was expected. The Ellingtons were more than glad to accommodate the Newcombs, not only because the Newcombs had been coming to Hobe Sound for thirty years against the Ellingtons' six, but because Gertrude Dinsmore was the kind of person who could disregard such things as the Newcombs' schedules.

Although she was to spend only one night at the Ellingtons', Gertie had six pieces of Vuitton luggage in the Newcombs' hall when Eve went to fetch her. She permitted Eve to carry the larger pieces to the station wagon, and waited on the front seat while Eve was coping with the tailgate. "You might think Walter Newcomb was Secretary of State," said Gertie, as the car got started. "He has all these damn people down here."

"Why Secretary of State?" said Eve.

"What?"

"Why did you say Secretary of State? I thought Walter was a Republican."

"I don't know what Douglas Dillon is if he isn't a Republican. Or is he? I don't know what he is, and I couldn't care less. Whose house have you got?"

"Our own."

"I meant, whose was it? You didn't build, did you?"

"No. We bought the Rodeheavers'."

"Oh, you're down at that end. I remember when there wasn't anything down there. Why did the Rodeheavers have to sell? Have people stopped drinking Coca-Cola?"

"They bought a house on one of the keys."

"What are we supposed to wear tonight? Nancy went off to Palm Beach without so much as telling me what we're to wear. I had her make a hair appointment for me for tomorrow. I hope I can get it changed. I have nothing to do this afternoon, unless you've planned something."

"No, I hadn't planned anything. My husband's playing golf, but I don't play. Actually Nancy didn't get your telegram till this morning."

"Oh, that's all right. I just wanted to get out of New York. I'm *sick* of New York. Three days of it, and really I've had it. I can see everybody I want to see in three days at the *most*. My dentist got through with me sooner than I'd expected, so I just told Nancy I'd be here today instead of tomorrow. They didn't always use to have a houseful of people. Who have they got, for heaven's sake? They have four bedrooms, so they must have—well, they could have eight, couldn't they? No, there's only a single bed in the downstairs bedroom. Seven. They usually give that to a man. What man is there by himself?"

"I really don't know."

"Some golfing friend of Walter's, no doubt. One of those dreary, *dreary* men, that Walter likes to play golf with. They get home from Palm Beach, so dead tired they barely last through dinner, in spite of all the Martinis they drink. And then they're off to bed because they have to get up early in the morning. Well, just as long as I don't have to play bridge with them. One of them cost me a pretty penny, I can tell you, the last time I was here. This place always makes me think of a friend of mine. He had a house here even before Walter and Nancy, and that's going back a long ways."

"I didn't know anybody was here before they were."

"Oh, Teddy was. Teddy Morris. He's a—"

"Oh, I know Teddy Morris."

"You *do?* Where would you have known Teddy—or I wonder if it's the same one."

"Oh, this is the famous one," said Eve Ellington. "Originally from Philadelphia, but lived abroad most of his life. He was at Harvard the same time my husband was, but I never met him till last year. A perfectly charming man, I thought."

"Well—I suppose that description could fit Teddy. This is your house, isn't it?"

"This is it. Would you like me to try to change your hair appointment while you're having your bath?"

"That'd be awfully nice," said Gertie.

Much later in the day, her hair set and her bags unpacked, Gertie joined her temporary hostess on the terrace. "Dinner's not till nine-thirty, I imagine," she said.

"Nancy asked us to get there at nine," said Eve Ellington.

"That's a trick of hers, so that I'll get there at half past. Which means we'll finally sit down at ten, and the golfers will go to bed at half past eleven. I hope there are some unsleepy bridge players. Do you play?"

"Yes, we play. My husband is quite good."

"Well, then there's some hope. I'm going to help myself to this Scotch, if you don't mind. I had only one at the hairdresser's and you really need something after a night on the train. Don't move. I'll help myself. Where did you actually meet Teddy?"

"Teddy Morris? In London. My husband ran into him in the elevator at Claridge's. They hadn't seen each other since before the war."

"Oh, your husband was a friend of Teddy's?"

"I thought I told you, they were at Harvard at the same time."

"You did tell me that, but Teddy's the least likely person I know to attach any importance to old college ties. So they must have been friends before the war."

"No. To tell you the truth, my husband wasn't too keen on Morris. A bit too much of the aesthete, I suppose you might put it. But Morris couldn't have been more friendly and terribly *nice*. We had an awfully busy schedule, with English friends, but we had supper with Morris every night we were in London. I thought he was perfectly charming, and my husband thawed out too. Cap—my husband—doesn't usually go for the international set, but they were certainly fun for a few evenings. A bit strange, some of them, but fun. There was one man, he must have weighed close to three hundred pounds, but he was one of the best dancers I ever danced with."

"Johnny Reddington."

"That's exactly who it was. He'd come off the dance floor absolutely wringing wet, but he was so light on his feet. He'd been a racing driver till he got so fat he couldn't squeeze into a car, and then he became a bob-sledder."

"Did you enjoy his conversation?"

"Not really, but I knew he was trying to shock me and I wouldn't let on. Is that his line?"

"Not only his line. He meant every word of it."

"But he's so fat. And he's definitely not young. Sixty?"

"Yes, he's sixty, or very close to it. Who else did Teddy have for you?"

"Have for us? I definitely got the impression that these were his constant companions."

"Teddy always hand-picks his groups."

"Oh, not this time. They were all different, a different group every night, and nothing at all like—well, like Cap and me. We met a movie actress that I've never seen in American movies, but I see her in British movies on TV."

"Kathleen Webberley."

"That's who it was. You really know all these people, don't you? How old is she? I couldn't be sure."

"Oh—fifty. Fifty-two."

"Yes, that's what *I* thought. Cap thought she was about forty. She invited him to her flat, without me. Specified without me. Cap said he never went to strange ladies' flats without me, and she said, 'Very well, then bring her, but she'll cramp our style.' They're all so outspoken, those people. They make absolutely no bones about what they're up to. Even one young girl, very young. Eighteen at the most. And her father is a member of the House of Lords."

"Tanya Greensdale."

"Right again. She propositioned Cap. I think so many of the men in that crowd are fairies that when the women meet someone like Cap, they go haywire. That was Cap's theory."

"If you think they're sex-starved, you're wrong."

"Well, maybe because my husband was new, a new face."

"Is he good-looking, your husband?"

"Yes. Not in any exotic, Rex Harrison way. Typically American good looks. Half German, half Scotch-Irish. You'd never mistake him for anything but an American."

"Who else propositioned you?"

"Of the men, only one. Gerald Somebody. He was the only one I definitely wasn't amused by."

"Jerry Wixted."

"Those loose lips, and eyes ready to fall out. And he *fancied* himself so. We got up to dance—this was at the 400 Club—and he danced a few steps and then guided me to an empty table. Sat me down and said he was going to be in Paris for the next few days, but when he got back he'd like to take me to dinner. I thanked him ever so politely, but said I'd be homeward bound on the *Queen Elizabeth*. Well, he said if I'd wait over a week, we could go back together on the *Queen Mary*. That would be really more fun, he said. When I said no, he said what about that same night? 'You're really quite attractive, you know,' he said. 'And you mustn't play hard-to-get with me.' Insufferable! Do the English women put up with that?"

"A great many have, with Jerry."

"But why?"

"Oh, Jerry's not so bad. There are so many good-looking Englishmen that Jerry's a welcome change."

"I thought he was horrible. I couldn't bear to have him touch me, let alone anything else."

"Then he got some response, didn't he?"

"No, he did not," said Eve Ellington.

"Well, Teddy must have had a wonderful time."

"Why do you say that?"

"Why not? He took you out to supper every night, so he must have been having a ball."

"I have a feeling that there's more behind your remark than just that. He did take us out to supper every night. Danced with me. Sent me flowers. He didn't treat us like a couple of hicks in the international smart set, if that's what you meant. Perhaps he did have in mind getting something started between me and one of those men. That occurred to me, the first night we went out with him. Or he may have been giving Cap a chance to kick over the traces with those girls. But he must know that Americans aren't hicks any more. As far as sophistication is concerned, we have that right in St. Louis. We don't shock as easily as we're supposed to. I've had the same things said to me that the fat man said, at some of our club dances back home. In Hobe Sound, too, but here you'd more or less expect it."

"Do you hear from Teddy?"

"Only once. We wrote and thanked him, at least Cap did. I thought it over and decided not to. But he wrote to me, not to Cap. He said that Mr. Wixted was going to be in the United States and wanted to know our address, but he wouldn't give it to him. What was it he said now? 'I don't think our Jerry ought to have everything he wants.' "

"An obvious double-entendre."

"Yes, I thought so."

"And that's all you've heard from Teddy?"

"That's all."

"Well, it's awfully hard to keep up with Teddy, and not worth it unless you happen to be one of his special people. He takes very special knowing."

"Does he? He seemed to me like a very nice person, charming, good manners and all that. With aesthetic tastes and the money to indulge them. I suppose he's a fairy. Cap thinks so. But his kind I don't mind. He's not going to do me any harm. Why are you smiling?"

"Well, you see I *know* Teddy, and I couldn't help but be amused at your oversimplified impression of him. But then you only saw him those few nights in London."

"I don't think my impression would change if I saw him every day for a year."

"Which isn't very likely, is it? I don't think our Teddy has made a new friend in twenty years."

"What about the young English girl?"

"Tanya Greensdale? She's second generation. Her mother was a friend of Teddy's—still is. Yes, we're getting into the second generation, and it's amazing how quickly some of them are—what's that word?—assimilated."

"I don't think I'd like our daughter to be assimilated."

"But she wouldn't be second generation, would she? You and your husband were never Teddy's friends."

"Mrs. Dinsmore, are you trying to snub me?"

"If I am, I won't admit it till tomorrow. I have no place else to sleep. Do you play canasta?"

It would hardly be accurate or true to include Teddy's mother among his special friends. And yet every year, on her birthday, he has dinner with her in whatever city she happens to be. It is not always Philadelphia, by any means. It is just as likely to be Paris or New York, London or Madrid. Wherever she may be, he never fails to make the effort to be with her on that one evening. Last April it was London, which did not require much of an effort; the taxi ride from Chelsea Embankment to the old lady's rooms in Claridge's Hotel. "Happy birthday, Mama," he said.

"Thank you, and what did you find to bring me? It gets harder every year, doesn't it? What is there to amuse a rickety old woman?"

"You've been calling yourself an old woman since you were in your forties."

"But not a rickety one. All right, give it to me, and hand me that pair of scissors, will you please? Will I need my glasses?"

"To read the card."

"*You* read the card, but first let me open my present. Or does the card come first?"

"You can open the present and then read the card," he said.

She hefted the parcel, which was about the size of a cigarette carton. "Can't tell anything from the weight of it, but it doesn't rattle. And it's not liquid." She held the parcel to her ear, and shook it. "No, it isn't heavy enough for perfume anyway."

"And I wouldn't buy you perfume. Whenever I've bought you scent you've given it away."

"That's right, we do call it scent when we're over here. All right, then, here goes." She snipped the gilt cord and tore away the tissue paper, and opened the glazed cardboard box. "Why it's a dagger. Is this a dagger I see before me?"

"It's not a dagger, it's a dirk, and it belonged to some member of your clan."

"My clan? I didn't know I had a clan."

"You're a Stewart, that's a clan."

"Yes, I guess it is, but how many generations removed am I? I never even think of myself as Scotch. But did a Scotchman carry this around with him? Where did they get that reputation for frugality?"

"This was worn tucked in the stocking on the right leg. It was worn on dress occasions."

"It's very handsome. And must have set you back a few dollars. This part is gold, isn't it?"

"It cost me a packet, but I thought you'd like it for your desk at home."

"I hope it isn't too sharp. Your grandnephews are just at that age. I'll have to keep it out of their reach. Well, thank you, Ted. I know you planned just where it would go on my desk, with all the other junk I keep there."

"This isn't junk, Mama."

"Oh, I know it isn't. Well, we're having pheasant. I can chew pheasant, and I can slosh it down with champagne so it won't stick in my throat. I hope that's all right with you. It's what I ordered, but we can change if you're not in any hurry. They're always very nice to me here. I'm seventy-nine years old, next year I'll be eighty. This is going to be my last trip abroad. I don't want to die in transit, so to speak. It'd be such a nuisance for everybody. Margaret wouldn't know what to do. She doesn't pack me properly any more. Forgets some things, and puts in two of things I don't need. I'd fire her, but she'll be all right as long as we stay put in Philadelphia. I often think, poor Margaret, she hasn't had much of a life of her own. A personal maid for thirty-five years, and now she's almost as old as I am, but hasn't a soul in the world except a grandson of her sister's, a Catholic priest in Africa. She put him through college, Villanova, and then he decided to be a priest. He came to see me before he went to Africa. I asked him why they sent him all the way to Africa when we have all those Negroes in Philadelphia and it'd be much less dangerous for a white man at home. He had some explanation, but I'm afraid I didn't pay much attention to it. But isn't this a bad time to send white priests to Africa?"

"In some places, I should think so."

"Margaret worries, every time she picks up the paper. Those Belgian nuns. I've often wondered about the after-effects on a nun that's been raped. I'm sure I'll never know, but it could be an interesting problem. I wonder if any of them ever give in, and if you gave in and enjoyed it, would you have to stop being a nun?"

"That kind of rape is usually followed by murder."

"Yes, men that do that are so ashamed that they have to kill the poor woman. So I guess it wouldn't do any good to give in. They're going to murder you anyway. But I remember a story I read during the first World War. A German officer raped a Belgian girl. Always the Belgians, isn't it? And then he fell in love with her. It was in a magazine. I remember thinking at the time, that girl must have given in. I was never quite convinced that it was a real rape. Most women I've talked to are inclined to be skeptical on the whole subject of rape. I am myself, having been married and the mother of two children. Your sister sent her love."

"Thank you."

"To think that she has grandchildren. It isn't so terribly long ago that I was able to accept it as a fact that she could reproduce. But now those that she reproduced have reproduced. My great-grandchildren. When you go home again you must make a point of seeing them. Marjorie has hurt feelings that you show so little interest in her grandchildren, and they are after all your grandnephews."

"Marjorie has such a strong sense of other people's family obligations. But I haven't had a letter from her in twenty years, not even when I was with the Field Service."

"Well, you know who to blame for that. Whatever you did to Joe, or said to him, Marjorie feels she has to string along with her husband. And she's right."

"I never said anything to Joe, or did anything to him. We were all those years at school together before he proposed to Marjorie, and we could never stand the sight of each other. But when he married Marjorie he had to make sure that everybody knew he didn't approve of me. Nobody cared what he thought of me, or I of him, but he made a big thing of registering his disapproval. And Marjorie *was* perfectly right to string along with him. But let's not have any of this hurt feelings because I refuse to say goo-goo to her grandchildren."

"I've given up trying to make you and Marjorie see eye to eye. But you could spare a few minutes with her children and grandchildren. It would look better."

"To whom?"

"There you have me," said the old lady. "I haven't seen what you wrote on the card. Will you read it, please?"

" 'To Mama, with love and no wish to cut the silver cord.' "

"That's very nice, Ted. You were always much more bothered by the silver cord than I ever was. But I'm glad you don't want to cut it at this late date. It never would have bothered *you* if you hadn't read Freud and those people."

"But I did read them."

"You understood yourself so well. Did you ever stop to think that you were also taking a lot of the mystery out of life?"

"I took the mystery out of my own life. When I was finally able to do that, I led a much more peaceful existence. I know all about myself, Mama, and I'm not unhappy. It took me about thirty years to come to terms with reality, and ever since then nothing has bothered me very much. I know I was a great disappointment to Papa, but for a long time he was a great disappointment to me, too. He really was my father, wasn't he?"

"Oh, yes. I never had a lover, or a love affair. You've asked me that before. I think in the hope of explaining to yourself why you and he were so different from each other. But you weren't so different, you two. He didn't know the things you know, the artistic things. But he was just as selfish as you. The difference was that he liked having a woman to go through life with. And you don't. That isn't as great a difference as it may seem. Instead of one woman, me, that your father had, you have all these friends of yours, that take up so much of your time and lavish their affection on you. I gave him what your friends give you, but it amounts to the same thing. When he wanted to get away from me he did, even though for thirty years we slept in the same bed. You shut off your telephone, or go on a trip to some other city. Well, I think you're old enough to be told this. Your father really didn't want to have children. I was the one that did. He could have gone through life with just me. Oh, later on he probably would have had a discreet affair with another woman, out of curiosity. But when you and Marjorie were born it was very hard for him to pretend to be a proud and loving father. It was all he could do to hide the fact that he considered you a damned nuisance, a threat to his comfort. You and Marjorie. He didn't start to love either one of you until you were able to walk and say a few words. 'Jesus Christ! Can't you make that child stop crying?' And you cried quite a lot as a baby. You were frightened of him. So was Marjorie. Does all this check with what you know about yourself?"

"Very much so."

"Well, that's good. Ring for the waiter, will you please?"

The old lady went back to Philadelphia right after her birthday, and at the final Friday afternoon concert of the Orchestra, while Mr. Ormandy was conducting the *Rosenkavalier* waltz, she fell peacefully and more deeply asleep than ever before. Teddy noted in letters to a special few of the special friends that she probably died in the midst of pretending to lead the orchestra; that her eyes may have been closed, but that she was not really asleep. The *Rosenkavalier,* he said, was one piece that did *not* put her to sleep.

Teddy flew home for the funeral, of course, and took a suite at the Barclay so that—he explained—he would not be a nuisance. Marjorie had plenty of room for him, she said, but she agreed that he probably would be more comfortable at the hotel. All those years of bachelor apartments, a man gets set in his ways. But there is no denying that Teddy has changed. He has stayed on in Philadelphia ever since the funeral—seven months, now—and doesn't seem to mind it as much as he used to. He gives little dinner parties, one a week, and has assumed the position in artistic circles that could always have been his. He has been a darling to his niece, Lydia Poffenberg, and her children, and his interest in Lydia could not have been more timely. Things have not been going too well between Lydia and Dale Poffenberg, and having someone like Teddy, with his immense culture, has been a godsend to Lyd. They lunch every

Friday at twelve-thirty, in plenty of time to be in their seats at the Orchestra before the doors close. And there is something very stabilizing in having Teddy and Lydia occupy those same seats that his mother occupied for so many years. He has not made any plans to go away this winter.

THE TWINKLE
IN HIS EYE

At this very moment, in a town in southwestern Massachusetts, a man who possesses all the information that has been handed down by Galileo, Watt, Millikan, Boyle, and Newton is planning to get rid of his wife. He does not contemplate divorce. He wants to murder her, and he has wanted to for ten years. Before that he was very much in love with her for four years, and it probably is too late to hope for any change in his intentions.

The love began in 1948, the year that Gordon Whittier received his Master of Science degree from the University of New Hampshire and his appointment as math and science teacher at the Consolidated High School of Rexbury-Hammonton–North Chintocket. If ever there was a young man ready to settle down, it was Gordon Whittier. He had graduated with honors in math and physics from his high school in Hartford, Connecticut, and more to please his grandmother than anything else, he entered Amherst. He was given draft deferment until he completed sophomore year; applied for officer training in the Navy, and was shipped out to Notre Dame. There he was commissioned an ensign, USNR, and through a foul-up due to a similarity of names, he was ordered to report to CINCPAC, which was then at Pearl Harbor, for duty in a seagoing tugboat. The Gordon Whitty whose orders he had received reported at Pearl two days after Gordon Whittier sailed for the Admiralty Islands as exec aboard the tugboat. Gordon Whittier had no combat, no decorations, no considerable length of service, and he was one of the last to be separated from the Navy. He came out a j.g., with a Pacific ribbon and the ribbon for pistol shooting. Gordon Whitty was killed at Iwo while in command of an LST, but Gordon Whittier learned this fact so many months later that it was an occasion for only momentary self-congratulation on his own good fortune. He wanted to get home, to finish his education, and become an assistant professor at some good college. But Amherst had no room for him, and after dozens of letters he managed to get accepted at Durham.

He was not much of a skiier, and in any case he worked so hard for his degrees that his extra-curricular activity consisted principally of beers with married students who were in college on the GI Bill. But during the New Hampshire winter carnival he met Norma Bull, who came from Springfield, Massachusetts, and she struck him as a girl he would like to see more of. Her date had told Gordon that Norma was a guaranteed lay, and it was a new experience for Gordon to sit and drink beer with a girl for two or three hours and know that when she got up to leave, it would be to go straight to bed with a man. Meanwhile nothing in her conversation indicated that she was that kind of girl, and as for looks, she was nothing special. She was not homely, but she was not pretty and *not* a sweater girl. It was hard to believe that such a girl—you could almost call her mousy—could one minute be joining in the singing of "I'm gonna buy a paper doll," and then say goodnight to everybody and head for the hay with her date. There were plenty of girls drinking beer and singing along with the juke box who were more flamboyant about their attractions, but girls like them did not interest Gordon Whittier. He was also prepared to concede that he did not interest them. He had been in Massachusetts, New Hampshire, Vermont, Connecticut, New York, Indiana, Illinois, and California; flown over or passed through various other states of the Union, and had spent some time in the Hawaiian Islands, and other islands and atolls in the Pacific Ocean. He had been an officer and by act of Congress a gentleman. He was an educated man. He had been around; at least he had not spent all his life in Connecticut. His experience with girls had been limited and, until now, somewhat unsatisfactory. But two weeks after winter carnival he still could not forget Norma Bull, and he gave up trying to. He got her address from the classmate who had been her date, and on the

way home after commencement he stopped in Springfield and
called her up.

She remembered him, and she said she would be willing
to have a date with him the next week, when he could borrow a
car and drive to Springfield. They had their date, and from his
point of view it was all that could be hoped for. She drank bourbon instead of beer, and she did not sing "Paper Doll," but this
time when they got up to leave it was to make love in his bor-
rowed car, *with him*. He did not believe that she was conferring
any special favor on him, but on the way up to Springfield and
during the early part of the evening with her he had been afraid
that in his case she would not live up to his classmate's guarantee. As he was saying goodnight to her outside her house, Gordon Whittier asked her when he could have another date. "I
don't know," she said. "Next week? Wednesday?"

She was twenty-five, and at the moment had a job as
cashier in a medium-size supermarket. She lived with her
mother and an older brother, Bruce, who was a salesman for a
building-supplies company and had the territory consisting of
western Massachusetts, northern Connecticut, and all of Vermont. He was beginning to make good money, and he was on
the road from Monday through Thursday. From certain remarks made by Norma it seemed to Gordon Whittier that
Bruce was a bit of a wolf. "My mother doesn't know where he is
half the time," she said. "He says to her he doesn't know
whether he'll be in Rutland or Hartford, your home town. He
doesn't tell *me* anything, either, but I don't *care* where he is."
Bruce and Norma contributed to their mother's support, but she
was not dependent on them. She had the income from four
two-family houses that were left her by her husband, and in
their particular neighborhood the Bulls were considered very
well-to-do. Mrs. Bull was active in the affairs of the Eastern
Star, the Methodist Church, and the Hampden County Women's
Republican Committee. She was not counted on for much financial support, but she gave freely of her time. Her first question
to Gordon Whittier was to get his opinion of Harry S. Truman,
and when the answer proved satisfactory she gave him her
qualified approval. She did not like Norma staying out late at
night when she had to get up early to go to work at the super-

market, but since Gordon had to drive back to Hartford after a date with Norma, he usually had her home at a decent hour. That, too, was in Gordon's favor.

Before the summer was through Gordon was so much in love with Norma that he asked her not to have dates with other fellows. He was taking a risk, but he was in love. "You mean *nobody* else?" she said.

"Well—if you just went to a movie," he said.

"God, how many times do I go to a movie with a fellow?" she said. "You're the same as asking me to go steady, like the teenagers."

"I know. Because as soon as I start teaching I'm going to ask you to marry me."

"Well, if I was going to marry you I wouldn't have other dates. If I married you would I have to keep my job?"

"Maybe the first year it'd be a good idea. I only get forty-eight hundred the first year."

"Yeah, I guess I would, on forty-eight hundred."

"I'll say this, you're not overanxious to get married. Most girls want to."

"Oh, I don't have anything against getting married, but I don't see where I'd be better off married on forty-eight hundred. I make that myself, or just about. The next thing they're going to have a union and I'll probably make more. My mother won't like it if I have to join a union, but they're going to get more money for us so I'm for it."

"All right, then you could work the first year."

"Wait a sec, I didn't say I'd marry you. In fact, you didn't even ask me. You said you were *going* to."

"Well, maybe there's no use asking you. I wouldn't ask you if you weren't willing to give up other dates. That's no more than fair. I don't have other dates."

"But you never did have many, and I did. I've been going out on dates alone since I finished high school. Before that my mother wouldn't let me go out alone. Little did she know."

"Norma, you're twenty-five years old."

"I know how old I am. You don't have to tell me."

"No, but think of how many fellows you had dates with."

"Why should I keep track of how many fellows I had **dates with?**"

"Because."

"You're afraid to say it, aren't you? You're not thinking of how many fellows I had dates with. You're thinking of something else entirely, only you're afraid to come out with it. Well, I didn't do it to make some fellow marry me, the way half the girls I know did. I could have got married five or six times, but thank God I didn't when I see what happened to some of them. Thank God. Well, Gordon, I have to go in now, it's almost one o'clock. Will I see you again next week?"

"How about if we have a date Sunday?"

"I'm sorry, I can't. I have a date."

"Who with?"

"Who with? You're not supposed to ask me that. Anyway, you wouldn't know if I told you, so why ask?"

"Is it the fellow with the Studebaker Lark?"

"How do you know he has a Studebaker? Have you been spying on me?"

"Only once. Last Sunday."

"Well, you have your nerve. Who gave you permission to spy on me?"

"Nobody. I gave myself permission because I was going to ask you to marry me. Does *he* ask you to marry him?"

"What if he does? At least he doesn't spy on me. You came all the way up from Hartford just to see who I had a date with?"

"Yes. *You* wouldn't tell me."

"Well, all you found out for your trouble, you know he has a Studebaker Lark."

"And where he lives."

"You must be crazy."

"Crazy about you," said Gordon.

For a moment she was silent. "Gordon, would you mind if I said something personal?"

"Go ahead."

"Why don't you start having dates with other girls? I wouldn't mind. I'd still have a date with you. I *like* you. But you got so now you have all your sex with me. You ought to try it with other girls."

"I have."

"No. I don't think you ever did. I'm almost positive, no matter what you say."

"You're only guessing."

"You won't admit it, but I'm positive. It's nothing against you. A fellow like Bruce, my brother, he's just a wolf. He'll never be able to settle down with one girl."

"Do you realize what you just said, practically?"

"That I won't be able to settle down. Well, maybe I won't."

"I don't want anybody else but you, Norma. I love you."

"Well, I wish you didn't, Gordon."

"All the same, I do."

"Oh, heck, I don't know what to say," she said. "Give me a cigarette."

He lit one and handed it to her. "Maybe you're the one I ought to finally settle down and get married. I can cook and all that, and one thing I learned at the supermarket, I know how to buy. I save my mother a lot on food bills. The early part of the week is always the best time to do the marketing, especially the meats. Monday and Tuesday is when they always have the specials, but the women put it off till Friday. If I held on to my job the first year that would be over nine thousand a year."

"Does this mean you *are* going to marry me?"

She turned to him and frowned. "You must think I like to hear myself talk. *Yes.*"

Through the first year and into part of the second Gordon Whittier could hardly believe that such happiness was happening to him. Everything, *everything* was working out. At school, in his classes, he was made to, allowed to, feel more like an officer than he had felt during his thirty-eight months in the Navy, where he could never orient himself with his skipper on the one side or with the enlisted personnel on the other. At Consolidated he had Thales and Copernicus, Faraday and all those others to back him up, and no high school student was going to dispute *their* granite authority. Since, in a manner of speaking, he was the living representative of the classic mathematicians and physicists, none of his pupils disputed him, and his life in the classroom was rewarding. Financially, too, his work had certain rewards, particularly the six hundred dollars he earned during the summer, tutoring some rich kids in plain and solid geometry. The six hundred dollars put him well over Norma's income-producing ability, and that extra money pleased him for that very reason.

On Bruce Bull's advice they bought a house in a new development in North Chintocket, which they financed through
the GI Bill and some help from the in-laws, Gordon's grandmother and Norma's mother. Norma's supermarket was 'way
on the other side of town, and they bought a second-hand
Pontiac for her transportation. Gordon could walk to school.
Norma had to be at work at seven-thirty, and Gordon still had
time to rinse off the breakfast dishes and put them away. In
the afternoon Norma would be waiting for him after school,
and they would ride home together and sometimes they would
make love before dinner.

Because of the tutoring jobs they could not go away during
Norma's vacation, but she did not mind. She put on a bathing
suit and got just as good a tan at home as she would have got
at a beach on Long Island Sound. She and Patsy Quillen, her
next-door neighbor, sunned themselves every afternoon, rub-
bing each other's backs with lotion samples that Norma had
foresightedly brought home from the supermarket. Patsy was
as changeable as the weather, chattery some days and full of
stories about the five movies she had been in as a chorus girl.
But other days she would hardly open her mouth, and for one
three-day stretch she would not get into her bathing suit, then on
the fourth day she came out wearing a little-girl sunsuit and
Norma noticed the bruises on her arms that body makeup could
not quite hide. Norma would have said nothing, but Patsy saw
she had noticed the black-and-blue marks. "Oh, all right," said
Patsy. "Frank gave me a going-over."

"You don't have to tell me about it unless you want to,"
said Norma.

"Well, what does he expect?" said Patsy. "He promised me
a mutation stole last Christmas. He'd pay half if my mother
paid half. But he didn't give it to me and he didn't give it to me.
So when I saw there was a sale, I went in to Springfield and
bought one myself. The August fur sale. A hundred and
nineteen-ninety-nine. I got it for forty dollars down and the rest
over sixteen months, I think it was. He wanted me to take it
back to the store, but all sales were final."

"And he beat you for that?"

"Here, on my arms. He hits me with his knuckles. That
can hurt, if you ever had it happen to you."

"I know. My brother did it to me, once. Right on the muscle."

"Now he's embarrassed for fear you'll notice it."

"Don't tell him I did," said Norma.

"Oh, I won't. I'll get something out of him, don't think I won't. I know just about how long he can last before he comes crawling back. But this time I'm not making it any the easier for him." She laughed. "Last night I bet he didn't have two hours' sleep. I took a bath about one o'clock. Maybe you saw our light on. I knew he was still awake when I went in the bedroom, but I didn't say anything to him. You know how hot it was last night, and I was all covered with perfume, but I didn't even say goodnight to him. I'm not going to speak to him till he apologizes. My arms were only sore the first two days, but I want to get him out of that habit. We're trying to have a baby, and what if he clouted me when I was pregnant? I could have a miscarriage, and then I think I'd walk out on him. I almost didn't marry him because he lost his temper. He was a marine, and I had this friend of mine in Casting at Metro. Frank hit him so hard he almost knocked him out, and that just about finished me at Metro. Not that I couldn't get a job someplace else, but I was living in Culver City and Metro was closest. You know he still gets these nightmares from being in the war, but I don't consider that an excuse. He doesn't have to act that way. Most wives wouldn't take it, and why should they? He didn't know whether I could get a job at another studio, and Sid Prell wasn't doing anything, just walking to the parking lot with me, and Frank came at him and let him have it. He thought Sid was somebody else that I did go steady with for a while, but my goodness they didn't even look alike. I'll tell you this much—Jack Healey wouldn't have just laid there. He could be just as mean as Frank."

"I don't like fights," said Norma.

"I don't either. Sometimes they can't be avoided, through some misunderstanding or something. But when it comes to hitting a man's wife, a man giving his wife black-and-blue arms, he promised me that stole last Christmas. I hope my mother remembers she was going to put up half last Christmas. That's a thought, you know. My mother owes me half. How much is that?"

"About sixty dollars."

"And I used forty I had! My own. Sixty and forty—what the hell was the fuss over nineteen dollars and ninety-nine cents? Oh, Mr. Frank Quillen, have I got a few words to say to you!"

Gordon Whittier was not afraid of Patsy Quillen, nor of the influence she might have on Norma. Patsy was cute, one of those young women who wear frilly little-girl playsuits and cheap Mexican peasant dresses, and who would go on wearing such clothes long past the time when they ought to change into more mature styles. Norma was not like that. Patsy was pretty, with a sexy little figure and a way of looking over her shoulder and pointing her behind at you. Norma was not like that. Patsy was a chatterbox and could not endure a moment's silence when there was a male present. Norma was not like that. Now that she was married, Norma wore her glasses all the time, or nearly all the time, and Gordon had begun to understand about Norma that she was submissive more than anything else. She had been promiscuous to a degree that he still could only guess at, since she refused to tell him the whole statistical truth about her relations with men. But she was not aggressive. Submissive was what she was; obliging whenever he wanted her, which was often; and in his love for her he had begun to comprehend his own theory that it was not a quantity of men that she wanted, but one man; that in the many men she had had and who had had her, she had not been seeking the thrills of variety, but only the reassurance and relief that she could have got just as well from one man as from a multitude. Since their marriage she had not missed the variety of men, and Gordon was pleased that in their own relations she appeared content with him and his admittedly inexperienced lovemaking. Her friendship with Patsy had given him moments of uneasiness. He had hardly made his private observations of Norma and her essential constancy when her friendship with Patsy was provided with its most favorable opportunity to flourish—the two weeks' vacation, with the two girls sitting together every day in the sun. But Patsy's stories about herself, which Norma reported to Gordon in tones of pity and distaste, had obviously done nothing to create discontent in Norma. "I could never live that way," she told Gordon. "I don't only mean him hitting her. I'll

bet you Patsy could try your patience. But they're always bat-
tling about something or else they're like honeymooners. No
wonder their nerves are on edge."

Gordon, with the diffidence of the non-combatant junior
officer toward the marine veteran of Guadal, and the hidden
sense of superiority of the low-paid schoolteacher over the
hustling salesman of California wines, was never at his ease
with Frank Quillen. The Quillens' scale of living indicated that
Frank unaided was making as much money as the Whittiers
jointly. Patsy spent more than Norma, but she did not have a
job, and when the two couples would sit together and drink
beer, Frank easily assumed the traditional posture of the self-
made man toward the educated contemporary of more modest
means. Although he was making close to ten thousand a year,
Frank still read comic books. Gordon Whittier wanted to be
friends with his neighbor; he would have wanted to be friends
with any man who was his neighbor; and he would have enjoyed hearing Frank talk about the war. But even when they
went on picnics together Gordon Whittier was made to feel that
he and Norma were always the Quillens' guests. They always
went in Frank's Roadmaster, and it was the Quillens who supplied the sets of vacuum bottles and plates and eating utensils,
the folding picnic table, the aluminum back rests, the cans of
beer in dry ice. If they stopped anywhere for food or drink—as
little as a Coke, as much as a steak dinner—Frank would not
let Gordon pay. "Frank, if you don't let me pay my share, we're
not going out with you any more," said Gordon, one day.

"Norma made the sandwiches, didn't she?" said Frank.
But it was the last time they went on an outing together. Frank
was hard to figure out, but when Gordon had figured him out he
did not tell Norma. Frank's generosity was a cover-up for his
true feelings; he would not accept anything from the Whittiers
because he wanted to be able to say he never owed them anything. Well, if that was the way Frank felt, it was all right with
Gordon. He was not going to let a thing like that bother him—
and Frank Quillen was practically a moron anyway, with those
comic books, that preoccupation with the baseball scores. When
the summer was over and outdoor activity curtailed, sometimes
a week would go by without Gordon's so much as passing the
time of day with Frank.

At the end of the calendar year Norma quit her job. She was pregnant, and so was Patsy. Both girls had their babies in May; Norma, a son; Patsy, a daughter. The husbands got no closer together, but the girls were more or less interdependent on account of the children, and Patsy and her little Lana were at the Whittiers' nearly every afternoon when Gordon got home from school. It was nice to know that the girls could count on each other for help and companionship, and Gordon began to get a new slant on Patsy; or perhaps it was not so much a new slant as the discovery that Patsy had changed. She had become a devoted mother to her own child and she was very sweet with little Brucie Whittier. It was impossible to be in Patsy's presence for ten minutes without hearing her say, "According to Dr. Spock . . ." Gordon often wished that Norma would show some of that California enthusiasm for motherhood, but she was rather listless and got nowhere near as much pleasure out of Brucie as Patsy got from both babies. The doctor told Gordon you had to expect that letdown in some women, and what, really, was he worried about? Norma never had been exactly effervescent, and why expect her to be now? The baby's name-sake and godfather came through with the money for the medical bills, and Mrs. Bull loosened up when she learned that Gordon's grandmother had given him a thousand dollars. Consequently, Norma's retirement from the supermarket was not immediately damaging to the family finances, but Norma occasionally would talk about getting another job as soon as the baby was old enough to be put in a day nursery. One thing she was sure of: there would be no more children until Gordon was promoted or moved to a better-paying job. But she had hardly announced this decision before she discovered she was pregnant again, and now it was Gordon's turn to worry.

In the first place, he was not in line for a promotion; in the second, he did not know how to go about looking for another job if by another job Norma meant a non-teaching job. If he had been better at chemistry, he could have applied for work as an industrial chemist in one of the factories that were starting up. In the third place, he did not want to give up teaching; it was his *profession,* and if the pay was small now, it did promise security for the future. If they could get through the next few years . . .

He could expect no help from his own parents. His father was a bus driver in Hartford, with steady work and fair pay, but Malcolm Whittier had had a lot of jobs in his day, and had become a bus driver only a few years ago, during the war, and he had neither saved his money nor acquired seniority. He had his bus driver's pay and that was all. It had galled him to have his mother-in-law send Gordon to Amherst, a college she selected because of her great admiration for Calvin Coolidge. It had to be Amherst or nowhere, too. Not Boston Tech, or the scientific school at Yale, either of which was a logical place for a boy who had taken honors in high school math and physics. It was the kind of dictatorial behavior that was typical of her ever since Malcolm Whittier married her daughter, and that had made it doubly galling when he had lost jobs and was compelled to accept her help. She was not one of the Farmington Avenue rich, either, but she always seemed to have five hundred or a thousand lying around loose, just enough to get Malcolm and his wife through various crises, as she had done a dozen times during their married life; and since boyhood Gordon had never gone to his father for money. Whenever the son needed money for a bicycle, for summer camp, for a new suit, he went to Grandma. "Well, we'll see," she always said, and always came through.

On the day that the doctor was sure that Norma was having another baby, Gordon Whittier took the Pontiac and drove down to Hartford to see his grandmother. "Isn't it pretty soon to be having another?" said the old woman.

"The doctor says she'll be all right," said Gordon.

"Oh, no doubt. But I hope you and Norma don't get to be like a couple of Italians. One a year. You ought to wait in between. I guess you want another thousand, is that it?"

"I could use more, Grandma. We can't name this one after Bruce Bull."

"No, I guess not. I *could* let you have a little more, but your mother's expecting something when I pass on. I don't know what age they retire bus drivers, but your father won't have that job much longer, and then what? It isn't as if you were going to be able to help *them*."

"I'm afraid not."

"Norma's mother is supposed to be well-off. Is she going to take care of Norma when she passes on? Or will it go to the son?"

"That I don't know, and I'm sure nobody does," said Gordon.

"If you could have stayed at Amherst you'd have a better-paying job now than teaching school."

"I don't know," said Gordon. "I like teaching."

"As a stepping stone. But it wasn't what I meant you to do. I always hoped you'd be a lawyer. You had a great-great-grandfather on our side was governor of Connecticut. Did you know that?"

"But I wasn't cut out to be a lawyer. Math and physics—"

"You could be good at those things and still study law. I always understood that you studied those things no matter what degree you were after. The math, anyway."

"You more or less do, for a B.A. But they were my specialty, and I wanted to teach. When I was in high school I used to be allowed to take over the class during experiments. That's when I found out I liked teaching."

"Then in a way you deceived me, Gordon. You knew I wanted you to be a lawyer."

"You never said anything."

"Well, if I didn't, you could have made a guess. Mr. Coolidge was never any teacher. *She* was, his wife, but I never cared much for her. A Goodhue, she was. I knew some Goodhues and I didn't have a very high opinion of them. Isaac Goodhue, drank like a fish. Got a girl in trouble over in West Hartford, and his brother was no better. He was a drinker, too. Well, I'll let you have one thousand dollars, Gordon. As for the rest, we'll see. But you won't always have me to come to, you know. You may be lucky you got here first, because your mother may have to have an operation, and you know who'll pay for that."

She was not quite right about the operation: it had been put off too long, and Gordon's mother died a few weeks before his second child was born. His father was so drunk the night before the funeral that it was doubtful he would make it, but Gordon and Norma got him through the morning with coffee and small amounts of whiskey, so that by two o'clock in the afternoon Malcolm Whittier was shaved and dressed and able to attend the services at church and grave. The family gathered at the house after the burial and Malcolm Whittier retired to his bedroom, and he was sitting on the edge of his wife's bed, bottle and glass in hand, when his mother-in-law came in, without knocking. He did not speak.

"Where I expected to find you," she said, not so much confirming her expectation of his whereabouts as implying the expectation of finding the bottle in his hand. "I would like to sell this house."

"I can't stop you," said Malcolm Whittier. "Go right ahead."

"Will you be ready to leave as soon as I find a buyer?"

"Sure."

"Some of these things are yours."

"I don't want them."

"You can make a list and I'll go over it with you, and I'll give you fair payment."

"Give me five hundred for the lot," said Malcolm Whittier.

"You should have more, by rights," said the old lady. "I'll give you a thousand and you can sign some kind of a quitclaim. But I'd like to sell the house as soon as possible."

"All right. Give me a thousand. I'll take whatever you give me. A thousand is all right."

"Are you going to keep your job?"

"Not if you give me a thousand dollars. I'll clear out. That's what you want me to do, isn't it?"

"Where will you go?"

"Oh, I know where I'll go, all right," he said. "I'm going down to Florida and get me a job on a boat. A fishing boat."

"That's what I thought," said the old lady.

"It's what I wanted to do thirty years ago. Maybe by now I'd own a couple of boats. But you had to have her here. She didn't like it here any more than I did, but you were her mother."

"You won't have to worry about Gordon. Not that you ever did. That's why I want to sell this place, when I can still get a good price for it."

"Well, Gordon leans on you. He always did," said Malcolm Whittier. "You get rid of me, and you hold on to Gordon, all in the same operation. But watch out for Norma, ma'am. She'll only take just so much of your bossing, and then you'll hear from her."

"I've never tried to boss Norma."

"So far," he said. "I'm not sore at you, ma'am. Maybe I could be if I thought about it, but I was never much of a money-maker, and I'll give you credit. You helped out a lot of times. Why you did is another story."

"Why I did was because I wasn't going to see my daughter and her son suffer, that's why."

"Yes, I know," said Malcolm Whittier. "Well, if you send me the papers to sign I can be out of here day after tomorrow. I'll draw my time at the bus company, and you can send me a cheque to Florida. I have enough to get to Florida, by bus."

"Are you taking care of the funeral expenses?"

"Oh—that slipped my mind," he said. "Then maybe if you sent me the cheque with the papers you want me to sign. I have about four hundred and fifty in the bank, but I guess there won't be much of that left after I get through paying Stillman-O'Brien."

"I'll pay Stillman-O'Brien. And I'll send you the cheque with the quitclaim."

"Then I guess I won't be seeing you any more," said Malcolm Whittier. He smiled. "Not if you can help it, eh, ma'am?"

"I'm too old to make jokes," she said.

"I'm not so young myself, a grandfather. But watch out for Norma."

The old lady left him, and Gordon and Norma came into the room.

"Are you all right, Pop?" said Gordon.

"You mean *this?* I'm not drunk. That's not saying I won't be by nightfall, but I'm not now."

"You ought to go easy on it," said Gordon. "Norma and I came in to say goodbye. We have to get back. The baby's with our next-door neighbors."

"Oh, sure, that's all right," said Malcolm Whittier. "And Norma, what is it? Another couple of weeks?"

"Three," said Norma Whittier. "According to the doctor."

"We'll let you know," said Gordon.

"I'll send you my address," said Malcolm Whittier.

"I'll phone you here," said his son.

Malcolm Whittier shook his head. "I won't *be* here. I'm clearing out for Florida."

"You're quitting your job and all?" said his son.

"Your grandmother wants to sell this place. I never owned it. And I always wanted to work on a fishing boat, so that's what I'm doing."

"Grandma isn't putting you out, don't try to tell me that. You just want to go to Florida. Be honest with me, if you won't be honest with yourself."

"I wouldn't know how to be honest with you, Gordon. With Norma I could be, but not with you. Norma, I'm sorry we never had a chance to get better acquainted."

"Well, maybe when you get back," said Norma Whittier.

"I won't *be* back."

"You mean you're going to live down there the year round?" said Gordon Whittier.

"Why not?"

"You're going to be a beachcomber in Florida?" said Gordon.

"I'm going to be a man that's doing what he wants to do, if you call that a beachcomber. You can call it anything you like —a bum, if you want to. If I had enough to retire, I'd buy me a boat and live on it, but being's I didn't amass a fortune, I'll just have to take what jobs I can get. Oh, don't worry, Gordon. I'm on my own. I don't intend taking anything away from you."

"I may never see you again," said Gordon Whittier.

"Yes, I realize that," said his father. "But it could have been me they buried today, instead of the person they did. So you can look at it that way."

"I don't know what to say," said Gordon Whittier.

"Then just wish me luck, and stay on the right side of your grandmother."

It had been so long since he had felt anything for his father that Gordon Whittier was a little surprised that he could even feel relief that his father was so conveniently and painlessly taking himself away, out of all their lives. Out of their lives that he had not been in.

"I never understood my father," said Gordon on the way back to North Chintocket.

"That shouldn't be hard," said Norma.

"I never knew he liked you so much."

"He doesn't," said Norma. "He's just looking around for one person to have on his side. Only he picked the wrong person."

"You don't like him?"

"To tell you the truth, no," she said. "He never did anything for anybody but Malcolm J. Whittier."

"Malcolm D. Whittier. His middle initial is D, for David."

"Don't try to feel anything for him now, just because he's going away. Just thank the good Lord you won't have to bother about him. He said it himself. He's a bum. My goodness, he didn't even own that ramshackle house, and what is he? Over fifty. The one you could feel sorry for is your mother, but now she's where he can't make her life miserable."

"There you're wrong, Norma," said Gordon. "He didn't give her much, but with him she wasn't miserable."

"How do you know she wasn't miserable? Did she ever say so?"

"No, she never said so, but I would have been able to tell."

"I doubt it," said Norma.

"She never uttered a word of complaint," said Gordon.

"I *don't* doubt *that*," said Norma.

Norma went into the hospital on schedule and produced her second child, a daughter whom they named Lorraine, after Gordon's grandmother. "She'll see through that," said Norma.

"Sure she will," said Gordon. "But she's as much entitled to it as Bruce was. More so."

"Bruce did all we could expect of him, more than a lot of brothers would do," said Norma.

She was weary after this baby, but it interested her more than the first child. Whenever Patsy Quillen or anyone else held the baby, Norma stood waiting impatiently until the baby was returned to her. Weary or not, she toted the baby around with one arm while she was doing her housework. If Brucie cried while she had Lorraine in her arms, she would say, "Oh, shut up," and the first time that Gordon heard her say it he began, just a little bit and without realizing it, to hate her.

"You shouldn't snap at him," said Gordon.

"He's jealous," said Norma.

"That's what I mean," said Gordon. "He doesn't understand that Lorraine is his sister. He used to get all the attention, and now he sees her getting it all. He used to be the king of the hill, then this new arrival comes here and gets all the attention. That's why he cries, Norma."

"You don't have to tell me about child psychology. I heard all about it," she said.

"Then practice it," he said.

He was extra nice to Brucie, to make up for Norma's neglect of the child, but he had to admit that whatever the reason might be, the boy was growing up to be a whiner. He was not yet two years old, but he cried at anything and everything— and nothing. He made it difficult for Gordon when there were papers to mark and lessons to prepare. "Well, I have to listen to it all day," said Norma, in answer to Gordon's complaining.

"You could do something about it instead of just listening to it. He's just as much your child as Lorraine is, and it isn't right to favor one over the other. You better do something before it's too late."

"He comes by it naturally, complaining."

"You never used to hear me complain."

"Oh, nuts," she said.

Now, when the Quillens and the Whittiers got together of an evening, Gordon could tell that Norma had confided in Patsy about the Brucie situation. There was a kind of *watching* him, as though Patsy were waiting for Gordon to criticize Norma in front of the Quillens. Anything less than bouncy friendliness amounted to hostility on Patsy's part, and now his earlier uneasiness about her friendship with Norma returned. Previously it had been uneasiness based on the fear that Patsy's frivolous outlook might make Norma's unprecedented fidelity seem stodginess; but now it was something different. It was disapproval of *him* and of his whole attitude toward Norma, shown by Patsy in her limited politeness to him. He was in a defensive position now, warding off silent criticism of an attitude that was wholly right and proper. Heretofore he had enjoyed Patsy's foolishness and chatter, especially when he was convinced he had nothing to fear; but to get those long, disapproving looks from this ex-chorus girl (and from her ex-marine husband, with his comic books) was a little too much.

"What have you been telling Patsy?" he asked Norma.

"I haven't been telling her anything," said Norma. And Gordon knew she lied; she had not even bothered to say, "What about?"

"You can keep family matters inside the family. I don't go around telling *my* friends what you're doing to Brucie," he said.

"Do I have to hear *that* again?" she said.

When one of the inevitable infant maladies touched Brucie it was now inevitable that Gordon would exaggerate the seriousness of it and charge it to Norma's neglect of the child. He knew he was being unfair, but he could not help himself. "Then stay home and take care of him," said Norma. "*You* change his diapers. The doctor says he'll be all right in two or three days, but I'd just as soon let you be his nurse the rest of the week. The child can't have a runny nose without you pulling this child psychology on me. Well, cut it out. Just cut it out. You're going to end up making me hate this child."

Her threat had an immediate effect because it was so naïve, and not uttered as a threat. The baby got well in two days, and though Gordon attributed the quick recovery to Norma's being forced to give the child an unusual amount of attention, he had been alarmed by Brucie's illness and by Norma's threat. The sense of relief from these crises lasted about thirty-six hours, and when it passed Gordon Whittier became conscious for the first time of the inert but real fact that he hated Norma. Once she had made him feel love, and she had been the first to do so. Now she had introduced him to hate, and it very soon became an exhilarating and satisfactory thing.

It was easy to hate her, once he began. At the bottom of it was the galling knowledge that no one had paid much attention to him until she let him make love to her. She, moreover, had instantly detected his lack of experience in such matters and therefore was able to take credit for rescuing him from the barrenness of his existence. And what had enabled her to be so astute? Nothing but her own record of promiscuity that went back he knew not how far or with how many. He had once said to her, "Well, were there twenty? Twenty-five?" and in the long moment she took before answering evasively he realized that she herself was wondering which was the closer figure. She had started in high school, more than ten years ago, and at the rate of two boys a year, twenty was a reasonable number. But it had been certainly no less than two a year, and not all of them were high school boys. There had been married men; there had been one grandfather, a politician friend of her mother's whom Gordon knew about because he had listened while Norma told the man over the phone that she did not want to see him any more. He owned the Studebaker Lark, she said; he was the one.

She was a scrawny girl, who dressed more quietly than most of the young teachers at Consolidated, and somehow gave the impression that her shoes were too big for her, as though her gait were governed by her fear that the shoes would fall off. She had dark brown hair and large front teeth, always visible because of the set of her upper lip. She never talked dirty or joined in the risqué songs. And yet men knew, without advance information from such as Gordon Whittier's classmate, that she would not waste their time. Nothing she said, nothing she wore, nothing she did was invitational—but sometimes the way she stood, something in her long, lean aloofness, made her the object of a first, tentative curiosity, and men would suspend their standards of ideals in femininity to find out why she attracted them. The worldly ones, the young roués, soon lost interest; but the grandfather with the Studebaker Lark had *wanted* to marry her, and Gordon Whittier *did*.

Gordon Whittier discovered, in his recognition of the new passion she provoked, that by letting himself hate her, he was achieving an emotional maturity that love had postponed. Love had actually postponed the virility and self-confidence that were now his. He would not repudiate the earlier emotion; it had been there, it had existed, it was betokened by two small children, and he could not have been wrong about any such deep feeling. But love had tied him to her, and hate had set him free, so that it was not long before his colleagues at Consolidated were seeing a rather different, somewhat new, more personable Gordon Whittier than the merely competent, conscientious man they had become accustomed to. If the keen-edged sarcasm had always been there, they had failed to notice it because until recently he had not spoken out much at faculty meetings. Before the school year was out he was a natural choice for faculty representative in dealings with the Tri-District board and the practical politicians among the board members were beginning to wonder how they could use a teacher who was a Yankee, an Amherst and University of New Hampshire man, who had an ancestor a governor of Connecticut, an untarnished if not brilliant record as an officer in the Navy, the husband of a Yankee family girl, the father of two lovely children, the son-in-law of Mrs. Bull. And there it ended. Gordon Whittier's career in public life never got beyond the politicians' early inquiries.

Brewster Lumsden, the man with the Studebaker Lark, was a party hack, who used his political connections to gain certain advantages for his insurance business, and used his insurance business as a protection against the charge that his business was politics. All his life he had resisted the temptation to run for office, and the firm of McIlhenny & Lumsden, a second-generation enterprise, was sufficiently well known to be continually in the public mind during the years when Brewster Lumsden's faction was out of power. But Brewster Lumsden was always active politically. Politics, he said, was in his blood, by which he meant no more but no less than that he enjoyed political activity—the small gatherings, the food and drink, the give-and-take of arguments, the sharing of power, and the financial profit. And he had a permanent excuse for staying away from home and the tiresome woman who for thirty years had been his wife. He had played tackle at Amherst, served as an infantry lieutenant in the 26th Division in 1918, and was possessed of such vigor and appetites as to make his attentions to his wife serve as mere stimulation for his curiosity in all other women. He could not understand why Norma Bull Whittier had such a lasting effect on him, but neither could he understand

why he had had no effect on her mother, in whom he had originally been interested. The mother was prettier, and had a more
womanly figure, but she had not responded to his unmistakable
(though discreet) indications of his interest. The girl, on the
other hand, understood exactly what he wanted, and because
she asked literally nothing of him, he became convinced that
she was in love with him, so helplessly in love with him that he
became convinced that he was in love with her. When she said
she would not marry him, he took it as additional proof that she
loved him desperately, since she went on seeing him whenever
he wanted her to. He began to pity her in her helplessness, and
his pity introduced an element of gentleness that had not previously been a part of his feeling for her, or for any other
woman. He did not blame her for rushing into a marriage with
the schoolteacher, but he wanted her to know that he was not
abandoning her to a life without love. Then when she refused
his invitation to meet her, he realized how desperately she was
trying to make a new life for herself, and that much he could
understand. He could respect that wish. She was young, and yet
not so young that she did not know what was best for him.

The politicians on the Consolidated school board, eager to
demonstrate their alertness, had a meeting with Brewster
Lumsden to acquaint him with their discovery. "Well, of course
I know who he is," he said, greatly to their surprise. "He mar-
ried Mrs. Bull's daughter, and I'm a great admirer of Mrs. Bull.
Have you said anything to him, Whittier, I mean?"

"Just sounded him out. Seemed interested."

"Let me handle it from here in," said Brewster Lumsden.

It was routine work to find someone who had known
Whittier before he came to Consolidated. A young fellow
named Jack Williamson, now working in a sporting-goods store
in Springfield, was a classmate of Whittier's at the University of
New Hampshire and had gotten a master's degree in the same
year. Brewster Lumsden decided to buy some golf balls.

"Say, Jack, when you were up at Durham did you know a
fellow named Whittier?"

"Very well, *then.*"

"*Then?* Did you have a falling-out or something?"

"Not exactly. But I used to lay the girl he married. He met

her through me. Naturally they didn't invite me to the wedding. Why do you want to know about Gordon?"

"Oh—he's been mentioned to me."

"Gordon's not a bad fellow. Kind of wishy-washy, but straight as they come. This Norma Bull, the girl he married, she was handing it out to everybody, as far back as high school. But as far as I know, she's stayed pretty close to Gordon. Of course I never see them, so I don't know. But they have a couple of kids, I did hear that. Gordon was always kind of a lonely fellow. I used to wonder how much he knew about her, although maybe it wouldn't have made any difference to a guy like Gordon. He never had a date all the time I knew him, till he asked me for Norma's phone number. I think her mother has something to do with politics. Maybe the old lady got Gordon interested."

"I don't know. He was mentioned to me," said Brewster Lumsden. "How much do I owe you?"

He was out of breath when he reached the sidewalk. In all sorts of political situations he had learned to keep his temper, to take advantage of men who lost theirs. But he had ordered his habits so that no woman had ever been in a position to betray him, and this tart had let him betray himself. Well, he would see about that. He would see about that, all right.

Gordon Whittier was made fully aware of the school-board politicians' plans for him. His faculty colleagues, who might have been envious of him, were instead pleased that a man who had been so typically a self-disciplined schoolteacher could blossom out as he had done. He gave them hope, and they kept him informed. He knew immediately when one of the politicians had been making inquiries about him among the other teachers; he learned in a few hours that the politicians were studying the superintendent's confidential file on him. All this was something he could not resist telling Norma, less in pride than in affirmation of his changed position in their relationship. "Bud Hickson thinks they may want me to run for Congress," he said. "But I think they'll want me for something else."

"What?" said Norma.

"Oh—local or county. Maybe the legislature. You don't

just suddenly put a man up for Congress. That takes a little time. I can just imagine what Grandma would think if she knew about it. But I won't tell her till I have something definite."

"Would you have to quit teaching?"

"Not *now,* for heaven's sake. That's the whole point, now. Having a schoolteacher for a candidate, instead of the usual politician."

"Maybe you ought to have a talk with my mother. She knows the ropes."

"Like the dickens I will. Right now I don't want to have a talk with anybody, but specially not anyone mixed up in politics. I'm not supposed to know anything about this. I'm going to act surprised."

"Well, I don't know the first thing about politics. My mother does, and Bruce. But you could never get Bruce to run for anything."

"No, but he'd run after anything if it had a skirt on. Can you imagine how many married men would vote for Bruce? With his record? Every husband would—"

"Oh, lay off Bruce. It isn't all his fault."

"They can search up and down, but they won't find anything like that in *my* record."

"No, they sure won't," she said.

He was especially careful not to antagonize her during these days, when a chance remark or even an unenthusiastic silence on her part would take on exaggerated importance to an inquiring politician. He had kept his hatred of her a secret pleasure, and now he could congratulate himself on his luck. The only overt quarreling had been over the child Brucie, but he had come out of that as a too devoted father rather than as a husband who was obsessed with hating his wife. He was certain she suspected nothing of that nature. If she wondered about some differences in his lovemaking—the disappearance of gratitude; some experimental cruelty—she was as submissive as always, and no doubt welcomed the variations. No woman today would find him, as she had found him, an inexperienced lover. Even there, hating her had matured him, and his fantasies were as much concerned with himself and a future of irresistibility with her as the symbol of Patsy Quillen and the rich young woman who brought her two kids to Consolidated in a Ford station wagon. Mrs. Weaver, the Consolidated dietician. Frances Mullaly, the cheerleader. Miss Goodman, the doctor's receptionist . . .

Summer came, and again he took on some tutoring work. One of the fathers offered to pay him in cash, to evade the income tax, but Gordon Whittier, the possible candidate, had to decline the cooperative gesture. Late in August, accepting the father's cheque, he was reminded of his reason for his costly honesty, and it occurred to him that months had passed since he had heard anything about a political future. True, his teacher friends were away on vacations, but he observed in retrospect that the entire summer had gone by without a single word from anyone, teacher or school-board member, that could be interpreted as even remotely related to the controlled enthusiasm of the spring. Two weeks later, back at Consolidated for the fall term, he joined Bud Hickson in the school cafeteria. "Well, it'll be Election Day before you know it," said Gordon Whittier.

"That's right," said Bud. "Fall always goes fast. Football games. Thanksgiving. Then the Christmas shopping."

"Have you been reading Eisenhower's speeches? I suppose he has a ghostwriter."

"No, I haven't. I haven't had the time."

"Thought you were interested in politics," said Gordon Whittier.

"Oh, I am. But the time it takes me to read a speech, or listen to one on the TV, I could be boning up on my Caldwell."

"You mean the single-wing? That Caldwell?"

"Yes. You're aware, I hope, that I took on the job of backfield coach this fall?"

"Oh, sure," said Gordon Whittier. "We should have had you last season, too."

"Well, I don't know about that. I'm only doing it this year because I get paid extra. Tri-District doesn't pay me. It comes out of the alumni fund."

"If I were in a position to do anything about it, the school board would pay you. Coaching is teaching, just as—"

"Yep. Well, I've got to run, Gordon. See you."

Bud Hickson was not the only friend who made transparent excuses to avoid the topic of politics. It became so obvious that Gordon Whittier decided on forthright action. He did what he was determined not to do: he paid a visit to Roy Barksdale, of the school board, who had a greenhouse and nursery business. "I came to see you, because I've been doing a lot of thinking this past summer. Maybe you can guess about what," said Gordon Whittier.

"No."

"Well, the talk last spring about me going into politics."

"Oh, yes," said Barksdale. "Mm-hmm."

"I thought it was pretty far-fetched when I first heard about it, but so many people mentioned it to me, and during the summer I gave it a lot of thought. I'm a schoolteacher first and last, but we all have some duty like I was thirty-eight months in the Navy. And my great-great-grandfather was governor of Connecticut."

"That so?"

"And you, for instance, you have this fine business, but you give a lot of time to your work on the Tri-District board."

"Too much, but this is my last term."

"Well, would you advise me to go into politics?"

"I wouldn't advise you to, or not to. The only advice worth anything is your lawyer's, maybe your doctor's. But they charge for it. What you want from me, I suppose, is an opinion. Right?"

"Yes."

"Then my opinion is, you're better off a schoolteacher."

"But I understood that you were one of the influential ones that had me under consideration."

"Quite right."

"What made you change your mind?"

"I didn't."

"Somebody did."

"Yes, somebody did. That is, somebody said you wouldn't do. I didn't ask why. I'm getting out of public life, such as I've been in. I just put a lot of money in a new thermostatic apparatus."

"Who said I wouldn't do? You could tell me that."

"Oh, I guess I could. I guess you're entitled to that. Brewster Lumsden. He's the one has the say. Go see him, maybe you can convince him otherwise."

Gordon Whittier remembered now that he had been jealous of Brewster Lumsden when Lumsden was not even a name to him, identifiable only as the owner of a Studebaker Lark. Something very special about Brewster Lumsden had made him stand out among Norma's former lovers, and it could only have been his influence on Norma. Not that she had said anything to that effect; and she had certainly brushed him off when he tried to get her to meet him. But this one man, this Lumsden, was bigger to her than all the others put together, whether she knew it or not.

The jealousy he had felt automatically when Lumsden was a man wearing a hat and driving a new Lark, and that had vanished when he heard Norma say she did not want to see him any more, did not now return. But in its place was a hatred of the man that was new, a distribution of the hatred he had been feeling for Norma and still not the less for its being shared now by Norma and Lumsden. There was enough for both. Together the two of them—and he knew this immediately—had condemned him to a lifetime of mediocrity and routine. For one brief moment he had been allowed a vision of another life, in which he would ask men and women to vote for him, and they would vote for him and in so doing would be telling him that he was a little better than they, a little their superior. They would send him on to other places and other things, to Boston and to Washington, where he would be one of the men whom big people, not little people, would have to cultivate. The Commonwealth would pay his fare, the federal government would give him a secretary, the President of the United States would have him in for breakfast, the French ambassador would invite him for cocktails, Amherst would give him an honorary degree, his father would boast about him and be called a liar, his grandmother would be satisfied, and Mrs. Bull and her salesman son would toady to him. So much for the vision, that he had been adding to all summer even while Lumsden was destroying its chance of coming true. It was a terrible thing to discover that he had been subsisting on dead hopes.

At Consolidated he had to start all over again, not as the man who could speak up in faculty meetings but as the man who kept his mouth shut. The Bud Hicksons and the rest of them had to be convinced that he had abandoned outside ambitions, the school board had to be convinced that he had never wanted to be anything but a teacher. He did so good a job of readjusting to recent developments that soon no one could remember that he had ever been looked upon as a potential hero. By the end of the first semester he was safe, liked but not admired, accepted and not envied. He was given chores to do that other teachers had refused, and a new woman was chosen to represent the faculty. "Everybody felt you'd kind of lost interest," said Bud Hickson.

"Well, as a matter of fact I'm carrying a pretty heavy schedule," said Gordon Whittier.

He could think of no way to kill Norma that would not also cause him suffering or death. Nevertheless he spent many hours in planning her murder and in finding fault with his plans. The reading lamp on his bed sent a shaft of light on his book and did not keep her awake. She was quick to fall asleep, and her sleep was deep. No primal instinct warned her that his thoughts were not on his reading matter but on her extermination. If he had minutes ago made love to her, she slept even more deeply, a tensionless animal of human origin, without an animal's fears or human visions. In the waking hours he would study her and watch the concentration she would put into her reading of a chain drugstore ad in the newspaper. A special price on Kleenex. A real bargain in bathmats. Giant economy-size soap flakes for twenty-six cents a box, tomorrow only. She would go to the telephone and advise Patsy Quillen of these opportunities. It was not a mind that he could work on by suggestion, so that she would achieve his purpose by committing suicide. And he did not want her to commit suicide. He wanted to be directly responsible for ending her life, just as she was responsible for his missing the chance to live his.

What did other men do who hated their wives? Frank Quillen beat Patsy, but Gordon Whittier did not believe Frank hated his wife. And if he did, and wanted to kill her, he would never get away with it. Patsy had shown her bruises too many times. At least once a week the newspapers contained articles that told of men in Massachusetts or Montana, Connecticut or California, who had got rid of their wives. But nearly always the women had been involved with another man, currently and not in the past as Norma had been. Gordon Whittier was not troubled by suspicion of Norma and, say, Frank Quillen or Bud Hickson or random telephone repair men and door-to-door salesmen. Nothing had made him change his analysis of Norma as a woman who got reassurance and relief from one man—himself —instead of a multitude. If he could find a way to kill Norma he could at least be sure that Patsy Quillen would have to tell the police that as far as she knew, Gordon Whittier was not one of your jealous husbands. He was almost as sure that Patsy would have to tell the police that Norma was a faithful wife. This was not to be a crime of passion, provoked by sexual infidelity. Gordon Whittier wanted Norma dead, exterminated by him, and put to death in some manner that would enable him at the last moment to give her his reasons for killing her. His hatred of her was passionate but self-contained, unguessed at by anyone but himself. She had made him experience love without herself loving; she had failed to respond to the natural experience of child-bearing—she did not like their son, and their daughter was sometimes a doll and sometimes a nuisance. She had humiliated him in his own eyes, casually and unforgivably contrasting her slut's past with his decency. And finally, and illogically, he hated her for something an old lover had done to him. So much of what he thought, nearly all his thinking, was governed by beautiful, orderly restrictions; proven laws, logical sequences. To hate Norma, to want to exterminate her, for Brewster Lumsden's pettiness, was an act of defiance to all law, all logic, all Coolidge-loving grandmothers and incompetent bus-driving fathers who had lived lives of orderly frustration.

It took a little time for Gordon Whittier to rationalize his hatred, and while the time was being taken it became blocks of months that became a wall of years. He liked to think of these blocks, this wall, and of himself behind it, alone. He would retreat behind it daily and oftener than once in a day, for as long as it would take him to recover from a slight, or to keep out of the trouble that he would get into by killing Norma without a plan. There was order of a kind even to the illogical, disorderly act that he contemplated, and he was not unaware of the humor of the situation. People noticed a twinkle in his eye.

THE WINDOWPANE
CHECK

Although the gate was not yet open, a crowd was gathered near it. Phillips, like all the others, had seen the attendant with the sign that would shortly be raised to indicate the track number, and they waited for the raising of the sign and the opening of the gate. It was now fourteen minutes before train time. No matter how early you were, you still had to wait for them to open that damn gate.

Thirteen minutes, and the crowd was a little larger. A newcomer now stood a few feet ahead of Phillips. A chiseler, getting that much closer to the gate, and it was someone Phillips vaguely recognized. He did not like to catch anyone he knew in the act of chiseling, getting ahead of people who had been waiting. You expected that of some people, strangers, but you did not like to see it done by someone you knew. Then Phillips got a better look at the man and realized that it was not the *man* whom he knew; it was the man's jacket. Unmistakably, without the remotest possibility of a doubt, it was a jacket that Phillips had once owned.

The material was from a shop in George Street, Edinburgh. Highland Home Industries, the shop was called, and the material was a brown homespun with a faint dark-brown windowpane check. Phillips had remarked that he had never seen a material quite like it, and the woman who waited on him said she hadn't either. He bought the last of it, enough for a jacket and plus-fours; he had had the jacket made up, and had given the rest to his wife for a cape, but she had not had the cape made, and now she never would.

The jacket had been a great success. Four patch pockets with inverted pleats, and old Schumacher had done a beautiful job of matching up the pieces of material so that the lines of the windowpane checks were not broken by the pockets. The jacket had a throat latch and cloth straps at the cuffs so that you could close the collar and sleeves on a windy day, and not have to wear a topcoat. It had a full enough skirt so you could wear it while hacking around, but it was not fitted like a riding coat, and it came in handy for general country wear. It became and continued to be Phillips's favorite jacket and was much admired through the years. He had had brown suede patches stitched on the elbows, and he noticed that they were still there. But he had never seen the wearer before. Never.

The man was in his sixties, possibly two or three years younger than Phillips. He was smoking a pipe and giving all his visual attention to the station attendant at the gate, who was fidgeting with the train sign. Phillips conceded that the jacket fitted him well. With it the man wore gray flannel slacks that were shabby beyond the acceptable stage; a Tattersall check shirt with a brown woollen tie, and a pair of those shoes that lace on the side and are most often worn by men and women who turn out to be enthusiasts for Adlai Stevenson and fluoridation. The man wore no head covering, but it would be hard to find a hat or a cap to immure that mop of hair. It was long, dirty gray, and was pushed back in a disorderly pompadour. The man had several newspapers folded under his arm, and at his feet was a musette bag. Phillips had seen all he wanted to see, and he turned away. The embarrassment he had felt upon first seeing the man in his jacket, and knowing that somehow the man had got hold of it through a white-elephant sale, had vanished as he studied the man. The man was a perfect specimen of a type that Phillips had avoided all his life, and he did not feel sorry for the man but for the fate of the jacket.

He had loved that jacket, but he had given it to the church eagerly. "Pa, this material was in Mother's cedar chest," his daughter had said. "Doesn't it match that old jacket of yours?"

"It came from the same bolt. We bought it in Scotland," he said.

"What was she going to do with it, do you know?"

"*I* was going to have a pair of knickerbockers made of it. A shooting suit."

"*Knicker*bockers? Pa? Not knickerbockers."

"Oh, a few men still wear them, at the Rod and Gun."

"And I'll bet I know who. Mr. Gwillem Jones and Doctor Inness."

"And Joe Bruce."

"Yes, I forgot Mr. Bruce. Mr. Bruce. Ee-eek. Haggis. And a piper at Mary's wedding."

"No matter what they wear, they're all damn good shots, all three of them, and you can get your husband to vouch for that."

"Billy can't hit the side of a barndoor, so he's no criterion," she said. "Anyway, I infer that you want to keep this material?"

"No, I don't. You can have it if you want it," said Phillips.

"Are you sure? I could have it made into a winter coat for Jeanie. What was Mother going to do with it?"

"Have it made into a cape."

"That would be cheaper. I could have a cape made for myself. It does seem extravagant to have a coat made for a girl that'll grow out of it in one winter. Would you mind if I did that?"

"I wouldn't mind at all," said Phillips. "I would mind if you were going to be here, but you're not here much. And I know your mother would like you to have it." He did not mention it, but at that moment he made up his mind to dispose of his jacket. He had very pleasant memories of that last trip to Edinburgh. "If you come across a gold thistle with some rubies in it, I bought that for your mother just a few doors away from the place where I got this material. Hamilton & Inches. I'd like you to save that for Jeanie when she gets older."

"I will, but meanwhile I'm going to wear it myself. That is, if you don't mind," she said. "I hope you don't think I'm grabby."

The jacket went, with a wagonload of stuff, to Phillips's church. There were, heaven knows, hundreds of other things to remind him of Ida; a houseful of things and the house itself. But that jacket, and the unused piece of material from the same bolt, disturbed him, or threatened to be disturbing. Some symbolism that he did not attempt to penetrate; the bolt of material signifying their marriage, the unused portion representing Ida's death. Life uncompleted because it had ended. He would have to talk to somebody about that sometime, if he ever found the right person to talk to. But as it turned out, once he had got rid of the jacket and the unused material, he never thought of either again nor of the symbolic significance that had threatened to disturb him.

The man who now wore the jacket bent down and picked up his musette bag and hung it from his shoulder. The gate was opening and the crowd moved forward. The man turned to have a look at the crowd, and he saw Phillips. There was some flicker of recognition, but Phillips was not unaccustomed to that. A rich man gets used to it in the area where his wealth is a factor, and presumably most of the people who were waiting to take the train were Philadelphians. The man in the jacket was surely a Philadelphian or he would not have the jacket, and he could even be a resident of the same parish. It did not seem likely that the man was a fellow parishioner or, for that matter, a member of any church. But the white-elephant sales at the parish house always offered bargains and attracted bargain-hunters of all and no denominations.

Phillips went to his reserved seat in the club car and the steward followed him. "Just over for the day, Mr. Phillips? I see you don't have any baggage."

"Just for the day. Could I order a bourbon and water in a tall glass, before the rush?"

"Yes indeedy, Mr. Phillips. You shall have it, first thing. Care for a paper? *Evening Bulletin?*"

"Thank you," said Phillips. Two men sitting across the aisle stopped talking until he looked in their direction, and he saw that he was expected to speak to them. They were faces that belonged in Philadelphia business or philanthropy. "Good afternoon," said Phillips.

"Good afternoon, Mr. Phillips," they said, and one added, "Beautiful day."

"Yes, 'tis," said Phillips. They had spoken to him, he had spoken to them; they had saluted a prominent fellow townsman, he had acknowledged their salute. If they saw him on South

Broad Street they would not speak to him nor he to them, but technically they all were still in New York City and owed this ephemeral cordiality to their common place of origin. No one expected the cordiality to continue after the train left the station, and by the time it reached Newark they would all be back on a South Broad Street basis. The men across the aisle were having a little difficulty resuming the conversation they had suspended, and Phillips now helped them by putting on his reading glasses and devoting himself to his newspaper. He had said all he was going to say, and they did not have to wait on the chance that he might want to say more. In a very short time he was absorbed in his newspaper and forgot about them.

As soon as the train began to move the steward brought Phillips his drink. Phillips put a dollar bill and a fifty-cent piece on the smoking stand, muttered a thank-you, and took a satisfactory sip of the drink. He became so intent on his reading of the newspaper article—a dispatch from London that concerned the prime minister's conversations with the American secretary of state—that he did not look up when a man seated himself in the next chair. He heard the man say, "Let me have a bottle of ale, please. And be sure it's cold, will you, laddie?" Phillips knew, without looking, that his new neighbor would be wearing his old jacket. And the train had not yet reached Newark.

Phillips took off his reading glasses and folded his newspaper and went to the steward. "Think I'd like to take a little nap," said Phillips. "Are all those other chairs taken? The regular Pullman-type chairs?"

"No, you just take any one you find vacant, Mr. Phillips. It's a drowsy time of the day, isn't it?"

"Yes. Thank you very much," said Phillips.

The upholstered revolving chairs, eight or ten of them, were in a section separate from the bar section, and he had his choice of four vacancies. He sat in one and turned it so that he looked out on the Jersey meadows. He still did not feel safe; the man in the jacket had passed up a couple of vacant chairs in the bar section to settle himself in the chair next to Phillips's. Phillips was now convinced that the man felt compelled to talk to him. And he was right.

Between Newark and Elizabeth the man took the chair next
to Phillips and lost no time in starting a conversation. "Mr. Phillips, I guess it gave you a funny feeling to see this old jacket."

"I don't exactly—"

"Oho, come on. You don't have to spare my feelings. I'm
not ashamed to tell you where I got it. Paid twelve bucks for
it at the rummage sale. Got any more like it, *at that price,* I'd
sure like to get hold of another."

"Why are you so sure that it was mine?"

"The same way I'm sure it was made by Schumacher.
Your name is inside the pocket. The date you had it made is
rubbed off, illegible, but you can still make out your name."

"Well, I hope you're comfortable in it."

"Not only comfortable. Makes me feel like the landed
gentry. When I was a young fellow I had a couple suits made by
Anderson and Sheppard. Hell, that was right after the war. Our
war. I had a few bob my old man left me, and I was hanging
around Europe then. I knocked around for three years, mostly
Paris. Just getting started painting, but not taking it too seriously while the money lasted. Funny I never ran into you, back
in those days.

"Oh, I don't know."

"Well, I knew *Ida*. That is, I met her. I couldn't say I
knew her, but I met her."

"Oh? Where was that?" said Phillips.

"Well, I was just trying to think. Who did she know in
Paris in those days, back around 1920-21?"

"A great many people, I should think. Her family took her
abroad every year, and she went to school in Florence for a
year."

"That was it. The school she went to in Florence, I knew a
girl went there with her. Miss Dixon's."

"Miss Nixon's," said Phillips.

"Yolanda McDermott. I was stuck on her. She came from
San Francisco. She was half Spanish on her mother's side. Obviously not her father's, with the name McDermott. And they
had plenty. They kept a suite at the Ritz all year round and once
a year they gave a party at Armenonville. It was kind of an institution, that party, and that was where I met Ida. I remember

now she was staying with the McDermotts and she and Yolanda both came in Spanish costume. Big high combs, black lace mantillas. It was fancy dress. I forget what I went as. What the hell did I wear? I remember some things so clearly, but my memory is in and out. I could tell you some 1920 street addresses. And phone numbers. But some of the easy things I have a hard time with. I cut out the booze a few years ago, and it affected my memory. When I had enough whiskey in me I could tell you every party I ever went to and who all was there, but when I had to give up the hard stuff I began to run into difficulty. Ale is all I ever drink now, and I'm not even supposed to drink that, but what the hell. I have to have something. I couldn't sleep without it. I went as a faun, by the way. No wonder I had a hard time remembering it. Me as a faun. But never mind, there are some pictures to prove it. Photographs. I always meant to leave them by your house. Thought they might amuse Ida."

"Oh? Do you live nearby?"

"Nearby to you? Yes. That is, about six or seven miles from your place. Near Downingtown. I have a farmhouse, nothing very elaborate. And I converted the old corncrib into my studio. Works out very well."

"How long have you lived there?"

"Since '35. I lived in New York for quite a while, but we had to get out of there. My wife couldn't stand the noise. Funny thing, she was born in New York. Stuyvesant Square, if you know where that is."

"Roughly."

"Well, you get the noise from the two elevated lines down that way, or you used to, when she was growing up. But suddenly one day, we were living on West Ninth Street, and she announced that we had to get out of New York. Couldn't stand it another minute. And I heard about this part of Pennsylvania and we bought the farmhouse without the farm."

"You never saw Ida in all that time?"

"She wouldn't have remembered me. And I know you and she would never buy a painting of mine. I know what you have, and those Laurencins and Mary Cassatts would fall off the wall if you ever hung one of my pictures in your house."

"I gather you're the modern school," said Phillips.

"Well, yes. You don't have to be young, you know, Mr. Phillips. Picasso was born in 1881. He's older than we are."

"His work doesn't interest me at all," said Phillips. "But you're somewhat of a neighbor, and you knew my wife. You haven't told me your name."

"Jack Roebuck. No relation to the mail-order family."

"Roebuck. No, I don't recall her ever speaking of you."

"Oh, she wouldn't remember me. If she did it would only be through Yolanda McDermott. And collecting Marie Laurencin and Mary Cassatt, she'd never take a second look at any of my paintings."

"But she might have been glad to see you. You should have stopped in, you and your wife. Ida was very fond of people."

"Well, as I say, I thought of it a couple of times. I had all those old photographs. But you keep putting those things off, and then of course the time came when it became impossible to plan anything ahead. I never knew from one day to the next how Willie was going to be. Willie was my wife. We didn't have anyone else in the house, and there had to be someone there to watch her."

"I see," said Phillips. He was afraid he saw only too well, and he wished he knew how to put a stop to Roebuck's ramblings.

"Just that one time, that was all she needed," said Roebuck. "Had to get a few things in Wayne, and I was sure it was all right to leave her. Only be gone an hour or so, and she'd been in pretty good shape. But when I got back, there she was."

"Dead?" said Phillips.

"Hanging from a beam in my studio."

"I think I did read about that, at the time. Yes. I'm very sorry."

"Yes, it was in some of the papers. Just a brief account. All the people that have any knowledge of such things said if it hadn't been then, it would have been some other time. So it didn't make any sense to blame myself, but I did anyhow, for quite a while."

"About five or six years ago, wasn't it?"

"Longer than that. Eight years in September."

"But you've gone on living there, in the same place, I take it?" said Phillips.

"Oh, sure. I don't say I make the bed every day, and I get a little tired of my own cooking. But nobody bothers me. There's a woman comes once a week to clean, and I have a sort of an understanding with the mailman that if I don't take my mail out of the box for three days, he'll go in the house and have a look. If I'm going away, like yesterday I had to go to New York, I won't be there longer than three days. But I expect to be around for quite a while. Both of my parents lived past eighty, and I had a great-uncle died at a hundred and three. That's a hell of a long time. He outlived three wives. As long as I can keep working I'll be all right. You probably feel the same way. As long as you can keep working."

"Yes, I go in to my office every day. New York once a month."

"I don't know about New York. I couldn't go there that often. New York is where Willie and I had our best times, and everywhere I go there depresses me. People wonder how I can live alone in that old farmhouse, but to tell you the truth, she was never herself there. I kept a constant watch over her there, and I gave away everything that would remind me too much of her."

"Yes, I can well understand that," said Phillips.

"Well, I think I'll go back and have another bottle of ale. Flush today, sold two pictures. But I'm going to hold on to this jacket, and I just wish I had another like it."

"Are you getting off at North Philadelphia?"

"No. Thirtieth Street. I'm going to treat myself to a good dinner and take a later train out."

"I have a car meeting me at North Philadelphia. How would it be if you came home and had dinner with me, and then I'd send you home in my car?"

"Yes, I'd like that very much, if it's not going to be any trouble. I understand you have an Eakins that Ida bought a long time ago."

"We still have it. That is, I have," said Phillips.

YUCCA KNOLLS

It is not a colony they have, and the circumstances of their choosing Yucca Knolls were different in all three cases, but for twenty years now Cissie Brandon, George W. ("Pop") Jameson, and Sid Raleigh have been, as they say, more or less neighbors. Weeks often go by without any two of them seeing each other, and as for the three getting together, it only happens at Christmastime every year and at much greater intervals when a picture magazine or a television program rediscovers Cissie or Pop or Sid and, quite by accident, learns that the other two also live in Yucca Knolls. But any time Cissie, or Pop, or Sid is in any kind of trouble, she, or he, lets the other know about it right away. They have never expressed it in so many words, but when the chips are down you go to your own people, and your own people are not your neighbors, or your family, or friends you have made in recent years. They are the people who were stars when *you* were a star. Well, if not quite a star, a featured player. Cissie was starred, Sid was starred; Pop never quite made it, his name above the title of the picture. On the other hand he lasted a little longer than Cissie and Sid. In fact, Pop still gets work in TV westerns. Cissie and Sid will not take such work; they don't need the money—nor, for that matter, does Pop. Cissie and Sid would consider it undignified of Pop to take those dirty-old-men parts in TV if he had been a star; but since he was always a character actor, they don't hold it against him now when he goes unshaven for four or five days and goes without a haircut and, six months later, appears on The Box. He is never on for very long. His longest scene usually shows him lying behind a rock, an arrow through his chest, and he is saying, "Think they got me this time, consarn it. But don't you wait around, Jeff boy. You still got time to head them off 'fore they reach the stockade," and *quick* his head falls and he dies with a smile on his face.

A few hours after seeing Pop die in prime time the television audience can see Cissie or Sid in full-length films; Cissie, for instance, in *The Humperdinks Abroad,* in which she played Jane Humperdink from Mountain Falls, Iowa, and had those hilarious sequences when she and Ezra Humperdink were invited to go on a fox hunt in England. That was the one in which it turned out that Lord Chesterton had always hated fox hunting and was delighted with Cissie's antics, so much so that he willingly gave his blessing to the marriage of Barbara Humperdink and young Eric Chesterton, who wanted nothing better than to go to Iowa and raise Poland Chinas.

Sid Raleigh was not a comedian. In his starring vehicles, visible on the late shows, he is a World War One aviator, an infantry lieutenant in the same war, a district attorney with a younger brother who has become a gangster, an idealistic architect, a peacetime test pilot, a bandleader, a forest ranger and, three times, a newspaper reporter. A Sid Raleigh picture seldom ran longer than seventy-five minutes, but with the insertion of commercials and station breaks followed by commercials Sid may be back and forth from one A.M. to two-forty-five, shooting down Fokkers, putting the ax to beer vats, making speeches to aroused taxpayers about the inferior materials in the new high school, and kissing June Wentworth, the former Mrs. Sid Raleigh, who is now married to a chiropractor in Redondo Beach.

Sid is not often recognized these days. The curly locks, that even thirty years ago were augmented by hair-pieces, have entirely gone, and there was nothing that could be done about the wattles. Nose jobs were still very much in the experimental stage in the early Thirties, and Sid could not resist legal imported beer and liverwurst sandwiches. "All of a sudden I was thirty-five years of age and looking like my Uncle Max," he says. "This is fine if I am making my living in the poultry business, a better-than-average living Uncle Max was making. But I am suppose to be the poor man's Ronnie Colman, a B-picture Warner Baxter, if you prefer. What the hell? I had a few bucks, some various income-producing properties out in the Valley. So a couple friends and I got together and started Yucca Knolls. Who needed Warner Brothers, and anyway they had Flynn. I don't have to care any more now how I look, a forty-two-inch waistline, and at six o'clock in the morning I'm getting my best sleep, instead of driving out to Corrigan's Ranch and monking around with some bronco that hates all human beings but particularly Jews. I swear to you, I seen more anti-Semitic horses than the Czar with the Cossacks. I made one picture where I was a big Mexican landowner, Don Something or Other, and I had this pure white steed that was suppose to come when I whistled, untie knots when I was bound with rope. You wanta know something? I have to have a double just for patting that horse on the neck. The first time I ever went near that animal he tried to chew my arm off. Ripped the sleeve off my costume, and they had to shoot around me till they got a new one. I said to Roy Risman, Roy was directing, I said, 'Roy, that horse don't like me. Already he don't like me, and before I had a chance to do anything to him. But if he can read my mind, what I'm thinking about him, tomorrow he's going to kill me. So you get another white horse or another actor.' Well, they solved it by having my double ride the horse in the long shots, and close shots and medium close shots they put the saddle on a white dummy. You couldn't tell the difference. But *I* could!"

Cissie Brandon's pictures are action-filled, as much so as Sid Raleigh's, but the action is directed to the task of creating laughs. Her pictures contain even more close-ups of her face than Sid's of his. The Cissie Brandon Burn and the Cissie Brandon Slow Burn were famous in the profession, often imitated but never equaled. It is impossible for any television comedienne to copy the Cissie Brandon Slow Burn because none of today's comediennes (or any other day's) has the Cissie Brandon face or the Cissie Brandon timing. One of the New York critics observed that Cissie Brandon always looked as though she had her hat on crooked even when she was not wearing a hat. Her hats, incidentally, were all sight gags, always good for an entrance laugh. But sight gags were surplus, laugh-getting insurance; the Cissie Brandon face, doing

a takem or a double takem, a burn or a slow burn or a fig bar,
registering sadness or any other emotion the situation called for
—that face was always the focal point of the scene, always better than the material they gave Cissie. She never had to be afraid
to have a dog or a child in a scene with her, and no human
performer, co-star or bit player, was allowed to do or say or
wear anything that would divert attention from Cissie. If a performer attempted to steal a scene and the attempt escaped the
notice of the director, Cissie would go through the scene uncom-
plaining, apparently unaware. But when the scene was finished
and the satisfied director said, "Print that," Cissie would say,
loud enough for everyone on the set to hear, "No you don't.
No—you—don't. That son of a bitch in the policeman suit.
When did he develop a tic in his face? He doesn't have a tic in
the long shots." The director would order the scene reshot, and
the man in the policeman suit would behave himself. Cissie
Brandon's pictures were family-type comedies, made on low
budgets, and retakes cost money. An habitual offender, a
performer who kept trying to steal a little of a scene from
Cissie Brandon, would find himself on her personal blacklist;
and yet it was an impersonal war that she carried on with bit
players. She fought them, protected herself, but it was a game
that minor actors played with stars, stars with minor actors, on
every set in Hollywood. Some of Cissie's friends among the bit
players were guilty of trying to steal scenes, and if they got
away with it, that was part of the game. No hard feelings, but
if they did it too often Cissie could keep them out of work. She
could also pull a few tricks of her own; she could tramp on their
lines without saying a word, merely by making a moue. Or she
could raise her hand to her head, pretending to smooth out her
hair, and get her elbow in front of the actor's face, between him
and the camera, and blot him out completely just as he was
reading the only lines he had in the picture.

     She could also use her powers to help a friend, and the bit
players knew about that, too. She had what amounted to her
personal stock company as well as a personal blacklist, and
since Cissie Brandon made a minimum of two pictures a year,
it was practically guaranteed income to be one of her favorites.
Cissie Brandon's films were the studio's bread-and-butter pic-

tures, cheaply made, making use of old sets, written by five-hundred-dollar writers. They never played the Radio City Music Hall, but they were box office all over the world, year after year after year. She did eight Humperdink pictures with Carl Buntley as her husband, Ezra Humperdink. When Carl died, the studio decided to take no more chances on the fragility of actors; the Humperdink series was abandoned, and Cissie had a new husband in every picture that had a story-line which called for a husband. There were not many; the studio preferred stories that had her unmarried or with a husband who was not seen. It was not studio policy to give an actor the buildup that he would get as husband of Cissie Brandon, and Cissie most heartily concurred. She was as firmly opposed to one writer's suggestion that she be given a female co-star. The studio tried teaming her up in one picture, and it was the only Cissie Brandon film that ever lost money. Audiences in Manchester, England, and McKeesport, Pa., resented the intrusion of Ruth Chalmers, her co-star, who was well enough known from other pictures. The trouble with Ruth Chalmers was that Cissie Brandon's fans came to see Cissie Brandon, and felt cheated when given so much of Ruth Chalmers. Thereafter Cissie went it alone, using the same catalogue of facial expressions in every picture, whether she played a housewife, a boarding-house mistress, the proprietress of a grocery, or the owner of a beauty parlor.

The people understood her, and made her the "well loved." She would step out of her rented limousine at movie premieres, bejewelled and beminked, and a roar would go up. "It's Cissie! Cissie Brandon!" The people would cheer her, and she would reassure them as to her appearance in the accouterments of wealth; she would stare at her Cadillac, as though surprised, and wink at her fans. She would take hold of her gown in the middle and hitch it up. She would pretend to stumble on the red carpet. The people knew that in spite of the limousine and the diamonds and the evening gown, she was their Cissie.

And she was nothing of the kind.

She would clown it up for the benefit of the crowd outside Graumann's Chinese, but at the party after the premiere she would be herself. Newcomers to the industry and non-professional guests would see her at these parties and ask incredulously if that could be Cissie Brandon. She had dignity and good manners, and she just missed being beautiful. As it was, she was a handsome woman, and if she had not been a star comedienne, she could have made a more modest living, in Hollywood terms, as a dress extra, one of those creatures who provide the human background at the embassy ball, the hunt breakfast, the society wedding. The face that she contorted to make the people laugh was, at rest, the face of an aristocrat. The facts were played down in her publicity, but she had attended a young ladies' Episcopal seminary in the Middle West and was the daughter of a Kansas City physician who drank himself into bankruptcy and death. She worked in stock companies and repertory theaters across the country, and eventually as a bit player in silent films. At twenty-five she was playing old maid schoolteachers and taking pies in the face. But no matter how degrading the slapstick action or the descriptions of her on the sub-titles, some trace of dignity was always left, and because of it she escaped from the custard pies and got into character acting. Earl Fenway Evans, an early director who was one of the first to see artistic possibilities in the motion picture medium, put Cissie in a straight part. He cast her as Doris Arlington's jealous older sister in a society melodrama. He thought that having Cissie's aristocratic face in the picture would provide authenticity to the fiction of Doris Arlington as a society girl. His theory did not work. The vast movie public were willing to accept Doris Arlington as a society girl, and Cissie Brandon, from long habit, could not overcome the temptation to make funny faces. Nevertheless Evans became Cissie's biggest fan among industry people, and for years he told his colleagues that some day he would find the right story for her and Hollywood would have a great dramatic actress. As a direct result of Earl Fenway Evans's enthusiasm for Cissie, she was given the part as Carl Buntley's wife in the first Humperdink story. She stole every scene from Carl Buntley, and he meekly shared star billing with her in the next Humperdink and the subsequent Humperdinks. Carl Buntley knew a gold mine when he saw one, and he had never heard about Art. He had hardly heard of Earl Fenway Evans.

The friendship between Earl Evans and Cissie Brandon
was a perplexing relationship for Hollywood. He was a perplexing man all by himself. He was given to violent outbursts
and many men were physically afraid of him. He had a
smashed nose and the scars of cuts that had been stitched
above his eyes and on his mouth. Four of his fingers had been
broken. On several occasions he had beaten up men who did
not realize that an argument had reached the violent stage.
When he fought he would not stop until he was beaten insensible or pulled away by at least two men. He fought to kill, and
he would fight anyone: smaller and weaker men, bigger and
tougher men. Whatever the odds, he would wade in with both
fists, heedless of what was happening to his face. It was generally (and hopefully) agreed that some night Earl Fenway Evans
would come up against a man who would kill him.

He was a drinker, but he got into fights sometimes while he
was perfectly sober. A man's attire, his gait, his voice, the way
he ordered a meal—any small thing could annoy Earl Evans to
such a degree that he would goad the man into a fight. In any
other community, in any other industry, people would not have
put up with him; in Hollywood, however, men who loathed and
feared him gave him jobs because he made money for them. He
was known as a woman's director. Other directors knew how
to photograph women to their best advantage, but Earl Fenway
Evans was one of the very few who would have long discussions
with a female star well in advance of the first day's shooting. He
would tell her things about the character she was to play that
could never, never be hinted at on the screen or described in
the script. He would analyze the character so thoroughly that
some actresses would wish they had not signed for the part. But
Evans knew what he was doing: he was directing the star even
before the picture was in production. Once he had implanted
the suggestion that the character was, for example, a nympho-
maniac, no actress of any intelligence would be able to dismiss
the thought entirely, and Earl Evans and the camera would get
at least a little of that thought on the screen. With some of the
more stupid actresses, he would wait until a scene was about to
be shot, and the assistant director had called out, "Quiet please!
This is a take. Shut the hell up back there, we're rolling." Then
Earl Fenway Evans would suddenly get up out of his chair and

go to the actress and whisper something naughty in her ear. She might be confused, irritated, or amused, but in some cases, with some actresses, the tactic worked. There was no denying that he had earned his reputation for putting animation and sex appeal into some of the most wooden women in the industry, and he did it without the help of tight sweaters and deep décolletage.

He had come originally from a small town in Nebraska, joined the Navy in time for service in one of Sims's destroyers in World War One, and bummed his way across the country to San Francisco. He had two or three fights as a middleweight, losing them all, and got interested in sculpture as a model. From sculpture he went into painting. For a while he lived with a woman who had a studio in San Francisco and taught him a few basic elementals of painting. He married her, or he did not marry her; his stories of his early years did not always check out. In any event he moved to Los Angeles and got a job as assistant to a vaudeville actor who was directing two-reel comedies. In Southern California he had his own bungalow, all the women a man could wish for, and time to read. He had graduated from dime novels to Rex Beach and Jack London, to Stephen Crane and Galsworthy and Bennett and the Russians, Maugham and Mann and Anatole France, Conrad and Anderson and Sinclair Lewis, Cather and Dos Passos and Mencken. He read only for entertainment; the men and women with whom he earned his living and had his fun were not bookish—or if they were they were as reticent about it as he. He was about twenty-seven years old and earning two hundred dollars a week when he discovered Havelock Ellis and Sigmund Freud, and the shock of discovering himself through them was almost too much for him. He was so fearful of turning up in one of Ellis's case histories that he wanted to kill Ellis. He was never again able to take a long look at a human being without wondering what she—mostly she—would confess to Ellis. In time he forgave Ellis for giving him a shock; indeed, he was grateful to the bearded old men for having lived at the wrong time in the wrong place, for keeping their prying eyes and irresistible questions out of his life. But he was also grateful for their having shown him that he was not alone in the world with his troubles, and that his troubles were not unique. Even men who had been to Eton and Oxford, lords and ladies who stood beside the king . . . As never before, he met the world with self-confidence. In less than a year he was directing a six-reeler.

He married three times in the movie industry, in addition to his yes-or-no marriage to the San Francisco painter. His actress wives ran to type: they were top stars, they were tall and slender, and in a community that was not renowned for quality, they were ladies. He once said, "I married three out of the four ladies in this business. I would have married the fourth, too, but she wouldn't spit in my eye." He would never identify the woman whom he considered to be the fourth lady; it was fun to let people guess, and one guess was that the fourth woman did not exist. The marriages, as well as the wives, ran to type: a brief, urgent love affair; an elopement; an exchange of extravagant presents; a reconciliation between public quarrels, and a friendly divorce. Once safely parted from him the women became genuinely fond of Earl Fenway Evans. He boasted that all three would take him back—for one night every six months or so. Only one of the three admitted there was any truth in his boast, but all three remained on fairly good terms with him and were unanimous in describing their marriages as an experience, if a nightmare.

In all three instances he had been the one to insist on the legal ceremony. Regina Knight, the second of his actress wives, said that Earl admitted to her that he was creating a public, formidable record of interest in women to offset his true feeling for them, which was contempt. "Well, I have no contempt for Reggie," he replied. "She used to come home from the studio so tired that she wished she was married to a fairy. And now she's convinced I was. Reggie can say what she pleases about me, just as long as I can go back there every six months or so for a re-take."

His first actress wife, Helena McCord, returned to her first love, the theater, and thereafter did only an occasional film. Whenever a studio approached her to do a picture in Hollywood she would telephone Earl for information and advice. She was a serious-minded woman who did not permit any references to their conjugal past. "I get a feeling that her husband is listening in on the extension," said Earl. "Maybe not, but I don't give him anything to complain about. She was a right guy, Helena."

Marietta Van Dyke, the third actress wife of Earl Fenway Evans, was a Southern California society girl who had been East to school. She started her movie career at the top because there was no other way that she could be induced to go into films at all. Her father was rich, her mother was rich, and Marietta Van Dyke, known to her friends as Van or Vannie, had accepted the movie offers to spite her Eastern schoolmates, who had been somewhat condescending to the rich and beautiful Californian. Almost overnight she became the most famous alumna of her school, and she got letters that began, "I don't know whether you will remember me . . ." from girls who would sometimes have trouble remembering her when they saw her at college parties and in New York restaurants, a year or so earlier. Having put those Eastern girls in their place, she set out to put the movie stars in theirs. They had resented her unearned stardom and were very outspoken about it. To them she represented the society type that the Eastern society types, her schoolmates, said she was not. She hired a dramatic coach, an English actress who had played Shakespeare and Noel Coward; a personal press agent; and a German gymnast who conducted her daily calisthenics. She undoubtedly would have cultivated Earl Fenway Evans, but it was not necessary; he saw her first, and with a few well-chosen insults he cut her down to size, seduced her, married her, and left her. She was the only one of his three Hollywood wives who hurt him financially. Although she did not need his money, she retained the Van Dyke family lawyer, who hated all picture people and got every cent that the law would allow. Earl did not call Marietta a right guy; she had not, in fact, played the game. The other women had not asked for money. But since it was part of his own pose to care nothing about money, he made jokes about the financial arrangements. "According to my figures, it comes to about fifteen hundred dollars a night," he said. "That's pretty high when you think of how much you can get free."

"You'd better stop saying those things," said Marietta, when his comment reached her. "I could tell a few stories about what kind of a man you are—or are not."

"Too late. Everybody knows by this time," he said.

"*I* didn't," she said.

"You didn't know *anything*."

"Well, I do now. I certainly do now."

"But you're not sore at me, Van."

"No, not a bit. When I was a little girl I had a broken arm and appendicitis at the same time. Everything all at once, and that's what it was like being married to you."

"Well, at least you won't have to have your appendix out again," he said.

"Exactly," she said.

"Although you could break your arm again."

"I'll try not to. I'll be more careful from now on."

He saw little of Cissie Brandon during his seven marrying years. She invited him to her own wedding; he accepted the invitation, then forgot to attend. He was too busy with the details of the divorce from Regina Knight, a new picture he was directing for Goldwyn, and the early curiosity about Marietta Van Dyke. His secretary picked out a nice pair of silver pheasants, six hundred dollars at Brock's, and it was the present of which Cissie was most proud. The silver birds adorned her dinner table on all important occasions, and Cissie could be coldly scornful of anyone who suggested that they had been a gift from Pathé, which had a chanticleer as a trade mark.

It was two years before Earl Fenway Evans saw his wedding present on Cissie Brandon's dinner table. By that time she had come up in the Hollywood society world. She was, in fact, more firmly established in that world than Earl himself. He was fully qualified as a director who had imagination and taste, and to whom pictures with high budgets and top stars were intrusted; but there were some homes to which he was not invited. Movie moguls, as they were then called, who had come from the garment industry, food products, wholesale jewelry, or the real-estate side of picture business, were afraid of Earl Fenway Evans. He had never actually struck one of them, but the threat was there; and they had good reason to be afraid of his outspoken comments on their value to the movie business. His sarcastic labels had a way of sticking. To one producer he said, "Joe, I hear you got the Last Supper in your new picture. Why?

Because you want to do the catering?" To another he said: "Well, now you can put your whole family to work, Harry. All those Levinsons, all that scrap iron in the one picture." This was a reference to a Levinson version of the currently popular railroad epics. The movie magnates could sit in sullen silence, or they could pretend to laugh off the insults, but they were afraid of a man who cared so little about the consequences *to himself* of the ill will he was creating. He knew they hated him; they knew that he knew they were waiting for him to begin slipping. But his pictures made money, and there were four or five of the biggest female stars who wanted no one else as their director.

It was impossible to deal with a man who was not afraid of scandal, who could not be threatened or blackmailed by bad publicity. The peculiarities of his sexual relations with women could not be exploited to his disadvantage without damage to his former wives and to the female stars of his pictures. "You dirty little bastard," he said to one producer. "You'd like to get at me through Reggie Knight, but you won't hurt me. You'll only ruin Reggie." He was totally lacking in the instinct for self-preservation, and when one producer hinted at evidence of homosexuality, Earl Fenway Evans destroyed the effectiveness of the threat by supplying names of his accomplices in all-male orgies. "Unless I'm very much mistaken, one of those boys is a nephew of your wife's," said Earl Fenway Evans. "He's going to be very cross if he isn't invited any more." He offered to notify the producer of the time and place of the next orgy, so that the police could be informed. "But if there's a raid, you can just push the whole damn picture business into Santa Monica Bay," he said. "Your wife's nephew is such small change he won't even get his name in the papers. But, oh boy, the names that *will* get in!"

His enemies could only hope that he would die, or, failing that, that his pictures would lose money. Meanwhile he was left out of parties to which his professional standing entitled him to invitations. But he came anyhow. "You didn't invite me, but here I am," he would say. "You can either try to throw me out, or you can make the best of it. Suit yourself." Hostesses slowly learned that if they made the best of it, he would behave himself and, even better, put a kind of hazardous life into routinely dull parties. There was always the danger that he would start a fight, but apart from that danger, he would often provide the only entertainment for a gathering of men and women who made their living in the entertainment business. He had a bitchy wit, he had a lifetime of unconventional behavior to draw from, and his lack of self-preservational instinct enabled him to tell stories on himself that a cautious man would keep secret. "I wish I could write like Jim Tully," he once said. "He's not the best writer in the English language, but he knows how to write the kind of things that happened to me. I was an errand-boy in a whorehouse in Omaha, Nebraska . . ." He was not bothered by fact, but he told his stories with an intensity that momentarily supplied the element of truth, and in all his stories that concerned women, the men were villains or chumps, the women no worse than sympathetic figures. "We were in Queenstown, or Cobh, they called it, and you could tell by the amount of stuff they were putting aboard that we were going to be gone at least a month. So another fellow and I smuggled this little Irish hooker aboard the *Smithfield*. That was the destroyer we were on. If you've ever been on a four-piper, you know there isn't room for an extra pair of socks, let alone a fat little Irish girl. Nevertheless . . ." Women liked to listen to his stories. He seemed to be their friend, and in the film business even the vainest, stupidest women would sometimes become aware of how much like cattle they were. (There was, in fact, one producer who referred to all performers, male or female, as his livestock.)

Cissie Brandon, increasingly famous through the Humperdink series and growing richer by the minute, brought her dignity to most of the parties that Earl Fenway Evans, invited or not, attended. A sense of gratitude to him, a sentimental belief that she owed it all to him, kept her in awe of him after she had ceased to be in awe of anyone else in the industry. She was secretly distressed to see him make a fool of himself, piling up scores of ill will that he would have to pay the moment he showed an inability to pay. The men and women he offended were not the only ones who were waiting to tear him to pieces: he was thoroughly hated by others, whom he had not specifically attacked, but who had not dared to defy the powerful and by their timidity had made tacit admission of their inferiority of talent and spirit. These, the uninsulted, were potentially his worst enemies, since he could not identify them and they did not identify themselves.

As time went on, and Earl Fenway Evans, invited or not, became a party entertainer, Cissie Brandon observed that her hero was enjoying himself in the role. She knew that hostesses frequently refrained from inviting him to their parties but carefully saw to it that he was informed that a party was to take place. "He's really more fun if he crashes than if you invite him," they said. "If you do invite him, half the time he doesn't show up." The men called him a nuisance, a pest, but the women were usually delighted when he appeared, and butlers were instructed not to turn him away.

He liked to show up while the guests were still at the dinner table. He would be dressed in jacket, breeches and boots, or in a yachting costume (although he owned neither horse nor boat); for Sunday luncheon he would come in a Tuxedo, as though he had not been to bed the night before; and at other times he had been known to come to dinner in white flannels and blue blazer, with an Old Etonian scarf about his neck. He would go to the hostess, kiss her hand, and pull up a chair beside her. "Bring me a plate of food, and a bottle of wine," he would say to the butler. If the guests included strangers to the movie business and one of them was seated on the hostess's right, he would watch for indications of the stranger's reaction. "Don't look goggle-eyed at me, Mister," he would say. "This kid happens to be my mistress." In most cases the stranger had been warned that Earl Fenway Evans, the eccentric genius, would most likely show up; one of the idiosyncrasies of Hollywood social life; pay no attention if he gets a little out of hand. First-time visitors from the East were delighted with this proof of the Hollywood legend of strange behavior among its geniuses. "There was this Earl Fenway Evans, the famous director, or at least we were told he was famous. Actually he was quite a good story-teller, if you don't mind hearing someone come right out with the real words. You know, the words you're not supposed to know till you ask your husband. I looked around the room and the only woman that seemed at all shocked was Cissie Brandon. Oh, she was there. And wait'll I tell you about *her*. Mrs. Schuyler Van Astorbilt. *Yes!* Cissie Brandon, no less. I don't suppose she's more than thirty-five, but she's the one they all sort of not exactly look *up* to, but *sort of* look up to."

Cissie Brandon's reaction to Earl Fenway Evans's stories was not lost on him. "Cissie, you don't even fake a polite laugh," he said. "What am I doing wrong? Punching my lines too soon?"

"No, not at all, Earl. You're the best story-teller I ever heard, bar none."

"Nobody'd guess that to watch your face."

"Come to dinner next Saturday. Just you and Lester and I. You can leave early, if you don't want to waste a Saturday night."

"All right," he said.

He arrived at her house on Beverly Drive at a few minutes past eight, dressed in a blue suit and black shoes. He was met at the door by Lester Long in a velveteen smoking jacket and black bow tie. "Well, how nice to have you at last, Earl. Cissie's been looking forward to this ever since we've been married, she's so proud of the silver pheasants. You remember the silver pheasants?"

"I sure do. How've *you* been, Lester?"

"Oh, I'm all right. I keep about the same. Outside of my sinus condition, but Cissie only has another week shooting and then we go to the desert for a month. That always does wonders, but it really isn't so bad. Cissie's out in the kitchen, but we're not supposed to go out there. What can I get you? I was just opening a bottle of champagne, but you don't have to have that."

"All right, I'll have a glass of champagne."

"It's the only thing I like with my sinus. I have to explain now, Earl, but I'm only going to sit with you through dinner. Then I'm going up to my room. So don't be surprised if I leave you two alone. I have a terrible lot of things to do that I have to finish up before we go to the desert. You know, I take care of everything. The ordering. The bills. You wouldn't think there'd be much with just two, but we have three servants and a chauffeur and a gardener, and it's quite a household. Just between you and I, we're getting ready to fire the couple. The butler and his wife. He thinks he's some kind of a Romeo and they fight all the time. The night before last he came home late and they went at it hammer and tongs, and Cissie has to get her sleep. So we're not taking them to the desert. Too bad, because as far as the work goes he's topnotch. He does all the silverware, takes care of my wardrobe. Serves beautifully, beautifully. But he gets a lot of personal phone calls. The maids in the neighborhood all have hot pants for him, and Irma, his wife, she shows her age much more than he does. He has a marvelous physique, Earl. I'll tell you who he resembles quite a lot—"

"Hel-lo, boys. Who resembles who?" Cissie Brandon Long made her entrance while raising her apron over her head.

"Hello, Cissie."

"Hamish, he resembles Tom Meighan."

"Not a bit. The dimple in the chin, otherwise no. Lester, pour me a glass of champagne too, will you, dear? Well, Earl, at last we've got you here in person. How do you like Humperdink Hall? That's what we ought to call it. We bought it because it was the only house in Beverly that looked anything like the house I was brought up in, in Kansas City, Missouri. They could have been done by the same architect, although this house is only about fifteen years old, if that. Do you remember houses like this back in Nebraska?"

"Yeah, but I never got inside of them."

"How do you like your steak, Earl? That's what you're getting. Good old Kansas City cut. We like ours rare."

"So do I."

"Swell. Then I won't have that to worry about. All three the same. Lester, how about if you put them on, dear? Everything else is ready. The potatoes are in the oven. String beans in the double boiler. You call us when the steaks are ready."

"All right, but you're wrong about Hamish. He does so resemble Tom Meighan. I saw Tom Meighan every day for years when I was with Mr. Lasky."

"If you want my opinion, I think he looks more like Mr. Lasky, but he doesn't really look like either one of them. Now go put the steaks on like a good boy, will you please? And call as soon as they're ready."

"Oh, don't hurry me, Cissie. I'll be so glad when we go to the desert. The last week of shooting she's always so bossy, it's a wonder I have the patience to put up with her." He left.

"That's the dearest, sweetest little fellow. I just love him. I finally got the studio to put him on the payroll, so now he has quite a nice income of his own. Of course he wants to spend it all on me, but I refuse to let him."

"How did you ever happen to marry him?"

"Oh, I don't know. Two lonely people, I guess. He took care of things for me at the Stern office, my bank account, my investments. And I don't exactly know when we got on a more personal basis. I didn't think I'd ever get married, and I don't have to tell *you,* Lester wasn't interested in me as a woman. But his sister died and left him all alone in the world, and I was the one that I guess you'd call it proposed. I'll say this, I've never regretted it, not for one second. And having him has probably kept me from making some very serious mistakes. I know it. When I have nightmares he comes in and gets in bed with me. He babies me, and that's what I need sometimes. But that's all we ever were to each other. Maybe *I* could want something more, but I don't miss it, and he more or less told me that he couldn't live with me if I made any demands on him."

"Would he care if you slept with another man?"

"That hasn't come up, and I don't guess it will. I'm not romantically inclined, and when I was I always had some kind of a sixth sense that warned me away from men. That's our protection, we plain Janes. I'll tell you later, if you want to hear about it. Oh, I like my little fellow, glad to see me when I come home from the studio, gets me into a hot tub—not that he ever sees me naked. And we have our dinner together in my room. Sometimes he reads to me, sometimes not. But I fall asleep knowing he's there, and if I have a nightmare he comes in and wakes me out of it and gets me back to sleep. When we reach a certain amount I'm not going to do any more Humperdinks. One picture a year, and the rest of the time travel."

"Glad to hear it. Maybe you and I'll do that one picture a year."

"I'll talk to you about that after dinner. Les told you he was going to leave us, didn't he?"

"Yes."

They hurried through the meal, the diffident Lester not wishing to keep the others from their conversation. "I may not see you again, Earl, but it was a pleasure having you," said Lester.

"The steaks were just right," said Earl Fenway Evans.

"Were they? I hope they were. Well, goodnight, kids. Not goodnight to you, Cissie. I'll come tuck you in."

The silence was heavy after he left. "Where do we start?" said Earl. "What kind of pictures do you want to do when you quit the Humperdinks?"

"I don't want to talk about that, Earl," said Cissie Brandon. "All this, this house and everything in it, I wouldn't have if it hadn't been for you. So let's talk about you."

"Don't start licking my hand, Cissie."

"I would never do that, and anyhow I wouldn't know how to any more. I'm a big star. I say that because I have to. I have to remind myself that I'm a star so I can give you a good talking-to."

"What about?"

"I need a writer for my next line," she said.

"You're a big star, don't forget."

"All right," she said. "Earl, why don't you quit going to those parties? Why don't you save your energy for your work?"

"I have plenty left over, that's why I go to those parties."

"That's not why you go."

"Why do I go, then?"

"I'm not sure. Loneliness, partly. But whatever it is, you aren't doing yourself any good. You're making yourself into a comic, an entertainer, and all those bastards are just waiting for you to stub your toe, then look out."

"I know that."

"Is it true that you went to Zimmy and Sylvia's in drag?"

"I didn't go there in drag, but I guess I spent most of the evening in one of Sylvia's dresses."

"And made a play for Eddie Blaine. Pretended to make a play—or was it pretending?"

"Half-pretending, I guess."

"There's no such thing as half-pretending in things like that."

"Maybe not."

"But you don't *like* Eddie Blaine. Did you do it to embarrass him?"

"Those kind of Arrow-collar looks annoy me."

"Eddie can't help how he looks," she said. "It used to be that you got in fights, then you changed into being a story-teller. But lately I hear it's the fag act. If you want boys, have them, but what's the use of flaunting it in people's faces? Nobody's going to hold it against you if that's the way you are. But the fighting, and crashing parties, and camping all over the place— you're just going out of your way to make enemies every way you can. Earl, you're not that good."

"Yes I am. Have you seen the figures on *Desperate Love?*"

"I have. But *Desperate Love* has Doris Arlington in it, and had four top writers doing the script. Don't take all the bows for *Desperate Love,* Earl. I could name you three other directors that could have done just as well as you did. There was nothing in that picture that had any particular Earl-Fenway-Evans stamp to it."

"Oh, come on, Cissie. You're not talking to Lubitsch."

"I wasn't talking about those little touches. I was thinking more of whole scenes, where in your best pictures you can get a girl like Doris to do two whole minutes without a cut."

"Who notices that but a few people in the business? If you can get the same effect in short takes, do it in short takes. That's what cutting is for."

"But you *didn't* get the same effect. You're getting lazy."

"Maybe I am. Not lazy, but I admit I'm not as interested as I used to be. I know exactly where you meant in *Desperate Love.* Where Doris doesn't know whether her husband is dead or alive, after the explosion. Is that where you meant?"

"No."

"It wasn't?"

"No."

"Where did you mean, then?"

"Long before that."

"Long before that? Oh."

"Where they're first married, and she realizes how much she loves him. Long before any explosion or any of that. The kind of thing you could always get out of Doris and girls like that. In this picture you skipped it. You dodged it. And it wasn't fair to Doris, because you could have made her a much more sympathetic person."

"See this? I don't hear any complaints from Doris," he said, and slipped off a gold wristwatch with a gold mesh band. "With 'Desperate Love,' Doris."

"Very original. And very expensive. But Doris gives presents to everybody. And I'm not impressed by the grosses on *Desperate Love,* either. I'm merely telling you that I can see you getting lazy, or indifferent, or blasé. Whatever you want to call it. I'll have it engraved on a gold wristwatch, if that makes more of an impression on you, Earl."

"I forgot to wind this. What time is it?"

"Twenty after nine."

"Well, at least you didn't say it's later than you think." He set the watch and put it back on his wrist.

"I didn't think of it or I would have."

"Or that you're telling me all this for my own good," he said. "You should have married me instead of Lester."

"Well, I would have."

"Maybe you ought to now."

"No thanks—if that was a proposal."

"Not exactly a proposal. I was just being agreeable. I thought maybe it was what you wanted."

"Would you tuck me in at night? Would you wake me when I had a nightmare?"

"What do you have nightmares about? You're all set."

"Well, you don't believe that, either," she said. "You know what my trouble is."

"No, I was never sure. I used to think you were a Lez, but if you were you kept it pretty quiet."

"I went through that. But it was only because I had to have somebody. It wasn't what I wanted, though. If I'd stayed home in Kansas City I probably would have married somebody, but I went in show business and then pictures, and when you're not pretty and you play the kind of parts I got, it isn't like being in one place all the time. You know. The less attractive men in a small town, they give up trying to marry the prettier girls and finally settle for girls like me. But then when I began making money in pictures it was an entirely different story. The gigolo types, men that wanted me to support them. They were always so surprised when they saw me without any clothes on, but that didn't flatter me. It infuriated me. It showed that they'd never really thought of me as a woman, but only a meal ticket. Then for a while I had a friend, she was a biologist. Older. The physical part wasn't very satisfactory to me, and therefore not very satisfactory to her. She said I was holding back, and maybe I was, and she introduced me to a friend of hers, a quite beautiful woman. Married. Wife of a musician, fascinating-looking, and any woman that had an affair with her was supposed to be through with men forever."

"Oh, I know who you're talking about. First name Naomi?"

"Yes."

"You were really getting into the inner circle."

"I didn't though. I shook like a leaf whenever she came near me. I made the mistake of going away with her for a weekend, but I was so nervous that she gave up in disgust. She slapped me in the face and sent me home. She was wrong about me, though. I was fascinated by her, and if she hadn't sent me home so soon, lost patience with me, I would have been in the inner circle. Once in a while I see her at parties and she glares at me."

"And you didn't go back to the biologist?"

"No. I would have liked to have her as a friend, but I think she was afraid of Naomi."

"They're all afraid of Naomi. She has them all hypnotized."

"Exactly."

"Is she the cause of your nightmares?"

"Some of them."

"Do you want me to speak to Naomi? I know her."

"What about?"

"Well—you could get rid of some of your nightmares."

Cissie shook her head. "They're not so bad. And I'd rather have the nightmares than be dominated by her all the time. I don't get them very often, and they're not all about her."

"Do you ever get them about me?"

"No. I used to have dreams about you, but never any nightmares."

"Used to have. Not any more?"

"No. At least not the same kind."

"Who do you dream about now? What man?"

"I wouldn't think of telling you."

"O.K. That means it's somebody I know."

"Know of. I don't think you know him personally."

"An actor, it must be."

"Yes, an actor. It's so ridiculous that you'd kid me about him, and it's too personal a thing. Some day you might say something to him. I don't trust your discretion, not in things like that."

"I think it's time I went home, Cissie."

"You're not cross because I said that?"

"Hell, no. No, it's because I feel like making a pass at you, and I don't think I'd get anywhere. Or would I?"

"You mean here, in this room?"

"Yes."

"No, Earl, not here. And not now. Some other time, and some other place, maybe. But not now. And never in this house."

"Because of the little guy upstairs?"

"I guess that's why. He's not really my husband, but I don't think he'd like it and I owe him that. He has his troubles, too."

"He sure has."

"I've seen him look at Hamish, the butler. And yet I know he'd never do anything while Hamish was working for us, in this house."

"Well, then I think I'll go home, Cissie. Would you ever come to my place?"

"I don't know. Maybe when I have time to think it over I'll decide against it. You have what you want, and maybe I want what I have. Not bad. You have what you want, and maybe I want what I have."

"But what you have is nothing."

"I know, or just about nothing. But what have I *ever* had? And I wouldn't want to lose my little fellow upstairs."

"You really love him, don't you?"

"He loves me, Earl. That's a hell of a lot, to me."

Earl Fenway Evans rose. "I have a feeling, Cissie, that I'm not going to see you any more. I don't mean that I'm going out and drive my car madly over some cliff."

"No, don't do that."

"Although damn little difference it would make to anybody if I did just that. But you and I have come close a couple of times and never got anywhere, and maybe we're not intended to."

"We're pretty close, considering. I've never talked to anyone the way I have with you tonight. That's pretty close."

"And I had a good time, regardless of your bawling me out."

"I'm glad."

"Will you kiss me goodnight?"

"No. I'm not used to that. That's all I'd need. Did you have a coat?"

"I never wear them."

"Not even when it rains?"

"It never rains here, in sunny California, you ought to know that."

"I forgot. I'll see you to the door. Where will you go now, not that it's any of my business?"

"I have no idea. Is anybody having a party that I could crash?"

"Do you want me to look in my book? I keep a record of all invitations, even when I'm not going."

"The old story. Hollywood. No matter how hot it gets in the daytime, there's no place to go at night."

"Never heard that one. If you really want to crash a dinner party . . ."

"No, I think I'll just drive around a while, and maybe end up losing some money at roulette. Or pay a call on Miss Francis. Always run into somebody there. Goodnight, Cissie. And say goodnight to the little fellow."

Cissie Brandon heard two nights later that Earl Fenway Evans had dropped twenty thousand dollars at roulette. He thereby became the heavy loser of that week, and while he

could afford to lose twenty thousand dollars, she heard a few
days later that he had gone back to the gambling joint and lost
heavily again. This time the loss was said to be thirty thousand
dollars, and he had had to go to the studio for an advance on
salary to cover it. The very next night he returned to the roulette wheel, lost again, and the studio refused to advance any
more money unless he renewed his contract for two years at
no raise in pay. He refused to sign the new contract on those
terms, and Cissie Brandon knew that they were beginning to
close in on him. She telephoned him.

"How much do you need?" she said.

"Where did you hear about it?" he said.

"Several places," she said. "Earl, you must let me give you
the money, and if not give it, lend it. Lester and I can lend you
fifty thousand, and you can pay it back any way you like."

"Cissie, you're a good girl, but I can't take your dough."

"But those gangsters—"

"Oh, they're not talking tough yet. They know I can
raise the money. And I have a year to go on the old contract.
I'm not broke, in spite of Miss Van Dyke. But I'll never forget
this, you and Lester. You two, and Doris, and one or two others
have come through for me."

"Earl, this is Cissie. Don't lie to me. I won't lie to you. Do
you know what I heard?"

"I'm not lying to you."

"I hear your studio has you just where they want you—"

"Over a barrel," he said. "Yes, in a way they have. They
want me to renew for two years at the same money I'm getting
now."

"I heard it's worse than that," she said. "Maybe you
haven't heard this, and maybe it isn't true. But someone told
me that they're not going to let you work for anyone else until
you do the picture you owe them. And they're not going to give
you a picture. Can they do that to you?"

"Yes, unfortunately they can. I haven't got a time clause
in my contract, a starting date. I didn't want one when I
signed the contract, and now it turns out I was a damn fool. I
didn't have a lawyer on that contract. I thought I knew it all
and was getting what I wanted. I have the right to turn down

stories, but they don't have to start paying me till I accept one. I guess a smart lawyer could fight them, but right now the smart lawyers aren't in when I phone them."

"Maybe the studio's just trying to teach you some kind of a lesson. Have you thought of that?"

"I've thought of it. That's looking on the bright side."

"You think they'll offer you nothing but junk?"

"I'm sure of it."

"Why don't you fool them? Why don't you take the junk, and make a good picture out of it?"

"Cissie, have you ever tried to buck a studio when they're out to ruin you? No, of course not. But you must know what they can do."

"I've heard. But it doesn't make any sense to ruin you. You're still one of the five or six best."

"Cissie, they did it to Griffith."

"Well—I don't know what else to say."

"You've already said some beautiful things. You and Lester. Doris. Two or three others. I'm going to sell my house, and that'll be more than enough to pay off the gamblers and enough to live on for a year or two."

"Please don't do any more gambling."

"That's easy. I have no more credit, and just now very little cash."

"How little?"

"Oh, five or six thousand, I guess."

"How much do you owe the gamblers?"

"Now, Cissie. Don't you go near them."

"I'd be willing to pay them, if they agreed to stop your credit."

"Thanks very much, but it's better this way. I was never much of a gambler. I never played for such high stakes before. I don't know how I got started now. But I've had a ninety-thousand-dollar lesson."

"That much? I thought it was less than that."

"No, this was one time when Hollywood didn't exaggerate. I lost thirty the first night, and I paid that. Thirty the second night, and the studio advanced me that. And the third night the gamblers took my marker, my I.O.U. So what it comes down to is that I owe the studio thirty, and the gamblers thirty. When I sell my house I'll pay the gamblers, and then I think I'll leave town for a while. I ought to get around seventy-five for my house. More than that, furnished. I'll be all right, old girl. I've been thinking I'd like to rent a little house down at the beach and try to paint some pretty pictures. It's what I've been wanting to do, and now it's forced on me."

"Do you think you can?"

"Paint? No, not well enough to earn my living at it."

"I didn't mean paint. I meant do you think you can leave town, and stay away for a while?"

"God, yes."

His house, she heard, was put on the market and in a quick cash sale brought sixty thousand dollars. "They say he had rugs worth almost that much," said Lester. "He should have waited."

"No, it's better for him to get away. Frankly I was afraid he'd hang around, crashing parties and so on. And I know he wasn't going to be allowed to crash. They weren't going to let him in, and if he tried to force his way, they were going to have him arrested."

"Who?"

"Practically all the people that give parties. I wonder where he went to?"

He vanished, and was not seen or heard of for a year. Someone had seen him, or a man who looked very much like him, coming out of a grocery store in Balboa, carrying a large paper sackful of provisions. He—if it was he—was dark brown from the sun, wearing a striped Basque shirt and blue jeans, and he did not return the wave or answer to the call of his name. He got in a yellow Ford roadster driven by a young man of college age. Someone else reported seeing him in an elevator in the Westlake medical building. Lester Long showed Cissie an eight-column newspaper photograph of the crowd at a movie premiere on which he had drawn a circle around one face. "Who does that look like?" said Lester.

"I see what you mean, but it couldn't be Earl. It says that these people had been waiting since six o'clock in the morning. Can you imagine Earl doing that?"

"Sure I can. He'd love it. And hope people would see his picture. You know, ironic sense of humor."

"Maybe," she said. "But I have a hunch that the Balboa rumor was correct. You may be right though. This picture, it doesn't look very much like him, but he has this wide-eyed exaggerated grin, just like the people that start lining up at six o'clock in the morning. If he did it, that's the kind of face he'd make. It might be Earl, at that."

"It's just the kind of thing would strike his sense of humor," said Lester.

"Well, at least he has that, if nothing else," she said.

One day the studio had made too many Humperdinks. It was almost possible to fix the exact date; it was a year or so after Cissie and Lester had seen Earl Evans's picture in the premiere crowd. Three Humperdinks had been released that year, and the confused public finally had had enough of them. The third of the three made money, but so little money compared to the anticipated profits that the studio considered the picture a loser. "Cissie, we're gonna have to think of a new format for you," said Arnold Bass, production head of the studio.

"So I gather," she said.

"You got any ideas of your own?"

"I have, but you wouldn't go for them."

"Like for instance? Try me," said Arnold Bass.

"Put me in a straight part. The kind of thing Aline MacMahon does, or Agnes Moorhead. I started out as an actress, you know."

"They'd never stand for it. It'd be a dreg on the market."

"Who wouldn't stand for it? Put me in a big picture, in the supporting cast. It'd be a year before you released the picture, and I'd be getting a whole new start."

"Do you have anything in mind?"

"No, but I have a director in mind. Earl Fenway Evans."

"Earl Fenway Evans. A long time since I heard that name. Where is he?"

"I haven't the faintest idea, but the studio can find anybody if they want to."

"The problem here being, do we want to? As far as I know

he's still under contract to Metro, and they don't make it a practice to loan out anybody unles you give them the moon. No, there's too many complications to it, Cissie. And anyway we don't even know if he's alive."

"That's one of the things I'd like to find out."

"Well, there's nothing stopping *you* from hiring a private eye, Cissie. Give me one reason why the studio should bear the brunt of that expense."

"The studio is richer than I am, that's all."

"No, I guess we better forget about that scheme. But I'll mull it over you doing a straight part. I'll take it up with New York. We want to use you."

"I know you do, Arnold."

"Why do you say it with that sweet smile?"

"Because I know Paramount's been making inquiries."

"Oh, you heard. I should go to more parties."

"You would go, if you were invited, Arnold."

"So I don't move in Hollywood society circles."

"That's right, you don't. Now the question is, do you find a straight part for me, or do you loan me out to Paramount, or do you just go on paying me till my next option comes up?"

"That's three questions, and I don't have the answer. That will be up to New York to make the decision."

"Well, you looked pretty good while the Humperdinks were making all that money. You ought to have some influence."

"I have the influence, but don't you look for any gratitude, if that's what you were thinking."

"No, I could tell that when you said I could hire my own private eye to find Earl Evans. A year ago a little thing like that wouldn't have taken you two minutes. What's next, Arnold? Am I going to have to pay my own secretary, or is it going to be the park-off-the-lot routine?"

"Those things are in your contract, and you got two more years to run, almost. However, since you bring it up, Lester is off the payroll as of now. He was only part of the Humperdink unit, and there is no more Humperdink unit. Still, at twenty-five hundred a week, that's a hundred and twenty thousand a year. That's pretty nice for you."

"Not if I don't work. You know that. My salary will be

charged off against the budget on the next picture I do, and the longer I'm idle the bigger that gets. If you put me in a picture now, my salary goes on that budget now. I could be in two pictures and split the charge against the two budgets."

"The voice is the voice of Cissie Brandon, but the words are the words of Lester Long. I can't promise you anything, Cissie. It's up to New York."

"Then is it all right if Lester and I plan a trip abroad?"

"What do you want to go *there* for? They're getting ready to have a war."

"Going abroad doesn't necessarily mean Europe."

"If you want my advice, this is a good time to stay home."

"Don't send me a bill for that advice, because I won't pay it," she said.

"Cissie, you shouldn't high-horse me that way. I been your friend a long time, and I'll do what I can to put you in a straight part. But don't expect me to enthuse if you start high-horsing me. All these things take time."

"What on earth has that got to do with it?"

"I don't follow you," said Arnold Bass.

"Exactly," she said.

No one underestimated the shrewdness of little Lester Long, no matter what jokes they made about his virility. He now proceeded to prove to Cissie, who needed no proof, that his devotion to her had its practical side. "What do we do now?" she said, after the conversation with Arnold Moss.

He pulled his feet up on the chair and sat tailor-fashion and grasped his ankle with both hands, rocking back and forth. He was grinning with delight at being in action again. "Why, we just fool them. We just outsmart them," he said.

"How? You mean get Paramount to put on some pressure?"

"Heavens no, Cissie. That's what they expect us to do," he said. "If we go to Paramount and ask them to put on the pressure, they will. No, sweetheart, what we do is I go to Paramount tomorrow and tell them that Arnold and the studio are being mean to us. They don't want to loan you out."

"What does that accomplish? I know it accomplishes something, or you wouldn't say it. But what?"

"It accomplishes as follows. First, it shows Paramount that the studio is afraid to loan you out. That makes Paramount want you the more. Second, it makes Paramount sore at Arnold and the studio. Puts us and Paramount in the same boat, we're allies."

"I see."

"The Humperdinks are all through, a thing of the past. So just sit tight and do nothing except draw your salary for seventeen more months."

"You mean I don't do a picture for seventeen months?"

"Not a thing. And all that time Paramount will be sizzling. And of course we'll get it around that Arnold is being a bitch, Arnold is the one we want to make the heavy in all this. Nobody likes him much anyway, and my Cissie will be known as a martyr. In and out of the industry people will hear about how Cissie Brandon is being kept out of pictures because Arnold Moss is a bitch. So when the seventeen months are up, you'll be in demand."

"Let's hope so. And what do we do in the meantime? I'm not so sure I want to leave the country."

"We're not going to leave the country. We'll stay right here in California, but we're going to move. I have some news for you. We're going in the real-estate business."

"Oh, Les. Stop teasing me."

"Sid Raleigh is starting a development out in the Valley. He's calling it Yucca Knolls, and we're in it. He's raised close to a million, of which a hundred and fifty thousand is ours. Do you know how much we pay out in servants every month?"

"I have a pretty good idea."

"Well, we're going to get rid of that headache. The houses at Yucca Knolls are going to be one-story, modren type, that you can get along with one servant. They're not going to be your Altadena type, little Glendale bungalows at all. Nothing cheap about them. But the day of the big house like this, where you need at least three servants, that's passé. The minimum at Yucca Knolls is going to be forty-five thousand that you can spend on a house, so it isn't going to be cheap at all. But all the domestics are starting to get jobs in new airplane plants, and the others are asking outrageous salaries."

"What do we do with this house?"

"We hold on to it and rent it."

"Furnished?"

He nodded. "All but things we care the most for. Most of our things wouldn't go in a modren type house, anyway."

"When did you start thinking about all this?"

"When they previewed the last Humperdink. Remember, they sneaked it in Westwood. You didn't go, but I did, and they were laughing at the wrong places."

"That's a college audience."

"No. No it isn't. The college is there, but the bulk of their audience is mostly young couples that live around there. And then I happened to run into Sid and he got me interested."

"Sid Raleigh. I never knew he had that much brains."

"He started out as a runner in Wall Street. A very good business head on his shoulders, Sid."

"I always thought of him as just a bedroom athlete."

"Well, that. But he never let it interfere. And he's worked steady ever since he came out here. He part-owns a chain of hamburger stands, and he has money in several other things. Did you ever notice that furniture storage on Santa Monica near Hacienda? Big white building? He owned that and sold it to go into this Yucca Knolls development."

"Is he going to live at Yucca Knolls? Will we have him for a neighbor?"

"Yes. But I'll bet you wouldn't know him if you saw him now. Don't worry about Sid. He's very conservative. The only other picture people will be George Jameson."

"Pop? That's a combination, Sid and Pop Jameson and us."

"Pop wouldn't be in it but for the fact that he and Sid were in the hamburger stands together. Sid doesn't want any of the so-called glamour crowd. Mostly business men in the twenty-five thousand and up bracket, but no divorcees or picture people. Only people he figures will stay. And it's a little out of the way, so we'll have seclusion. And yet only twenty minutes from downtown L. A. Or, if you want to go through Cahuenga Pass, maybe a little less than that from Beverly, when you want to go to a party."

"Are you retiring me, Les?"

"In a way I am. But it's what you want. These last couple years, it was the same thing over and over for you. Work hard, go to the desert for a rest. Back to work. A few parties, with always the same people. It's time you got what you wanted out of life."

"And what is that?"

"Kansas City, without going back there. You could never live there again, I know that, but you'll like Yucca Knolls. I got an architect coming here Sunday, and you can have fun planning your new house."

"Our new house. Never forget that, Les. Now tell me the truth, Mister Man. Is all this because you were worried about me and the studio? Did you think I was upset over my so-called career?"

"No. Yes."

"Which?"

"Well, you're not used to long stretches without working, and you have to have something to do. But I don't think you care much for acting, and I don't blame you. Maybe if you and Earl could have got together it would have been a different story, but the Humperdinks were drudgery, irregardless of the financial security."

"I was getting so I could do them in my sleep," she said.

He paused before speaking. "Maybe you did do them in your sleep. All those nightmares."

"No, they were never about the Humperdinks."

"I know that much, sweetheart. You didn't have nightmares about the Humperdinks, but half the time you'd go to the studio so tired that you were only partly awake."

"Now I see what you're doing," she said.

"Do you mind?"

"Lord, no. I want you to take care of me. Who else have I got to?"

"We're well off, Cissie. Very well off. You never have to work again unless you want to."

The house at Yucca Knolls was a great success, both as a place to live and as a means of occupying her time and energy. It was situated high enough above the floor of the Valley so that the only sounds that reached them were the shrill cries of locomotives, softened by the intervening distances, the scornful laughter of transport planes on takeoff, the droning of airliners coming over the mountains on their way to a landing. At night they could look down on the lights of Glendale and Burbank and the continuous beams of automobile headlights, all equally impersonal and remote. It became harder to get Cissie Brandon to leave her house for a party in Beverly, and she put off her own housewarming until her friends stopped asking her about it. "It's Kansas City, all right," she said.

"Only more so," said Lester. "I understand Kansas City is pretty wild."

"Yes, I suppose it was, even while I was there. I didn't see much of that side of it. My father did."

"What was your father like, Cissie?"

"If you want to see my father all over again, take a good look at Pop Jameson."

"On or off screen?"

"Either. Both. When I first started working in pictures I had such a crush on Pop that I was ashamed to talk about it. The other girls were trying to get to meet Valentino, or Jack Holt, or Wally Reid. Not me. I was dying for Pop Jameson."

"Good grief, if I'd known that I never would have bought in here."

"That's all past and done with."

"How did you get over it? Don't tell me you had an affair with Pop Jameson."

"No. It was about as unromantic as anything you could imagine, how I got over Pop. I'm almost embarrassed to tell you."

"Oh, *tell* me, Cissie."

"Well, I was working for Universal. That was when they were still in Hollywood, but we were on location for a week. Horse opera. Two other girls and I were living in a tent, and there was one tent they used for the ladies and another for the men, only they weren't very far apart. And every morning for a week I could hear Pop Jameson going to the can. He had the noisiest bowel movements you ever heard, and he'd come out of there pulling up his suspenders and looking as if he'd just won the Academy statue. That cured me of my romantic notions

about Pop Jameson. He was too much like my father in that respect, I guess. My father made a lot of noise in the bathroom, too.
So you don't have to worry about me and Pop Jameson. Or anyone else."

"The only thing I ever worry about is because there *is* no
one else."

"If I don't worry about that, why should you? I'm the neu-
ter gender, I guess."

"No. I am, but you're not. You could always fall for some
man."

"Not any more. Maybe once I could have, but not any
more."

"Didn't you ever want children, Cissie?"

"No, I never did. Children never liked me when I was a
young girl. Babies never liked me. My face is too big, probably.
After they got used to seeing me in pictures they weren't so
afraid of me, but before that I used to frighten them, when I
was just Cecilia Brandon, nobody. That had its effect on me. I
got so I didn't like kids any more than they liked me, and the
thought of having one of my own, in my tummy—well, you can
imagine. I would have been a lousy mother, even if I'd been
married. One time I thought I was knocked up, and all I could
think of was what I would do with the baby."

"You mean like—drown it?"

"Yes! Or do away with it somehow. It wasn't only the dis-
grace I was afraid of. It was the thought of having a child and
not caring for it, and especially if it was a girl that looked like
me."

"But people love you, all over the world."

"Mm-hmm. Or at least they love Jane. But Jane isn't me,
and I'm not Jane. How much would they love me if they knew I
went away with Naomi Sobleff? Or that I was Virginia Dim-
ming's girl friend?"

"The people that love you, or Jane, don't know that people
like Naomi and Virge exist."

"Or me. They don't even know that people like me exist."

"Well, if they do, they'd rather not. The secret of the Humperdinks' popularity isn't because they're home folks. Every
damn one of those families have their own troubles. Little

Johnny won't stop playing with himself, and Cousin Judy does naughty things to the iceman. The old man probably gets drunk every payday, and Mom can't do without her patent medicine. My own sister used to take Bromo-Seltzer four times a day, if not more. When I was a kid and one of the other kids showed up with a nickel ice cream cone we used to holler at him what did he have to do to get a nickel cone. Mr. Thompson upstairs from us, every Saturday night he used to beat the hell out of Mrs. Thompson, as regularly as clockwork. And how do you think *I* got started? You know that story. No, the people that love the Humperdinks like to pretend that that's the way *they* are. It's the same way with the rich society people that go to see those plays by Philip Barry. You can't tell me that society people talk as witty as that."

"Well, not Kansas City society."

"No, and not Newport, Rhode Island, either. Or Pasadena, for that matter. But the average person goes to see a Humperdink, and they see you in an apron and Carl Buntley, dear old Carl, smoking his pipe and can't find the sports section, and then there's a couple of sight gags and you do the famous Cissie Brandon Burn. Home folks. They can't go home pretending they're rich society people, but they can pretend they're Jane and Ezra and life isn't so bad after all. That is, till they have to get up the next morning and *he* looks at *her* and *she* at *him*, and they think good God! Only they don't really look at one another, do you know that? They don't have to. Only too well they know what's there, her with her bosoms flopping down on her big fat belly, and him blowing on his coffee to cool it off but if it wasn't hot he'd hit her with his lunch pail."

"My public?" She chuckled.

"Sure it is," he said. "I wouldn't of said this if you were going to make any more Humperdinks, but now the Humperdinks are all washed up, and I don't want you to miss them. The home folks will miss them, but don't you, Cissie. You made a lot of money out of them, you earned every damn cent and more."

"Well, it's over a year since I put on that apron," she said.

"Just don't brood over it."

"Do I?"

"Oh, now and then."

"It's the ham, I guess," she said.

"Save the ham for when you sign to do a straight part. And that won't be long, now." He rolled back in his chair, and the momentum as he rolled forward carried him to his feet. He looked down at her. "Pop Jameson, eh?"

"Uh-huh."

"I used to think it was Earl."

"Well, it isn't anybody any more. I haven't had a nightmare since practically since we moved here. Have I?"

"No. No."

"There's one too many no's there, Les." She reached for his hand and held the back of it against her cheek. "You're a sweet, sweet man. You are. A sweet man."

"Often a sweet man, but never a sweetheart," he said. "I'm going out and have a look at the glads. Mr. Yokohoma says they're dying. Personally I think he put a curse on them. Maybe I ought to just fire Mr. Yokohoma, and I'll bet the place would be overrun with glads."

He was spared the trouble of firing the part-time gardener, Mr. Yokohoma, when Mr. Yokohoma's compatriots dropped their high explosives on Pearl Harbor. Mr. Yokohoma vanished completely, not even bothering to collect a day's wages that were owed to him, and presumably was placed in an internment camp. The outbreak of war at first made remarkably little difference in the daily lives of Cissie and Lester. They owned three cars— Lester's Buick coupe, a Dodge station wagon, and a Cadillac limousine-sedan—and gas rationing, in Southern California where nearly everyone used an automobile, was loosely enforced. "Any time you run short, I guess I can take care of you," said Sid Raleigh, who was on the local gas-rationing board. Cissie and Lester never ran short. They would use their cars to drive in to Los Angeles or Beverly Hills, park the car, and take taxicabs; and on special occasions they would hire a Tanner limousine. The special occasions became more special because they were fewer in number, and during the first year after Pearl Harbor Cissie could not make up her mind what to do in the war effort. She did a few shows at army camps and naval installations, and the young service men were politely appreciative, but they saved their roaring enthusiasm for the glamour girls. "If I were a soldier I'd be the same way," she told Lester.

"Maybe we ought to put you there in an evening gown. You have the shape."

"No, that's not my forte. They don't know I have a shape and it's not what they're looking for from me. Not that the shape is that good anyway, although thanks for saying so. I'm not competing with Rita Hayworth, Lana Turner, those girls. I want to find something else, not these little sketches at the camps and the defense plants. And what the hell are we doing, entertaining those jerks in the airplane factories? Who gives a damn about their morale? I'd like to go overseas with the Red Cross."

Lester took a job with the Red Cross, investigating the wants and needs of service men's families, and he was conscientious and made to feel useful. He was sympathetic, but after his years in the motion picture business, not easily fooled. He enjoyed the work, and he forgot that Cissie was not accustomed to being home alone. She grew bored and restive when he tried to tell her that she would find something she really wanted to do. At this stage Earl Fenway Evans re-entered her life.

She answered the doorbell one day, and there he was, tacky in a cheap double-breasted suit and a plaid shirt without a necktie. "Why, Earl! It's you, come in," she said.

He was half grinning, in a way that could quickly change to a real smile or to no smile at all. "Hello, Cis," he said. "Long time."

"Forever. Where have you been keeping yourself?"

"Oh—what I have been doing? Well, I was walking hots at Santa Anita, the last job I had."

"You were what? Come in. What did you say you were doing?"

"Oh, what the hell difference does it make? Got any cigarettes?"

"Yes, we have some. What kind do you smoke? You know I don't smoke and Les doesn't very much, but they save us a couple of cartons a week at the market. Sid—Sid Raleigh—owns the market."

"If you can spare a pack or two of Philip Morris."

"Of course. We may have a carton. Yes, here's a carton.

Les smokes Chesterfields, but sometimes the market is out of them and they send us another brand. How about a cup of coffee? I was just going to have one."

"With sugar and cream?"

"You have sugar and cream. I take saccharin. A sandwich. Would you like a sandwich?"

"What kind?"

"Well—fried egg?"

"You wouldn't have a steak sandwich on the bill of fare?"

"Not today. We had a steak but we ate it last night for dinner. There was enough for three, too, darn it. Let's go out in the kitchen."

"Where's the little man?"

"Has a job with the Red Cross. He's gone from seven in the morning till sometimes eight or nine o'clock in the evening. How did you know where we were?"

"Oh, once in a while I read the papers. I guess it must have been about a year ago I saw where you were living out here. You all shook free of Arnold Bass?"

"Oh, yes, long ago."

"You haven't quit pictures, have you?"

"No. But I haven't been offered anything I wanted to do. Sit down and I'll make you an egg sandwich."

"Why don't you ask me to stay to lunch?"

"All right, will you? It's only half past ten. You could still have a sandwich."

"Yes, and I guess I look as if I needed one."

"Now *I* didn't say that, Earl."

"No, you didn't have to. I can read you like a book. Well, all right, I'll have a sandwich, and I'll fill you in on what I've been doing."

"We often wondered about you. Les cut a picture out of the paper that he thought was you. Some opening at the Chinese, I think it was. Was he right? Was it you?"

"Christ, I forgot about that. Yes, I did that for a gag. I went and sat with all the hyenas, and I thought it would be a laugh if I got my picture in there with all the rest of the boobs."

"I didn't think it was you, but Les was positive. Then I think somebody said they saw you down in the Westlake medical building."

"They could have. I was in there quite a lot."

"Oh, were you sick? Why didn't you let us know?"

"I was getting rid of a dose of clap. It hung on for quite a while."

"Sorry to hear it."

"Well, it could have been worse. At least I didn't get Big Casino."

"Is that syphilis?"

"Yes."

"Then I guess another report we got wasn't true."

"What was that?"

"That you were living in Balboa with a young boy. Somebody thought they saw you, but they weren't sure."

"That was true. That was before I picked up my dose. You know me. I'll take on anybody, if I'm in the mood. Sometimes when I'm *not* in the mood. I wasn't in the mood when I took on the little girl from Olvera Street, so I ended up with my dong in a sling for six months."

"Where have you been living all this time? Balboa. Santa Anita. And we also heard you were up north, Carmel or some place."

"Say, they kept pretty good track of me. Yes, I was up there for a while, trying to paint. But *they* wanted to talk about Hollywood, and I *didn't,* so I came down here again."

"Has your money held out?"

"What do *you* think?"

"Well—you didn't get that suit at Eddie Schmidt's."

"Leo Sunshine Fonarow. Eighteen dollars. Do you ever listen to Jack the Bellboy, on the radio?"

"I have, when I have trouble sleeping. But you had a lot of money, Earl, for the kind of life you seem to've led. Where did it all go, if it's any of my business?"

"That's a good question. When it's all going out and none coming in, you'd be surprised how fast it can go. And in addition to that, I went down to Tia Juana a couple of times with Duane, that was the young boy I was seen with. He could go through a bankroll very fast. Anybody can, at roulette, but he had it down to a science."

"And what have you been living on since? I'm surprised they haven't drafted you."

"When that happens, we've lost the war . . . What have I been living on? Haven't you heard of the manpower shortage? It isn't hard to get jobs. Do you know how much they pay an undertaker's assistant these days?"

"Have you done that?"

"No, but that's a sure thing. And you can walk into any restaurant in L. A. and get a job as a waiter. Plenty of jobs, especially if you're slightly decrepit and don't look as if you're going to be drafted."

"Egg sandwich. Some ketchup?"

"Sure."

"So you're all right for money?"

"I didn't say that. I said there were plenty of jobs. But I only work when I have to."

"And where do you live?"

"Everywhere. A couple of years ago I would have been picked up for vagrancy, but now the cops are so used to seeing people with no place to sleep that they don't bother you. Stay out of fights, don't get caught committing a crime, and the law pays no attention to you."

"You. Have you committed any crimes?"

"I haven't been caught."

"What kind of crimes do you commit?"

"Well, when things get tough I can usually pick up a few bucks as a lush-roller."

"A lush-roller. That means you roll lushes. Take money away from drunks? Is that it?"

"Yes."

"I should think you might get killed that way."

"You forget that I can throw a pretty good punch with either hand."

"Oh. You beat them up first?"

"No. I pick a soldier or a sailor, preferably an officer because they usually have more money. I follow them to see if they're soused, and then I usually tap them on the chin to make sure. My best customers are the fly-boys, the aviators. They like to get stewed, and they collect flight pay."

"I'm surprised at you, Earl. I would have thought you'd be more patriotic. You were in the Navy yourself."

"I certainly was. And when I see an ensign or a j.g. with aviator's wings, it all comes back to me how I used to hate those ninety-day wonders, in '17 and '18."

"Won't it be nice if you get caught?"

"You mean I'll be disgraced? Famous film director a lush-roller? Can you imagine how much sleep I lose over that? If I ever get pinched I'm gonna make damn sure the papers know who I am. Damn sure."

"Oh, then this is sort of your way of getting even?"

"It'll be some consolation if I have to go to jail. I don't want to go to jail, but if I do, the movie business will have to take part of the rap with me."

"I never knew you hated us that much."

"Us? What the hell is this us? It's two years since you did a picture, and you got a screwing."

"Maybe, but I can't help thinking that it was the movie business that paid for that sandwich you're eating, this coffee I'm drinking."

"Well, I'll be a son of a bitch. You *are* a chump, Cissie."

"Oh, I don't know. Maybe you're a chump, too," she said. "Tell me, why did you want to come see me?"

"Well, I tell you. This morning I woke up and I don't know how I got to thinking about you, but I did."

"Where was this?"

"A flophouse downtown. A kind of a luxury flophouse. A dollar and a half a night. Not exactly a room, but your bed is partitioned off. The walls don't go all the way up to the ceiling or down to the floor. It isn't the Beverly-Wilshire, but you don't have to be afraid somebody'll steal your shoes while you're asleep."

"Would anybody steal *those* shoes?"

"I did. So anyway, I woke up and I didn't feel so damn good, and I got to thinking about a lot of these bastards that weren't even awake yet. In the flophouse you have to be out of your room by eight o'clock, and this was about ha' past six. These no-talented bastards that I made millions for. The butler would come and bring them their cup of coffee and orange juice, and they could have a steak if they wanted it. And here I am, getting close to fifty years old, and the only thing I can make a good living at, they prevent me. And living in a flophouse. It's no-smoking in the flophouse and I like a cigarette the first thing when I get awake, but I couldn't even have a drag on a cigarette because that's one thing they're strict about. If they catch you smoking they kick you right out and don't let you come back. So I had to get all dressed and go outside before I could even smoke a lousy cigarette. And believe me, it was a lousy cigarette. Some wartime brand I never heard of till recently.

"So I checked out my hotel and went to the hamburger stand for a cup of coffee and a roll. Seven cents. Nickel for the coffee, two cents for the roll. Then I started walking up towards Pershing Square, you know, where the rest of the bums hang out, near the Biltmore."

"Uh-huh." She noticed now that while he was speaking, telling a story as vividly and with the same enjoyment he always got out of telling a story, his right hand was not still. It moved continually, back and forth, slowly, as though he were trying a key in a lock. He was not at all conscious of his spastic condition, and Cissie could also safely observe in detail other marks of time and dissipation that had been less obvious during the early minutes of his visit. His eyelids were heavy, slumberous even while he told his story, and he could not breathe through his nose. He seemed to reach for air with his mouth, like a fox terrier that had learned to catch tossed morsels of food.

"I go there every so often," he continued. "I almost expect to see Percy Marmont turn up there some day. You know, *The Street of Forgotten Men*. They don't know who I am or anything about me except what I tell them, and I've told them some beauts. No worse than some *they've* told *me*. One guy there that claims to be a Harvard graduate. About my age or a little older. He told me to call him Larry Lowell. Said it wasn't his name, but it would do. He knows me as Spike Evans, which was what they called me in the Navy. He only has one eye. Says he lost the other in a street fight in Paris, but I doubt it. He does speak French. He and another guy, a White Russian known as the count, talk French together when they want to say something about me. I don't know any French but it's easy to tell when they're talking about me. I called them on it one day and they didn't deny it. The count said it was all very complimentary, and offered to

tell me what they'd been saying. So I said all right, if they told
me separately, so I got the count off to one side and he told me
what they'd been saying, and then I got Lowell alone and he told
me the same story. They didn't have any chance to get together
on a story, so what I got was the truth."

"What were they saying?"

"That I was either a writer or a painter, and that if I told
them my real name they'd probably both recognize it. So I said
they were right, I was a painter, but I was on the lam, and didn't
trust them with my real name because they'd turn me in for
the reward. They knew that was crap, that part of it. Nobody
on the lam would ever sit in Pershing Square. The flycops go
there every day to have a look around, and I never knew them
to make an important pinch there. The first thing you think of
when one of the regulars doesn't show up for a couple of days is
that he's either dead or in trouble with the law. If you sit in the
Square it's pretty certain that your conscience is clear, at least
as far as breaking the law. In a big way, that is. I'm *always* there
when I've lifted somebody's bankroll the night before, and on
those days I usually let Lowell buy me a bowl of soup."

"You *like* that kind of life."

"The hell I do. But I make the most of it. I get a few laughs,
and that's why I came to see you."

"To give me a few laughs?"

"No, no, for Christ's sake. I want to make some money.
I want to make some big money. You always said you owed
everything to me, didn't you?"

"Yes, I did," she said.

"Well, that was an exaggeration, but still there was *some*
truth in it. Through me you got out of the slapstick two-reelers
and the bit parts, and so forth and so on. Right?"

"Absolutely."

"All right. Now *you* can do something for *me*. You still
have an in with the big shots. At least you can get to see them.
I can't. Or anyway, I don't want to. The last couple of years I
did a few things that I more or less got away with because nobody knew who I was. But if I got back into pictures and started
getting some publicity, some people that are sore at me would
say, 'Hey, isn't that the son of a bitch that did this and that?'

And I'd be in for a couple of lawsuits. As far as that goes, Marietta Van Dyke could attach any money I got from a studio. I owed her thirty or forty thousand bucks when I blew town. That's why I was so anxious to get out quick, with the cash, before her lawyer could get wise. There's another matter, too. I'm still in hock to the gamblers, and they have long memories. If I collected any money from a studio, the boys with the black shirts and white ties would be around calling on me. In other words, Cissie, with Marietta and the mob and the income tax people, and not to mention those other creeps that would come up out of the ground, it could easily take me a half a million dollars to get in the clear. And then I'd only be in the clear. I wouldn't have any money."

"That much?"

"I beat up a guy in San Diego. He was a fag that was after my friend Duane. He didn't know who I was, so he was willing to settle for six hundred dollars I paid for the hospital and the doctor bills. But if I suddenly made some money from some studio, he'd sue me for sure. And I had a little trouble with a young girl in Pedro."

"What kind of trouble?"

"Rape. Whether it was rape or not, she was fifteen years old and Duane and I had her down at the shack for about three weeks. That was going to be real trouble. I didn't wait around to pay off her old man. I just blew. But can you imagine if they found out who I was and saw in the paper that I sold a story to a studio?"

"That's what you want to do? Sell a story."

"Not me. You. I'll write the damn thing. I'll write an original and a treatment, and give it to you and Lester to peddle to the studios. You can tell them it was written by your nephew, back in Kansas City, or some unknown novelist. They don't have to know who wrote it. You can say you wrote it in collaboration with Ernest Hemingway, if you think you can get away with it. You can say it was written by somebody that doesn't want to have his name on the picture. Tell them you stole the idea from some Nazi. I don't give a God damn, just as long as we sell the story and don't get me any publicity."

"And the story is about your friends down in the Square."

"More or less. I'd give anything if I could direct the God damn thing. There's a woman in it that you could play, if you have the guts. I can cast the whole picture, sitting here."

"How much have you got written?"

"On paper? None. It's all up here," he said, tapping his forehead with a quivering hand.

"How long would it take you to write a six-page original?"

"Two weeks, maybe three. Then I'd do about a thirty-page treatment. So—wuddia say?"

"Well of course I'll do it. I'll talk about it when he gets home this evening, but I know what his answer will be."

"I'll know what it better be, the little son of a bitch. I don't owe Les anything. I don't owe *you* anything, as far as that goes, but if you swing this for me I'll call it square. We'll be even."

"Do you need some money now?"

"Sure I need some money. I want to get a shack somewhere, get away from Skid Row and write this thing. Let me have five hundred dollars. Do you have that much in the house?"

"Yes, most likely. If not I can get it quickly enough."

"Give me whatever you have."

"It's in the wall safe," she said. She rose, indicating that he should follow her. "Do you know what would be wonderful? If you sold this story and they wanted more, and then maybe we could take the studio into our confidence and somehow work it out so that you could be back in pictures."

"Be wonderful, all right, but it'll never happen."

She moved the sliding panel in the wall and turned the dial of the safe. "Do you want to tell me any more about the story? I mean, it's a dramatic story, isn't it? Not a comedy."

"It's a murder story. Not a murder mystery, but there's a murder in it. It's not a whodunit, and it's not a Mr. Moto. Not that we're going to see many Mr. Moto's from now on. Bogart would be the man I'd want to see in it, so maybe we better try Warners first."

"Not a war story?"

"I wouldn't waste my time on one. Propaganda slop. Did you ever see *The Kaiser: the Beast of Berlin?* Irene Castle, in *Patria.* And there was one by Hudson Maxim, the inventor of the Maxim silencer. I was an ignorant, unsophisticated kid from Nebraska then, but I didn't go for that crap."

"Here you are," she said. "Five hundred."

"Thanks. Do you want a receipt?"

"A receipt? Oh, come on, Earl."

"I wish it wasn't all in hundred-dollar bills."

"Do you want me to take it down to the bank and have it broken into smaller?"

"No, never mind," he said. He folded the banknotes and stuffed them in his pants pocket.

"More coffee?" she said.

"No, I was just looking around at the setup you have here. For you it's kind of—modest. Don't you have any servants?"

"Right now, a woman that comes in three days a week. Les and I manage."

"That's not what you should be doing. I always said you were an artist, one of the few real ones."

"Oh, I don't mind the housework."

"The hell you don't."

"Well, I won't say I like it, but it's wartime."

"There's a part in this picture for you," he said.

"So you said."

"The wife of one of the principal characters. If they buy it I know who they'll think of right away. ZaSu. But don't you let them put her in it. Maybe you ought to make the sale conditional on you playing it."

"That might hold up the sale."

"On the other hand, it would explain why you were trying to sell the story."

"Yes, that's true."

"We don't want them asking too many questions."

"Les will know how to handle it," she said.

"Les. Les. You and I should have teamed up. If I'd had any sense I would have married you instead of those three long-stem beauties. I could have made you into one of the real greats."

"Well, it's too late now."

"Not for you. If you play the wife in this picture, and maybe Tod Browning to direct, this could be a whole new start for you."

"Tod Browning? That's a long way from anything you or I ever did. Tod shoots everything in the dark."

"The longer away the better. And he *doesn't* shoot everything in the dark. Nobody uses lighting better. Tod Browning. Bill Howard. Tay Garnett. Either one of those fellows would be almost as good as me. Where I'd be good is getting you to forget Mrs. Humperdink."

"Stop talking that way, Earl," she said. "You're making me miserable." She smiled, to show how miserable she was not, but she convinced neither herself nor Earl.

"How do you think *I* feel, giving my picture to some other director?"

"It's kind of exciting, though, isn't it? To be getting back to work again. To be doing something."

"Write down your number, in case I have to call you. You know, I may run out of money before I finish the original. This should last me for five weeks, easily, the scale I've been living at. But I may want to call you about something. I sure as hell will. I'll want to call you tomorrow, to hear what you and the little man are going to do."

"I'd like it better if you stopped calling him the little man. He's my husband, and you know his name."

"Your husband. You know damn well you could get this thing annulled any time you felt like it."

"But I never will feel like it."

"How about you and me trying a little experiment?"

"What kind of an experiment?"

"You start by taking your clothes off."

"Don't be silly, Earl."

"I could take mine off and where would you be?" he said. She looked at him steadily for a count of four or five. "Earl, what if I *did* take my clothes off?"

"Then we'd have some fun," he said.

"No we wouldn't," she said. "You wouldn't get any pleasure out of looking at me. I wouldn't get any pleasure out of looking at you."

"Are you trying to talk me out of raping you?"

"Oh, cut it out. If I had any real desire for you, or you had any for me, there's nothing to stop us. Nothing or nobody,

and you know it. You insult me. The last time you were in our
house you insulted me the same way. You always get around
to insulting me. Does it make you feel big when you do that?
When you call Les the little man? You come here wanting money
and wanting us to help you sell a story, and when I show you
I'm willing to help you, you insult me because you think that
makes you a big man. Asserting your independence. Listen, why
don't you just take your five hundred dollars and your carton of
cigarettes and go away? I really don't want to see you any more.
You bore me."

"I don't bore you. Maybe I scare you, but I don't bore
you."

"No, you don't scare me," she said.

On an impulse, but acting slowly, he picked up a heavy
crystal ash tray and hurled it through a picture window. He
hardly bothered to observe the damage, but he watched keenly
the effect on her.

"What was the point of that?" she said.

"What was the point of it? I'll tell you what was the point
of it. Don't start treating me like some bum that you just gave
a sandwich and a cup of coffee. I don't have to be grateful for
your lousy handouts. That's the point of it."

"I think you'd better go now, and don't come back."

"What about my story?"

"I've lost interest. Keep the five hundred dollars, but just
go away."

"You don't seem to realize."

"What don't I seem to realize? All I realize is that I don't
want to see you any more."

"God damn it, you don't seem to realize, I'm dangerous.
Do you realize I could take a butcher knife and hack you up?"

"You could, but you won't."

"You're bluffing," he said. He then went about the room,
systematically breaking small and large objects of glass, porce-
lain, jade and earthenware. After each act of destruction he
would look at her before going on to the next. She watched
him, but said nothing. His tour of depredation took him finally
to the dining alcove, where, on the table, rested the silver
pheasants he had given her as a wedding present. "These are
mine," he said.

"Yes, they're yours," she said.

"I'm gonna take them with me."

"All right, take them."

"The hell I will. Do you think I'm gonna walk down the street with them under my arm? The first time a cop saw me. And don't you phone them when I leave, or do you know what I'll do? I'll give out a story that will be in every newspaper in town. All over the country. I'll ruin you."

"That's if anybody would believe you," she said.

"They wouldn't have to believe me. They'd print it anyhow. Where did I put those cigarettes?"

"Right there in front of you," she said.

He tucked the carton of cigarettes under his arm. "Don't you give anybody my idea," he said. "I'm going to watch the papers, and if I read anything about you selling my idea, you'll be sorry. You won't get away with it."

He left the house then, and she watched him walk down the road. He was laughing, and she was almost sure he was talking to himself. Her first telephone call was to Pop Jameson, but he was working at RKO. She tried Sid Raleigh and after several calls she reached him. He promised to come right out to her house.

"No police," she said, when she finished her account of the visit.

"I don't know if you're doing the right thing, Cissie," said Sid. "On humanitarian grounds he ought to be put away."

"Not through me, though," she said.

"But when I survey all this damage, just look at the destruction. I would say he's downright demented. Are you gonna feel safe, alone here so much?"

"I don't think he'll ever be back."

"Hard to say."

"I wish there was some way I could keep it from Les, but unfortunately most of the things he broke were things Les bought."

"Oh, you can't keep it from Les."

"He'll want to quit his job with the Red Cross, and he mustn't do that."

"Well, we'll find some solution. Like if you say checked in with my office ten o'clock every morning, three o'clock every afternoon. If my operator didn't receive a call from you she'd send someone out to investigate."

"That could get to be an awful nuisance for all concerned," she said.

"Well, I'll take it up with Les and maybe he'll have some ideas," said Sid. "You'll be home this evening?"

"Oh, sure."

"Meanwhile anything I can do? You could spend the rest of the day at my home. Bitsy would enjoy your company I'm sure."

"Oh, thanks, Sid, but I'll be all right, I know I will. You and Bitsy come out this evening. Les is usually home by nine."

"We'll do that," said Sid Raleigh. "Take care."

In the evening Bitsy Raleigh and Cissie Brandon stayed in the kitchen while their husbands conferred. "So's to put your mind at ease, Les," said Sid Raleigh. "I didn't say anything in front of Cissie, but Earl's gonna be picked up. What happened today isn't gonna figure in it. I simply thought it over and picked up my phone and called this friend of mine I happen to know in the L. A. Police Department. Lew Berger. I knew him from ten, fifteen years or more, and I did him a lot of favors. So I presented him with the whole picture of what occurred today and said we didn't want any publicity or nothing like that, but I said if he wanted to pass the word along that this party was a lush-roller, not to mention a fag, not to mention what sounded to me like an advanced case of the syph, and Lew said yes, they had several reports of service men getting rolled and it tallied with Earl. Somebody that knew how to throw a punch, and mostly young officers. Now they have a full description, and it's only a question whether he gets picked up by the cops or the M.P.'s or the Shore Patrol. As soon as he blows the five hundred he got from Cissie he'll be back to his old habits. Lew called me back and said Earl didn't check in at the fleabag up till about an hour ago, but now they knew where to look for him. There, and Pershing Square."

"Well, that finishes Earl Fenway Evans, I guess," said Les. "A pity."

"Well, yes and no. He didn't work any harder than the rest of us, and he made a hell of a lot more money. Don't feel too sorry for him."

"Oh, I don't. I really hated him. He put some sort of a spell over Cissie. I wish he'd taken those silver pheasants with him. Still, he was a good director."

"Now there's where I differ with you, Les. I never considered him topnotch, considering the calibre of people he had to work with."

"You better not say that to Cissie. She worshiped him. And very likely still does, regardless of today."

"Very possibly. But he couldn't have bought his way into Yucca Knolls if he came to me with a certified check for a half a million dollars. As the fellow says, I never liked him and I always will. It's all right to have talent, mind you, but you don't have to go around insulting people."

"We sound as if we were talking about a dead person."

"Well, maybe that's only a question of time, too," said Sid Raleigh. "While I'm here, Les, we're thinking of taking an option on a hundred acres just this side of the fire break. For after the war, that is. Would you and Cissie be interested? We can get it for practically nothing now, whereas if we wait till later somebody else may beat us to it. It's for protection as much as anything else. We want to keep Yucca Knolls the way it is."

"Well, I was gonna suggest that, Sid. You mean and keep out the Hollywood riffraff?"

"Strictly, Les. Strictly. That's what we wanted to get away from."

"It sounds like it might be a good investment, if the price is right."

"We can't miss. I have a lot of faith in Southern California real-estate values," said Sid Raleigh.